Critical Failures IV

ROBERT BEVAN

For Meghan and Jack

Pinas: (from Wikipedia) "The *pinas*, sometimes called "pinis" as well, is one of two types of junk rigged schooners of the east coast of the Malay peninsula, built in the Terengganu area."

Junk rig: (from Wikipedia) "The **Junk rig**, also known as the **Chinese lugsail** or **sampan rig**, is a type of sail rig in which rigid members, called battens, span the full width of the sail and extend the sail forward of the mast."

You can probably see where this is going.

CONTENTS

Chapter 1

Spirits were high at the Whore's Head Inn. There was plenty to celebrate. The Horsemen were gone. Enough of the roof was rebuilt so that anyone who didn't mind the noise could sleep somewhere other than the cellar. And, of course, there were the new arrivals.

Frank had personally welcomed Stacy, Randy, and *Denise* (as she was now calling herself) from his seat atop the bar. His little red shoes swung back and forth at the bottom of his blue and red striped pants as he cordially explained the no violence against fellow Player Character policy of the inn and poured them each a glass of beer. He raised his own glass, which was the same size as everyone else's, but looked comically large between his little gnome hands. Once Stacy, Randy, and Denise raised their glasses in return, they all took a sip of beer and the initiation ceremony was complete.

After that, it didn't take long for Randy and Denise to fade out of the spotlight. In fact, Julian couldn't recall seeing either one of them for at least thirty minutes. Frank's attention, (as was the attention of most of the unclaimed male residents of the Whore's Head Inn), was fixed on Stacy. Her skin-tight black leather "armor" drew a lot of attention, which Julian found ironic, considering it was probably designed to help her hide in the shadows.

"So then this big doofus," Frank said, nodding down the bar at Cooper, who was sitting on the stool on Stacy's left, "he gets right up in Eric's face and says *I must have left it in your mom*."

Stacy was a rowdy drunk, and laughed like she was being stabbed with a hot poker. It was almost more than Julian's elf ears could take. It didn't help that she punched him in the arm as well. It was a jovial gesture to be sure, meant to invite him to share in her mirth, but damn could that girl pack a punch.

And she could drink like a sailor as well. She sucked back a shot of stonepiss, slammed the glass down on the bar next to half a dozen other fallen soldiers, and wagged a finger at Cooper.

"Bad Cooper!" she said in mock sternness. "No Funyun!"

When she finished laughing at her own joke, Frank continued his story. "I thought we was all gonna die right then and there. But with nothing to lose, every person in the joint with a bow or a Magic Missile spell focused their aim on him. The big bastard turned tail and walked out. It was a turning point for us. That's when we realized we didn't have to be afraid anymore."

"That's very inspirational," said Stacy. She slapped Cooper on the back.

"Ow!"

"Sorry."

"Of course," said Frank. "He and his pals came back later and burnt the place to the ground, killing two of us."

"Oh!" Stacy clapped her hands over her mouth. "I didn't know. I'm so sorry."

Frank smiled and waved his hand dismissively. "Nah, don't be. They pulled through. Ain't that right, Rhonda?"

"Yeah," said Rhonda, filling up two beer mugs. "I'm just hunky-dory." She still wore a scarf around her head. Her skin wasn't scarred or anything, but her hair was taking its time growing back to a length she was comfortable with.

Julian felt a tug on the back of his serape. He turned around, but there was no one behind him.

Tug, tug.

Julian looked down. Tim was staring up at him through drunk, bleary eyes.

"Hey, Tim. What's up?"

Tim gestured for Julian to lean down. Julian obliged.

"Dave's out back taking a shit," Tim whispered into his ear. Before Julian had time to thank him for the update, he continued. "The wipes are too high up for him to reach. You think you could go out and give him a hand?"

"Uh...okay." Julian welcomed the idea of stepping out for a bit of fresh night air, but seeing Dave squatting over a hole wasn't exactly what he'd had in mind. "Save my seat?"

Tim smiled. "Gladly."

Julian helped Tim up onto the stool. Tim slid his hip flask across the bar for Frank to fill up. He didn't even bother with glasses anymore.

"Hi, Stacy," said Tim.

"Tim!" Stacy ruffled his curly hair. "How's my favorite little drunk?"

"I'm actually a full-grown adult, you know."

Julian sensed a punch coming, and stood ready to catch Tim if he should go flying off the stool.

Stacy's punching arm, however, was occupied with getting her glass refilled. "I'm just fucking with ya!" Her focus shifted to Julian. "Where do you think *you're* going?"

To give my ears a break.

To help Dave wipe.

"I gotta pee," Julian lied. "I'll be right back."

Stacy grinned and winked at him. "Don't get lost."

Julian slipped through a section of unfinished wall at the back of the inn. The air outside was refreshingly cool and crisp, more so than he remembered it being before their brief sojourn in the real world. Autumn must be on its way. He hoped the winter here wouldn't be too cold. One of the best things about moving from Buffalo, New York to Gulfport, Mississippi – indeed, maybe the *only* good thing – was the weather. If Julian never saw another flake of snow for the rest of his life, he could die a happy man. He made a mental note to ask Ravenus what winters here were like. Rounding the corner to the back of the building, he spotted the outhouse, one of the first parts of the building to have been rebuilt, probably even before the bar. It was situated next to the kennel where the wizards' and sorcerers' familiars, and the druids and rangers' animal companions stayed. The animals didn't mind the smell, and the constant din of animal noises gave the occupant a little bit of privacy while they were doing their business.

Julian knocked on the door. "Dave? You in there?"

No answer. Maybe he was concentrating.

Julian knocked harder and raised his voice. "Dave?"

Still no answer, and the door didn't feel locked.

Julian cautiously pulled on the handle. The door opened a bit, and nobody screamed from inside, so he opened it the rest of the way.

Of all the modern conveniences the residents of the Whore's Head Inn had collectively decided they could live without – cars, HBO, electricity used as anything but a means to blast your enemies to smoldering bits – toilet paper was the one thing nearly everyone insisted upon. Julian hadn't yet had the opportunity or the nerve to inquire as to how the locals cleaned up after themselves, but he made sure to wash his hands thoroughly at his first opportunity after shaking anyone's hand.

Frank had worked out a deal with a nearby tailor who agreed to save scraps of fabric that he would have otherwise thrown out in exchange for Frank's agreement to have all of their tailoring done at his shop.

The stack of irregularly shaped scraps of linen and wool was on a shelf mounted inconveniently high for a dwarf, halfling or gnome to reach, which was an oversight that should certainly be addressed, but Julian didn't think it looked impossible. There was even a small wooden crate on the ground, presumably put there as a temporary solution until someone got around to actually remounting the shelf.

Conspicuously absent from the lavatory, Julian observed with some curiosity, was Dave. Had Tim deliberately sent him on a wild goose chase, or –

"Hey!" came a voice from the other side of the animal pen. It was barely audible over the collective murmur of wolves, cats, owls, and other assorted animals, so Julian assumed it was not directed at him. His elven ears were much more sensitive than his human ones had been, and he had learned, through many a trial-and-error, to stop answering every address he heard. Still, it was a female voice, and Julian thought he might have heard a trace of distress in it.

Julian cleared his throat as he approached the alley between the Whore's Head Inn and the charred remains of the abandoned building next door.

"God dammit, Randy! Lower!" Dennis's female dwarf voice was not entirely dissimilar to the voice he'd had before. "If I wanted it in the pooper, we'd have done this a long time ago."

"I'm sorry," said Randy, whose voice hadn't changed at all. "It's all slippery down there. It feels weird."

By the time Julian had formulated an image in his mind as to what he was about to walk into, the image was right there in the pasty, hairy flesh, holding him trapped like a deer in headlights.

Dennis, or Denise as she was now known, stood on a hastily stacked pile of lumber, bent over forward, pants around the ankles, bracing herself with one arm on the wall of the building. Randy was behind her, eyes closed, listlessly thrusting his pelvis.

"That's how it's supposed to feel, you fuckin' queer. Hey, now! Don't you go soft on me, Randy. Just think about Caillou, or whatever it is you jack off to at home, and –" He looked up, right at Julian. "Mother of Fuck!"

"Wha-wha-wha?" was all Julian could stammer out.

Denise lost her balance and fell forward off the stack of boards.

Randy stopped tugging on his semi-erect penis and started crying. "I told you, I ain't like that! He said he was twenty-two! He had an I.D.!"

Denise scrambled to pull her pants up. The left side of her beard was caked with shit. With the high concentration of familiars and animal companions, it was wise to watch where one stepped.

"What the fuck, Confucius?" said Denise. "What's a lady got to do for a little privacy 'round here?"

Julian snapped out of his trance. The game might have switched Dennis's gender, but he was still the same racist redneck asshole on the inside. "My name is Julian. And you've got shit on your face."

Randy choked back a sob as he pulled up his pants. "You ain't gonna tell no one, is you?"

Julian shook his head. "I'm going to do everything in my power to erase this from my memory. Have either of you guys seen Dave?"

"Is he the husky one with the big beard?"

"That's him."

"He said he was gonna turn in early, on account of he wanted to get a good night's sleep without no more bad dreams."

"Is that right?" Julian bit his lower lip thoughtfully.

"You got wax in those big ears, Charlie?" said Denise. "Your little butt buddy ain't here. Show's over. Take a hike."

Julian nodded, and walked back briskly in the direction he had come from. After clearing the outhouse, he nearly ran right into Stacy.

"Stacy!" cried Julian. "What are you doing back here?"

"I was looking for you," said Stacy. "I thought you might have gotten lost." She cocked an eyebrow. "I *told* you not to do that."

"Where's Tim?"

"He fell asleep on the bar. Frank said it happens all the time, and to just leave him there."

Julian nodded. "He'll be out for a while."

Stacy tried to look past Julian, and Julian shifted his stance to block her view. This, of course, only served to make her even more curious. "What are you doing sneaking around out here in the dark?" She feigned left and stepped past his right.

Julian grabbed her by the arm. "Please, Stacy. Don't go back —"

She stopped him with a cold stare. She looked down at his hand on her arm, then back up into his eyes.

Julian released her. "I'm sorry. It's just that there's —"

Stacy grabbed him by the arms, shoved him against the wall, and thrust her tongue into his mouth.

Julian's thoughts grew fuzzy as all the blood in his head raced down to his groin.

Chapter 2

Tim had laughed when Katherine told him she was stepping out for some air.

"You don't even breathe," he said.

Well fuck him. Why should she even bother reporting her comings and goings anymore? Nobody ever consulted her before making decisions. *Just stuff the bitch in a bag. Toss her a rabbit from time to time.*

She beat the air with her leathery wings, climbing higher into the sky. What the hell were they doing back in Nerd World? She wanted so badly to be angry with her brother and his idiot friends, even if she knew in her cold, dead heart that everything they'd done was to protect her.

They killed her fiancé, Millard. Sure, he'd killed her and magically coerced her affection, but Tim didn't even listen to her objections.

They killed Ginfizzle. Sure, she'd been trying to kill him as well, but they didn't even let her say goodbye.

And now they brought her back here, in a fucking bag, without even asking her opinion on the matter. Sure, the bag was only there to keep her out of the sun, but she still wanted to punch something.

The mountain grew closer as she flapped. Millard's keep, her home for most of her previous stay in this world, was a jagged silhouette against the moonlit clouds.

She emitted a screech as high and loud as her dire throat could force out. A second later, the image formed in her mind, as clear as if she was seeing it with her eyes. At least two dozen shambling corpses guarded the keep, still obeying the command of a master who had long since turned into dust. They'd do nicely.

Spotting a relatively zombie-free landing spot, Katherine changed from her dire bat form to her half-elven form about ten feet from the ground. She hit the ground harder than expected, and skinned both of her knees. No big deal. They'd heal by the time she got to her feet. But she really needed to work on that entrance before trying it in front of anything living.

The nearest zombie was on top of her before she could stand up. A farmer, she judged by his torn, decaying clothes. He lunged toward her, his dried, pruny eyeballs pointed in opposite directions, both arms raised to strike. She drove her heel up into his crotch, sending him flying onto his back. That was mildly satisfying.

She tried to do that martial arts move where you spring from your back to your feet in one fluid motion. She had the Strength and Dexterity for it, but lacked the knowledge of exactly how it was done, so she spent a few seconds flopping around like a fish before giving up and standing the conventional way. Meanwhile, the zombie got to its feet like a marionette in the hands of an unskilled puppeteer.

Keeping aware of the other approaching zombies, she judged that she had sufficient time to enjoy the first one properly before she had to start fighting for real.

The zombie she'd kicked in the dick stumbled toward her, snapping its jaws, its bone and muscle tissue showing through holes in its rotting skin.

Katherine cocked her right arm back, then let her fist fly as the zombie came within range. She savored the crunch of bone as she punched through its face, taking its head clean off above the lower jaw. Now *that* was satisfying.

Catching the collapsing zombie by the wrists, she spun around, making two full rotations before connecting its foot with the head of the next one that got too close. She let go of the body, temporarily putting two more approaching zombies on their rotting asses, then charged into the horde in a whirlwind of fists, elbows, and feet.

She punched through sternums and skulls, cracked pelvic bones with kicks so hard they should have shattered her own bones.

"I am *not* a piece of luggage!" she shouted into the face of a zombie she held by the throat.

It opened its mouth wide and reached for her with its dried out tongue.

"That's fucking disgusting." She grabbed a second zombie by the throat and smashed their two heads together.

After she uppercutted the head off of the last zombie standing, Katherine stood back and surveyed the carnage. There was no way she was ever riding in a bag again, only to be pulled out at the convenience of others. She was a motherfucking badass.

The bodies were literally piled on top of one another, and she felt like she could go ten more rounds. A few of them had gotten in some lucky punches or bites, but her skin was entirely clear of bruises or scratches.

Her dress, however, was a different story. The thing was done for. Perhaps she'd underestimated just how few zombies had gotten in a lucky bite after all. No matter. Millard had spoiled her during her stay here. She had plenty to wear.

The main entrance to the keep was too secure for her to break through, so she turned into a bat and flew in through her old window. Strange as it was, it reminded her of high school, sneaking back into her room at three in the morning after making out with Tommy Hodges. *Ha! What a fucking loser.*

Katherine's room was just as she left it. The open closet showcased a number of dresses which Millard had given her, as well as the druid clothes and leather backpack she had entered this world with. Even her bath was still running. The giant, hollowed-out pumpkin overflowed with water constantly pouring out of a magical silver pitcher.

She settled on a black turtleneck sweater and a pair of pants not entirely unlike blue jeans. She'd had the hardest time explaining the concept of blue jeans to Millard, and he'd had at least as hard a time trying to re-explain it to his tailor. There was a pile of horrendously failed attempts sitting in the corner.

After peeling off the remains of what had once been a dress, but could now be better described as an assortment of torn strips of fabric glued to her body with zombie gore, Katherine ascended the steps next to her pumpkin and dipped her toe in the bath, then immediately jerked it back. The water burned her skin. She remembered a lesson she'd learned on her first day as a vampire. *Do not touch running water.* She tipped up the pitcher and waited until the water was still, then tested the water again. It wasn't exactly what she'd call refreshing, but at least it didn't burn.

Not long into her bath, the water became murky with coagulated blood and rotted chunks of flesh. That was an unpleasant surprise she'd leave for the next occupant of this manor, as Katherine had no intention of leaving behind a magical pitcher of endless water. That sort of thing could come in handy.

After she scrubbed as much zombie gore off of her body as she could, she dried off with some of the worst interpretations of blue jeans, got dressed, and gathered together a few changes of clothes, her bottle of bath salts, and the silver pitcher, and packed them into her backpack.

Katherine's departure wasn't a sentimental one. She didn't look back at Millard's keep as she flew back toward the city. Her short bat neck didn't allow it. Not wanting to draw any unnecessary attention to herself, she flew back to town in her normal bat form. Her belongings were absorbed into her body during the transformation.

The Collapsed Sewer District was easy to spot from the air. None of the city was particularly flashy by her modern standards, but the CSD stuck out like a burn scar on an otherwise hairy chest.

The Whore's Head Inn was still alive with drunken, noisy idiots. She wasn't ready to go back in there. Not yet. Part of the reason she'd gone out on her zombie-punching rampage in the first place was that she'd grown tired of hearing all the Twilight jokes. Her annoyance was only compounded by her discovery that, having no bloodstream, she was unable to join them in getting drunk. The beer, the harder stuff — What were they calling that? Rock Piss or something? —it all tasted the same to her. It was a dull, flat taste she could only describe as *not blood*. Eternal life just got a hell of a lot longer.

Katherine flew to a nearby sycamore tree and found a branch high enough to keep an eye on the inn, but with enough leaf-cover to keep herself hidden. Standing up was awkward. She was top-heavy and had to brace herself up against the trunk with her wing in order to stay upright. She sighed. Everything sucked.

"Having a rough night, are we, Miss Katherine?" said an unexpected British voice.

What the fuck? Katherine turned to her left. Julian's big, black bird friend was sharing her branch.

Judging that the branch would hold her weight, she morphed back into her standard, half-elf vampire form. The bird could only understand her if she spoke in a British accent, so she did her best.

"How did you know it was me?"

"Real bats hang upside down," said the bird.

Katherine nodded. "Good point. What are you doing hiding out in this tree?"

"Just keeping an eye on my master." He turned toward the inn. "Making sure he keeps out of trouble."

Katherine followed the bird's gaze and spotted Julian walking hurriedly from the far side of the building. Someone else was walking around from the front side, on a course to intersect his.

"Oh great," said Katherine. "Is that the skank Tim's got the hots for? Did she get a boob job?"

"Boob job, M'lady?"

"Shut up for a second. What's going on here?"

After a little bit of flirty talk, Julian grabbed Stacy by the arm.

"Whoo," said Katherine. "Boy, you better *watch* that shit. You try to grab *me* like that, and that'll be the last thing you – Oh, *snap!*"

Stacy turned the tables on Julian, shoved him up against the wall of the building, and pressed her body and face against his.

"Good heavens," said the bird. He swayed on the branch and had to flap his wings a little to keep from falling over. "I'm all overcome with a wave of emotions which I don't understand. What's she doing to him?"

"I believe that's what your people call *snogging.*" Katherine had hooked up with an English tourist in NOLA a couple of years back, and she picked up a few colorful expressions.

"Is she regurgitating food into his mouth?"

"Ew, I hope not."

When Stacy finally stepped back from Julian, the bird regained his composure. "I must say, I'm glad that's over. I felt lightheaded, and tingly around the cloaca."

"I really don't need to know that."

"The sun will be up before long, Miss," said the bird. "Perhaps it's time you should be getting inside?"

Katherine hopped down from her branch. "I'm not going inside." She sat down on the ground.

The bird puffed and fluttered his feathers. "But, Miss Katherine, —

"

"Shush," said Katherine. "I need to concentrate." She focused her mind on vermin. The site of a sewer collapse should be crawling with just what she needed. She closed her eyes and waited for the sound of a squeaking army of walking blood bags. What she heard instead was a scream.

"RATS!" The voice came from behind the far side of the building. A squat, naked man followed shortly after, his boobs bouncing with each step, and... Was his junk tucked back? No, on second thought, this was clearly a woman with a bushy brown beard. "Jesus Christmas, they're everywhere!" He almost sounded like...

"Come back!" said a tall man in leather armor from the chest up. Below that, he was struggling to pull up a pair of pants as he stumbled after the bearded woman. "It's just a couple of rats. Come on, Dennis!"

Dennis? Holy shit! Were these two the cop and the pedo? Had they just been fucking? That's hilarious.

More screams followed, these even more horrified than Dennis's had been.

"Jesus Christ!"

"My eyes!"

"Put some clothes on!"

If Katherine didn't want the rats to give away her position, she had to act fast. She grabbed the first couple that arrived and bit their heads off. Just as she was about to suck the life-juice out of them, she spotted what must have been the granddaddy of all rats. It was almost as big as her brother. She dropped the rat in her right hand and pointed at the big one.

"You, come here. The rest of you, fuck off."

The congregation of rats scattered back out into the alleys and sewers where they'd come from. The big rat approached Katherine and lay down obediently before her.

Katherine sucked the blood out of the rat in her left hand, then tossed the body aside as she focused on her prize.

"Roll over."

The rat rolled over, exposing its belly, sparsely covered in grey bristly fur. The neck appeared to be the least furry part of it.

Katherine picked up the rat with both hands, bared her fangs, and tore into its throat. It put up a brief struggle, but she held it firm and greedily gulped its life down her throat. By the time the blood stopped pouring out of its neck, requiring Katherine to squeeze and suck for more, she'd had enough anyway. She set the rat corpse down and lay on her back.

Julian's bird was still up on the branch, looking down at her. "Feeling better now?"

"Much," said Katherine. "Sorry you had to see that."

"It's quite all right, M'lady. Are you going to eat the eyes?"

"I hadn't planned on it."

"Do you mind, then?"

"Knock yourself out."

The bird flew down, plucked the rat's left eye out, and slurped up the trail of nerves and veins that followed it.

Katherine wanted to tell the bird how disgusting that looked, but figured her own display didn't leave a whole lot of room for criticism. She just turned her head away as he went after the other eye. Merely hearing it made it no less disgusting.

"Miss Katherine," said the bird after the slurping stopped. "A word about the impending sunrise and your sleeping arrangements?"

Katherine picked up the bloodless, eyeless giant rat, held it up against the tree trunk, and punched it in the head until she felt its skull crunch.

"Or not," said the bird, stepping back slowly. "I suppose I'll just leave you to it, then."

"Wait," said Katherine. "I'm going to need your help."

"I don't know how I could possibly —"

Katherine dropped to her hands and knees, face to face with Ravenus.

"M'lady?" Ravenus sounded uncomfortable. "Are we about to do *snogging?*"

"Ha!" Katherine grinned and rolled her eyes. "Keep dreaming, bird." She closed her eyes and concentrated.

When she opened them again, she was in her giant wolf form. She sniffed the earth. It was rich and moist. It would do nicely. She chose a spot and started shoveling into the ground with her massive forepaws. Within a few minutes, she had a nice big bowl-shaped hole, about three feet in diameter and four feet deep at the center. Satisfied, she morphed back into her default form.

Katherine removed a pair of not-blue-jeans out of her bag and tossed it into the hole. She strapped on the backpack so that it would be absorbed into her when she transformed again.

"I need you to bury me."

Ravenus looked at the hole. "In there?"

"Yes," said Katherine. "And I need you to keep this between you and me. Don't tell anyone where I am."

"I won't lie to my master."

"Okay, fine. But you don't have to go volunteering the information either."

"If you don't mind me saying so, Miss Katherine, this hole doesn't look very accommodating. How flexible are you?"

Katherine smiled at him. "Silly bird." She kissed the tips of her fingers and gave him a light slap on the cheek. "If you have to tell Julian, make sure and tell him *not* to tell Tim. At least not until sundown tomorrow." She morphed into her normal bat form and hopped into the hole. Once she had gotten herself snugly inside the pants, she looked up at the bird and squeaked.

The sky was just beginning to lighten as the bird shoved wing-loads of moist dirt on top of her. The thought of being buried alive had always given Katherine the willies, but now that it was actually happening, it wasn't so bad. In fact, it was the most at peace she'd felt all day.

Chapter 3

"Hey!" said a familiar voice. "Hey! Come on, man. Get up."

Tim ignored it.

"Don't you roll over on me. Rise and shine, bucko!" The slapping and kicking was more difficult to ignore.

Tim opened his eyes and swatted Frank's hand away. "Chill out, dude. I'm up. Why's everything got to be at the crack of dawn with you?"

"You went to sleep at the crack of dawn," said Frank. "Right now is the crack of mid-afternoon, and we've got some brainstorming to do." He held out a mug. "Drink this."

"Brainstorming?" said Rhonda, carrying some dirty breakfast dishes behind the bar. "With this group? My forecast is mostly cloudy with slim chance of brain."

Cooper yawned and scratched his balls under his loincloth. He looked about as rough as Tim felt. "Fucking hell. Can somebody go and put a dick in her mouth?"

"Uh-uh," said Frank. "You two lovebirds knock that shit off. We've got a real shot at getting out of here, and we need to focus."

"Is this supposed to be coffee?" asked Tim. "It tastes like river sludge. It's not even hot."

"It was hot when I started trying to wake your sorry ass up."

Tim closed his eyes and choked back the rest of the lukewarm liquid. "Start without me. I've got to take a piss."

As he got to his feet, his blurry vision sharpened on Stacy. She was sitting at a table next to Julian and smiling down at Tim.

"Charming."

"Sorry," said Tim. "I mean I've got to take a *leak.*"

"Oh, that's much better."

Tim set his empty mug down on Stacy's table and stumbled outside through the unfinished section of wall that most everyone was using as a door. It was probably a good place to put one.

He eyed the outhouse as he walked past. If he caught one whiff of it, he'd puke for sure. Puking while pissing was no easy task if you didn't want to be soaked with at least one of the two, and he didn't think his bladder could hold out much longer. Better to water the tree.

Pulling Tim Jr. out for a bit of fresh air, he aimed at a knob in the tree trunk that he hadn't yet reached. His tank was full. Today could be the day.

"Pardon me, sir."

"Jesus Christ!" Tim looked up.

Ravenus was perched on a branch, looking down at him. "Apologies, sir. I didn't mean to startle you."

"Well you startled the shit out of me!"

"You know I can't understand you when you talk like that."

Tim bottled his frustration. "Hi-ho, cheerio, pip-pip! What the fuck do you want?"

"Umm…" said Ravenus, like he was choosing his words carefully. "What, exactly, are you doing here?"

"Well blimey, guvnor. I thought I might squirt me ol' trouser snake on this here tree trunk. Now be a good chap and turn the fuck around. I can't concentrate with you looking at me."

"Does it have to be here, sir?"

"I piss here all the time."

"*Do* you?"

"Dude, what the hell is wrong with you? Give a bloke some privacy, hey?"

Ravenus lowered his head. "Very well, sir." He turned around.

Tim considered taking aim at Ravenus, but his stream would never reach that high. He focused on his original goal, and soaked his target knob with his initial blast.

"Aaaaahhhhh," Tim sighed as what felt like half of his body weight darkened the tree trunk. "Now *that's* how you start a day."

The stream flowed down the trunk, pooling at the base of the tree before meandering onto a patch of freshly-turned earth, where it seeped into the loosened soil.

What was that? Was someone starting a garden here? Why would —"Holy shit!"

Beyond the urine soaked patch of earth, an emaciated dire rat stared at him through empty eye sockets. Its dead body was suspended in a threatening pose inside some dying bushes. Its mouth hung open, showing off its spiny, needle-like teeth.

"Jesus Christ, Ravenus!" said Tim. He could see the thing was dead, but he still had the memory of those teeth raking through his flesh, scraping against his bones. "Why did you have to —"

It was too much. He dropped to his knees and threw up all over the upturned patch of earth. Since he'd drunk much more than he'd eaten, most of what came out of him was liquid, and seeped into the ground to mingle with his piss, but a few solid chunks stayed on top. Hopefully, a mixture of recycled booze and stomach acid was nutritious for seeds.

"Are you quite done, sir?" Ravenus sounded uncharacteristically stern.

Tim hopped to his feet and pointed up at the bird. "Don't you take that tone with me, you eyeball gobbling freak. What do you expect a person to do when they see..." He couldn't bear to look at the thing again, so he pointed blindly in its general direction. "...*that?*"

"I didn't... It wasn't..." Ravenus flapped his wings and ruffled his feathers before settling down. "I'm very sorry, sir."

"You'd better stick to smaller prey. I was nearly killed by dire rats. It looks like you got lucky with a skinny one, but those things are dangerous."

The experience had not been pleasant, but Tim walked back to the Whore's Head Inn with a much clearer head. His hands were sticky with vomity mud, and his knees were stained with piss-soaked soil, but at least he could think straight.

"But what makes you so sure he's a first level scrub?" asked Tony the Elf. "For all we know, he could be a twentieth level wizard."

Tim climbed onto a table, then onto a crossbeam in the gap of unfinished wall he'd walked in through, to get a better look at the crowd.

Julian stood in front of the bar, the inn's residents gathered in a semicircle around him. Cooper was behind the bar, near the cellar door. When he spotted Tim, he looked down and said something to whoever was standing next to him, most likely Dave, as the person was too short for Tim to see.

"*We* all started at level one, right?" said Julian.

Tony the Elf rolled his eyes. "That was *his* decision. What's so hard about writing *Level 20* on a character sheet?"

"He didn't have a character sheet," said Julian. "He didn't plan this out. He just threw the dice to avoid falling to his death."

"Besides," said Stuart, the monk who had helped them confront Millard the vampire, "if he were a twentieth level wizard, don't you think he'd have paid us a visit by now?"

"That doesn't mean anything," said Tony the Elf. "Maybe he's staying away because he's afraid of facing all of us together."

"Bullshit!" said a voice that Tim couldn't identify.

"Why not?" Tony the Elf addressed Frank. "That's how we faced down Eric. We stick together and defend the Whore's Head."

Frank shook his head. His little gnome fists were balled up in frustration. "Eric was no twentieth level wizard. I agree with Julian. If we sit here and wait for him, we're going to regret it. We've got the dice, and he's the only one who can use them. He's going to come after us sooner or later, and he has knowledge of this world that can help him grow very powerful very quickly."

"What about the gnome?" said Tony the Elf. He was sounding more and more desperate. "Mr. Goosewiggles?"

"Professor Goosewaddle," Julian corrected him.

"Whatever. Can't he figure out how to work the dice? We could all just go home and ditch Mordred here."

"He already told us that the magic involved was more powerful than anything he'd ever seen."

"He knew enough to recognize how they were bonded to Mordred, didn't he? Maybe he just needs to study them more. Do some reverse engineering?"

"No," said Frank. "If the professor thought he could do it, he wouldn't have dismissed the idea so quickly. He's a gnome. We're curious by nature. Anyway, you don't need to be a computer programmer to be able to recognize the on/off switch on the monitor. We need Mordred, and we've got something he wants. Our only chance is to get to him before he's so powerful that he doesn't have to bargain with us."

If Tim had to assign someone the title of Leader in the Whore's Head Inn, Frank would be the guy. But it wasn't a political position. Frank didn't actually wield any power over the others, nor did he seem to want to. He was one of the founders, though, and he had a combination of Charisma and Wisdom that made him easy to talk to and well worth listening to. But his word wasn't law, and as the discussion wore on, quite a few of the inn's residents were siding with Tony the Elf, who stood firm that they should stay together and defend their home away from home.

While fear was certainly a factor, Tony the Elf had presented some strong arguments to support his position, the strongest of which was that none of them had any idea where to look for Mordred anyway. A few of the more accomplished wizards and sorcerers among them attempted Scrying, but none of them could get a lock on him. They were looking for a fat, bearded guy in a cape. But wherever Mordred was, he was someone else now.

Cooper had either shoved or farted a path through the crowd. He, Dave, and Chaz came to meet Tim.

"What's up?" asked Tim, trying to stay half-focused on the Mordred debate.

"It's your sister," said Dave. "We can't find her."

"It's daytime, dingus. She's asleep in the Bag of Holding."

"We looked in there," said Chaz. "*I* looked in there."

Tim's attention was now firmly fixed on Chaz. His colorful silk clothes hung a little more loosely on his body, and he had a streak of grey in his hair. His encounter with the troll and his time with Millard had taken their toll on him. "What about the cellar?"

Chaz and Dave shook their heads.

"I asked around a little," said Dave. "Nobody remembers seeing her since early last night."

"Goddammit, Katherine." Tim looked around for something to punch. Coming up empty, he just shook his fist. "This is the second time she's done this. Last time she went and got herself murdered. Why can't she just hang out in a bar and drink herself to sleep like a normal person?"

"Well what the fuck are we standing around here for?" asked Cooper. "Let's go find her."

Tim shook his head. "Fuck that."

"Dude, she's your sister."

"And where do you suppose we look, Cooper? There's a big world out there, and she's got to be hiding in the dark. She could literally be anywhere. Shit! I never should have let her out of that goddamn bag."

Dave frowned. "It's only a couple of hours before sundown. Maybe she'll come back."

Tim guessed Dave was trying to be comforting, but he really sucked at it. *Maybe she'll come back*. The unspoken implication, of course, was that maybe she was a pile of ashes on a scorched bit of street somewhere. All he could do was wait and hope.

While he wasn't in the mood for company, Tim didn't want to be alone with his thoughts. Best to drown them out. He hopped down onto the floor, stomped away from his friends in a manner which he hoped made clear that he didn't want to be followed, and settled into a little nook at the back of the inn. There was no room for a table or stool. This was probably meant to be a supply closet or something when it was finished. Tim sat on the dirt floor, retrieved his flask from his vest's inside pocket, and swigged back as much stonepiss as he could gulp. It burned in his throat, and failed to block thoughts of Katherine from his mind.

Katherine wasn't a stupid girl. She was just naïve. She didn't know this game. As badass as a vampire could be, its weaknesses were numerous and severe. Tim should have kept a closer eye on her. He'd already failed to protect her once. His chest started tightening as the thought of never seeing his sister again really started to weigh in. He tried to keep his emotions at bay with another swig, but he choked it up through his nose as the tears started pouring out of his eyes. He buried his head between his knees and tried to muffle his whimpers and sobs.

"Hey, man. You all right?"

Fuck. Cooper.

The last thing Tim needed was Cooper catching him crying like a little bitch. It was bad enough he was trapped inside the body of a toddler. He faked a cough, but it came out like a squeaky dog toy.

"I'm good," Tim's voice was raw and raspy. He rubbed his face into the crook of his arm and held up his flask. "I just took some down the wrong pipe."

Cooper sucked in air through his teeth. "Shit. That must burn like a motherfucker."

Tim determined the tears still in his eyes could sufficiently be explained by the choking-on-stonepiss story. He looked up at Cooper. "Tell me about it."

Cooper's face didn't look quite as stupid as it usually did. He looked serious. "Kat'll come back. She's smarter than you think."

Tim shook his empty flask and flashed a halfhearted smile. "Time for a refill."

The Mordred debate was still raging as Tim crawled under people's legs to get behind the bar. Factions had further divided, but it didn't sound like anyone was contributing anything new to the dialogue. It was the same old bullshit, but now that the drinks had started to flow a bit, the same old bullshit was starting to heat up. Frank called Tony the Elf a coward for wanting to hide from Mordred, and Tony the Elf called Frank a coward for not wanting to defend the Whore's Head Inn.

It had always been such a chill atmosphere. Tim had never seen these guys at each other's throats like this before. He climbed up onto the bar, filled his flask from a bottle of stonepiss, necked back what was left of the bottle, then hurled it down between his feet.

The shatter of glass against the bar brought on a swift ceasefire in the arguing, as all eyes turned toward Tim.

"Shut the fuck up already!" he yelled.

Frank glared up at him. "Do you have an insight you'd like to contribute to the discussion?"

"No," said Tim. "Because you and Tony the Elf have already contributed the only two facts that matter, and they both lead to the same conclusion."

Frank's plump little gnome face was turning redder. "And what's that?"

"Mordred could be anywhere," said Tim. "There's a big world out there, and that asshole knows every inch of it. If he doesn't want to be found, we're never going to find him."

"That doesn't mean we shouldn't at least try."

Tim shook his head. "Fine. Try. Let me know how it goes." He hopped down off the bar. The crowd parted to let him pass. He walked toward the rear of the building.

"Where do you think you're going?" said Frank.

"I'm going to see if Mordred's in the toilet. I'll report back soon."

While Tim did need to pee, he was more relieved to be walking away from the Whore's Head Inn than he was to be walking toward his favorite pissing tree.

"Tim," Cooper called out after him. "Wait up." It felt suspiciously like his friends didn't trust him to be alone.

"What? Do you want to watch me take a piss?"

"Uh… sure."

Tim couldn't help but smile a little to himself. Suicide watch was a sweet, if unnecessary, gesture. He stopped smiling when he looked ahead and saw Ravenus still perched on the same branch of the pissing tree. He couldn't put his finger on why, but he kind of expected to see him there. There was something peculiar about the way that bird was acting today.

"Good day, gentlemen," said Ravenus as Tim and Cooper approached the tree.

Tim ignored him and pulled out his sad little dick. If the bird wanted to watch, so be it. Knowing his bladder wasn't full enough to try for a new height, he pissed a lazy zig-zag pattern on the lower trunk.

When he was done, he didn't feel like going back to the inn just yet.

"Hey, Coop. Why don't you head back in? I could use a little alone time. It's thoughtful of you to worry about me, but —"

"Who said I'm worried about you?" Cooper squatted, holding onto the tree trunk for support. "I came out here to drop a deuce."

Tim turned away and hoped it wouldn't be noisy.

"Oh dear," said Ravenus. "Is he about to…"

"Dude," said Cooper. "Could you ask the bird not to watch? He's breaking my concentration."

"Hey! Bloke!" Tim shouted up at Ravenus. "Stop being creepy, huh?"

"A thousand apologies, sir," said Ravenus. "But do you think you could ask him to do that somewhere else?"

"Fuck you, Ravenus! Nobody's begging you to watch. If you don't like it, then get the fuck out of here."

"Oh, that's good," said Cooper. "Keep shouting at him. I've got my concentration back."

"Please, sir," pleaded Ravenus. "Literally *anywhere* else would do."

Un-fucking-believable. "Listen, Ravenus. I've got a lot on my mind right now, and you're really starting to weird me out, so I'm going to make this as plain as I can. Please go away, you fat, feathered fuck."

Ravenus stared down at him for a moment, his beak wide open. He ruffled his feathers and took a few deep breaths. "My diet… is different here… than it was in the wild." His voice cracked as he spoke. He took another deep breath. "And I feel I should point out that you've put on a bit of weight yourself." He stuck his chest out defiantly, ready for whatever further insults Tim had to hurl his way.

"Ahhhhh," said Cooper. "There it is. Nice and smooth, like soft serve."

Ravenus buried his head under a wing.

Tim didn't need guilt heaped on top of the pile of emotions that was already weighing him down. "I'm sorry, Ravenus. That was wrong of me. I'm just worried about my sister, and I took it out on you."

Ravenus peeked out from under his wing. "Your sister?"

"She's been missing all day, and I'm worried about her getting caught out in the sun."

"Hmph," said Ravenus. He lowered his wing and glanced down at Cooper, who was humming to himself and swerving his hips in a circular motion as the shit continued to flow. "That's the least of her worries."

Tim looked curiously up at the bird. "What do you mean?"

Ravenus turned sharply back to Tim. "What? Nothing!"

Tim didn't need a Sense Motive check to see the bird was hiding something. "Ravenus." He spoke calmly but sternly. "Is there something you're not telling me? Do you know something about Katherine?"

Ravenus shifted his weight from one foot to the other. "Of course not, sir! Nothing at all! Who's Katherine?"

"Bullshit!" Tim hurled his flask at Ravenus, hitting him in the face and knocking him off his perch. The stunned bird landed with a thud on the ground, and Tim pinned him down with both hands.

"Holy shit!" said Cooper. "Tim! What the fuck are you doing?"

"Stay out of this, Cooper!" Tim stared into Ravenus's eyes. "Tell me what you know."

Wrestling a bird was harder than Tim would have imagined. Flapping wings repeatedly smacked Tim in the face, and he had to practically lie down on top of Ravenus to keep his talons pinned to the ground.

"I can't, sir!" Ravenus shrieked. "I'm sworn to secrecy!"

"I don't want to have to do this, Ravenus. But you're not leaving me any choice." Tim plucked one of Ravenus's tail feathers.

Ravenus squawked. "Stop that! I need those!"

"Where is she?"

"Please, sir! If you'd just calm down, the whole matter will be resolved in a few —"

"You think I'm fucking around?" *Pluck. SQUAWK!* "You better start talking, bird, or you're going to be as bald as my fat little ass! What do you know abou—"

Tim got tackled by what felt like a speeding freight train. The world spun around his head. When it stopped, he was staring up at Julian, who was pinning his arms to the ground. Ravenus flew back up to the safety of his branch.

Tim squirmed under Julian's weight. "Get the fuck off of me!"

Julian held him down firmly. "What the hell do you think you were doing to Ravenus?" He looked up at Cooper. "Why didn't you stop — Ugh!" A knee in the nuts loosened his grip.

Tim pushed Julian off and rolled away. "That bird's holding out on me!"

Julian stood up slowly on shaky legs, cradling his balls. "What are you talking about?"

"He said it himself. He's *sworn to secrecy*. Ask him."

Julian looked up at his familiar. "Ravenus?"

Ravenus lowered his head. "I'm sorry, sir."

"You see?" said Tim. "I told you! He's been sitting on that fucking branch acting suspicious all day."

Julian looked up at the branch, and from there back to the Whore's Head. His eyes widened.

"I can't betray my —"

"Shut up, Ravenus!" said Julian. "Don't say another word."

Tim tugged at handfuls of his own hair. "What?"

Julian shifted his gaze from Ravenus's branch to the inn and back again before glaring at Tim. "How dare you torture my familiar for information. He's got as much right to privacy as any of us."

"Are you fucking kidding me!" said Tim. "His feathers will grow back! Katherine's life might be on the line here!"

Julian looked genuinely puzzled. "Your sister? What does she have to do with any of this?"

Tim shook his fists. "That's exactly what I want to find out!"

Julian pursed his lips and furrowed his brow. "Do you mind if I have a word alone with Ravenus?"

Tim sighed and rolled his eyes. "Whatever. Sure." He bent over to pick up his flask while Julian walked off with his crazy-ass bird on his shoulder, whispering in his ear.

All Tim could hear was Julian's side of the conversation, which wasn't very informative.

"Oh? *Oh*. Ohhhhh…. Oh!"

"What the fuck!" said Cooper. "Did I accidentally shit out a pentagram?"

That was enough to pull Tim's attention away from Julian and Ravenus's conversation. "What set of circumstances could possibly compel you to ask – Holy shit!"

The patch of freshly turned earth on which Cooper had just finished defecating was shifting, as if some living thing was buried underneath, and trying to get out. Tim had already spent his default reaction to such a situation on the tree trunk. Before he had time to come up with a new reaction, a fist burst out of the ground.

"Fucking zombies," said Cooper. He casually walked over to the unearthed forearm and started stomping on it.

"NOOO!" Ravenus cried. He flew into Cooper's face and squawked and cawed.

Cooper tried to swat at him while continuing to stomp on the zombie arm. "Ravenus! Knock it off, you stupid fucking – Whoa!"

The hand grabbed Cooper's ankle and pulled his foot right out from under him, sending him crashing onto his back straight into his own pile of shit.. It balled up into a fist again and punched him square in the junk.

Cooper groaned and rolled out of the way before the hand could strike again.

But the hand didn't even try to strike. It rubbed its fingers together, then shook violently, as if it realized it was tainted with Cooper's nut musk. The hand felt around in flattened poo until it found a patch of clean grass, then wiped itself, its slender white fingers twitching the whole time.

Finally, the hand dissolved into a wisp of vapor. This was no zombie.

Tim looked at the patch of earth. His own dried chunks of vomit were still visible in Cooper's fresh turdcake. "Shit."

A column of red vapor shot out of the hole the hand had created; a geyser of pissed off Katherine. It formed a mushroom cloud ten feet in the air.

Tim took a step back. Cooper crawled away from the cloud as well, one hand still cradling his balls.

Once all the mist had ejected itself from the hole in the ground, it started to condense into larger droplets about ten feet away from Cooper's shit pile. In a matter of seconds, the mist had coalesced into the recognizable shape of a red, liquid woman. The finer details, such as whatever was going on on top of her head, were not revealed until the transformation was complete, and her normal colors returned.

"What the hell is *wrong* with you people?" asked Katherine as soon as she was whole again.

It had been pretty messed up to see her explode out of the ground in a bloodmist and come together as a person like a red T-1000, but it was somehow stranger to see her standing here now, in blue jeans and a black, damp turtleneck, and a pair of pants not entirely unlike blue jeans on top of her head.

"Katherine?" said Cooper, apparently only now catching up to what was going on.

Katherine pulled the strange pants off the top of her head and flung them on the ground. "Why does everyone in the world suddenly decide to relieve themselves on the spot where I chose to sleep?"

"You've got no room to complain," said Tim. "Not after what you put me through. I've been worried sick about you all day!" At least for as much of the day as he'd realized she was missing. "Anyway, how the hell were we supposed to know where you were? Next time maybe you should tell someone before you up and decide to bury yourself under the pissing tree."

Katherine glared at Ravenus. "I *did* tell someone."

"I'm sorry, Miss Katherine," said Ravenus. "I tried to dissuade them."

"Don't apologize to her," said Tim. "She got exactly what she deserved." He looked up at Katherine. "None of this would have happened if you'd slept in the Bag of Holding. Nobody ever pisses or pukes in there."

Katherine raised her eyebrows at him.

"I mean, not since that first time."

"I'm not getting back in that bag. *Ever.*" She took off her backpack and pulled out a silver pitcher.

"Please," said Tim. "You won't survive long if you keep trying to hide in shallow holes every day. Sooner or later a dog is going to dig you up or something, and you'll be fried in the sunlight. Just play it safe until you've got a better idea of what you're doing."

"I know *exactly* what I'm doing," said Katherine, running her fingers through the tangles of her filthy hair. "I'll figure out a better sleeping arrangement after I figure out how I'm going to get the pee smell out of – Yow!" Katherine dropped the pitcher. The hand that she'd been holding her hair with was sizzling and smoking. "Fuck, that hurts! What was I thinking?"

Water continued to flow from the mouth of the pitcher. The expanding puddle crept toward Katherine's feet. Of course, she was too busy nursing her burning hand to notice.

Tim waited a few seconds before alerting her. "Katherine?"

"What?" she snarled, baring her fangs at him.

"Look down."

"Huh?" She looked down just in time to see the puddle nearly touching her toes. "Shit!" She jumped up in the air, transformed into a bat, and flew up to the branch Ravenus had been sitting on all day, where she once again took her half-elf/goth/beatnik form.

"Is that acid?" asked Julian, stepping cautiously up to the border of the expanding puddle.

"Nope," said Tim, stepping into the water to demonstrate how little harm would come to him. "Just plain old water. My sister, who knows *exactly* what she's doing, is learning a valuable lesson about how running water affects vampires. From the sound of it, this may not be her first time learning this lesson."

"It's not a big deal," said Katherine. She held out her hand. "See? It's already healed."

"So what are you going to do in your hole when there's a heavy rain, or when a dire bear decides to take a piss on you?"

"That was really the second danger scenario to pop into your head?"

"Hey guys?" said Cooper. "How much water does that fucking thing hold?" The puddle had spread out to reach him by this point, and water was still freely flowing out of the pitcher.

Tim picked up the pitcher, and the water stopped. When he tipped it sideways again, water poured out, but the weight didn't decrease at all. "Is this a Decanter of Endless Water?" He looked up at Katherine. "Where did you get this?"

"I picked it up while I was getting my things at Millard's place. I thought it might be useful."

"Oh shit," said Tim. He dropped the decanter on the ground and looked at Cooper and Julian. "I know where Mordred is."

Chapter 4

Stacy didn't know what the motivation was behind Tim's outburst. The little self-loathing drunk was constantly trying to bring people down to his level, and it looked like he'd succeeded. Tempers had been high in the Whore's Head Inn, but at least everyone had been trying to come up with a solution to their common problem. Now they all just seemed hopelessly apathetic.

She and Julian had done their best to keep the discussion going until Julian suddenly and inexplicably screamed "Ravenus" and ran out of the building. He was an odd one, but Stacy found it charming how much he cared for his silly talking bird.

There was nothing more adorable, however, than a gloomy gnome. Frank sat at the bar on a stool taller than himself, swinging his little legs and propping his head up with one fist, quietly nursing a beer. His red cap and rosy cheeks highlighted the whiteness of his bushy beard.

Stacy pulled up a stool next to Frank. "Wanna talk?"

Frank sighed without looking up from his beer. "Not really."

"Wanna blow job?"

Frank's eyes lit up like two little emeralds as he looked up at her.

She grinned at him. "Not gonna happen, but it's nice to see that sparkle of hope in your eyes that you had when you were talking about finding Mordred."

"Hmph," said Frank. He sipped his beer. "Hope in one hand, shit in the other. See which one fills up first. It's just like your boyfriend said, we don't even know where to begin —"

"I'm sorry," said Stacy. "My boyfriend?"

"Yeah. Tim."

Stacy laughed. "Tim and I aren't... Wait, are people saying that?"

"Gorgonzola told me that Tim had been sitting at their table before joining us here at the bar last night, and he told them to quit staring at you. You were *his*."

Stacy narrowed her eyes. "*Did* he now?" She had a hunch it was going to come to this sooner or later. That was half the reason she'd accosted Julian as indiscreetly as she did the night before. She didn't want to slut it up right there in the bar, but if someone had been walking around outside and happened to see them, and word started to spread... It might have given Tim the hint he needed before he publicly declared his undying love or whatever.

She went to the other side of the bar and helped herself to a beer. "That little prick's got some nerve."

"That he does." Frank spoke as if she was talking about an admirable quality.

"Hey, Frank," said Frank's main adversary during the Mordred debate. *Tony the Elf*, Stacy seemed to remember people calling him. "I'm sorry things got so intense before. I shouldn't have said some of the things I said. No hard feelings, huh?"

"Nah," said Frank. "We both just want what's best for everyone. Sit down. Have a drink."

Was that it? Stacy still wanted to cut bitches from high school over less heated exchanges.

"You were right," Frank continued. "There's no point in fighting if we haven't got the first clue as to where to start looking."

"Stacy!" cried a shrill, inebriated voice from outside. Tim stepped down hard on the edge of a loose plank by the unfinished section of wall. The plank tilted upright and slammed into Tim's face. "Ow! Fuck!" It should have been hilarious, but the gloomy crowd just watched in stunned silence as the board fell back into place and Tim stumbled into the room, his nose bleeding into his mouth. "Stacy, I need you!"

Oh. My. God. Every person holding a drink suddenly found something fascinating inside it. Those without drinks took some time to appreciate the grain patterns in the nearest pieces of lumber. They were embarrassed for him. They were more embarrassed for her.

"Tim, this is neither the time nor the place for –"

"I know where Mordred is."

"What?"

"Was he in the toilet?" asked Tony the Elf. "Or did you find him at the bottom of your flask?"

Tim wiped his sleeve across his face, leaving behind a long red stripe. "I'll tell you where he is, motherfucker. If he started out at Level 1 like the rest of us, and he doesn't want to stay there for long, he'll be heading for the biggest stockpile of weapons, armor, magical accessories, and gold in the world."

"And where's that?" Tony the Elf's tone suggested he still wasn't taking Tim seriously.

Stacy, however, was suddenly taking Tim very seriously. "The Horsemen's villa."

"Do you remember where it is?" asked Tim.

"Not exactly, but if we follow the river, I'll recognize it when I see it."

"Well, Tony the Elf," said Frank. "You about ready to start fighting again?"

"Frank," said Tim. "We're going to need the Flying Carpet."

"And the Bag of Holding," said Julian, stepping in from outside. Both Tim and Frank looked at him questioningly. "It's the best tool we've got for taking him alive and keeping him under our control."

"It *is*, isn't it?" said a female voice from above.

Stacy looked up. Tim's sister, Katherine, was sitting on a partially completed section of the roof. She was wearing a black turtleneck sweater and a pair of blue jeans. Her icy blue eyes were staring straight at Stacy. When their eyes met, Katherine gave Stacy a casual smile, one that wouldn't have been at all menacing if performed by a person with normal teeth.

"They're in the cellar," said Frank. "Take what you need."

Tim and Julian started moving toward the cellar.

"But how about you leave those dice behind?" said Frank.

Tim and Julian stopped and looked at each other. "What?" said Julian. "Like, collateral?"

"You don't trust us, Frank?" said Tim. "You really think we'd fuck off back home and ditch you here?"

Frank sipped his beer. "I trust you. I just don't think it's a good idea to have Mordred and the dice in such close proximity before we do have him under our control. You know, just in case things go south."

Tim looked at Julian.

Julian paused, his right hand tucked under his serape. Eventually, he nodded. "It makes sense." He pulled out a small black pouch and set it on the bar in front of Frank. "Keep these on you at all times."

Frank nodded and put the pouch in his pants pocket.

Stacy was interested in seeing the cellar. She reminded herself not to expect all the wonders she'd seen at the Horsemen's villa, but there could still be a few neat things. She allowed Julian to go first as they followed Tim to the cellar door.. Tim opened the door and started walking down the stairs.

"Why yes, Mr. McConaughey, I *do* like it rough," said a gruff female voice from below.

Stacy, Tim, and Julian stopped halfway down the stairs and exchanged a glance. Tim shrugged. There was no time to waste. Stacy and Julian proceeded hesitantly, but Tim seemed to be in even more of a rush than he'd been in before.

Reaching the bottom of the staircase and turning right, Tim's jaw dropped like he was looking at a shiny new bike under the Christmas tree. He waved excitedly for Stacy and Julian to follow.

Stacy glided swiftly and silently down the stairs, surprised at how nimble she was. When she reached Tim, she peeked around the corner to see what he was so giddy about. Denise, the cop who had drawn the game's short straw and turned into a short, fat, bearded woman, was standing with her back to them, bare-ass naked from the waist down. She had one leg jacked up on a crate full of weapons, and seemed to be trying to shove a large black rod up her cooch.

"Give it to me like I'm Jodie Foster!"

That was Tim's breaking point. He started laughing his ass off.

"Wha! Who!" said Denise, hastily removing the rod and turning around. The rod, as it turned out, was actually a giant wooden dildo. "You fuckin' perverts! Get the fuck outta here!"

Stacy suspected Denise was only trying to cover her girly bits while still holding on to her toy, but the position she was holding it in was disturbingly anatomically accurate. The effect was such that she looked like a short fat man holding up his massive black member.

Tim fell into a fetal position and laughed even harder, tears streaming down his red cheeks.

"Oh, Dennis," said Julian. "Not again."

Stacy looked at Julian. "*Again?*"

Tim's fit of laughter escalated even further. He punched the dirt floor.

Stacy nudged Tim with her foot, careful to avoid any blood or urine. "Tim! Get a hold of yourself." In retrospect, it was not the wisest selection of words, given the circumstances. Tim stopped laughing just long enough to open his eyes, see Denise, misinterpret Stacy's meaning, and fly into another fit of giggling.

"Go on now!" cried Denise. "Y'all get the fuck out!"

"I'm so sorry," said Stacy. "We'll be out of your hair in no time. We've just got to get a couple of things. Julian, let's hurry this up."

"And listen," said Julian. "I know you'd rather us all just pretend we didn't see anything, but I feel I should warn you. Make sure you give that thing a good scrub down before you... um...*use* it. You don't want to know where it's been."

Denise let the dildo drop to the floor as she sat down, buried her bearded face in her hands, and started sobbing. Stacy noticed that the other end of it was sharpened to a point. That seemed unnecessarily dangerous.

Stacy wanted to comfort her, or at least give her some privacy, but precious seconds were slipping away. While Julian grabbed the magic carpet and bag, she helped herself to a sword, as the one she'd arrived with had been quickly taken from her by the Horsemen. She chose a similar one, lightweight with a long, slender blade. It slid nicely into the leather sheath she had strapped to her back. Somehow, this made her feel more whole.

Having procured what they'd come for, Stacy and Julian stepped over Tim and toward the stairwell. Stacy had half a mind to leave Tim behind in his pee-soaked dickishness, but he had been the only one to come up with a viable theory as to where to find Mordred, however obvious it seemed in retrospect. That counted for something.

"Are you coming?"

Surprisingly, Tim stopped laughing. He looked at Denise, then at the big dildo. He hopped to his feet and scurried past Stacy and Julian and up the stairs.

"What was that about?" asked Stacy.

"Nothing!" Julian abruptly responded.

"What's taking so long?" called Cooper from the top of the stairwell. "Are you guys getting your freak on down – Hey! Tim! Watch where you're – Fuck! Ow! Shit! Motherfu—Ow!" He crashed down the stairs with all the grace of a sack full of bowling balls, landing on his back at the bottom of the stairs with his head in Tim's pee puddle.

"Cooper!" said Julian. "Are you okay?"

"Never better." He cracked his neck one way, then the other, and his gaze fell on the dildo lying on the floor next to a still-weeping Denise. He snorted out a laugh. "Brings back some memories, eh Julian?"

"Dude, shut up!"

"Fuck, my ass hurts just *looking* at that thing."

Silence engulfed the cellar as Denise stopped crying, stopped breathing, and her heart probably stopped beating.

"What's going on?" asked Cooper. "What'd I say?"

Stacy stared at the dildo, then at Denise. "Oh no."

Denise stared back at her with red, glistening eyes. She gulped. "I need a moment alone."

Stacy nodded. "Yeah. Sure thing." She grabbed Cooper's outstretched arm by the wrist and yanked him to his feet.

"Goddamn, girl," said Cooper. "What's your Strength score?"

"You just march your ass up those stairs."

Julian looked like he'd rather be showering with Hitler than spending any more time in this cellar, but he was having an awkward time maneuvering the bulky, rolled-up carpet.

Stacy rolled her eyes and grinned at him. "Use the bag, dummy."

"Oh," said Julian. "Good idea." He wrapped the mouth of the Bag of Holding over the top end of the carpet and pulled down. The bag easily managed the impossible task of swallowing up the entire thing. Julian smiled at her. "Very clever."

Stacy shot him a wink and a kiss. From the look on his face, you'd think she'd stabbed him in the gut with the tail end of that dildo. She thought she might be able to ignite a torch on the tips of his ears.

Julian hurried up the stairs, and Stacy followed and hurriedly closed the door behind her.

"NOOOOOOOOOOOOOOOOOOOOOOOOOOO!" cried Denise from the bowels of the Whore's Head Inn. If she thought she was being discreet by waiting for the cellar door to close, she was mistaken.

"What happened?" asked Frank.

"Is that Denise?" asked Randy, standing up at the table where he'd been mingling with the other patrons far more successfully than Stacy thought he was capable of. "What's wrong with hi—er?"

"She's just having a little trouble adjusting to all this," said Stacy. "Maybe you should stay behind and be there for her once she composes herself."

Randy nodded. Stacy could tell he didn't need much convincing. She knew people like him. Sweet folks with big hearts who had, for whatever reason, been marginalized by society and stripped of their confidence. Sitting here, in this half-completed bar, shooting the breeze with a few guys over a beer, seemed like a luxury for him. Here he was an equal, and he was relishing every moment of it.

"You coming, Dave?" asked Julian.

Dave and Chaz were sitting at another table with three people unfamiliar to Stacy. Unlike Randy's table, the five of them looked to be merely tolerating each other's company for the sake of having somewhere to sit and drink.

Dave sighed and stood up. "I guess." Chaz followed.

"We're going after Mordred," Stacy announced to the room. "I know I'm a newcomer here, but I think it's safe to say that none of us know what to expect when we find him. If anyone would like to join us, we've got a little more room on the carpet."

Stuart, the bald man who had introduced Stacy to the Whore's Head Inn when she'd first entered the city, stood up. "I'll go!"

"No!" cried the woman next to him, grabbing his wrist. She was dressed in what looked like shiny, metallic underwear. "It's too dangerous. Last time you left, you almost died."

"Sit down, Stuart," said Tony the Elf. "Stay with your wife. I'll go, if for no other reason than to personally make sure these idiots don't screw everything up."

That seemed unnecessarily harsh to Stacy. She looked at Cooper picking his nose while Tim drank from his flask, not even bothering to try to hide the wet spot on his pants, and conceded that Tony the Elf might have a point.

Frank slapped Tony the Elf on the shoulder. "You're a good man."

Tony the Elf let out a loud, high-pitched whistle. "Dave!"

"What?" said Dave, who was standing right next to him.

Tony the Elf didn't even look at him. His eyes were fixed on the rear exit of the inn. After a couple of seconds passed, a big shaggy sheepdog came bounding through. Tony the Elf crouched down, and the dog put its front paws on his shoulders and licked his face.

"Oh!" said Stacy. "Look at you!" She stroked the fur on the dog's back, which it didn't object to at all. "What's your name?"

"It's Dave," Dave grumbled.

Once Dave the dog had greeted his master long enough, he turned his attention to Stacy, knocking her down on the floor and licking her face until he stopped suddenly. He backed away slowly with a low, rumbling growl.

Katherine had hopped down from the roof. She stood, looking down her nose at the growling sheepdog. "You're bringing your dog with you?"

"He's my Animal Companion," said Tony the Elf, putting a calming arm around his dog. "Where I go, he goes."

Katherine bared her fangs at Dave the dog. "This rug is getting too crowded. I'll just fly separately." Stacy couldn't help noticing that Katherine seemed to harbor some kind of special resentment toward this poor dog which couldn't be entirely explained by the mere fact that she was a hateful bitch. "I'll be outside," said Katherine. She turned into a bat and flew through the open roof.

The assembled crowd oohed and aahed, like they'd never seen a bitch turn into a bat before. They were only slightly less impressed when Julian pulled a giant, rolled up carpet out of a bag much too small to physically contain it. They backed out to give him room as he unrolled it on the floor.

By the time Stacy, Julian, Tim, Cooper, Dave, Chaz, Tony the Elf, and his dog took their seats, Stacy confessed to herself that Katherine had been right about it being too crowded. It didn't help that Cooper and Tim smelled like bus station toilets.

Julian placed his palm flat on the surface of the carpet, then raised it slowly. As he did so, the carpet lifted off the floor, soliciting another round of oohs and aahs.

"You kids be careful," said Frank, saluting at Julian.

Julian returned his salute, then traced his finger in a clockwise, circular pattern on the surface of the carpet, causing it to rotate until they were facing east. Moving his hand, he positioned the carpet so that they weren't under any part of the roof that had already been completed. Once he was satisfied that they were clear, he raised the carpet at least thirty feet in the air.

In spite of the smell, everyone huddled a little closer to the center.

"Whoa!" said Stacy, taking in the aerial view of the city. It was still early enough in the evening for her to make out the streets and buildings, and just getting dark enough to notice all the street lamps were lit. "Do those run on electricity?"

"Magic," said Julian. "Inside each lamp is a permanently enchanted Light stone."

"You wanna get this thing moving?" said Tim. "I've got a whiz to throw as soon as we clear the city walls."

Stacy considered telling him to just pee his pants again, but she held her tongue. It was a little too mean, and she didn't want to risk the chance of him taking her up on the suggestion.

Julian slid his hand forward on the carpet, and they started moving. It was a slow start, like a car in first gear. But unlike a car, the carpet remained crawling through the air at a snail's pace. Katherine and Ravenus flew in circles around the carpet like little moons until Katherine finally broke free from her orbit.

She landed on the roof of a building just ahead of them and morphed into her standard form. "What's with this funeral procession bullshit?"

Julian slid his palm forward a couple more times. "I'm giving it all she's got."

Cooper farted. "I could walk faster than this."

That sounded like a fine idea to Stacy. She tried in vain to wave away the cloud of fart that surrounded them. "You might have to do that," she said. "We're carrying too much weight."

"How do you know?" asked Tim.

"When the Horsemen first caught me, they'd already done some adventuring that day. We were flying slowly like this until they started dumping treasure over the side."

Julian held up the Bag of Holding. "Anyone feel like riding in here?"

Everyone looked at Chaz.

Chaz shook his head. "No fucking way, man."

"All right," said Julian. "I'm taking her down." The carpet descended until it was hovering three feet above the street. They'd only made it about two hundred yards from the Whore's Head Inn. "Hop down, Cooper."

"Dude!" said Cooper. "You're making me fucking walk?"

"Of course not," said Julian. "We're in a hurry. Horse."

Stacy was confused by the last part of what Julian said until she turned her head and saw a big brown horse staring back at her.

"That's more like it," said Cooper. He stepped off of the carpet and mounted the horse.

"Let's see if that's enough," said Julian. He stroked the carpet. It crept slowly forward. "Apparently not. We'll have to dump someone else."

All eyes turned to Chaz again.

"Seriously," said Chaz. "Screw you guys."

"Cooper," said Stacy.

"Huh?"

"Catch!" She grabbed an unsuspecting Tim under the arms and tossed him at Cooper.

"Shit!" cried both Tim and Cooper. Cooper caught Tim and placed him on the horse in front of himself.

"What the hell was that for?" asked Tim.

Stacy shrugged. "We had too much weight. You two can ride together."

"I barely fucking weigh anything!" Tim protested. "You should know. You just fucking threw me. How big a difference could I possibly make?"

Stacy turned to Julian. "Give it a try?"

Julian slid his hand forward. The carpet moved so fast that Dave fell off the back.

"FU—" It was a short fall.

"I guess that answers that," said Julian. He ran his hand backwards on the carpet, and they flew back to pick Dave up. "Sorry about that, Dave. Still getting a feel for this thing."

"You okay?" asked Stacy.

Dave stood on trembling legs. "If we had been higher up..."

Stacy offered him her hand. "Don't think like that." She pulled him back onto the carpet. "Just sit tight and don't look down. You can hold my hand if you want."

Dave nodded and held her hand tightly.

"Jesus Christ," said Tim. "Why don't you breastfeed him while you're at it?"

Stacy ignored Tim, satisfied with his reaction.

"Let's move!" said Tony the Elf. "We've wasted too much time as it is."

Julian raised the carpet high enough so that they could see over the rooftops, but he flew along the streets so that Cooper and Tim could follow on horseback.

Once they passed over the city walls, Katherine took the form of a much larger bat, comparable in size to the horse Julian had called into existence. Where she had been struggling to keep up before, she now overtook the horse and carpet with ease.

Stacy was able to spot her place of captivity long before she'd expected to, and her heart sank. It was the one on fire.

Chapter 5

The fire was big for sure, but not quite so big as Julian had first thought. Now that they were closer, he could see that a portion of the flames he'd thought he was seeing was actually the reflection from the surface of a large swimming pool next to the house.

Chaz whistled. "Sweet digs."

"Not so sweet anymore," said Stacy. "It looks like we're too late."

Julian frowned. "Maybe we should have visited here before spending the night getting shitfaced."

"Don't fucking pin this on me," said Tim. "I'm the one who thought to come here."

"I'm not trying to pin anything on you. I'm just –"

"Shut up, the both of you," said Tony the Elf. "What's done is done. Bring us down next to the pool and we'll form a bucket brigade. We don't know how long this fire has been going. There may yet be something we can salvage, if only a clue as to where Mordred may have gone from here."

"Ravenus!" Julian called out.

"Up here, sir."

Julian looked up. Ravenus was perched atop his quarterstaff.

"Oh, good. Ravenus, I want you to circle the perimeter and see if you can spot Mordred."

"At once, sir! What does he look like?"

"I have no idea."

"Right!" Ravenus nodded his head decisively. "I'm on it!" He flapped off into the night sky.

Julian brought the carpet down on the opposite side of the pool from the burning building. The heat given off by the flames was pretty intense, and the smoke stung his eyes.

Having no bucket, Dave volunteered his breastplate. It would hold a decent amount of water, and maybe keep him from baking alive inside his armor.

Cooper took the position closest to the pool, followed by Dave, then Tony the Elf, and ending with Stacy. She was as close to the fire as anyone dared get. Much to Julian's surprise, it looked like it might work. Cooper scooped up as much water as he could, and they only lost about half of it by the end of the chain, at which point Stacy hurled whatever was left into the fire and tossed the breastplate back to Cooper. She was stronger than she looked, and barely breaking a sweat next to the raging fire.

"What should I do?" asked Chaz.

"Play a song!" said Tony the Elf.

Chaz folded his arms. "I know I'm not the most useful member of the party or whatever. But I want to help. You don't have to be a dick."

Tony the Elf's eyes were tearing up from the smoke. He passed Dave's breastplate to Stacy. "If you want to help, then play a goddamn song!" While waiting for the breastplate to cycle back to him, he wiped sweat and soot from his face with his sleeve. "You're a bard. Your purpose is to play music to bring out the best in others. Give us a rhythm to work to."

Chaz pulled the lute off his back and bit his lower lip. Finally, he looked up. "I think I've got something." When he started picking at the strings, the tune wasn't entirely unfamiliar.

"Nice one!" said Stacy.

Two lines into the lyrics, Cooper stopped mid-scoop. "*Nine to Five?*" he said. "Fucking Dolly Parton? That's the best you've got?"

"Cooper!" Stacy shouted.

Cooper resumed the task at hand, and they actually seemed to become more efficient, the breastplate moving more smoothly and quickly from person to person, and spilling less water.

"Well how about that?" said Julian.

"It's still going to take forever," said Katherine, startling Julian. He hadn't even realized she was standing right behind him. "Take us up over the house. I've got an idea."

"Me too," said Tim, hopping back onto the carpet as Julian guided it into the air.

"Okay," said Katherine once the carpet was directly above the house. "Stop here."

As she rummaged through her bag, Tim pulled his idea out of the front of his pants and stood at the carpet's edge. "Suck it, fire!"

"*Workin' nine to*– Hey, man! What the fuck!"

Tim looked over the side. "Oh shit. Sorry! It got caught in the wind!"

"Get out of the way," said Katherine, holding a silver pitcher. When she tipped it over, a small, but steady stream of water flowed out.

Julian maneuvered the carpet to adjust for the wind until the stream was pouring right into the fire. It wasn't going to make a huge difference, but he guessed every little bit helped.

"What are you doing?" asked Tim. "Don't you know that thing has different settings?"

"Settings?"

"Here, give me that."

"Wash your hands first."

Tim rolled his eyes and rubbed his hands together as Katherine poured water over them. "Satisfied?"

Katherine handed over the pitcher.

"Back up the carpet," Tim told Julian. As Julian backed up, Tim nodded and grinned. "Now get a load of this shit." He aimed the pitcher down, its mouth pointed directly at the fire. "Geyser!"

A second later, Tim disappeared, having been replaced with a jet of water and the word "FUUUUUUUUUUUUCK!"

"Tim!" cried Katherine.

Julian followed the collapsing trail of the stream. Tim was lying motionless on his back, in the middle of a field, the silver pitcher resting next to him. Julian guided the carpet down.

Katherine didn't waste any time. She jumped down off the carpet without even bothering to transform into anything. She hit the ground running and was at her brother's side in seconds. "Tim! Are you okay?"

Tim sat up slowly. "Fuck, that hurt."

"That was really stupid of you!" Katherine scolded him.

"I'm too small," said Tim. He looked up at Julian.

Julian nodded, and they both spoke in unison. "Cooper."

Katherine and Tim climbed back aboard the carpet, and Julian ferried them back to the swimming pool.

"Cooper!" Tim shouted as they approached.

"Huh?" said Cooper, turning toward him. Dave's breastplate hit him in the back of the head and fell into the pool. "Ow!" He looked down at the sinking breastplate. "Shit!"

"Leave it," said Tim. He held out the pitcher. "Try this."

"Dude," said Cooper. "I don't want to be judgmental about your drinking problem or whatever, but we're kind of in the middle of something here."

"What? I don't... Fuck you. Just point this at the fire and brace yourself."

Cooper took the pitcher and held the opening out toward the fire. "Now what?"

"Say *geyser.*"

"Geyser?" The force nearly knocked Cooper back into the swimming pool, but he managed to steady himself and hold the pitcher firmly as a torrent of water blasted continuously out of it. "Oh *hell* yes!"

After a minute, Tim could already see the flames receding. The heat was noticeably less intense.

Stacy stood back and smiled, her white teeth and eyes shining from her blackened, sooty face. "Way to go, Tim!"

Tim's face turned red as he smiled back at her, looking quite pleased with himself. Julian was happy for him. If anyone needed a win, it was —

Tim snapped his fingers. "It's still not enough. I've got another idea."

"Oh yeah?" said Katherine. "Is it better than your pissing-on-Chaz idea?"

"Maybe. Julian, give me the Bag of Holding."

Julian brought the carpet down next to Tim.

Katherine narrowed her eyes. "This plan better not involve me."

Without a word, Tim took the bag from Julian and jumped into the swimming pool.

"Hmph," said Julian. "That was underwhelming. I was expecting something… I don't know. A little more –"

"Holy shit!" said Dave. "Check it out!"

Julian looked over the edge of the carpet. The swimming pool had turned into a swirling vortex of water, with Tim at the center of it. On the sides of the pool, he could see the water level rapidly receding.

As quickly as the water was draining into the Bag of Holding, it still took over a minute for Tim's purple face to break the surface. He sucked in as much air as his little lungs could hold, then breathed heavily until the water leveled off with the mouth of the bag.

"Give me a lift?" he called up to Julian.

Julian took the carpet down and Tim climbed aboard. They flew back up over the house, and Julian helped Tim hold the bag upside down. He braced himself for upward force as Tim reached up into the bag's mouth.

"All the water!" shouted Tim.

Much to Julian's relief, the Bag of Holding didn't propel him into the sky. The water didn't shoot out like it did out of the magical pitcher. Instead it just flowed out as gravity allowed. The mouth of the bag, however, was much wider than that of the pitcher, and made short work of the fire on the second story of the building.

By the time all of the pool water was spent, Cooper had gotten the fire on the bottom story of the building under control enough so that the group on the ground could start to make their way into the building.

As the smoke dissipated, Julian could see that the fire on the second floor had actually been fueled by the floor itself. The rooms were empty. They were either never furnished to begin with, or all of the furniture had been used to act as fuel for the main fire downstairs. Made of sturdier beams than the roof, the floor hadn't completely burned away, but there was still a wide enough hole to guide the carpet down through.

Chaz said something into Cooper's ear that Julian couldn't make out over the rush of the water. Shortly after, the geyser slowed to a trickle. Charred debris floated in pools and puddles all over the floor, but it wasn't hard to reconstruct the scene. The walls of one corner of the room were completely blackened. It was also this corner from which the second floor had burned away. Everything had been piled up here and set aflame.

"He wasn't trying to burn the house down," said Dave. "The fire was too focused. What was he doing?"

"Getting rid of stuff," said Katherine, looking down at them from the edge of what was left of the second floor.

"What stuff?" asked Tim.

"All the stuff. Remember when Robby dumped me and I burned all of his shit in the backyard?"

"Of course I remember. You took down half the fence."

Katherine nodded. "That's what went down here. Spite burn."

"That doesn't make sense," said Tony the Elf. "He had to know that, once we got our heads out of our collective asses, this is one of the first places we'd come looking for him. Why waste all that time? Judging by the state of that fire, we only missed him by a couple of hours as it is. He couldn't afford to take that kind of risk."

Stacy picked up a warped, blackened sword blade. "He couldn't afford not to. Look at this."

"What about it?" said Tony the Elf. "It looks like it used to be part of a katana or something. You'd need an Exotic Weapon Proficiency to use it, not that it makes much difference in its current state."

"That's what I'm talking about," said Stacy. "This place was cluttered with all kinds of magical weapons, potions, trinkets, you name it."

"So he burned it?" asked Tony the Elf. "That stuff is worth a fortune."

"Which is why he couldn't let us get our hands on it," said Dave. "He armed himself to the teeth, packed up as much as he could carry, and burned the rest."

"Detect Magic," Julian mumbled to himself. His vision grew darker, and he could see the remnants of magical auras everywhere. The blade in Stacy's hands was emitting a soft purple vapor glow as the last of its magic drained out. The burnt rubbish heap at the site of the main fire was cloudy with a mix of different colored auras.

"Stacy and Dave are right," he said. "There was a whole lot of magic around here, but it's dissipating even as we speak."

"NO!" cried Tim. "We could have been total badasses! Is there nothing left?"

Julian frowned at the burnt pile. "Not here." When he turned around to look at the rest of the interior, however, he was bombarded with strong magical auras. "Hang on!"

"What is it?" asked Tim.

"The walls over there," Julian said, pointing at the far end of the room, which hadn't been damaged by fire. "There's magic all over them! Red and green and purple and orange. It looks like a Motel 6 for clowns."

Tim jumped off of the carpet and splashed through the puddles toward the far wall.

"FUCK!" he cried, collapsing on the floor just three feet short of the wall. "Goddammit!"

The others approached cautiously. Julian guided the carpet toward Tim just above the floor.

"Stay back!" warned Tony the Elf. "It's obviously some kind of magical trap."

Julian shook his head. "The magic on the floor is too weak. It's only strong on the walls."

"It's no fucking magical trap," said Tim, showing them the bottom of his bleeding foot. "It's broken glass. It's all over the place."

"What a jerk," said Stacy.

"Give him a break," said Cooper. "He's fucking bleeding."

"Not Tim. Mordred."

Tim hopped on his good foot back to the carpet. "Thank you though, Cooper, for jumping to that conclusion."

"You got it, buddy."

Julian continued to stare at the multi-auraed wall. "What was that about Mordred?"

"Potions don't burn," said Stacy. "So he must have thrown them against the wall."

"What a fucking asshole," said Cooper. He'd gone back to dig through the pile of burnt garbage. He kicked aside scorched, twisted blades and misshapen plates of what used to be armor. "It looks like he took a hammer to some of this armor."

Chaz sighed. "Just in case the fire didn't burn hot enough to ruin it."

Cooper hurled a dented helmet at the wall. "I don't think I've ever met someone who I've wanted to punch repeatedly in the dick as much as I want to – Hey, what the fuck is this?"

Julian looked over. Whatever Cooper was holding wasn't magical, so he ended his Detect Magic spell. It was a metallic tube, about a foot long, and about as wide around as the Masterwork dildo. With all of the vaguely cylindrical objects at his mind's disposal, he wasn't pleased that *Masterwork dildo* was the first association it made.

Cooper poured some water from the pitcher to clear away the soot. The tube looked familiar, and appeared to have suffered no damage from the fire.

"That's mine," said Stacy abruptly.

"Says who?" asked Katherine.

Stacy frowned. "I don't know. I just have a very strong suspicion that it belongs to me."

"Fuck your suspicions," said Katherine. "You can't just call dibs. Cooper found it first."

"Give it a rest, Katherine," said Tim. "It's hers."

Everyone stared awkwardly at Tim, even Stacy. It was common knowledge that he had a thing for her, but this seemed like a very odd moment for him side with her against his own sister and possibly even Cooper.

"What the fuck are you all gawking at?" said Tim. "It's her character sheet. It would have been with the rest of her belongings when the Horsemen captured her."

Everyone let out a collective sigh of relief.

"Oh."

"Right."

"Yeah."

"Of course."

"My what?" asked Stacy, looking from Tim to Julian.

"Here," said Cooper. "Check it out." He lobbed the tube at her while she was still looking the other way, but she snatched it out of the air just before it would have hit the back of her head.

Stacy unscrewed the top of the tube and pulled out the single sheet of paper inside. Unrolling it, she frowned at what she saw. "It's me, all right. But my scores kinda suck."

Tim shrugged. "Ability scores aren't everything. What's your highest?"

"Eighteen."

Dave and Cooper laughed. Even Tony the Elf cracked a smile.

"You're moaning about your scores when you've got an 18?" said Tim. "That's the highest you can get!"

Stacy continued frowning at her sheet. "That seems highly unlikely."

"It's simple math," said Tim. "You roll your stats with four six-sided dice, and drop the lowest roll. Between the three dice that are left, the highest possible total is eighteen."

"What's your 18 in?" asked Cooper. "I'm thinking Strength."

"Uh-uh," said Tony the Elf. "She's dressed like a rogue, and did you see how she caught that tube you threw at her? It's Dex."

"My money's on Charisma," said Tim.

Julian noticed that Stacy was still frowning, staring intensely at her character sheet. "Stacy? So which is it?"

Stacy finally looked up from the paper. "All of them."

Chapter 6

"Bullshit," said Tim. He hopped down from the carpet and limped to Stacy. "Let me see that." He jumped and snatched the paper out of her hand.

"Isn't that kind of personal information?" asked Julian. "Should we really look at each other's —"

"Jesus Christ," said Tim. A quick scan was all he'd needed to confirm Stacy's stats. Just as she said, all of her ability scores were marked 18. "That's impossible."

"It's not *impossible*," said Julian.

Tim rolled his eyes. "Yes. Thank you, Commander Data. I know it's not technically impossible. Would you feel better if I said *highly improbable*? I mean, seriously, do you have any idea of the fucking odds?"

Stacy looked at the ceiling and tapped her fingers randomly against her thumb. "About one million, four hundred twenty thousand to one."

"Holy fucking shit!" Tim dropped Stacy's character sheet like it was made out of spiders.

Stacy deftly snatched the paper out of the air with a cartwheel and a somersault, rather than just leaning over, which would have done the job just fine.

Dave, Julian, and Tony the Elf gave her a polite round of applause.

Cooper pushed Dave, who had just gotten his breastplate back on, onto the floor from behind.

"Ow!" cried Dave, his beard soaked with sooty water. He started to get back up, but Cooper held him down. "What the hell are you doing?"

"They burned all the furniture," said Cooper, putting his elbow on Dave's back. "Stacy, come here. I wanna arm wrestle you."

Dave spit out some dirty water. "If you think I'm going to let –"

"Dave, shut up!" said Tim. "I want to see this."

Dave sighed. "Fine. Can I at least lie on my back so I can watch?"

Cooper accepted. He and Stacy knelt on the floor, positioned their elbows on Dave's breastplate, and gripped each other's hands.

"You're quite certain this is the best use of our time?" asked Tony the Elf.

Stacy and Cooper locked arms and eyes. Her petite human hand was buried inside Cooper's enormous half-orc fist.

"On three," said Tim. "One. Two. THREE!"

For a moment, Tim wasn't sure they'd started. Their hands barely moved at all. Then Dave started groaning. It was most likely due to the extreme amount of pressure bearing down on his armor from the force of both Cooper and Stacy's elbows, but it might have been due to Dave coming to the realization that, no matter how this contest ended, it was going to involve him getting punched in either the face or the dick.

The tendons in Cooper's neck stretched as his face trembled.

"Come on, Stacy!" said Julian. "You've got him!"

Tim circled around Dave to see how Stacy was faring. Her face showed more disgust than struggle. It must have been rough trying to breathe that close to Cooper's mouth.

Stacy let out a slow grunt, and their hands began to tilt in her favor.

"I swear to God, Cooper," said Katherine. "If you let her win, you will never live this down."

"Nnnnnnnnnnnnnngggggggggggggggggggg," said Dave.

Tim didn't care who won. If Stacy beat Cooper, it would make an awesome spectacle. If she lost, well… She could stand to be taken down a peg. But from the looks of it, Cooper had given up too much ground, and Stacy was starting to lean into him.

Cooper's nostril's flared. "I'm… really… angry." His body grew fifty percent bigger, his forearm even further dwarfing Stacy's. His added Strength sent their hands slowly moving in the opposite direction, but Stacy was still doing an impressive job of holding her own.

As Cooper was energized by the sudden surge of adrenaline provided by his Barbarian Rage, Stacy's face betrayed her exhaustion. "What... the... fuck... is..." She exhaled, and both their hands smashed into Dave's crotch.

Cooper stood up and let out a victory roar. As he raised his arms, his temporary muscle deflated back into fat, and his roar changed in pitch from grizzly bear to redneck.

Stacy also stood up. She had on her serious face. Tim hadn't seen that look since she'd slapped him over the head with a Slim Jim.

"My balls," groaned Dave.

"What was that?" Stacy demanded.

"Barbarian Rage," said Julian. "He gets to use it once per day."

"That sounds like cheating to me."

"Hmph," said Tim. "What do you call having all your ability scores maxed out at 18?"

Stacy put her hands on her hips and looked at Cooper. "Best two out of three."

"Oh, hell no!" said Dave, starting to sit up.

"Lie the fuck down, Dave," said Stacy, without taking her eyes off Cooper.

Dave lay flat on his back.

Stacy continued to stare at Cooper, waiting for his response to her challenge.

"Fine," said Cooper. "Let's get this over with."

They sat back down on either side of Dave, placed their elbows inside the dents on his breastplate they'd made during their previous match, and joined hands.

Cooper grinned at Stacy. "You ready to lose again?"

"Don't get too cocky," said Julian. "She was about to kick your ass before you Raged."

Stacy narrowed her eyes at Cooper in steely determination. "Count!"

"All right," said Tim. "One. Two. THREE!"

"I'm really angry!" Cooper quickly shouted.

"What?" cried Stacy.

A second later, Dave took another blow to the junk.

When Cooper stood up again, it didn't look very celebratory. He was stumbling and sweating like he'd just gone fifteen rounds with Apollo Creed.

"What the fuck?" whispered Tim.

"Oh my God!" said Julian. "Do you know what this means?"

Stacy stood up and glared at Julian. "It means you're a lying asshole?"

Julian grimaced. "I can see how, from your point of view, there could be two possible interpretations. But no, that's not the correct one."

"Spit it out, Julian," said Tim. "What's your interpretation?"

Julian looked around at a room full of anticipating faces. "I can't believe *I'm* the only one who knows. Have you forgotten where we are? *What* we are?"

"Come on, Julian," said Dave. "Just say what you've got to say before Cooper punches me in the nuts again."

"Cooper leveled up."

Tim thought for a moment. *Could that be true?* "From beating Stacy in arm wrestling? You think he got experience points for that?"

"I don't know *when* it happened," said Julian. "But it's the only thing that makes sense. When's the last time any of us looked at our character sheets?"

"Not since before we teleported to Earth. Do any of you have yours on you?"

Julian shook his head. "I've been keeping mine in Frank's safe box at the Whore's Head."

"Me too." Tim turned around. "Dave?"

Dave propped himself up on his elbows. "Safe box."

"Cooper?" It was worth a shot.

Cooper was swaying, his eyes pointed in different directions. He tried to speak, but whatever he was going to say was replaced by a thick stream of yellow vomit. It gushed out of his mouth and spilled all over Dave's head. Stacy jumped backwards in time to avoid being splashed.

"Ugh," said Tony the Elf. He turned his head away quickly, looking like he was making an effort not to give up his own guts.

Dave wiped his face with both hands, scooping away globs of what looked like week-old pancake batter.

"Oh shit," said Cooper. "Sorry about that, dude. Back to back Barbarian Rages, bad idea."

Dave spit out some chunks. "You don't say."

"It's cool. I feel much better now."

"I don't give a fuck how you feel!" cried Dave. "Look at me!"

"Don't be such a pussy," said Cooper. "It'll wash off."

"And what do you propose... Ugh, my eyes are glued shut!"

If Dave's eyes hadn't been glued shut with half-orc puke, he would have seen exactly what Cooper proposed. Cooper pointed the Decanter of Endless Water at Dave's face.

"Cooper!" cried Tim. "Wait! There's more than one set—"

"Geyser!"

The blast of water knocked Dave flat on his back again as a circle of yellow radiated away from him. Tim had to give Cooper some credit. If Dave still had a face when this was over, it would no doubt be a clean one.

Stacy leapt onto the flying carpet to avoid the widening circumference of vomit spreading across the floor.

Dave waved his arms and kicked his legs like an upside-down turtle.

"I gotta bring back one of these for my dad!" Cooper shouted over the rush of water. "His power washer sucks!"

"That's enough!" Tim shouted back. He swiped his fingers across his throat. "Turn it off!"

Cooper deactivated the decanter, and the torrent slowed to a trickle.

Dave's face was as red as his beard, but it was still there.

"You okay, Dave?" asked Julian.

Dave opened his eyes. "Been worse. Been better."

The vomit situation had been resolved. Back to more important matters. Tim drew his dagger and stabbed at the air. Nothing noteworthy in that. He tried a couple of karate kicks. Nothing special there. He tried Moving Silently, but couldn't tell if he was any more silent than before.

"I don't feel any different," he said. "How are we supposed to know if we leveled up or not? Dave, did you get any new spells?"

Dave sat up. His face looked like that of a drowned cat, but a clean one. "My praying time is at dawn. I slept through it."

"How about you, Julian. Did you prepare your spells today?"

"We were... There was a lot of excitement this afternoon..." He lowered his head. "I forgot."

"You only need to concentrate for twenty minutes, right? Go outside and meditate while we figure out our next move."

Julian nodded. "Okay." Stacy remained on the carpet as he guided it up through the hole in the ceiling.

"Next move?" Tony the Elf laughed with disdain. "You are, without a doubt, the worst C&C party to ever disgrace this game. Every move you make is a complete and utter disaster."

Tim glared at Tony the Elf. "Didn't you say something about wasting time earlier? Why don't you look for clues or something?"

"There's nothing here," said Tony the Elf. His tone had changed from disdain to despair as he looked around the scorched, soaked shell of a house. "We should get back to the Whore's Head and report this."

As much as Tim would have liked to disagree with Tony the Elf, he had to admit that he couldn't think of much else they could do here. Mordred's trail had gone cold, and they really needed to check their character sheets anyway.

"Tony the Elf is right," said Tim. "Let's pack it up. We'll regroup, have a drink, and decide what —"

"Ravenus!" Julian shouted from outside. His voice was filtered through the wall, but Tim thought it sounded more like panic than happy welcome.

Tim looked up through the hole in the ceiling. He couldn't see Julian, Stacy, or Katherine. "Katherine!"

Katherine peaked her head over the edge of the hole. "Yeah?"

"What's wrong with Julian?"

"I don't know. He just shouted *Ravenus*, and then he and Stacy just fucked off toward the road on the flying carpet."

"Did you see Ravenus?"

"The bird?"

"Yes, the fucking bird!"

"No."

"Damn it," said Tim. "Ravenus got himself into some kind of trouble."

"How would Julian know that?"

"He and Ravenus have an Empathic Link. They can sense each other's feelings."

"I never had that with Butterbean," said Katherine. "I mean, even before I turned into a vampire and he started hating me altogether."

"Butterbean is an Animal Companion. Ravenus is a Familiar. The bond is stronger or something. Look, I don't have time to recite the whole goddamn rulebook. We need to go after them."

"It's pointless," said Dave. "We'll never catch them on foot, and Julian was our only source of horses."

"I can catch them," said Katherine. "I fly faster than that carpet."

Tim shook his head. "No way. You can't go out there alone. This isn't Gulfport. This place is crawling with all kinds of dangerous monsters."

"I know," said Katherine. "I'm one of those dangerous monsters. I'm the biggest badass on the block. And I don't recall asking your permission."

Shit. Tim had all but dared her to go off after them. There was no way she was going to back down now. She'd go just to spite him. He looked up at her. "At least take the Bag of Holding."

"I told you, I'm not –"

"Damn it, Kat! Just listen to me. You don't have to use it if you don't need it. I'd just feel better knowing you have it." A little bit of practicality might seal the deal. "And what if they've found Mordred? Remember we need him alive."

Katherine jumped down onto the first floor. "Fine. Give me the goddamn bag."

Tim handed it over, trying not to look too over-satisfied.

She leaned down and shook the bag in his face. "This is only for nerd storage. I'm not sleeping in this."

All Tim could focus on were her fangs. He nodded his head vigorously. "Good. Good." He felt terrified of her and for her at the same time. Suddenly, he was overcome with the memory of how he'd felt when he learned of her death. He hugged her leg tightly and tried to keep from crying. "Please be careful."

"Oh please." Katherine ruffled his hair. Her fingers were icy cold, but her touch was gentle. "I'll be fine. You take care of the rest of these idiots."

The next thing Tim knew, he was hugging a giant bat. He freaked out a bit, his whole body shaking as his skin crawled when his sister's cold, smooth skin grew prickly fur. He let go of her and fell backwards on his ass as Katherine flapped through the hole in the ceiling.

"You all right, man?" Cooper asked Tim.

Tim continued sitting on the wet floor and nodded.

"I'm going after them, too," announced Tony the Elf. "I'm a ranger. Dave and I can track them."

"How the hell are we supposed to track them?" asked Dave.

Tony the Elf smiled. "I was referring to the useful Dave." He whistled, and his sheepdog came bounding in from outside.

"Hmph," said Dave. "Nice setup."

Dave the dog sniffed around until he found the ring of Cooper's vomit, which he proceeded to lick.

"Dave!" said Tony the Elf. "Stop that!"

Cooper and Dave laughed. Tim would normally have joined in, as it was fun to see that condescending prick get put in his place from time to time, but he was still worried about Katherine and Stacy... and even a little bit for Julian, he supposed.

"How are you going to track them?" Tim asked Tony the Elf. "It's not like they're leaving a trail of footprints or broken twigs. They're all flying."

Tony the Elf sighed. "I don't know. We'll do our best. But it's just like you said. If the bird is in trouble, Mordred might have something to do with it."

"I was just saying that so she'd take the Bag of Holding."

"It's a longshot, perhaps, but it's the closest thing to a lead we've got. In the meantime, I need someone to report back to the Whore's Head. Tell Frank what happened here, and return with all your character sheets."

"I'll go," said Cooper. "Without any horses, I'm the fastest option we've got."

"But you're too stupid to trust with relaying information."

Cooper nodded. "You make a fair point."

Tim didn't want to put anymore distance between himself and his sister, but he couldn't think of a better alternative. "I'll go with Cooper. I'm small enough for him to carry without affecting his Movement Speed."

Tony the Elf nodded. "Very well."

"Excuse me," said Chaz. "What the fuck are Dave and I supposed to do? Hang out here?"

Tim took a moment to consider the options. There was only one. "You guys go with Tony the Elf."

"Shit," said Tony the Elf. "Fine. I move at half speed when I'm tracking anyway. I suppose you can tag along with me if you promise to shut up and stay out of my way."

"Ooooh!" said Chaz. "Did you hear that, Dave? We get the honor of being able to accompany Tony the Elf!"

"*The* Tony the Elf?" said Dave, just as sarcastically.

"The one and only!"

"It makes no difference to me," said Tony the Elf. "Stay here if you like." He walked out the front door with his dog happily trotting along behind him.

Dave and Chaz looked at each other, then at the door. "Wait! We're coming!"

Chapter 7

When a half-orc who had introduced himself as Gus went back to the bar to refill his beer, Randy seized the opportunity to take his seat. He wanted a better view of the door leading down to the cellar and figured Gus wouldn't mind switching seats.

Randy was having a hell of a time, the best he could remember ever having in his life. He hadn't been to a party since he was sixteen, and he'd had such a lousy time that it put him off parties for good.

He looked at his current situation as a chance to reinvent himself. Dennis – *Denise* – might have as well if he – *she* – hadn't been *reinvented* quite so severely.

"What did you do before you came here?" asked a dwarf called Burton. He kept his cylindrical helmet on while he drank, claiming it helped keep his beard in check.

"Nothin' much," confessed Randy. "Mostly just sit around, smoke weed, and watch COPS."

The whole table erupted with laughter. It was like there was literally nothing he could say that these people didn't find either mesmerizing or hilarious. It occurred to him, of course, that they could all be laughing *at* him for reinforcing the stereotype of southern white trash, but he really didn't think so. He'd been laughed at before, and this felt different.

"You didn't get abs like that smoking weed and watching COPS," said Gus, who had returned to the table apparently unaware of or unbothered by the seating change.

The gnome who called himself Gorgonzola laughed. "Maybe you two should get a room."

"Grow up, Gorgy," said Gus, suddenly looking as menacing as a half-orc was supposed to look. "Just because I'm gay, it doesn't mean I can't compliment a man's abs without wanting to hose him down with man-sauce."

Gorgonzola quickly hid his reddening face behind his mug of beer. "I'm sorry. It was a stupid… I didn't mean…"

"It's cool," said Gus. "I totally want to hose him down with man-sauce."

Everyone at the table, Gus and Gorgonzola included, resumed laughing. Everyone, that is, except for Randy. He was confused and a little scared.

Was this all for real? Was Gus being serious about being openly queer? Was everyone else really that cool with it? Or did they all have suspicions about Randy, and they were trying to lure him into coming out so that they could berate him? The idea that they'd go to all the effort seemed preposterous. And from what Randy remembered from high school, a gang of bullies didn't require that level of certainty to slap you with a label and make your life hell.

Still, Randy kept quiet, nursed his beer, and glanced at the still-closed cellar door.

"Come on," said Gus. "Pull out your tube. Let's see what you've got."

Randy felt like a deer in headlights. "I… uh…what?"

"Knock it off, Gus," said Burton. "He's from Mississippi. Your barrage of gayness is freaking him out."

Randy tried to find the words to object without actually giving anything up. "No, it… I don't… It's…" *Shut up, Randy. Shut up, Randy. Shut up, Randy.*

"Gus is talking about your scroll tube," said Burton. "It should have your character sheet inside it."

"Actually," said Gus. "I was purposefully leaving it open to interpretation."

"My character sheet?" said Randy, feeling both genuinely curious and relieved to be able to steer the conversation away from sexuality.

"Oh my God," Gus said to Burton. "He hasn't even looked at it yet." He looked at Randy. "What are you waiting for? Pull it out."

"Where is it?"

Burton smiled. "Look in your bag."

Randy looked down at the backpack sitting on the floor next to his stool. Along with his sword, it was the only other possession he'd come into this world with. An initial glance at the contents within had revealed nothing more spectacular than a change of clothes and some rope. With all of the commotion since he'd arrived, he hadn't thought to dig any deeper.

Reaching as deep into his bag as far as his hand would go, he felt a hard metal cylinder. He pulled it out.

"All right," said Gorgonzola. "Open it up. Let's find out who and what you are."

Randy leaned back as the rest of the table leaned in. He didn't know exactly how much of *who and what he was* this tube would reveal, and he wanted to look over it once alone before he showed it to anyone else.

Burton took the hint and leaned back. "Come on, guys. Give him some space."

The rest of the table grudgingly obliged. Randy unscrewed the cap on one end of the tube and found a paper rolled inside.

He unrolled the sheet and skimmed over a bunch of numbers and statistics which he'd inspect more closely once he scanned the rest of the paper for words like queer, gay, homo, fag, fudgepacker, or anything similar. He paid special attention to a list of Skills on the right side of the paper. It included things like swimming and horseback riding. Once he was satisfied that it didn't include things like cock-sucking and handjobs, he relaxed a little.

He looked back up at the top of the page. "It says I'm a paladin."

Burton let out a long, low whistle. "Don't see many of those."

Randy looked at Burton. "Ain't that like a knight?"

"Yeah," said Gus. "Think of it like a crusader."

Burton laughed. "You better watch yourself, Gus. Make another move on Randy, and he might smite your evil gay ass."

Gus smiled. "I'm already smitten."

Randy could tell that Gus was toying with him, and his smile was having the desired effect of making him feel uncomfortable, but not for the reasons Gus likely thought it was.

"Can't fault you for that," said Gorgonzola, who Randy was annoyed to discover standing on a stool behind him, looking over his shoulder. "He's got a Charisma score of 18."

"What's wrong with paladins?" asked Randy.

"Nothing's wrong with them," said Burton. "They're pretty awesome."

"You said you don't see too many of those. Why don't nobody want to play them?"

"You need some pretty high stats in specific ability scores to make a good one," said Burton. And they're kind of hard to play because you have to adhere to a strict code of conduct or risk falling out of favor with your god and losing all your powers."

"Who's my god?"

"Whoever you choose."

"Can I choose Jesus?"

Gus rolled his eyes. "Oh you're adorable."

Burton laughed. "I think you probably need to stay within the pantheon of gods in the game."

But even as Burton spoke, the words *Jesus Christ* appeared in the box labeled DEITY.

"Holy shit!" said Gorgonzola, still looking over Randy's shoulder.

The rest of the table leaned in to look at Randy's character sheet, and he let them look. His interest had shifted to the cellar door which had just swung open.

Denise stumbled into the common room with a double-bladed ax in one hand and a large flask in the other. She tilted her head back to gulp down the last of whatever was in the flask. From the state of her, Randy could only assume it was some strong booze.

Most of the people between Denise and the bar got out of her way, and she shoved aside the ones who didn't. She handed her flask to Frank and said something that Randy couldn't hear because of the sudden clamor of bells ringing outside.

Frank sniffed her flask, nodded his head, and produced a bottle from a shelf above the bar. As he refilled her flask, the ringing of bells grew louder.

Conversations stopped. Everyone in the bar seemed curious to know what all the bells were about.

Randy didn't care about bells. He was focused on Denise, who was stomping toward the front entrance of the building, blind drunk and wielding an ax. Randy didn't know quite what to make of that, but it couldn't be anything good. He had to follow her and keep her from hurting herself or another. It was his duty as a friend and as a paladin.

He turned to address the group at his table and say a hasty goodbye, but they were all gawking back at him.

"What's wrong?" said Randy, nearly shouting to hear himself over all the bells. "What'd I do?"

Gus stared at him, all the mirth and playfulness gone from his face. "You created a god."

Chapter 8

"What are you doing?" Stacy shouted as the carpet soared higher into the night sky. She looked back at the shrinking house, then up at the bright, full moon. A thought occurred to her. "Is this, like, an *Aladdin* thing? Cause that's really sweet, but —"

"Something's wrong with Ravenus," said Julian. "We have to find him."

"What's wrong with him?"

"I don't know."

"Then how do you know anything's wrong with him?"

"We can sense each other's feelings," said Julian. "Right now, he's terrified and confined." He lowered the carpet until they were gliding just above the trees. He peered down into gaps in the foliage. It was clear that he had no idea where to look.

"What if Mordred's got him?"

"Then I'll kick his ass."

"With what?" said Stacy. "A stick?"

"I'll figure it out when we find Ravenus."

"What was that about you needing to recharge your spells or whatever?"

"I need to spend fifteen minutes concentrating, and I get all my spells back."

"Then do that," said Stacy. "I'll drive."

"You know how to fly this thing?"

"I'm awesome, remember?"

"But you don't know where to go."

"Neither do you. But I know how to optimize the search so we can cover more visible ground in less time." She was mostly talking bullshit, but Julian didn't know that.

Julian nodded. "That sounds good. Okay, let's switch positions."

Stacy crawled to the front of the carpet and grabbed the two front tassels. After a shaky start, she got a feel for how to steer, how to ascend and descend, and how to adjust the speed. She looked back. Julian's eyes were glazed over. He'd either put his faith entirely in her and was now in a trance, or he'd somehow managed to get stoned in the time it had taken her to get the hang of flying.

She hadn't been talking out of her ass completely. They'd be able to see a lot more over open ground than they would with this needle-in-a-haystack-peeking-through-the-trees bullshit. That wouldn't help them if Ravenus's captor was actually hiding in the woods, but as long as they had no idea where to look, it was the more logical option.

Stacy raised the carpet and made for the main road. The forest was kept clear for about ten meters on either side. Spotting nothing noteworthy upon first reaching the road, she was forced to choose a direction. If the captors were heading north, back toward Cardinia, finding Ravenus would be next to impossible once they reached the city. So that was the direction she chose. If she was wrong, she could always double back and hope there wasn't another large city further south.

She traveled low, flying just a few feet above the road. It felt safer that way. The carpet they were flying on was no doubt very valuable, and there was no point in giving the whole world a big flying target to shoot out of the sky. Anyway, she might get lucky and spot a campfire through the trees that the bird's captors had carelessly lit too close to the forest edge.

Squinting, she peered into the forest on her left, trying to spot any hint of a light source. No such luck. She turned her attention back to the road ahead of her and nearly had a heart attack.

The beast running at them from the two o'clock position looked like Sweetums, the giant shaggy ogre from The Muppets. But in place of Sweetums's bulbous orange nose and pouty lower lip, this thing had a beak. When they made eye contact, the creature let out a roar that was something between a goose and Chewbacca.

Stacy pulled up on the fringe at the front of the rug, just in time to avoid the beast's massive, clawed hands.

"What the fuck was that?" she said after she settled on a higher cruising altitude.

When Julian didn't respond, Stacy looked over her shoulder, fearing he'd fallen off the back. But he was still there, his concentration unbroken, blissfully unaware that they had nearly been torn apart by some furry, beaked nightmare.

The creature howled after them. Looking past Julian, Stacy saw that it was still trying to chase them, despite the carpet being faster and well out of its reach. Ferocious thing, for sure, but none too bright.

Stacy's heart had only just gotten back to its normal rhythm when Julian spoke up.

"Turn us around."

Stacy looked back at him. "That wasn't fifteen minutes."

"I had to break my concentration because we're heading in the wrong direction. Please turn around!" There was desperation in his voice. He didn't like giving direct orders.

Stacy veered left, then swung the carpet around in a wide arc to the right, making a lightbulb pattern before straightening out southward along the road. "How do you know we were going the wrong way?"

"Because I can't feel Ravenus anymore. He's gone."

"You don't mean he's…"

Julian shook his head. "I don't think so. I think he's just out of range. We'll know soon enough."

When she got to the point where Julian had told her to turn around, Stacy was impressed with herself for having made a mental note of exactly where that point was.

"Do you feel him yet?"

Julian shook his head.

Stacy smiled. "That means he's moving southward, probably along this road." *Or dead.*

She increased the carpet's speed to as fast as it would go, keeping a wary eye out for the bear-bird monster as they flew over the spot where she'd encountered it. There was no sign of it. She chose not to mention the encounter to Julian. He had enough on his mind.

While Stacy had every expectation that Julian would alert her as soon as he felt his bird's presence again, she kept glancing back at him, just to make sure. Each time he looked a little more worried than the last.

"I've got him!" he finally said.

Stacy nodded and did some quick math in her head. "If both we and Ravenus maintain our current velocities, you should have just enough time to get your spells back before we catch up to him. I recommend you do that."

Julian went back into his meditative state, and Stacy flew the carpet just above the treetops, maintaining full visibility of the road on her left. Whenever the road curved, Stacy cut across the trees, picking up what precious few seconds she could.

Having a rough idea of how far away the bird was, Stacy kept her attention on avoiding danger. She scanned both the ground and sky for signs of monsters. While she was thankful not to see anything in the air, she was kind of disappointed not to spot any terrestrial creatures. Now that she knew better than to fly so close to the ground, she would have liked to get another look at Sweetums.

"I've got some good news," said Julian after a few more minutes had passed. "And I've got some bad news."

"What's the good news?" said Stacy, feeling they could really use some. Now that fifteen minutes had passed, it was time to start looking for Ravenus. She took the carpet up a little higher to get a better view of the road ahead.

"I think I'm a third level sorcerer now."

"Congratulations. What's the bad news?"

"I'm still limited to first level spells."

Stacy shrugged. As bad news goes, this wasn't so bad. "If you're third level, why can't you cast third level spells?"

"Spell levels are different from caster levels."

"That seems unnecessarily complicated."

"I know, right?"

"So how do you know you leveled up?"

"Because I was able to prepare one more first level spell than I could before."

"Cool. What did you get?"

"A couple of Mount spells, and I filled up the rest with Magic Missiles."

Magic Missiles sounded cool. "So what's the plan?"

"We find Mordred, and I blast the shit out of him with Magic

Missiles. If he's a Level 1 character, he should be easy enough to take down."

"Don't we need him alive?"

"You don't truly die until you reach negative ten Hit Points, but you fall unconscious at zero. Since a Magic Missile only does a maximum of five points of damage, I figure it'll be impossible to kill him outright as long as I stop shooting him as soon as he drops."

"That sounds pretty lame for something called Magic Missile."

"I thought so, too."

"Look!" said Stacy, pointing down at the road ahead of them. A covered wagon, pulled by two horses, was making its way southward down the road.

Julian put his hand on Stacy's shoulder and leaned over for a look. He smelled like nutmeg, which was surprising, given the filthy state of his clothes. "Let's try to get a closer look before we're spotted."

Just as Stacy pushed down on the front of the carpet, a flash of white light shone from the back of the wagon. A glowing orange bead shot out like a bottle rocket, heading in a trajectory that would have intercepted them if they had maintained their previous cruising altitude.

The night sky lit up like the sun had just exploded thirty feet above their heads. The heat and force from the shockwave was tremendous. The carpet shook violently but remained airborne.

Stacy did a quick check to make sure that neither she, nor Julian, nor the carpet was on fire. "I dunno. We may have been spotted. What do you think?"

Julian narrowed his eyes. "Take us down."

He wasn't normally the angry sort... not like Tim. That's what Stacy liked about him. He bumbled his way through ridiculous situations with childlike curiosity and wonder. Life hadn't yet worn him down like it had the others. In the short time they'd been acquainted, she didn't recall ever seeing a spot of malice in his heart... until now.

She took the carpet down as Julian had requested, but in the back of her mind, she wondered if he had put any thought into this, or if an equally childlike sense of immortality was causing him to recklessly endanger both of their lives to save his pet bird.

The road curved to the right just ahead, allowing Stacy to cut across the treetops and close a bit more of the gap between them. As they drew closer to the wagon, she counted at least four sets of legs through the flapping canvas. A driver brought the minimum body count to five, not including the bird. If one of these people was Mordred, and not just some random birdnapper, he wasn't alone. Strangely enough, none of the passengers she could see in the back of the wagon seemed the least bit concerned about being chased. All of the legs sat as still as statues.

"Don't shoot anyone until you know which one's Mordred," said Stacy.

The horses pulling the wagon picked up their pace when the road straightened out again. Stacy felt like they might be losing ground.

"Come on, you fat bastard," said Julian. "Show yourself."

An elf seated on the left side of the wagon pulled back the canvas flap and smiled at them. He wore black linen robes, the same style Julian wore under his serape, but they looked like they'd just come back from the laundry. Not a smudge or tear on them. The same went for his silky blond hair, carefully styled to look tastefully disheveled. The combination of that and his cold blue eyes made him look like the frontman for an Aryan boy band. He might have been handsome if Stacy couldn't see right through him.

"Mordred!" shouted Julian. "Just give me Ravenus, and I'll let you go!"

Smile unwavering, the elf pointed a small wand at them.

"Shit!" said Stacy. "Lie flat and hold on!"

Stacy knew that both their lives depended on her timing and successfully not telegraphing her next move. She glared at the elf like she was coming to get him, wand be damned.

Then, just as she sensed he was about to fire, she yanked up one corner of the carpet as hard as she could, sending them into a corkscrew spiral, through the center of which passed another glowing orange bead.

Once they were right-side-up again, Stacy looked back just in time to see the explosion. The spell detonated far enough behind them that she felt no increase in temperature and barely a tremor in the carpet.

"Magic Missile!" said Julian. A golden arrow of light shot out of his open palm and soared through the air until it struck the torso of the elf, who didn't so much as flinch as green bolts of electricity crawled over his body from the point of impact.

"Nice shot," said Stacy, thinking it wouldn't be unreasonable to expect a similar recognition of her sweet carpet-driving skills.

Julian frowned. "It didn't hit him."

"Sure it did."

"We're losing him," said Julian. "Can't this thing go any faster?"

This was not the recognition of her carpet-driving skills that Stacy had in mind. "This is as fast as it goes. We'll get them. Those horses can't keep up this pace forever."

"Horse!" cried Julian. "Brilliant!"

"Um... thanks?"

"Do you remember how much time passed between those two fireballs?"

"About a minute and forty-seven seconds."

"*About?*"

Stacy smiled and shrugged.

"And how much time has passed since that last fireball?"

"Twenty-six seconds."

"It'll be close." Julian turned and looked at the ground. "Horse!" he cried again.

Out of the corner of her eye, Stacy thought she saw something whiz by. She looked behind them, and was surprised to see that a brown and white speckled horse was standing on the side of the road, getting farther and farther away as they kept flying, veering off to the left with the curve of the road.

Then Julian whistled. The horse broke into a full gallop, and rapidly began to catch up with the carpet.

"Stacy! Steer!"

Stacy faced forward. With her attention on the unexpected horse, she had neglected to keep the carpet over the road, further widening the gap between them and the wagon.

Julian got on his feet in a squatting, steadying-himself-on-a-surfboard position, his eyes fixed on the approaching horse.

"Julian," said Stacy. "What do you think you're doing?"

"I'm going to get Ravenus."

"Come on, Julian," pleaded Stacy. "Think this through. If we stay on the carpet, I might be able to keep dodging his spells. You can't dodge shit on a horse."

Julian gave her a quick glance and a smile. "If I can get close enough, he won't be able to use his fireballs without them blowing up in his own face. There's obviously a lag time between uses, or he would have been blasting us with them a lot more frequently."

Julian's theory made some kind of sense, and it was too late to reason with him anyway. Julian readied himself as the horse caught up to the carpet, then jumped onto the horse's back. Oddly enough, the mysterious horse was already equipped with a saddle and bridle.

Stacy focused her attention back at the elf they suspected to be Mordred.

The Mordred elf appeared to come out of some sort of trance. That must be an elf thing. The smug expression that had been frozen on his face turned into one of alarm as he saw Julian on horseback pulling ahead of the carpet. He leveled his wand at Julian.

"Shit!" said Julian. That was *not* what Stacy had wanted to hear.

Doing a bit of math in her head, Stacy calculated, based on the approximate size of the previous two fireballs, that the one about to hit Julian was easily going to engulf her as well. She couldn't save Julian, so she did the only thing she could. She rolled the carpet around her body like a burrito and braced herself for a great deal of pain.

Chapter 9

Popular culture hadn't adequately prepared Katherine on the finer points of being a vampire. She thought back to all of the vampire movies and television shows she had seen as she lay on her back, staring up at the trees, reconstructing the fall in her mind, wondering which branches she had hit on her way down.

Every goddamn one of them.

All the shows and movies had covered the basics. Stay out of the sun. Don't walk into people's homes uninvited. Try not to get stabbed in the heart. None of them, that she could recall, had ever warned against changing bat forms mid-air without an ample amount of open space beneath you.

The transformation from huge bat to normal sized bat had only taken a second, but it was enough to throw off her wing-flapping rhythm. For her panicky effort to regain her orientation and maintain flight, she'd been rewarded with a faceful of pine needles, one of which poked her right in her little bat eye.

From there she bounced from branch to branch without knowing which way was up, slamming her right ear on a particularly large bough, before her fall was finally broken by the ground.

She took her half-elf form, sat up, and was annoyed to find that her ear still hurt. She needed some life juice. Concentrating on the creatures of the night, she willed them toward her.

The first customer who lined up to die was a rust-colored wolf. He bounded toward her, tail and tongue wagging, and lay down at her feet. Having a wolf not hate her made Katherine think of Butterbean. She'd tried the creatures-of-the-night trick on him, willing to regain his affection, even if only temporary, by any means she could. But Butterbean had only growled and snarled louder at her.

She couldn't bring herself to kill the wolf lying in front of her, though it was so eager to serve. She stroked the fur on top of its head until Option Two came along. A lean, brown rat, much healthier looking than the city rats she'd grown accustomed to, scurried forward to do its master's bidding.

Katherine allowed the rat to crawl onto her hand. Its fur was soft, sleek, and not crawling with fleas. Gripping its unresisting body tightly around the belly, she tore its head off with her teeth.

When she'd sucked the last fluid ounce of blood she could squeeze out of the poor creature, she was left wanting more. But at least her ear felt better.

Sadly, she didn't have the time for an all-out feeding frenzy. She had to get back above the forest canopy to keep an eye on Julian and Stacy, which is why she'd switched bat forms to begin with.

They'd been easy enough to find. Julian was wasting his time trying to find his bird by peeking through gaps in the foliage. Katherine had a much better view of the area from here on the ground, and it was lacking in talking birds.

Not really having any helpful advice to give, she'd decided not to announce her presence. After seeing them kiss, it felt really awkward to barge in uninvited on their romantic, moon-lit magic carpet ride. Stacy would probably think she was just trying to vag-block her for Tim.

Katherine had no time for that drama. She would hang back, observe, and only intervene if they got into the sort of trouble that could only be resolved with fists and teeth.

Taking her normal-sized bat form again, she flew to the top of the tallest tree in the area and found a branch that would support her meager weight. The carpet had barely moved. Julian was still hopelessly peering down into raven-less forest.

Standing was still awkward, so Katherine tried taking Ravenus's advice and hung upside down. It felt more natural, but at the same time extremely stupid.

She didn't have long to ponder that quandary. Stacy took control of the piloting, and the carpet zoomed away.

Katherine took off in hot pursuit.

The carpet moved faster than her little bat wings could take her. She'd need to take her big bat form again if she was going to keep up. Having learned her lesson about changing forms midair, she climbed higher into the sky. When the air was noticeably cooler, and the flying carpet was little more than a tiny red speck zipping across the shag carpet of forest, she changed forms.

She only fell about twenty feet before regaining control of herself in the air. She'd probably overdone it with the altitude, but at least she wasn't crashing through the trees again.

The main road was just up ahead, and it looked like Stacy was making a beeline for it. When your target could be anywhere, head for the place where you can cover the most open ground as quickly as possible. Katherine and Cooper had used the same logic to find Ginfizzle.

Upon reaching the road, Stacy turned right, back toward the city. She flew curiously low to the ground. Katherine would have opted for more height, but the reasoning behind Stacy's choice of altitude became apparent when Katherine observed her peering into the trees as she flew. Not a bad plan, but telling of just how hopeless a goose-chase they were on.

While Stacy was preoccupied staring into the empty forest on her left, some horrible monster broke from the treeline on the right and ran toward the carpet. It looked like Sweetums, from The Muppets, but with a beak. They were flying too low. If Stacy didn't turn around, that thing would tear them to pieces.

Dammit, Stacy! Turn! Look!... Fuck.

Katherine would have to step in, which was all the more awkward now as she would have to admit she'd been stalking them this whole time.

No. Fuck that. It wouldn't be awkward at all. It would be vindicating. Keeping their stupid asses from getting killed had been the whole point of following them to begin with.

Katherine started her dive. She had spent too much time deliberating. Hopefully, Stacy would have enough Hit Points to allow her to survive a single attack from that thing. Flapping harder, she thought she might just make it in time to ram the beast before it intercepted them. For that to work, there was no time to try to catch it from the side. She had to count on the carpet being at least high enough off the ground so that she could swoop under it without planting her face into the road.

The monster let out a terrible howling scream as it moved in for the attack. Just as Katherine was able to make out just how narrow a gap she was dealing with, it widened. Stacy had pulled the carpet up out of harm's way. This, of course, put Katherine on a collision course with the beast, which wasn't a terrible thing in and of itself. It was a giant, walking bag of much needed blood. But she didn't want to face it in bat form if she didn't have to, and she also didn't want to give away her presence now that not giving away her presence was once again an option. She banked a hard right and made for the trees. The combination of her great size and speed made it impossible to maneuver between them, and she caught a trunk with her left wing, spun around counter-clockwise, and crash-landed in the dirt.

Her whole body hurt like a son of a bitch, and she couldn't move her left wing. Transforming back into her half-elven form was excruciating. Her bat screech transitioned to a half-elven groan.

"Screeeeeeaaaaaauuuuuunnnnggggghhhhh... fuck."

The payoff was less than she'd hoped for. She was hoping her limb would have righted itself as it morphed from wing to arm, but she knew as soon as the process was complete that the bone in her upper arm was broken.

She'd give it a few minutes and see if her regenerative powers would kick in. After a few seconds without even a trace of relief, she knew it wasn't happening. She needed blood.

Trying her best to ignore the pain, Katherine closed her eyes and focused her mind on rats and wolves. In her current state, she'd be more than happy to kill a wolf, thoughts of Butterbean be damned.

CRASH CRASHCRASHCRASH

"Shit."

Katherine opened her eyes just in time to see the terrifyingly ridiculous beaked bear-man monster lunging at her. She rolled onto her back and slammed both heels into its furry, feathery chest, launching it backwards into the air. Its head connected with a low branch, somersaulting it so that it landed on its head.

The beast was disoriented long enough for Katherine to struggle to her feet, but not much longer. Its eyes were wild with rage. This wasn't a creature that hunted for food. It lived for the sole purpose of killing anything it came across.

Katherine bared her fangs and brandished the nails on her good arm. Those crazy-ass eyes were coming out. She kept close to a tree, shielding her gimpy arm behind the trunk while trying not to advertise it as a weakness.

The beast ran at her, beak open and arms spread wide like she was its long lost lover. She kept her own mouth open and her right arm raised, purposely telegraphing an impending bite or slash. But when it was close enough, she gave it a foot in the crotch.

Katherine was gambling on it being male and mammalian enough to have a set of testicles buried somewhere under the tangle of fur and feathers between its legs, and from the way the thing doubled over, her gamble had paid off. Now that its head was within reach, she drove her middle three fingers into its left eye, reached up for its skull from the inside, and pulled it toward her. She tore into its neck with her teeth, ripping away a mouthful of fur, feathers, and flesh.

With the angle she was gripping the beast, her arm was out of its beak's reach. It made a wild punch at her side. Katherine barely felt it. The blood was flowing, and she was gulping it down. The pain in her left arm subsided and she found she was able to move her fingers again.

With every gulp of hot, salty blood, Katherine grew stronger as the beast's desperate punches grew less and less substantial until it stopped punching altogether. By the time it was no longer able to stand, Katherine's left arm was fully functional again, and she supported its great weight with both hands until she felt bloated with blood.

She let the body fall on the ground, and pulled the eyeball she'd been gripping out of the creature's head. It came out with a goopy trail of bloody nerves. She stared at the eye in her hand and thought of Ravenus. He'd made good on his word, and even hung around to see that she wasn't disturbed, so long as one didn't count being urinated and defecated on in your sleep disturbing. He was a good bird, and Julian was lucky to have him as a friend. She decided to save the eye for when they finally caught up to him.

The Bag of Holding would be as good as Tupperware for food storage. Katherine opened the bag and put the eye inside.

"Gwaaaa..." groaned the creature on the ground.

Shit. It's still alive. Katherine looked at it and had a second thought.

Or it's alive *again*.

If this giant asshole vamped out on her, their differences in size might put her at a disadvantage.

It was too heavy to lift up and smash its head open against a tree trunk. Katherine looked around for a decent sized rock to brain it with, but came up wanting.

"Waaaaaarrrg…"

"Shut the fuck up!" said Katherine. "I'm trying to think." She looked at the moaning creature, riding the line between life and death, or possibly death and life, and found the solution was staring her right in the face. It was an icky solution, but only slightly ickier than ripping out its eyeball had been.

Katherine rolled up the sleeve on her right arm. She pinned the beast down by the throat with her left hand, thankfully cutting off its ability to continue groaning, and plunged her right fist into the open eye socket.

The creature's body convulsed wildly as she invaded its skull. She dug her fingers deep into what felt like a combination of cake and Jell-O, grabbed a hefty fistful, and pulled her arm back out. The creature lay still as Katherine held what must have been a good third of its brain in her hand.

She considered saving this for Ravenus as well, but wasn't sure if he was into brains or not. She decided against it, and tossed it away.

Discarding the brain didn't bother her as much as leaving behind all the blood still left in the thing's massive body. She didn't know how fresh blood had to be in order to nourish her, but it felt irresponsible to let all of this extra blood go to waste. Who knew when she'd be in another emergency?

Katherine opened the Bag of Holding. It was going to be a tight squeeze. She decided to go feet first. The feet were curios things. They were padded on the bottom, like paws, but the toes were scaly, more closely resembling bird talons than bear claws. But then, what the fuck did she know? She shoved both feet into the bag and started pulling the mouth up its legs like a pair of pants.

The creature's waist stretched the limits of the bag's opening, making it clear that its significantly broader chest wasn't going to happen.

"Shit," said Katherine, then thought for a moment.

If she broke the ribcage, she could probably squeeze enough air out of its lungs to lessen his girth. It was worth a shot.

Katherine straddled the beast over the abdomen and rained down both fists in a flurry of punches, smashing ribs like they were made of wicker.

The creature let out one final lifeless groan as Katherine sat on its chest, pressing the air past its vocal cords. Tugging on the bag, she found her plan had worked. With some effort, she was just able to stuff the chest into the bag's stretched opening. That is, until she got to its arms.

"Goddammit!"

She'd gone too far to give up now. The solution this time was a simple one. Those fucking arms were coming off. The joints came out of the sockets easily enough, but it took a bit of gnawing to separate the sinew and flesh.

Once the arms were off, the rest of the creature's body slid into the bag with ease. Satisfied with her accomplishment and a belly full of blood, Katherine took her giant bat form and started flying northward up the road as fast as her wings could take her. At the rate Stacy and Julian had been traveling before, she figured she'd catch up with them in no time.

Chapter 10

As the only member of the party who could perform healing magic, Dave resented being lumped together with Chaz as a couple of useless spare parts. Sure, he wasn't fast or stealthy, but he wasn't supposed to be. He was a cleric. His role was to fight and heal, which, now that he thought about it, seemed kind of contradictory. He was good for a hell of a lot more than belting out a Dolly Parton tune.

Tony the Elf might be a little more appreciative of having him along if they ran into some monsters out here. No more of this *I suppose you can tag along with me if you promise to shut up and stay out of my way* business. He'd be more like *Oh, Dave! I need your healing!*, to which Dave would reply *Your mom needed my healing last night after I poked her with my dwarf dick!* No, that sounded stupid. Tony the Elf would say *Oh, Dave! Please lay your hands on me!*, and Dave would come back with—

"What do you think?" asked Tony the Elf.

"How 'bout I lay my *balls* on you?"

Tony the Elf and Chaz stared blankly at him.

"I'm sorry," said Dave. "I was thinking about something else."

Tony the Elf looked down at Dave with the air of a babysitter who isn't getting paid enough. "Which way do you think we should go?" He spoke loudly, over-annunciating every word, as if English wasn't

Dave's first language.

"How should I know?" asked Dave. "You're the tracker."

"We haven't picked up any trails yet. It's tough to track when all the quarries are flying. I figure we should keep to the road so that we have a better view of the sky. You've got a high Wisdom score. Do you think we should travel north or south?"

They had come from the Horsemen's villa back to the main road. Dave looked north and south, but saw nothing but trees. "With our chances of finding anyone equally dismal in either direction, I vote we travel north. We know what's in that direction at least, and we may intercept Cooper and Tim along the way."

"Some incentive."

"You asked for my opinion."

"Fine," said Tony the Elf. "We head north."

Dave had no trouble keeping up with Tony the Elf, who stopped frequently to examine an errant animal turd or make a judgement on the freshness of a footprint on the road. More than once, they'd all gotten their hopes up when Dave the dog started sniffing at the base of a particular tree, but all he ever did was piss on it and move on.

They'd been traveling for over an hour when the dog jerked his head up and let out a sharp bark. Before anyone had time to react, it charged off into the woods.

"Dave!" Tony the Elf called out after it. After a few seconds without a response, he darted into the woods himself.

The night felt a lot scarier with only Chaz to rely on for mutual protection.

Dave looked up at Chaz. "Should we —"

"Yeah," said Chaz, apparently feeling the same way about the protection Dave had to offer him. He took off into the woods after Tony the Elf.

Dave waddled after him. "Hey, man! Wait up!"

Fortunately, he didn't have to walk far to find where the others had stopped. Dave the dog was approaching from the opposite direction dragging an arm behind him. The arm was about the size of a gorilla's arm, and covered with a mix of fur and feathers. The dog lay it down at Tony the Elf's feet and excitedly wagged his tail.

"Holy shit!" said Chaz. "What level is that fucking dog?"

Tony the Elf ruffled his dog's shaggy fur as he examined the arm. "Dave didn't do this. Let's go find the rest of the body."

Seeking out a creature big enough to tear the limbs off a creature as big as the one this arm had once been attached to hardly seemed like a wise idea to Dave, but he knew it was the closest thing they had to a lead, and it was pointless to argue with Tony the Elf now that he might finally be able to use his Tracking skill. He followed in terrified silence as Dave the dog led them deeper into the woods.

A few minutes later, they arrived at the scene of… something. All Dave saw, with his untrained eyes, was another fur-and-feather-covered arm lying on the ground. Tony the Elf, however, barely even glanced at the arm. He was more interested in scratches on a nearby tree trunk, flattened saplings, and fresh footprints.

"Combatant A took a defensive position here," said Tony the Elf, placing his own feet inside a set of footprints near the scratched tree. "While combatant B approached from where Chaz is standing."

Chaz looked at the ground at his feet, then took a step to the left.

Tony the Elf did a few squats, kicks, twirls, and air-sword swings, recreating a hypothetical battle in his mind. Finally, he straightened.

"Gentlemen, I have good news."

Dave was skeptical, but he'd take what he could get. "What is it?"

"The battle which took place here was between an owlbear and a high-level paladin, and the paladin was the victor."

"How is that good news?" asked Dave. "At best, it seems like inconsequential news. We're not looking for a paladin."

"It means that somewhere, perhaps very close by, there is a strong force on the side of goodness. He may be able to help us. Maybe he's seen someone in our group."

"Wait a minute," said Chaz. "How could you possibly know it was a paladin? Was that like a game thing, where you rolled high and the information just popped into your head? Or did you reason this out on your own?"

"Just a bit of detective work," said Tony the Elf. "If you pay close enough attention, there are clues everywhere."

Chaz put his hands on his hips. "I'm listening."

"The owlbear was easy enough to figure out just by looking at the arms."

"I have no idea what the fuck that is, but go on."

Tony the Elf pointed to a spot on the tree trunk. "You'll notice there's blood here, but not as much as there should be for such a vicious battle. Between that, and the lack of the rest of a body, what happened here is pretty obvious."

Chaz looked at Dave. Dave shrugged.

"Here's how it went down," said Tony the Elf, sounding more exasperated than Dave thought was fair. "The owlbear attacked the paladin here where I'm standing. It gripped the tree with its right hand while taking a swing at the paladin with its left." He ducked, twirled, and swung an imaginary sword down hard with both hands on an imaginary owlbear. "Then he cut the owlbear's entire left arm off at the shoulder."

"Like King Arthur and the Black Knight?" asked Dave.

"Exactly," said Tony the Elf. "And just like the Black Knight, the owlbear kept on coming. They're known for being wildly ferocious. The paladin waited for the attack, stepped out of the way of a frenzied, desperate charge, and chopped off the other arm."

"You sound very sure of yourself," said Dave.

"Do you have a better explanation?"

"Well, no," admitted Dave. "Your theory is plausible, I guess. But it doesn't concern you that it seems heavily influenced by a Monty Python movie?"

"And I still don't get how this all adds up to a paladin," said Chaz. "Why not a fighter or barbarian?"

"Allow me to continue," said Tony the Elf. "The owlbear, having lost both of its arms, probably dropped below zero Hit Points, and collapsed here." He gestured to the flattened saplings. "Where a fighter or barbarian would have just finished the thing off, a paladin might show mercy on his fallen foe. He used his healing powers to stop the creature from bleeding to death, at which point the owlbear woke up, recognized it was outmatched, and ran away. That explains the relatively little blood and the complete lack of a body."

Dave nodded his head slowly, considering Tony the Elf's theory.

"That's fucking retarded," said Chaz.

"Do you have an alternative theory you'd like to share?" asked Tony the Elf.

"No, but just because I don't know for a fact what actually happened, it doesn't mean I have to accept the first crackpot theory somebody pulls out of their ass. That's how religions are formed."

Tony the Elf cocked his head to one side. "Shut up."

"And that's how they're perpetuated," said Dave.

"Seriously, you two. Shut up and listen. Do you hear that?"

Dave and Chaz stopped talking. Dave knew his ears were no match for Tony the Elf's, but he strained to pick up any unusual sound he could. All he got was frogs and crickets. He was about to say as much when a faint ringing sound mingled into the croaks and chirps.

"Are those... bells?" asked Chaz.

"Hundreds of them," said Tony the Elf. "It's coming from Cardinia. Every temple in the city must be ringing them."

"Does that happen a lot?" asked Dave.

Tony the Elf shook his head. "Not once in the whole time I've been here."

"We should get back on the road," said Chaz.

It was all well and good to doubt religions in the real world, where faith was more often than not just a pretext for bigotry. But the gods in this game were real enough to grant Dave magical spells. He hoped that he and Chaz hadn't pissed them off.

"Water," said Dave. A stream of water flowed out of thin air, as if from an invisible pitcher, puddling in the footprints of the alleged paladin.

"What was that for?" asked Tony the Elf.

"Just testing a theory."

Tony the Elf nodded, as if he understood what Dave was up to. "Good idea. I agree with Chaz. Let's get back on the road." He kept his voice low, as if suddenly doubting his own friendly paladin theory.

Retracing their path back to the road, Dave kept his eyes open for scratches on tree trunks, or any other signs of owlbears, or creatures large enough to tear the arms off owlbears. Fortunately, all of the trees appeared to be relatively unmolested.

"Continue heading north?" Chaz asked upon reaching the road. "See what those bells are all about?" The night air was still filled with the sound of distant ringing.

"Absolutely," said Dave. He was less concerned with bells, and more concerned with getting back behind the city walls. He looked back for confirmation from Tony the Elf, who seemed in much less of a hurry as he fingered a piece of bark on the trunk of a nearby pine tree.

"Look at this," said Tony the Elf, fixated on the tree like he'd only just become aware of these tall leafy things growing out of the ground.

"That's fascinating," said Dave. "But we really should go

investigate those bells."

"How did I miss this before?" Tony the Elf continued as if Dave hadn't spoken. He flicked the piece of bark off the trunk. "This bark is loose. And look at the ground. The density of pinecones at the base of this tree is significantly greater than that of the trees in the immediate vicinity."

"Come on, man," said Chaz. "Either give us a reason why we should give a shit, or let's get moving."

"Something hit this tree," said Tony the Elf. "Hard, and not too long ago."

Dave was getting impatient. "Do you want me to heal it?"

Tony the Elf looked down at Dave with his I-shouldn't-have-to-deal-with-this-idiocy face. "Of course not."

"Then what do you want – Holy crap!" The sky to the south lit up with a ball of fire just above the horizon. It was if a tiny sun had been born and collapsed in on itself in the space of a second. "What the hell was that?"

Tony the Elf turned around, but the sky was dark again. "What?"

"You saw it?" said Dave. "Didn't you, Chaz?"

Chaz nodded.

"Was that a Fireball spell?"

Tony the Elf frowned. "Was it orange and spherical?"

Dave and Chaz nodded together.

"That's a Fireball all right. We're going the wrong way."

Chapter 11

Randy was able to keep as discreet a distance as he liked, as Denise was all but impossible to lose track of. There were other dwarves on the streets, and no shortage of drunks, but Denise was by far the least coordinated and the most belligerent. Whichever way she stumbled, fearsome creatures and men who looked tough enough to kill her with their thumbs alone, stepped out of her path.

"What's the matter with you mother—" She paused to vomit on the street. "—*fuckers*? Ain't you never seen a bitch with a beard before?" She swerved her hips and waved her axe above her head like a feather boa. "Who wants to show a lady a good time?"

It was amazing that her antics hadn't attracted the attention of local law enforcement before now, but they had presumably been preoccupied with the burst of chaos that had been incited by the clamor of those godawful bells, which had thankfully stopped ringing a short while ago. Her luck had just run out, though. Two soldiers, identically dressed in shining armor and golden cloaks marched briskly toward her.

"In the name of His Majesty, King Winston the Wise," said the older of the two soldiers, a dark-skinned human with stern eyes, a deep, commanding voice, and an immaculately trimmed salt-and-pepper beard. "I demand that you lower your weapon."

Denise put down her arms and ceased her embarrassingly anti-erotic dance. She wiped some vomit off of her beard with her arm and turned to face the soldiers. "In the name of his black, commie ass, King *Obama*, how about I lower my pants?"

The two soldiers glanced at one another. The younger of the two, blond-haired and clean-shaven, was obviously a rookie on the force, and looking to his superior for guidance on how to proceed, but it was clear that neither of them knew what to make of Denise's proposition.

The younger soldier cleared his throat and took the initiative, addressing Denise cordially. "That, um… will not be necessary, M'lady."

Denise staggered toward the young soldier. "What's the matter, boy? You holdin' out for one of those skinny Disney bitches up in a tower? Let me tell you, son. You ain't never had a woman like me. I'll make you come like a fuckin' Howitzer."

The distressed young soldier stepped backward, his spear held defensively in front of him, obviously not wanting to stab this sad dwarf woman, but possibly considering it. "Sir?"

"Good Lady," said the black soldier with the forced politeness of law enforcement officers engaging drunks that Randy had witnessed on countless episodes of COPS. "I demand you stand down at once!"

Denise shifted her stagger in his direction. "Oh, I ain't forgotten 'bout you, big daddy. Don't you worry. We gonna get that beard of yours good n' sticky."

The seasoned veteran's face betrayed a flash of embarrassment and outrage as he glanced at the small congregation of onlookers who had stopped to see the spectacle. It lasted only a second, replaced by tenuous professional stoicism.

"I warn you, Good Woman. Advance any further, and I'll have no choice but to charge you with disrupting the King's Peace."

"If the king wants a piece, I got plenty to go 'round." Denise stumbled at the older of the two soldiers and grabbed him by the crotch.

In the space of a second, Denise was whirled around, her face planted into the street and her crotch-grabbing arm pinned behind her back.

"Oh snap!" Randy said to himself.

"Motherfucker, that hurt!" cried Denise.

The soldier held the shaft of his spear against the back of Denise's neck. "I charge you with assault on a Kingsguard and —"

"Get your hands off me, Kunta Kinte," shouted Denise, fruitlessly kicking her little fat legs. "I'm a fuckin' *American!*"

"And disrupting the King's Peace," the soldier bellowed. "You are to be tried by the High Court and awarded whatever Justice they deem fit for your —"

"Excuse me!" said Randy, stepping forward, hands raised non-threateningly. "Might I have a moment?"

The soldier looked up at him impatiently. "Sir, I am currently occupied. Perhaps you might address my partner?" He looked at the younger soldier, then back at Randy.

"It's about your prisoner," said Randy.

"Randy?" said Denise, her cheek still smushed against the street. "What the fuck are *you* doing here? Did you follow me?"

"I'm here to help you," said Randy. "So mind your tongue."

"I don't need help from no cocksuckin' que—hmmphgrrmphstrfff." The last part of her sentence was muffled by her face being pushed into the pavement.

"Do you know this woman?" demanded the soldier.

"She's a friend of mine," said Randy. "And I would like to personally apologize for her atrocious behavior."

"She may speak her own apologies when she stands trial."

"Please, sir," pleaded Randy. "I beg the King's Mercy." He tried to think up a story to inspire sympathy in the guard, but found he was literally unable to tell a lie. Relying heavily on metaphor, he came as close as he could. "She has recently lost someone very dear to her," he said, referring to the person Dennis was before being stripped of his manhood. "It's driven her mad with grief." *No embellishment needed there.* "If you release her to my custody, I swear by my Lord and Savior, Jesus Christ, that I will —"

The soldier stood up straight, pressing the tip of his spear against the back of Denise's neck. He scrutinized Randy. "You claim to be a follower of the New God?"

"I am a paladin in His name, sir."

The guard smiled broadly, his white teeth gleaming against his dark brown face.

Randy smiled back, thinking maybe he should have opened up with that little name drop.

"You see, Sir Pip?" the older soldier said to the younger. "Did I not tell you that, within hours of the announcement, the streets would be filled with charlatans claiming to represent the New God?"

"That you did, Sir Walter," said the younger soldier.

"I beg your pardon," said Randy, just a little indignantly. He wanted to remain respectful, but could not allow his integrity to be called into challenge.

"I would remind you," said Sir Walter. "Blasphemy is also a crime."

Randy looked Sir Walter in the eye. "While I may disagree with that in principle, I have committed no blasphemy."

Sir Walter nodded. "Very well."

"Ow!" cried Denise. A trickle of blood leaked from the back of her neck where Sir Walter's spear had pricked her. "I was already in custody! I'll have your ass in chains before you can say *police brutali—*ugh." She was cut short by a kick in the gut.

"I'm afraid I have to agree with her on that count," said Randy. "That was an unnecessary use of force."

"If you are what you claim to be," said Sir Walter. "Treat your friend's wound."

"Um... okay," said Randy, kneeling next to Denise. "If that's what it takes. Do you have any gauze? Or maybe just a strip of clean cloth?"

"What use of these worldly remedies has a paladin? Heal her wound with the power granted through you by the New God."

Randy laughed. "Oh, that's not how it works. Believe me, I pray for Dennis's soul every day. Those faith healers you see on TV, those are the charlatans."

The two soldiers glanced at each other. Sir Walter shifted the focus of his spearhead from Denise to Randy. This time, when he spoke, his voice was loud and impatient.

"Lay your hands on the dwarf and invoke the power of the New God, or you shall stand trial before the High Court together."

Well, shit.

Seeing no other option, Randy got on one knee and placed his hand on Denise's neck. It was warm and sticky with sweat and blood. He looked up at Sir Walter.

"My patience grows thin, paladin."

Randy nodded and looked back down at Denise. "In Jesus Christ's name, I heal you." A surge of warmth flowed from his chest, down his arm, and out of his hand.

"Oh damn," said Denise. "That felt nice."

Randy removed his hand. Denise's neck was still smeared with blood, but the wound was clearly gone. He jumped back and landed on his ass. "Jesus Christ!"

Sir Walter and Sir Pip each took a knee and spoke together, "Jesus Christ!" Theirs seemed more out of reverence than surprise.

Sir Walter was the first to stand back up. He looked down at Randy. "I beg your forgiveness. Please accept my humblest apologies, Sir..."

"Randy?" said Randy.

"Please accept my humblest apologies, Sir Randy."

"It's cool, man," said Randy, getting to his feet. "Jesus is always ready to forgive when you's ready to ask him to."

Sir Walter bowed his head. "I thank you, sir."

"Can we, um... Can we go now?"

The two soldiers looked at one another. Sir Walter seemed as unsure of himself as Sir Pip. The latter was not prepared to take the initiative this time, deferring to the wisdom of the former.

"It is not my place to detain a paladin of the New God against his will," said Sir Walter. "But the temple leaders will have questions, as might the king himself. May I ask, at least, where I might find you?"

"We're staying at the Whore's Head Inn," said Randy.

"Is that a brothel?" asked Sir Pip. "Do you mean to tell me the New God approves of his paladins consorting with prostitutes?"

"Jesus enjoys the company of prostitutes." After a moment of awkward silence, Randy felt the need to elaborate. "I don't mean that like it sounded. I just mean He don't judge people by their past mistakes. He welcomes sinners with open arms, so that they might come to know His forgiveness. Also, the Whore's Head Inn ain't a brothel."

"I know the place of which you speak," said Sir Walter. "It's a ramshackle tavern in the Collapsed Sewer District, rumored to be inhabited by foreigners and misfits."

Randy nodded. "That's the one."

"I heard tell that that place had burned down."

"They're building it back," said Randy. "Folks is really nice there. You two ought to stop by sometime."

"You can count on it, Sir Randy. We shall leave you now to go about your business. May you continue to walk in the Light of the New God."

"Y'all do that too, now!" Randy called out as the two soldiers walked away. He hunched down next to Denise, offering her his hand. "How do you like that? *Sir Randy.*"

"You get your blasphemin' faggot hand away from me," said Denise, backing away from him.

"How can you say that, Dennis?"

"Don't call me *Dennis!*" Denise whispered, her eyes on the small crowd of people who were still lingering around.

"I'm sorry, *Denise.* But you just got healed by Jesus Christ himself! It's an honest to God miracle!"

Denise pointed a finger at him. "You shut your mouth, Randy! Don't you dare drag Jesus's good name through the mud like that."

"But your neck!"

"That weren't Jesus. You said so yourself, that ain't how He works. And even if He did, your hand's jacked off more cocks than a Thai masseuse. Ain't no *healin' power of Jesus* comin' through there. That's Devil magic, plain and simple."

"Devil magic? Come on, Denise."

Denise shook her head. "Uh-uh. You had your chance for that, softy. You just stay the fuck away from me, you hear?" She struggled to her feet. "I'm getting the fuck out of this madhouse."

"Where you going?" said Randy.

"That's none of your goddamn business," said Denise. "And don't you follow me again. If I so much as see you again, I'll kill you."

As Denise stumbled away, some of the less timid bystanders approached her.

"Is it true?" asked a person who looked to be half-lizard.

"Were you touched by the New God?" asked a fur-covered man with tusks jutting out of the bottom of his mouth.

Denise brandished her axe, keeping the curious onlookers at bay. "You freaks stay away from me!"

Looking past her, Randy saw a gate in the city walls. Denise was headed out of town. Randy felt compelled to follow and protect her, at least until she sobered up, but two male dwarves stepped in front of him, blocking his path. Each of them wore a blood-smeared leather apron, wielded a bloody dagger, and had a generous spattering of blood all over their faces and coarse black beards.

Randy took a step back and looked for the soldiers. They were gone.

"Fear not, servant of the New God!" said the dwarf on Randy's left. "We mean you no harm. We are but humble butchers." He pointed his dagger at Randy's eight o'clock position.

Randy glanced that way, and was relieved to see a butcher shop. Flies buzzed around the half-dismembered carcass of an elk, sprawled out on a table in front of the shop. Beyond that, inside the shop, the carcasses of unidentifiable animals hung from hooks.

"My name is Akrok," said the dwarf. "And this is my son, Torg."

"Pleased to meet you," said Randy, impatiently searching for Denise in the crowd now that he was mostly certain he wasn't being mugged.

"We wish to know the healing power of the New God," said Torg.

These two would waylay him until they got what they wanted, but Randy couldn't see any sign of either of them being injured. "Are you hurt?"

"Not yet, sir!"

"Don't damage me apron," said Akrok. He faced away from his son and balled up his fists. "Give me your best shot, son!"

"What?" said Randy. "No!"

Torg stabbed his father in the back.

"Rrrrrgggggghhhh," said Akrok, his fists trembling and face reddening. "You stab like your mother!"

"My turn, Pater!" said Torg. He removed his knife from his father's back, turned around, and gritted his teeth.

"Stop that!" cried Randy.

"Yerrrrrrgggggggghhhh!" cried Torg as his father plunged his dagger, and God only knows how many elk diseases, into his back.

When they were done stabbing each other, father and son dwarf knelt before Randy, breathing hard, hair clinging to their foreheads with sweat. Randy was horrified.

"Let us bear witness to the power of the New God!" said Akrok.

"I'm only gonna do this once," said Randy. "So don't you two go stabbing each other no more, hear?"

"As you command," said Torg. His voice was weak, and his face was turning pale. His *pater* had stuck him pretty good.

"Oh for Pete's sake." Randy placed a hand atop each of the dwarves' heads. "In Jesus Christ's name, I heal you." The healing warmth flowed from his heart, down both of his arms, and out of his hands.

"Praise be to you, righteous paladin!" shouted Akrok.

"And to the New God!" said Torg.

Randy nodded. "All right, all right. Y'all go on now."

The two dwarves punched each other in the shoulder as they happily made their way back to the shop.

Randy looked for Denise, though she'd be long gone. She didn't stand a chance alone in the wilderness. Seeing no sign of her, Randy sighed and headed for the gate.

Chapter 12

If there's one thing worse than being carried through a city, under the sweaty arm of a half-orc, with ten thousand bells clanging at once, it's being carried through a city, under the sweaty arm of a half-orc, with ten thousand bells clanging at once while sobering up.

In their haste, Tim had accidentally left behind his hip flask. That would be remedied once they made it to the Whore's Head Inn, where he kept a spare flask hidden in the cellar. But for now, the bells and the menacing specter of impending sobriety were more than he could stand.

"We get it already!" Tim shouted up at the unoccupied windows of a temple they were passing. "It's a million o'clock! Please knock it off with the goddamn bells!"

A second later, while the ringing inside his ears kept going, he was pretty sure the bells had all stopped.

"Hmph," said Tim. "I honestly didn't expect that to work."

"What the fuck was all that about?" said Cooper, not yet taking into account that he no longer needed to shout to be heard.

"Have you not heard the good news?" The voice behind them was suspiciously cheery, but a little muffled.

Tim and Cooper turned around. If the happy conversationalist's voice was suspicious, his manner of dress was doubly so. He wore tall, black leather boots, the tops of which were obscured by a thick, brown trench coat. His gloves matched his boots, and his wide-brimmed hat cast a shadow over his face, which was completely bandaged except for the eyes, which, despite the late hour, were covered by dark goggles. He must have been sweating like a rapist under all that shit.

"What's wrong with your face?" asked Cooper.

"Cooper! Don't be rude!" Tim elbowed Cooper in the leg, but was secretly glad he'd asked.

"Not rude at all!" said the improbably cheery potential burn victim. "It's a good honest question. Most people just dance around the topic, but I can tell it's at the forefront of their minds. I prefer to just get it out of the way from the start." He turned his face toward the light from a nearby street lamp, raised both hands to his left cheek, and pulled the bandages apart.

Tim cringed and held his breath, expecting to see some nasty scarring, but he didn't see anything at all. Just a hollow space leading to the inside of the bandages on the other side of his missing head.

"Fuckin' A!" said Cooper. He reached out and poked his finger into the gap in the bandages. It stopped where the man's face should have been.

"Ow," said the man. "Please don't do that. I'm *invisible*, not incorporeal."

"You had yourself turned permanently invisible?" asked Tim.

The invisible man tucked his bandages neatly back into place. "It's a boon to my line of work."

"And what line of work would that be?"

"Oh, I dabble in this and that."

The invisibility thing was cool, but Tim didn't have time to go fishing for answers to questions he didn't actually give a shit about. "You said something about *good news?*"

"Ah, yes!" said the man. "A New God has joined the Holy Pantheon."

"A new god?"

The invisible man took a cautious glance left and right, then opened the left side of his coat, revealing wooden and steel pendants in a multitude of different shapes. "Never too early to get in on the ground floor when it comes to god-worship, am I right?"

Tim took a closer look. There were suns, and stars with varying numbers of points, and cloverleaves, and joined rings. There was even one that looked like a curvy swastika. "Are these holy symbols?"

"Indeed they are! Now the question is, when your day of reckoning comes, will you be able to stand before your god and say that you were among the first few hundred to follow him? Opportunities like that are rare indeed. Gods aren't born every day, you know."

"Which one represents the New God?"

The invisible man shrugged. "Take your pick. The effort alone should be enough to stick."

"You're just selling randomly designed holy symbols?"

"Little is known of the New God but his name."

"And what's that?"

"The temple leaders call him Jesus Christ."

"Fuck me," said Tim, mentally profiling the patrons of the Whore's Head Inn, trying to narrow down a list of potential Mormons.

"It's caused quite the uproar, as you might imagine," said the invisible man. "With so little to go on, the common folk have started filling in the gaps with their own wishful thinking. See for yourselves." He nodded across the street.

Tim and Cooper turned around. On the other side of the street, a kobold was having a heated argument with a goblin.

"He was born under a full moon," shouted the kobold. That symbolizes the egg from which he hatched!"

"And you think it's just a coincidence," retorted the goblin, "that the moon was at the center of the Great Gobloid constellation at the time of the announcement?"

"It's the Great Gobloid to you. To everyone else, it's the head of Rapha's staff."

"How many reptilian deities do you know?"

"Just the new one," said the kobold. "How many filthy gobber deities do *you* know?"

"Your *mother*!"

From there the conversation continued in fists.

"You see?" said the invisible man. "It's all a bloody mess. No one knows what to do."

"No," said Tim. "It looks like they've pretty much got the gist of it."

The invisible man looked down at Tim, curiosity showing through his empty goggles. "How do you mean?"

Tim let out a shallow laugh. "Good luck selling your crap. We've got to be on our way. Come on, Cooper."

As Tim and Cooper continued toward the Whore's Head Inn, they witnessed several more fights break out in the name of Jesus. What did he look like? Was he male or female? How many arms/legs/fins/tentacles/wings/heads did he have? Did he favor Good or Evil? Was he inclined toward Law or Chaos? That last question seemed easy enough to answer at least.

"Has everybody lost their goddamn minds?" Cooper wondered aloud.

"What do you expect?" said Tim. "We're bearing witness to a socio-political revolution. Polytheism is turning into monotheism right in front of our eyes."

"Doesn't that usually happen a little more gradually? We went from zero to shitstorm in the space of a few hours."

"I'll tell you exactly what happened. There's a group of Jesus freaks at the Whore's Head who have been going around trying to convert locals."

"I didn't know that."

"I didn't either until just now, but it's the only thing that makes sense."

Cooper scratched his head. "That still doesn't explain how it happened so suddenly."

"That's easy," said Tim. "They've been at this a long time, but everyone's ignored them."

"As you do."

"Right. But tonight they got lucky. They reeled in a big fish. Maybe an influential nobleman. Maybe a famous bard. Think Tom Cruise and Scientology."

"Okay."

Tim couldn't tell if Cooper was processing this or just nodding while thinking about tits, but he didn't care. He was fleshing out this theory more for himself than for Cooper.

"So this gullible yet charismatic asshole makes a big announcement about how he's just come to know the One True God or whatever, and all of those people who ignored our little band of proselytizers before start to wonder if maybe there was something to all of that fire and brimstone talk after all. *Your old gods are false! Convert now, or burn in the fires of Hell for all eternity!* Throw in a little mob mentality, and this is what you get?" He thrust his hands in front of him to display the chaos unfolding.

Most of the action centered around temples, and the fighting was largely limited to shouting matches. But the city patrolmen had their hands full breaking up fistfights, swordfights, and the occasional magic duel.

The confusion was understandable. It had to be close to two in the morning, which is a lousy time for a new religion to manifest. The entire population of the city fell into two groups. Those who were far into the process of getting shitfaced, and those who had just been jolted out of bed by thousands of clanging bells. When Tim thought about how this kind of shit would go down in a major U.S. city, he deemed it a testament to the king's peacekeeping abilities that the whole city wasn't on fire by now.

The chaos lessened as they crossed into the Collapsed Sewer District, where the citizens stayed true to their reputation for having no fucks to give about anything.

"Knock knock," said Tim as he entered the Whore's Head through the gap in the wall. "Do you have a minute to talk about Jesus?"

"Tim!" said Frank. "Did you find anything? Did you find Mordred? Where is everyone else?"

"One thing at a time, Frank." Tim climbed on top of a table and glared accusingly around the room. "I'd like to know which one of you born-again, bible-thumping morons, —"

"Excuse me, Tim?" said Frank, but Tim was not going to be interrupted.

"They are literally rioting in the streets, Frank! You know where this leads. Holy wars! Inquisitions!" He picked up a half-drunk glass of beer, ignoring the objection of its owner and raised it above his head. "Fucking prohibition!"

As he necked back the beer, Frank tried to squeeze some more words in. "Actually, it was —"

"You can't just dump a monotheistic god into a polytheistic society like that. Which one of you mouth-breathing, holy-rolling rednecks thought it was the right time to bring Jesus to C&C?"

Frank chimed in again as Tim swiped someone else's beer and sucked it back.

"That's getting just a little bit out of —"

"Which one of you toothless, tongue-speaking, snake-fondling motherfuckers thought that *now* was the time, with Mordred out there gathering an army to come kick our asses, to start preaching the

Good Word on the streets of –"

"TIM!" Frank shouted.

"WHAT?"

"It wasn't any of us," said Frank. "It was the new guy that *you* brought back with you. The paladin."

"Randy?"

"When he was looking over his character sheet, he asked if Jesus could be the deity he followed. The game accepted it."

"Oh." Tim looked around the room. The faces looking back at him showed little in the way of warmth. "You can forget everything I just said. Where is Randy?"

"He took off after the new dwarf girl," said Frank. "I think she's having a hard time adjusting."

"Harder than you know."

"Now if you're done insulting us all, how about a little news? Where the hell is everyone? Did you find Mordred?"

"No... well, maybe. It's complicated. Cooper and I came back to get everyone's character sheets. You mind opening the safebox?"

"Fine," said Frank. "Follow me."

As Tim and Cooper followed Frank down the cellar stairs, Tim started recounting to him the highlights of the night's events. The fire, the arm-wrestling, Julian suddenly losing his shit about Ravenus.

"So they sent me and Cooper back here to get our character sheets while they tried to track down Stacy, Julian, and his goddamn bird." As he talked, Tim dug through a crate of miscellaneous pieces of armor. "Where the fuck is it?"

"Your character sheets are here," said Frank.

"Grab those, would you, Coop?" Tim tossed a dented helmet out of the crate and shoved a pauldron to one side, revealing nothing.

"Dude," said Cooper. "What are you looking for?"

"I hid a spare flask of stonepiss down here, just in case there was an emergency and we had to go on lockdown."

"You must have been an Eagle Scout," said Frank.

Tim had no time for Frank's sarcasm. He tossed out gauntlets and leg pieces until enough of the bottom of the crate was exposed so that he knew the flask wasn't in there. "Where the hell could it have gone? Nobody uses any of this shit."

"The new dwarf girl spent a while down here," said Frank. "She had a flask when she finally resurfaced."

Tim turned to Frank. "That fucking prick swiped my booze."

"Hey hey. That's no way to talk about a lady."

"Sorry," said Tim. "That fucking *bitch*."

Frank looked at Tim with his weary, I've-had-enough-of-your-shit face. "Shouldn't you two be on your way now?"

Tim considered the long walk back to the Horsemen's house. Sticking around for a quick drink here was out of the question, given the current temperament of the crowd upstairs. He could hold out until they reached their destination, but the flask he'd left there was running low. No general stores were open at this time of night. He looked at the floor and saw the dented helmet. He could turn it upside-down and fill it with enough stonepiss to fill up his flask, but he wasn't quite ready to reach that new depth just yet, not in front of all those judging eyes, anyway.

"Fine," said Tim. "We'll be on our way." He and Cooper started up the stairs.

"You do that," said Frank. "I'll just clean up all this junk you threw everywhere."

Tim didn't know whether to apologize or give him the finger. Which one of them was being the bigger asshole right now? He wasn't thinking straight. He needed to get the hell out of there. Reaching the top of the stairs, he swung the cellar door open harder than he'd meant to. Everyone was staring at him. Every single person in there thought he was a complete dickhole, a Grade-A fuckup.

As he staggered between tables, their gazes converged on him like walls closing in. They moved their feet out of the way and held their drinks in their hands as he stumbled from table to table like a pinball. Finally spotting a clear path between himself and the gap in the wall, he made a break for it.

Crossing the threshold, Tim stepped down hard on the loose board in the floor, which smacked him in the back of the head. He should have heard laughter coming from inside. The silence was far worse.

Chapter 13

Stacy lay on her back for a moment and caught her breath. She was still breathing. That was a good thing. The force of the impact upon hitting the ground had knocked the air out of her lungs, and it had really hurt. But oddly enough, the collision pain was the only pain she felt.

She raised her hands in front of her face to confirm that they weren't on fire. No sign of even the slightest burn. The carpet must have absorbed the fire damage like she was hoping it would. Upon impact, it had unrolled and spat her out like a watermelon seed.

Aside from being a bit banged and bruised, Stacy felt like she had made it through the ordeal completely unscathed. It could have been a lot worse. What the hell was Julian thinking to go charging full throttle at —*Julian!*

Stacy sat bolt upright and looked back up the road. The carpet was charred and smoking, as was Julian's body ten yards beyond it. Ignoring her minor aches, she sprang like a cat over to Julian's side.

The first thing she noticed was two hoof prints just in front of where Julian lay. The blast had left a perfect black circle of char on the road. Perfect, that is, except for these two prints, which were the road's natural color. From what she could deduce, it looked like the horse had reared up on its hind legs shortly before being completely vaporized by the explosion. It seemed unlikely that anything short of a nuclear bomb would be powerful enough to vaporize a horse, but then she thought back to the horse Julian had summoned back inside the Poison Control Center, and how it had rapidly starved to death until it winked out of existence, and the current lack of a roasted horse body made some kind of sense.

Julian's face and hands were splotched with second and third degree burns, but his chest was the hardest part to look at. The fabric of his robes had fused with his flesh. Stacy forced herself to look. His chest was moving, as were his eyelids, as if he were in REM sleep. He was alive.

Stacy ran back to the carpet and retrieved her bag. She dumped it out on the ground next to Julian, looking for anything she could use to help treat his wounds. A first aid kit being too much to hope for, she picked up a canteen and a small cloth pouch. She unscrewed the canteen's cap, poured just a drop of the contents onto the back of her hand, then tasted it. Water. Good.

She'd only picked up the pouch for the clean fabric, so she spilled the contents on the ground. A pile of four-pronged metal doo-dads fell out. She would have compared them to jacks, but somehow she knew they were called caltrops. She also knew that, instead of being used in a game played by six-year-old girls, they were meant to impale the feet of the owner's pursuers. Where this knowledge came from, she had no idea, as she'd never heard of any such thing before. She cringed at the thought.

Having soaked the pouch with water, Stacy patted the burns on Julian's face. He twitched and moaned a little, but didn't wake up.

"Come on, Julian. Wake up." She poured a little water on his forehead. "Please say something."

"Rrrrr…" Julian groaned.

"There you go!" said Stacy. "Talk to me!"

"Rrrrravenus…"

Stacy sighed. "Seriously? The fucking bird again?"

She continued applying water to his face and hands until the canteen was empty. He seemed stable enough, but his burns were just begging for infection. He needed some serious medical attention, and soon.

Somehow, Stacy already knew that the magic had burnt out entirely from the carpet, but she still had to test it, just to make sure. She sat on the scorched fabric and willed it up. It didn't comply. She pulled up on the burnt nubs of what used to be tassels, and the carpet lay still.

Stacy assessed her situation. "Shit."

As stupidly strong as she was, she didn't think she'd be able to carry Julian all the way back to the city, and he might not survive all the jostling. The next best alternative was to place him on the carpet and drag him toward civilization. In its current condition, she dared not hope the carpet would survive being dragged all the way back to the city, but she had to work with what was available until the thing finally wore away to a useless burnt rag.

As gently as she could, Stacy ran her arms under Julian's neck and knees, and raised him forklift style. He let out a labored groan but remained asleep. His head lolled back and his arms hung limp.

His body was so light. Stacy reasoned that elves have a more slender body style, and that she was much stronger than she was accustomed to being, but she couldn't shake the feeling that he was dying right there in her arms.

"Come on, Stacy," she said to herself, willing the tears to hold their ground. "It probably looks worse than it is. You just need to keep your shit together, and get him to a healer. He'll be good as new in no time." She wished she sounded more convincing.

She laid him gently on the carpet and took a few deep breaths. When she felt she had her emotions in check, she lifted the front of the carpet by both corners and started to pull. The carpet moved about six inches before the tassels of both corners ripped off in her hands. Julian grunted as his torso landed with a thud.

Her emotions were suddenly no longer under her control. Her cheeks became warm with tears as she began to sob.

No, no NO!

More deep breaths. *Get a hold of yourself, Stacy. He's counting on you. You can do this, because you're awesome. Of course the tassels came off. Why the hell were you dragging it by the tassels anyway?* She nodded, calmed herself, and grabbed the front of the carpet proper.

She stayed hunched over at first, keeping the edge of the carpet low to the ground in case it ripped. But she wasn't going to be able to keep going like that for long, and the carpet felt like it was holding together okay, so she stood a little straighter.

"Hang in there, Julian," she said. "You just rest easy. We're gonna get you all fixed up." She knew he couldn't hear her, but talking kept her distracted. "We'll find a wizard or something, brew you up a magic potion. You'll be back to your old self in –"

Somewhere in the distance, in the direction she was headed, a dog barked.

Shit!

Stacy had been so caught up in Julian's survival that it only now occurred to her that her own was by no means guaranteed. She was alone in the hostile wilderness of an unfamiliar world. What if she ran into another Sweetums?

Not likely. The bark sounded like it came from a domestic breed, and Sweetums didn't strike her as a pet lover. That other elf guy they'd been traveling with had had a dog with him. It wasn't too much of a stretch to think they might have come looking for her and Julian.

But then, that wasn't something she was going to bet their lives on. It might just as easily be bandits, rapists, or squid people for all she knew. She dragged Julian off the road, back near the site of the explosion, hoping that the overwhelming smell of char in the area would mask the scent of barbequed elf.

It was a much bumpier ride once she went off road. She cringed to herself as Julian's head bounced over roots and rocks. When he started groaning again, she knew she couldn't drag him any further into the woods. If he woke up now, he'd give away their position for sure.

It wasn't a great hiding place by any stretch of imagination, but a few strategically placed dead branches would be enough to shield Julian's body from a casual glance at least.

Once Stacy was done with Julian, she set to work choosing the best tree for her to hide behind based on concealment, observability, and ease of climbing. This final criterion was more for her hypothetical attackers than for herself. She was confident that she could scurry up any tree in the forest with one arm tied behind her back, but wanted to make it easy for her pursuers to follow her. She reasoned that if a person was really hell-bent over getting another person out of a tree, they had three options. Chop it down, set it on fire, or climb up after them. By making the third option preferable to the time and effort involved with the first two, she would increase her odds of surviving the hypothetical battle. She'd have the advantage of higher ground, and the probable advantage of a higher Dexterity, which would likely count for more in a tree branch-based battle than it would on the ground. Additionally, she would negate the possibility of being surrounded by multiple attackers, forcing her adversaries to confront her one at a time.

"Fuck, I'm smart," Stacy whispered to herself. This was some real Sun Tzu type shit happening in her mind. And while she hoped it would all be unnecessary, she was also kind of eager to see how it played out.

The dog's barking grew louder and more excited. They were close. Stacy drew the sword from the sheath on her back, squatted behind her chosen tree, and focused on the road.

Part of her was a little disappointed when she made out the shape of a big shaggy sheepdog, identical to the one which accompanied the other elf in the party. Still, maybe it was just a popular breed. She continued to wait.

"This is it," said the elf as he, a human, and a dwarf caught up to the dog. He put his hand on the dwarf's shoulder. "I'm sorry, man."

The dwarf shrugged the elf's hand away. "Don't act like you know what happened here."

"It's obvious what happened here," said the elf. "I mean, don't get me wrong. They were the only ones in your group I actually kind of liked. I'm sorry to see them go, but we've got to face reality."

She and Julian being two exceptions to a mostly unlikeable group. The evidence was piling up for these guys being from the Whore's Head.

"I don't know, man," said the human. "It looks pretty cut and dried to me."

"Oh please," said the dwarf. "After that CSI bullshit about severed owlbear arms and paladins?"

What the fuck is an owlbear?

"This isn't the same," said the elf. "There's no mystery to solve here. This is O.J. with the bloody knife in his hand. You said you saw a Fireball in the sky. Our friends were in the sky. They obviously got hit by the fireball, fell to the ground, and got blasted with a second Fireball. I don't care how tough they were. They didn't survive two Fireballs and a fall from that height."

"Then where are the bodies?" asked probable Dave. Mentions of O.J. and CSI had removed most of Stacy's remaining doubt, but after her tangle with the Horsemen, she couldn't be too careful. "And look over there. Are those hoofprints?" Stacy suppressed a giggle as Dave waddled excitedly to the epicenter of the blast.

"If a horse was incinerated here, you can bet your ass that Julian was – OW!" Dave collapsed.

"What's wrong?" asked Chaz, ducking low to the ground and scanning the trees.

"My fucking foot!" cried Dave.

Oops. Stacy had forgotten to pick up her caltrops. Time to come out of hiding. "Hey! Sorry guys. My bad!"

"Stacy!" said Dave. He glanced snidely at the elf guy before quickly turning back to her. "Where's Julian? Is he okay?"

Stacy frowned. "He's in bad shape. He took a direct hit from that Fireball. Do you think you can heal him?"

Dave tossed away the caltrop he'd removed from his boot and unsteadily rose to his feet. "I won't be able to pray for my spells until dawn."

"Are you, um…" said the elf. "Are you sure he's alive?"

The question angered Stacy, perhaps more than it should have. "I'm not stupid. He's breathing. His heart's beating. I got him stabilized." She walked over to where Julian was fitfully sleeping and kicked away the branches she'd concealed him with.

"Jesus Christ!" said Chaz. Dave and the elf averted their eyes.

Stacy started to tear up again. Julian's face looked even worse than before. The water she had applied had completely evaporated, leaving his skin burnt, scabby, and dry.

"Dawn's only a couple hours away," the elf said somberly. "We'll camp here until then."

Chapter 14

Katherine huffed as she beat her little bat wings defiantly against the wind. What the hell was with all the attitude?

All she'd needed was a simple answer to a simple question. *Did Tim and Cooper stop by here?*

Instead, with valuable minutes of night slipping away, they gave her a lecture on how her brother was becoming more and more of a degenerate drunken idiot. She knew this. He was going through a rough time. He had probably figured out what was going on between Julian and Skanky, and was dealing with his problems the best way he knew how. Tim never had handled rejection well.

Even if he was a degenerate drunken idiot, he was her brother, and they could all go fuck themselves. Katherine grinned as she flew, hoping they were all having a good time dealing with their mysteriously sudden rat infestation.

According to the information she'd finally been able to drag out of the judgmental pricks, Tim and Cooper had about a thirty minute head start on her. Not a problem. She had a clear path, while they would have to walk around buildings through unusually crowded streets full of people shouting at each other. There was no point trying to find them in that mess. It would be much easier to wait at the South Gate until they passed through it.

She arrived at the gate sooner than she'd expected to, then kept flying above the road for a while, just in case Tim and Cooper had been traveling improbably fast, or the lazy bums at the Whore's Head had underestimated how much time had passed.

After flying down the road for five minutes and seeing no sign of the boys, she took on her half-elven form mid-air and dropped to the ground, landing with her right fist in the air, and her left leg extended sideways.

A bit too high. Her left knee hit the pavement pretty hard, and she knew she probably had a nasty burn under her jeans. The pose was all wrong anyway. Something to keep working on.

She walked back to the South Gate, where she immediately caught the unwanted attention of the guards on duty.

Dull as it must have been, guard duty wasn't a slacker's position. The two men standing at either side of the gate were both tall and muscular. Personal hygiene, however, was held to a lower standard.

The guard on the left side of the gate grinned at Katherine with yellow teeth. "Now what's a fine young miss doing out alone at this time of night?"

"It ain't safe for a lady to travel unaccompanied at night," said the guard on the right, abandoning his position to move in closer to her. "There be predators out here, don't you know?"

"And scavengers," Katherine said flatly.

"Will you be needing a place to stay, m'lady?" said the first guard, crowding in just a little bit closer. "Mayhap, I can put you up for the night. My shift ends at dawn."

That wasn't all that would end at dawn. "I'm trying to find my brother. Maybe you've seen him?"

The two guards glanced knowingly at each other, grinning even more broadly as if sharing a secret.

"I don't know," said the guard with the yellow teeth. "What does he look like?"

And then Katherine understood their secret. They were closing in on her with their creepy intimidation thing, and thought that she had pulled the brother thing out of her ass to get them to back off. Just like a man. Always thinking 'Don't you know it's dangerous for a little girl to be out alone at night?', and never stopping to think 'How is it that this little girl was able to survive out there all alone at night?'.

"He's a halfling," said Katherine. "He would have been traveling with a half-orc."

The two guards halted their advance. They looked at one another, and Katherine shifted her gaze back and forth between them, trying to read their thoughts on their faces.

If she made up the brother, why would she invent such a preposterous tale?

Can a halfling even breed with other races?

And why a halfling? They're not very intimidating. Could it be she's telling the truth?

How would you even go about fucking a halfling?

This is one of them mind games. She tells me a story that's so ridiculous that I have to doubt her motivations for even telling it...

Would you stand her up on a chair? You could lay her down on a table, I suppose.

...and therefore have to entertain the possibility of it being true...

I don't think I could bring myself to do it. They're so tiny.

...which lends credence to the half-orc companion, which is then supposed to frighten me.

Bloody hell, now I can't stop thinking about it.

She's a clever one, I'll give her that.

How much would a halfling and an orc together cost me. Would they charge by the quarter-hour?

Katherine cringed, reminding herself that she did not, in fact, have psychic power, and that the thoughts she had been projecting onto the second guard had been born in her own mind."

"Bwa ha ha ha!" Yellowteeth finally blurted out.

His partner followed his lead, though with less conviction.

"Have you ever heard of such a thing, Mosley?" said Yellowteeth. "A halfling, sibling to a half-elf?"

Mosley's laughter grew a touch more genuine. "Don't forget about her other brother, the half-orc."

"What?" said Katherine. "I didn't say the h—"

"Dear old Dad really gets around, eh?" said Yellowteeth. They both had a good, hearty laugh about that.

"Who said it was the dad?" asked Mosley. "A man might have ten bastards around the city, all unaware of the others' existence, especially given the racial diversity. A low-rent whore, on the other hand, might be bringing up half a dozen such mongrels under the same roof."

"Gods bless her," said Yellowteeth. "The old girl must have a cunt like a Bag of Holding."

Katherine gasped. The situation had changed.

She could handle the double-team intimidation game they were playing before. She'd dealt with that shit enough back home. *Yo whassup, baby girl?* It was more macho posturing to impress their buddies than it was a sincere effort to get anywhere with the girl. *That's the way I talk to bitches, yo.* That sort of thing.

And that's the same vibe she'd gotten from these two creeps, until now. Given that there was always the chance, however slim, that the target in the bars and clubs back home would have low enough self-esteem to welcome that kind of attention, the scumbag wannabe predators took care to not overtly insult her. But these two motherfuckers had just dropped a C-bomb on her.

They weren't even thinking of her as a sexual object anymore. She'd just been demoted to crazy bitch, object of ridicule, village idiot.

Katherine was no village idiot, but she could be Crazy Bitch, if that's how they wanted to play it. She considered tearing one of their heads off, just to teach the other a lesson about how to treat a lady. It would be *sooooo* easy. They weren't even paying attention to her as they continued to make crude jokes about her imaginary mother. But she soon thought better of it. That's how Cooper had gotten himself into trouble.

A vampire's gifts were not limited to brutality, after all. Katherine cleared her throat. When they bothered to glance her way, she batted her eyelashes like Bugs Bunny in drag.

"I just love a man in uniform." Katherine added a bit of southern twang to her voice to keep herself in character. "But do you know what I love even more?"

"What's that?" asked Yellowteeth. Both of their attention was fixed on her like she was about to unravel the mysteries of the universe.

"A man *out* of uniform."

After a few seconds to process the insinuation, the two men began frantically scrambling to remove their armor as if it was crawling with ants underneath. Piece by piece, plates and chain garments haphazardly littered the ground just outside the gate. When they removed the thick padded shirts that buffered their skin from the metal, they revealed scars of battles past.

Katherine almost felt bad for what she was coercing them to do, in a *Support Our Troops* kind of way, but those scars could have come from a drunken bar brawl just as easily as they could have come from defense of their homeland. But even if they had spilled blood for their country, it didn't excuse the disgraceful behavior they'd displayed toward her.

"Whoa ho ho ho!" said Katherine as both men began to unlace the front of their underpants. "That's enough fellas. Leave a little to a girl's imagination." She had no desire to see any more of their dicks than the tents they were both pitching.

"Apologies, miss," said Yellowteeth. Both men stood erect, pun very much intended. Yellowteeth had quite a nice body on him, and appeared to be very well endowed. Pity about the teeth.

"How would you have us further *serve* you?" asked Mosley. Both men grunted out laughter like Butthead.

Katherine thought back on how she'd lost control of Ginfizzle back at the Chicken Hut. She'd refused to let him eat Butterbean. Her vampiric domination ability was not absolute. It competed with the target's baser instincts. Ginfizzle's thirst for blood was stronger than Katherine's will to control him.

These guards, however, were all too eager to tear off their clothes at her command. The base instinct guiding them was lust, and her request only served to stoke the fire. This was useful information to keep in mind.

Now... What to do with them?

She could test her baser instinct theory by commanding them to perform sexual acts on one another, but that was going too far. They hadn't earned that kind of humiliation. She needed a punishment that fitted the crime.

"Dance for me."

Both men's smiles vanished instantaneously.

"I... I beg your pardon, miss."

"Dance," Katherine commanded a little more sternly.

"A thousand apologies, miss," said Yellowteeth. "We ain't never danced before. We don't know how."

Katherine grinned. This was interesting. They were completely unbothered by stripping naked in public, but petrified of the thought of having to dance. Perhaps it was time to test her theory after all.

"You may dance for me," Katherine said to Yellowteeth. "Or you may suck your friend's dick."

The sexual acts thing didn't feel quite so reprehensible when she provided dancing as an alternative.

Yellowteeth swallowed hard, glancing down briefly at Mosley's fading erection. Mosley shook his head nervously.

"Very well," said Yellowteeth. He bent his knees slightly, then stood up straight again. Repeating that, he raised his elbows and shrugged his shoulders as well. Mosley followed his lead, and the pair of them looked like a couple of robots trying to invent the Charleston.

"What the fuck do you call that?" asked Katherine.

"I'm so sorry." Yellowteeth lowered his arms, dropped to his knees, and turned to his partner. "Come on, Mosley. Undo your britches."

"Uh-uh," said Katherine. "Get back on your feet, soldier." When Yellowteeth stood up again, she continued. "Now both of you, put your hands in the air and move your hips back and forth like this."

Katherine demonstrated, humming to herself, and her two students followed her example.

"That's it!" Katherine smiled as they caught on. She'd seen plenty of worse dancing by far more confident people back home. "You've got it."

Yellowteeth grinned nervously. "It ain't so bad, eh?"

"Of course not," said Katherine. "Now just keep doing like you're doing, and move in a little closer. Mosley, you get behind me."

They loosened up and grew more confident as they followed her lead, thrusting their pelvises at her just short of dry humping her on both sides. They had the hang of it now. Aside from smelling like spoiled meat marinated in liquid fart, they were ready for the clubs.

The timing of approaching boots on the wall above them couldn't have been better. Katherine dropped to the ground and whispered, "I release you."

"Huh?" said Yellowteeth, looking down at her, presumably wondering why he was dancing nakedly in front of the South Gate.

Katherine smiled and winked at him, then started shrieking. "Help! Help me! Somebody please!"

"What in the name of..." the booming voice sounded familiar, but Katherine couldn't think of where she might have heard it before. "You two! Step away from that woman at once!"

"I didn't..." Yellowteeth stammered. "We weren't..."

"Where are the South Gate guards?" demanded the voice from the wall. "Why is no one manning the – Gods have mercy! Jennings!

Mosley! Is that you?"

"I'm sorry, Commander Righteous! I don't know what –"

"How dare you disgrace the king's good name with such depraved acts of harassment on the peasantry! A New God has been born this day, and this is how you greet him?"

Yellowteeth – or rather *Jennings* – and Mosley competed to out-apologize one another, and Katherine remembered their commander's name.

Righteous. He was that hard-ass who'd tried to lock them all up and execute Cooper. Fearing he might recognize her, she refrained from looking up at him.

"Enough of your blubbering!" said the commander. "Report to Major Portheus at once! No, as you are. Leave your uniforms strewn about the dirt for dogs who are more fit to wear them."

As Jennings and Mosley hurried nigh-nakedly through the South Gate, Katherine pretended to get her sobbing under control.

"Are you harmed, good lady?" the commander called down to Katherine.

Katherine lowered her voice an octave. "No, sir. You arrived just in time. Thank you, sir."

"Your gratitude is unnecessary. I'll not have such behavior from the men under my command. You may rest assured that their punishment shall be swift and just."

"Oh," said Katherine. "That's nice." She felt like he was waiting for a response, but she didn't know what to say. She continued not looking at him, trying to play it like a meek victim, rather than someone who wanted to avoid being recognized.

"Be on your way, good lady. May you walk in the Light of the New God."

That was the second time he mentioned this New God. What was that all about?

"The New God, sir? Is that what all the bells were about?"

"Indeed!" said Commander Righteous. "Have you not heard? A New God, Jesus Christ, was born this day!"

"Isn't it a little warm for that?" Katherine was so thrown off by the news that she forgot to keep her voice disguised.

"I beg your pardon?"

Shit. She continued in her disguised voice. "Nothing. Just seemed like more of a winter thing."

"Have we...*met* before?" His tone was bordering on accusatory.

Shit. Shit. Shit. "No, I don't think so. I really should be on my way now. Thank you again, and praise Jesus."

"Stay where you are, woman," said the commander. "I'm coming down."

Commander Righteous may have been an asshole, but from what Katherine had witnessed, he only acted according to what he thought was right. She could probably take him in a fight, but she didn't want it to come to that. Nor did she want to try to dominate him. He was nothing if not strong-willed, and might be able to resist her power anyway. There was only one thing to do.

As soon as she heard the commander's boots on the wooden stairs of the right tower flanking the gate, she took her normal-size bat form and flew up to the roof of the tower.

"Where are you, woman?" Commander Righteous called out as Katherine lay still, her wings pressed flat against the tiled roof. "Reveal yourself at once!"

About thirty seconds passed.

"Where in the seven hells did she go?" the commander murmured to himself.

When she heard – and felt – his boots on the tower stairs again, she bolted off into the night. She could wait for Tim and Cooper a few miles down the road.

Chapter 15

Denise was surprisingly more difficult to keep up with in the forest than she had been in the city. Thankfully, she was a noisy walker; the sound of her stomping through the underbrush was the only means by which Randy had to follow her. With the trees blocking the moonlight, Randy could only see about three feet in any direction. He had no idea how Denise was managing to make such good time with no source of light.

Randy stopped to listen for Denise's footsteps, but the forest was silent. Maybe she'd stopped to pee. Come to think of it, this seemed like a perfect opportunity for Randy to relieve himself as well.

He set to work unlacing the front of his pants, hoping that Denise might be doing a Number Two. Somebody in this world needed to invent the zipper, or Velcro. Taking a pee shouldn't be this much of a chore. Maybe that Cooper had the right idea. The loincloth, that is. Not constantly pissing himself. Randy wondered if he could pull off the loincloth look. Just lift up the front and pee away. It'd be so much easier than these gosh darned laces.

Finally, his willy was free. He exhaled as the tension drained out of his bladder, soaking the trunk of a tree. He took care not to spray the path of a wandering beetle as he listened for Denise's footsteps to start up again.

"Turn around and put your hands on your head." Denise's voice came from about ten feet behind Randy, who was so startled that he accidentally hosed down the beetle.

"Can I lace up my pants first?"

"Hands on your goddamn head, right fucking now!"

"All right, all right." Randy put his hands on his head and spread his knees apart to keep his pants from falling any lower.

"I warned you not to follow me, Randy. Now turn around."

Randy wasn't particularly shy about being naked in front of Denise. But turning around was still awkward while trying to keep his knees apart. He rocked from side to side, like a penguin on a turntable, until he was facing Denise. "Listen, I know you're upset, but –"

"*Upset?*" Denise held her axe toward Randy like she was going to shoot him with it if he made a wrong move. He took a quick swig from his flask. "Upset don't begin to cover it. I'm fucking *pissed off.*"

"But Denise. It's dangerous out here. It's pitch dark, and there's no telling what kind of monsters are –"

"I can see in the dark," said Denise. The anger was gone from her voice. "It's wicked cool, man. We got a pair of old night vision goggles down at the station. Don't nobody never use them, though, on account of they're heavy as shit, and you can't barely make out what you're looking at anyway. This is *way* better."

"That's nice," said Randy. "I can't hardly see at all."

"That's because you're a fuckin' queer." The malice had returned to her voice.

"I don't see how that has anything to do with –"

"What the fuck are you doing out here, Randy?"

"I was worried about you. Like I said, there's monsters out here."

"And what was you gonna do, huh Randy? Suck their cocks while I run away like a little bitch?"

"Well, no. That actually didn't even occur to me. I thought maybe we could fight together."

Denise took another swig from her flask. "Oh, we's about to fight together. I told you if I ever saw you again, I was gonna kill you."

"Come on, Denise. Don't be like that."

"You should have gone back to the Fag Shack with the rest of your little faggot friends."

"That ain't a nice thing to say, Denise."

"Nice? Do I look like I'm trying to be fucking *nice?* I came out here to fuck shit up. I wanna see those monsters. I wanna smash their faces in with this here axe." She looked left, then right. "But I ain't seen a goddamn thing."

"Why don't we get some sleep," suggested Randy. "We can come back and try again in the morning."

Denise smiled and shook her head. "You still don't get it. You ain't gonna see the goddamn morning. Go on. Pick up your sword."

"I ain't gonna fight you."

"Then I reckon this is gonna be a short fight."

Randy mentally prepared for what was to come. He didn't like the thought of hitting a woman, but it was certainly preferable to stabbing her. He'd have to let his pants drop to his ankles, which would limit his evasive maneuvers to pivoting out of the way. All he'd need was one solid punch to the face, and hopefully he could knock her out without hurting her too bad.

Randy sighed. "All right, Denise. If that's really the way you want to –"

A sudden outburst of barking and snarling interrupted their pre-fight banter.

Randy looked to his left, where the sound was coming from, but couldn't see anything but darkness. He turned back to Denise, who could obviously see the source, because her eyes were as wide as her gaping mouth.

"What is it?" Randy whispered.

"It's a wolf," Denise whispered back, looking more awestruck than something as mundane as a wolf should warrant in a fantasy world.

Randy took Denise's diverted attention as an opportunity to pull up his pants.

"Man, you just don't know. This ain't like any wolf you ever seen. I'm telling you, man. It's bigger than a goddamn horse."

Randy grabbed his sword. "What's it doing?"

"I don't know," said Denise. "It's just barking up a tree, but I can't see what it's looking at. Maybe a squirrel or something."

"Help!" cried a high voice. Randy estimated it to be coming from directly above where he heard the wolf. "Somebody help me, please!"

"Come on, Denise!" said Randy. "Let's go!"

Denise shook her head.

"What's wrong, man?" said Randy. "Someone needs our help."

Denise backed up a step. "That someone can go fuck himself." Her crotch was soaked.

"You said you wanted to fight monsters," said Randy. "Here's your chance."

"I was talking about an orc or a goblin or some shit. You go ahead. Let's see what kind of hero you are. I'm telling you, you're gonna shit a brick when you see this thing."

"Please!" cried the voice from up in the tree again. "Is anyone out there?"

Randy frowned. "I gotta say, Denise. I'm a little disappointed in you." He didn't have time to lace his pants, so he held them up with his left hand while wielding the sword in his right. Mustering up courage he didn't realize he had, he stepped toward the snarling giant wolf.

Forcing one foot in front of the other, he moved closer and closer to what would probably be the last animal he'd ever see.

Denise had not exaggerated this creature's size, but she had neglected to mention its glowing red eyes and matted black fur. Whatever kind of hell-beast it was, *wolf* did not even begin to do it justice.

"Thank the gods!" cried the voice from up in the tree. "Please, sir! Save me!"

Randy glanced up quickly, not wanting to take his eyes away from the giant demon-wolf ferociously clawing the bark off the tree. A little girl in a red dress clung to the wobbling tree trunk.

Terrified as he was, he would rather die than abandon this child, which came as a bit of a surprise to him. He'd never thought of himself as the brave sort.

Randy took a deep breath, then shouted at the beast. "Wolf! Go away!"

He probably could have come up with something better, given more time and less urgency. Not that it mattered much. The wolf didn't even seem to hear him. It remained focused on the little girl up in the tree, not even bothering to glance his way.

"Kill it, sir!" cried the girl. "Use your sword!"

Randy would normally be averse to killing an animal, even a dangerous one, but he was surprised to find that the little girl's words sounded strangely appealing to him. He wanted to kill this animal. It wasn't just huge and terrifying. It disgusted him. Not like a possum or a sewer rat, but on a deeper, more personal level. He hated this thing. It was an abomination, an affront to his god. It was, for lack of a better word…*evil?*

Righteous anger stacked on top of Randy's resolve to save the innocent child. He held the front of his pants high and ran at the creature with his sword out in front of him.

"Yah!" he shouted, thrusting his blade at the foul creature's hind leg.

The attack didn't play out like Randy had envisioned it, skewering the leg and crippling the animal. The tip of his sword barely penetrated the thing's skin.

But if his attack was a let-down, the wolf's reaction was even more so. It let out a small yelp, glanced down at Randy, and then bolted off into the woods in the opposite direction.

Randy lowered his sword. "That was... underwhelming."

"Oh thank you, sir!" cried the little girl as she climbed down the branches of the tree. "You are so brave!"

"What kind of bullshit was that?" said Denise, stomping into Randy's limited field of vision.

The girl hopped onto the ground. "This gallant hero has saved me from certain death at the hands of a fiendish dire wolf." She looked at Denise's crotch. "I can only assume you were on your way to assist."

Denise held her axe blade in front of her crotch. "I saw that shit with my own eyes. He barely touched it."

"Please, Denise," said Randy. "I must insist that you mind your language in front of the child."

The girl's face flashed with annoyance. "I'm not —"

"What the fuck are you doing out here in the woods at night anyway, little girl?" asked Denise. "You bringing a basket of goodies to Grandma's house?"

"I'm not a little girl," insisted the little girl. "I'm a full-grown *male* halfling."

Randy squinted, trying to see a man standing before him. "You mean like Tim?"

The allegedly male halfling rolled his eyes. "Yes, like — Wait... Who is this Tim you speak of?"

"I just don't see it," said Denise. "Do you really mean to tell me you're packing a sausage under that dress?"

"It's not a dress!" said the halfling. "I'm a wizard! These are the Red Robes of Neutrality!"

Denise sipped from her flask, staring at the halfling. "You mean, like, *gender* neutrality? 'Cause let me tell you something, son. You show up to school wearing that shit where I come from, and the other kids will beat your ass."

The halfling took a deep breath. "I'm going to say this one last time. I. Am. Not. A. Child. Here, see for yourself." He pulled down the front of the garment, revealing a mat of chest hair to rival the wolf's fur.

"Jesus Christmas, boy!" shouted Denise. "That shit could stop a twelve gauge round."

The halfling covered his chest hair. "Are you satisfied now?"

"Well I don't know, Sasquatch. What kinda heat are you packin' down south?

"My name is Wister," said the halfling. "And I do not appreciate this line of questioning."

"You ever been with a dwarf?"

"Denise," said Randy.

"Don't you pull this shit again, Randy. We's two consenting adults."

"Denise," Randy repeated. "I need to talk to you...*alone.*" He turned to the halfling. "Would you excuse us for a moment, Mister Wister?"

"Just call me Wister, brave hero. And please, take all the time you need."

Randy took Denise by the arm and guided her far enough away so that they could whisper without being overheard. Denise raised no objection.

"You notice anything peculiar about that guy?" Randy whispered.

Denise snorted out a giggle. "You mean besides the fact that he looks like Tom Jones's bastard granddaughter?"

"I think he's hiding something."

"Like a wooly mammoth?"

"I'm serious, Denise! You remember my cousin Ronnie?"

"The one with the harelip?"

Randy nodded. "*Cleft* lip, but yeah, that's the one."

"What about him?"

"When we was kids, I used to borrow some of his fantasy novels. I distinctly remember the term *Red Robes of Neutrality.*"

Denise looked like she was starting to understand where Randy was going with this. "You think he's... not from this world?"

"Maybe."

"And that whole Little-Red-Riding-Hood-Big-Bad-Wolf scene was all an act?"

"Could be."

Denise's eyes went wide as she advanced to the next step. "You don't think he's..." She whispered very quietly, "*Mordred?*"

"I just don't know," said Randy.

"What do we do?"

"We proceed with caution and tact. If it *is* Mordred, we don't want to let on that we know."

Denise nodded. "I'm all over that shit." Having said that, she disengaged from the conversation and stomped back toward Wister.

"So, *Wister!*" Denise spoke as if she were addressing a witness before a jury, exactly the opposite approach of what Randy had had in mind. "If that really *is* your name. Please tell us more about these *Red Robes of Neutrality!*"

"Are you implying I'm not who I say I am?"

"Oh ho ho! Grandma, what big balls you have! You think you can pull one over on me, son? I'm a cop. I can sniff out a lie faster than you can... I don't know... roll a...Hit Point or whatever." Denise had lost a little momentum, but she brushed it off and got right up in Wister's face. "I know exactly who you are, *Mordred!*"

Wister backed up against the tree he'd been hiding from the wolf in. "Please calm yourself. I honestly don't know what you're talking about. I know no one of that name."

"Let me see if I can't jog your memory."

As Denise cocked her fist back to punch Wister in the face, Wister's eyes rolled up in his head and he collapsed to a heap at Denise's feet. Denise, enraged and probably still drunk, followed through with her punch, completely missing Wister's face, and instead smashing her fist directly into the tree trunk.

"MOTHER *FUCKER*, that hurt!"

A stick fell from the tree, bounced off Denise's head, and landed on the ground next to Wister.

"Stop!" cried Randy before Denise had a chance to take her anger and frustration out on the stick.

"What?"

"That's no ordinary stick," said Randy. "Look. It's polished." He picked it up. It was crooked and irregular like any branch but its surface was shiny and smooth. "I think it's some sort of *magical wand*."

Denise massaged her injured hand. "What does it do?"

Randy shrugged. "Beats me. What do you reckon happened to Wister?"

"I don't know," said Denise. "But I'm gonna check out his junk." She bent down to pull back his robes.

"Uh-uh, Denise," said Randy, stepping between them. "I can't let you do that."

"You're a goddamn hypocrite, Randy. Do you remember what I hauled you in for."

"I ain't gonna talk about that again. Now help me think. What are we gonna do with him?"

"This ain't a head-scratcher, man. We wake his narcoleptic ass up and beat the truth out of him."

Randy shook his head. "That don't sound right to me."

"Trust me on this one, Randy. I'm an officer of the law, remember? I'm trained in the art of interrogation."

"You beat him hard enough, he'll tell you whatever he thinks you want to hear. That don't make it true. We don't know he's Mordred. That's just a theory I pulled out of my ass."

"I believe *I* said it first."

"Who gives a shit?" said Randy. "All right, fine. *We* pulled it out of my ass. Are you happy?"

"I'll be happy once I can start my interrogation."

"I ain't letting you beat on him."

Denise stood up, looking like she was going to shove Randy, and then thought better of it. "So what do you propose we do, Mr. High and Mighty?"

"We'll tie him up and bring him back to the Whore's Head," said Randy. "Those other folks got a lot more experience with this game than we do. We can present them with what we know, and what our suspicions are, and we can have a civilized discussion on how to proceed."

"And what if they agree with me?" asked Denise. "What if, after all the gums are done flappin', they all agree I should beat the ever-livin' shit out of him until he starts sending folks home? You know most of them folks is eager to get back to their real lives. They side with me, and all your liberal hippie bullshit ain't gonna sway them."

"They're good people," said Randy. "They'll make the right decision."

"Don't kid yourself, Randy. I seen good people do some terrible shit when the stakes are high. They'll beat your ass down too before they give up their only hope of going back."

Randy frowned. He could only imagine the sorts of things Dennis had seen on the job, and he didn't doubt her words for a second. "We'll cross that bridge when we come to it. Let's get him tied up. We should try to make it back into the city before the sun comes up."

Chapter 16

"Stacy's problem," said Tim. He paused briefly to hiccup, punch himself in the chest twice, and belch. "Stacy's problem is that she's still looking at me like I'm some little kid."

The bartender was a bald man in a tight-fitting sleeveless tunic which displayed the numerous jagged scars on his meaty arms, each telling the story of a broken-bottle bar fight he'd personally broken up. He nodded sympathetically. "Love is a foggy sea. The right woman, an elusive fish." Business was understandably slow at four in the morning, and he was going to milk the only two saps still left at the bar for all the coin he could.

"Maybe she just doesn't like you," said Cooper. He kept an eye on Tim's fourth one-for-the-road. The level of stonepiss in Tim's cup was equal to the level in his own.

Tim slapped his hand down on the bar. "That's because she doesn't *know* me! Not the *real* me."

"You tell him, brother!" said the bartender. Addressing Cooper, he said, "This little guy's got plenty to offer a woman."

"He's a college dropout who co-owns a failing chicken restaurant with his sister who Stacy can't stand."

Of the three of them, Tim had had the most potential to make something of himself. Cooper was never going to amount to much more than a pizza guy, and he was okay with that. Whatever Dave accomplished in life, it wasn't going to make him any less Dave. But

Tim could have been something. He'd breezed through high school without ever cracking open a book. The physics teacher, Mr. Daniels, told him that he scored the highest grade, per unit effort, of any student he'd ever taught.

That was Tim's problem. Everything had always been so easy for him, he couldn't be bothered with anything that required any effort. He couldn't coast through college like he had in high school, so he dropped out and talked his sister into going in with him on that goddamn Chicken Hut.

Cooper had encouraged it at the time. He had also dropped out of college, and entrepreneurship sounded like a great idea. But then, what the fuck did he know?

"Those are things I *do*," said Tim. "That's not who I *am*. She said my Facebook profile picture was cute."

The bartender flashed a wide smile and punched the air encouragingly. "Well there you go!"

Cooper pointed at the bartender. "You. Quit pretending you have any idea what the fuck we're talking about." He pointed at Tim. "And you. I'm only saying this because I'm your friend. You're no prize in our world and you're starting to blow it in this one."

"Hmph," said Tim. "This coming from a guy... Tell me, how many times have you pissed yourself since we've been in this bar?" He and Cooper both looked down at the puddle at the base of Cooper's stool.

"Gods have mercy!" said the bartender. "Is *that* what that smell is?"

"We ain't talking about *me*," said Cooper. "We're talking about you and Stacy. She's smart, and funny, and nice, and smokin' hot, whereas you're a miserable little turd of a person. You can either get your shit together, or set lower standards for what kind of woman you expect to attract."

Tim nodded toward something behind Cooper. "You mean like her?"

Cooper could have sworn the bar was empty. He turned around, but saw nothing but empty tables and stools. "Who?" When he turned back to Tim, he was swapping his empty glass to the bartender for a full one. "Goddammit, Tim! You know we need to get back on the road."

"You've still got half a glass. I couldn't let you sit there drinking alone. You look like a fucking alcoholic."

The Alky-loop. Cooper knew this gambit all too well. Hell, he might have even invented it. The instigator is at the bar with a buddy, and it's long past time they both should have gone home. Maybe they have to get up early for work the next morning. Maybe it's only the sixth of the month, and their bar tab is already dipping into the money they've got earmarked for rent. Maybe their friends are lost in the wilderness, potentially chasing down someone with the means and motive to murder them. Whatever the reason, they've got no business being at the bar this late.

As a means of defying good judgment and extending this brief reprieve from the miserable reality of what their life has become, the Alky-looper will wait for his companion to reach just below the halfway part of his drink before finishing his own. Under the pretense of not wanting his companion to have to drink alone, the Alky-looper will order a fresh drink for himself. He will then slowly nurse his new drink until the companion has finished what remains of his. Whether the companion is a silent fellow conspirator in the gambit or not, he will find himself with an empty glass and his friend with a full one, leaving him with three choices: 1. Sit there without a drink until his friend slowly sips from his full glass, which can be soul-crushingly boring. 2. Abandon his friend and go home, which makes him look like an asshole. Or 3, the Alky-looper's choice of preference, order another drink, thus perpetuating the cycle. His booze-addled brain may not have the capacity to make sure his dick is all the way out of his jeans before he pisses down his leg, but it's capable of some shrewd calculation when it comes to getting in just one more drink.

Tim eyed Cooper's glass while taking a hummingbird-worthy sip from his own.

There was only one way to end the Alky-loop.

Cooper raised his glass, clinking it against Tim's. "Bottoms up." He tilted his head back and gulped down what was left of his drink. When he looked down again, he saw that Tim had only managed to gulp down about a quarter of his drink.

Tim smiled and shrugged, his eyes pointing in different directions. "Sorry. I'm smaller than you are."

Shit. Cooper had forgotten to factor in their vast differences in size. A quarter of a glass of stonepiss in one gulp was actually a pretty solid effort for a person Tim's size. Cooper was in exactly the position Tim wanted him to be.

"Why don't you have one more drink," said Tim. "And then we'll get out of here."

Cooper nodded. "Good idea." He grabbed Tim's glass off the bar and necked back the contents.

"Hey!" cried Tim. "Not cool, man!" As he turned back to the bartender, he barely managed to keep from falling off his stool by grabbing hold of the bar. "Good sir. Another round of stonepiss, if you please."

"Fuck that," said Cooper. "It's time to go."

Tim's head wobbled as he laughed. "Don't listen to him. He's drunk." He leaned in closer to the bartender and whispered, "Between you and me, I think he has a proBWLAAAAARF!" The vomit shot out of his mouth like the Decanter of Endless Water on 'geyser' setting, only green. The bartender got the worst of it.

"I've got a probwlarf all right," said Cooper. "His name is Tim."

Tim fell forward, his face splashing in the pool of vomit he'd left on the bar.

The bartender, to his credit, refrained from repeatedly smashing Tim's face into the bar. He didn't look amused, exactly, to be dripping in halfling puke, but he didn't look angry, exactly, either. Cooper took the stoic resignation on his face to suggest that this wasn't an uncommon occurrence. Just an occupational hazard.

"Will there be anything else for you gentlemen tonight?" A polite way of saying *Pay the tab and get the fuck out of my sight before I cut you.*

"No, I think we're good," said Cooper. He removed the Decanter of Endless Water from his bag and poured some water on the bar. "I'm real sorry about the mess. Tim, pay the man. Maybe throw in a couple extra gold pieces."

"Talk to Julian," Tim mumbled, barely awake. "He's got the money."

"Dude!" said Cooper. "Julian isn't here."

"Shit. Where'd he go?"

"Goddammit, Tim! Wake the fuck up!" Cooper pointed the Decanter of Endless Water at Tim. "Geyser!"

Tim flew off his stool and onto the hard, wooden floor. Cooper deactivated the Decanter.

"What the fuck, man?" cried Tim, soaking wet but wide awake. "Show a little courtesy, huh? I don't feel good." He closed his eyes and curled into a ball on the floor.

The bartender looked at Cooper. "Am I to understand that you haven't the coin to pay for your drinks?" His voice was calm. Maybe even a little hopeful.

"Umm..." said Cooper. "That would appear to be the case."

"That is unfortunate." The bartender lowered his gaze from Cooper's face to where Cooper was instinctively hiding his crotch behind the Decanter of Endless Water. "Maybe we can come up with an alternate means of payment."

Shit. Cooper had reached some pretty low depths in his life, but he'd never had to fuck a dude to pay a bar tab before. His mind started racing for a compromise.

"Uh.... How about a crossbow?" This was Tim's mess. He could be the one to surrender his weapon.

The bartender shook his head. "I don't believe in them."

"What? Like, that they exist?"

The bartender reached below the bar and pulled out a long, curved sword that looked sharp enough to slice a cow in half. "When I kill a man, I like it to be up close and personal."

"Listen, dude," said Cooper. "I'm real sorry about all this. I swear I didn't know we were broke when we came in here. But I'm not going to have sex with you. It just ain't gonna happen."

The bartender looked at Cooper with disgust. It was the first genuine negative emotion his face had betrayed all night. "How could you... Why would you even... I don't want to have sex with you."

Cooper pursed his lips and tried to think. "Then what are we talking about?"

"I want the Decanter of Endless Water."

Cooper breathed a long sigh of relief. "Well, this is awkward."

"Just put it on the bar, pick up your friend, and get out."

While it was nice that sex was now off the table, paying a bar tab with a permanently enchanted magic item was hardly a more favorable solution. Cooper didn't know how much a Decanter of Endless Water was worth, but he guessed it might be around the same amount of money he might consider fucking a dude for.

"Don't get greedy, dude," said Cooper. "Even if you unload it for half its value, that crossbow is worth way more than the price of a couple bottles of stonepiss." He reached behind his back and wrapped his hand around the handle of his battleaxe.

This would either count as a Diplomacy or Intimidation check, both of which were based on Charisma, which was not Cooper's strong suit. Still, the Difficulty Class might be low if the bartender was at all concerned with self-preservation. He was a big guy, sure, and he'd seen a few fights in his day. But he was still just a bartender, a second level fighter at best. Was he willing to put his life on the line for a quick score?

"Fine," the bartender finally said. "Leave the crossbow, and don't you ever show your ugly faces in this tavern again." He lowered his sword.

Cooper could live with a last-ditch face-saving insult. He placed Tim's crossbow on the bar, slung Tim's inebriated unconscious body over his shoulder, and exited the tavern.

Chapter 17

Katherine spat out a rat head, then joylessly sucked blood from the body as she pondered what the hell could have happened to her idiot brother and his idiot friend. How do you get lost when the only direction you need to follow is 'go south'?

A horse-drawn wagon was approaching from the south. Katherine scooted around to the north side of the tree she was leaning against to stay out of sight. It wasn't that she was afraid of some random turnip peddler. She just didn't want to be bothered with any more men asking her what she was doing out here all alone and defenseless in the middle of the night.

Was it still the middle of the night? It was still really dark.

Katherine wished she had brought back her cell phone, just for the clock. She tried to do some rough calculations in her head to make a guess on what time it might be, and speculate from there how much time she might have left before the sun came up.

She made her calculations in reverse chronological order, starting with her freshest memories. It had been about ten minutes since a southbound cart had passed her, and maybe another twenty before –

"Those stupid, lazy assholes!" Katherine said aloud as it occurred to her what must have happened. They had hitched a ride. The cart from ten minutes ago was small enough so that she would have spotted them. But the wagon that had passed twenty minutes before that was covered. They were all probably sound asleep at the

Horsemen's house by now.

She placed the Bag of Holding on the ground and lifted the mouth open. "All right guys. Hop in." Two dozen rats, what remained of the ones she'd just summoned to snack on while she waited for her brother, scrambled eagerly into the bag. They'd probably all asphyxiate to death, but their blood would still be fresher than that horrible feathered monster thing.

Not giving a shit about the turnip peddler seeing her, she took her giant bat form and flapped into the night sky. As soon as she rose above the treetops, she noticed a tingling sensation in her left wing. Glancing to her left, she saw the forest silhouetted against the dull orange glow of the distant eastern sky. Dawn was approaching.

Fuck.

She flapped harder, ignoring the gradually intensifying tingle in her wing. She didn't have much time. It didn't take more than a minute for the tingle to escalate into a burn. She could feel it on the left side of her face now too.

Flap! Flap! Flap! SCREECH!

Katherine's left wing burst into flames. She spiraled down and hit the ground hard. The shadow of the trees eased the tingle on her face, but her wing was still on fire. Flapping only fanned the flames. Struggling to think through the searing pain, she took her half-elven form. Her arm was still on fire, but she was now in a better position to do something about that.

"Ow! Ow! Ow! Ow! Ow! Ow! Ow! Ow!" she said as she opened the Bag of Holding with her right arm. Hoping the rats had consumed most of the oxygen inside the bag, she plunged her burning arm into it, all the way up to the shoulder. After a few seconds, the pain began to die down.

Removing her arm from the bag, she found it to be a black, horrifying mess. The skin was crispy and flaky, and her fingers were all fused together. This poor arm had been through some shit tonight.

It hurt a lot, but not as much as she thought it would. She'd heard about people going into shock after a traumatizing experience, their bodies not allowing them to feel the pain until they'd gotten themselves out of immediate danger, at which point the pain would really start to kick in.

Fuck that.

Katherine reached into the bag with her good hand. "Rat."

The rat she pulled out was gasping desperately for air. She bit its head off and greedily gulped down its blood. The tingle she felt in her arm this time was a good one. She squeezed the rat hard and kept sucking until her fingers separated and the skin had completely regenerated. She frowned. Her shirt was fucked, completely burned away all the way up to the shoulder. She must look ridiculous.

"Keep your head in the game, Kat," she said to herself. These trees weren't going to protect her much longer. She could already see their shadows beginning to creep toward the road. What the hell had happened? It was pitch black out not five minutes –

"The darkest hour is just before…" The Mamas and The Papas had been right all along. She was fucked. There was no time to dig a hole, and no one to shovel dirt down on her.

As much as she hated to admit it, the Bag of Holding was her only option. But with nobody to let her out, there was no escaping it. All she'd be doing was buying herself time until she starved to death. She could place it by the road, and someone might pick it up. But even then, they wouldn't know she was inside. Then she got an idea.

She reached into the bag again. "Rat!" This poor little guy barely had life enough in him to gasp. She bit its head off, but didn't drink the blood. Instead, she dipped a fingernail into its neck hole to use as a pen. She spread the Bag of Holding flat on the ground and carefully wrote the letter *K*, large and legible, in rat blood on the side of the bag.

She dipped her fingernail into the rat's neck again, then scrawled out the letters *A* and *T* as quickly as she could. She was starting to feel that familiar tingle on the back of her neck. Dawn was breaking through the trees. Their shade wasn't going to protect her much longer. Her *H* was sloppy due to blood dripping from another fresh dip, but it could be made out in the context of the rest of the word. Doing her best to ignore the pain, spreading to her head and back, she held her finger steady as she wrote the letters *E* and *R*. Why the fuck was her name so goddamn long?

As the tingle intensified to a burn, Katherine knew she only had a few seconds left. The last three letters she scribbled out were just a big, illegible mess, but they would have to do. Katherine was out of time. She hoped her name was as common in this world as it was back home.

Holding the bag out open in front of her, she ran as fast as she could toward the road.

"Ow! Ow! Ow! Ow! Ow! Ow! Ow! Ow!" she said once more as she felt her skin sizzle.

"Fuck! Fuck! Fuck! Fuck! Fuck! Fuck! Fuck! Fuck!" she added when what remained of her shirt ignited in flame.

She was only about halfway to the road, but that was going to have to be close enough. The bag would be easily visible to anyone passing by. She pulled it over her head and let it consume her.

Chapter 18

Dave and Chaz snored away as if they were having the best sleep of their lives while Julian, still barely clinging to life, wheezed softly like a one-stringed violin. Stacy sat helplessly next to him, her refusal to give into exhaustion the only token of support she could offer.

Branches shook on the tree above her. Tony the Elf was coming back down. He, too, had spent the night awake. Stacy told him it wasn't necessary, but he said elves didn't sleep. That did little to comfort her about Julian's likelihood of pulling through. Perhaps having regretted his choice of timing with regard to letting her in on that morsel of elven physiology, he shortly thereafter decided that he'd be able to keep watch over a larger area from a higher vantage point.

"It's time," said Tony the Elf when he was far enough down to whisper it.

Stacy looked up through the forest canopy. The sky still looked pretty damn dark to her. "Are you sure?"

"The light is faint on the eastern horizon, but the treetops are now visible against the sky. Dawn is upon us."

That was good enough for Stacy. She walked over to Dave and nudged him in the belly with her foot. "Dave! Wake up!"

Dave groaned. "Just five more minutes."

"No!" said Stacy, nudging him harder. "It's time for school. Get your ass up now!"

"Please, Jessica," Dave pleaded.

He calls his mom Jessica?

"I got... excited," said Dave. "I didn't know you... touch it..."

What the fuck? Stacy looked up at Tony the Elf. He shrugged.

"Five minutes... have it up again..."

Ew.

"Don't go... At least... wash your hands?"

That was all Stacy could stand. She wrapped her hand around as much of Dave's beard as she could grip and gave it a good hard yank.

"OW!" Dave cried, his eyes wide open. "What the hell was that for?"

"It's dawn," said Stacy. "You need to heal Julian."

Dave yawned and rubbed his chin. "Okay. I'll go pray." He was obviously not yet completely awake, still in some kind of half-dream state.

"Hello in there?" Stacy grabbed Dave by the shoulders and shouted into his face. "Earth to Dave! Do you copy?"

Dave nodded, his brow furrowed in fear and confusion.

Stacy held his gaze in hers and spoke as clearly as she could. "Your friend, Julian, has been severely burned."

Dave nodded again. He was responsive. That was good. She was getting through to him.

"He doesn't need your prayers, your thoughts, or for you to share a Facebook post. He needs his fucking epidermis. Can you treat him?"

Stacy felt a hand on her shoulder.

"Sta–"

Her elbow flew high and back, connecting hard with something crunchy. She spun around to face her would-be assailant. Tony the Elf held his hands over his bleeding nose.

"Oh shit!" said Stacy. "I'm sorry! I'm just a little on edge because I haven't slept, and I thought you were still in the tree, and –"

"Don't worry about it," said Tony the Elf. "It was my fault. I shouldn't have sneaked up on you." He nodded at Dave. "Go do your thing."

"But..." Stacy started to object as Dave scooted away. Then she thought better of it. She could at least give Tony the Elf a chance to explain himself since she'd just elbowed him in the face. Still, Julian was going to die if none of them did anything. "I don't want to dump on you guys' religion or anything, but Julian is covered in third degree burns, and prayer just isn't going to grow his skin back. He needs real medical attention, and he needs it now."

"Dave's going to give him much better than that," said Tony the Elf. "He's going to heal him with *magic*."

"That's what I want him to do!" said Stacy. "But he said he was going to go pray. Julian never has to pray before he does magic."

"Dave is a cleric, a *divine* spellcaster."

"Well, I'm glad you hold his work in such high regard, but I'll wait to form my own opinion."

Tony the Elf smiled and shook his head like he wanted another elbow in the face. "No. I mean *divine* as opposed to *arcane*. Wizards and sorcerers use arcane magic. It's either something you learn through study and training, or it's just something you innately know how to do. *Divine* magic, on the other hand, comes directly from the gods. That's why Dave needs to pray."

Stacy looked over at Julian and frowned. "How long's it going to take?"

"About an hour."

"An hour?" cried Stacy. "Is he delivering his prayers by carrier pigeon? Julian's lucky to have survived this long. He might not have another hour."

"You need to relax," said Tony the Elf. "Julian's fine."

Stacy couldn't believe the audacity of the bullshit coming out of his mouth. "Don't you *tell* me to relax. And don't try to placate me by telling me everything's going to be fine."

"I didn't say everything's going to be fine," said Tony the Elf. "I said Julian's fine right now."

"Have you studied medicine? Because I have, and I'm telling you, he is touch and go, Mr. *the Elf*. Touch. And. Go."

Tony the Elf smiled, his teeth outlined in blood. "You're not thinking about this in game terms. Let me explain it to you. When the Fireball hit him, it reduced his Hit Points to somewhere between -1 and -9. He's breathing, so we know he hasn't reached -10, because that would mean he's dead. But he's also not awake, so we know he's not up to 0. When you treated his wounds, you stabilized him. He's hovering somewhere in the negatives, but he won't actually die as long as he doesn't get attacked by anything. Even without magic, he'd gradually recover Hit Points over time, and even wake up eventually."

Stacy had to admit, that explanation did make her feel a hell of a lot more hopeful. A second wave of exhaustion began to sweep over her.

"You should try to squeeze in a nap," said Tony the Elf. "Dave's going to be a while, and you need the rest."

That sounded just fine to Stacy. She sat against Tony the Elf's scouting tree, closed her eyes, and quickly fell asleep.

*

"Stacy," a soft voice called out from the peaceful oblivion. "Stacy." Gentle fingers brushed against her cheek. Someone was... touching her?

Stacy snapped wide awake and head-butted her attacker in the face.

Julian fell on his ass and cupped his hands over his nose. "Shit!" His skin was clear and healthy. Even his clothes, while still discolored, were whole again.

"Julian!" Stacy cried. "You're all healed!"

"I *was*." His voice sounded like Donald Duck's.

Stacy held back a laugh. "Sorry about that. You really shouldn't touch a sleeping person."

"What?" said Dave. "You almost pulled my beard off waking me up!"

Maybe it was just a symptom of her gratitude, but this was the first time Stacy thought of Dave as cute, in a flustered, cranky dwarf sort of way. "You did a good job, Dave. Thank you."

Dave lowered his head. "It's what I do."

"It's interesting that his clothes got healed as well," said Stacy. "Does the game consider a person's clothes as part of the person?"

Dave perked up. "That's a good theory. It's wise of you to recognize that the game often interprets certain things in an unconventional manner."

Stacy shrugged and smiled. "What can I say? I'm wise."

"But wrong in this case," said Dave. "I filled up my zero level spell slots with Mending spells so that Julian wouldn't have to walk around naked."

"I appreciate that," said Julian.

"We all do," said Tony the Elf from about ten feet above Stacy's head.

Stacy looked up to find Tony the Elf squatting on a branch. "You don't speak for all of us." She flashed a grin and a wink at Julian, whose eyes were wide and furtive, like his parents were about to catch them making out in his bedroom.

"Um... okay," said Dave, clapping his hands. "So what do we do from here?"

"We've got to keep going," said Julian, as if he were shocked that there was even any question.

Stacy stood up and put a comforting hand on Julian's shoulder. "Julian, you almost got killed."

Julian shrugged off her hand. "He can't take all of us. Not at the same time."

"Some of us aren't willing to risk our lives to rescue a bird," said Tony the Elf. "We need to regroup, have a look at our character sheets, and rationally consider our options."

"How's this for rational?" asked Julian. "*That* Mordred, the one that just blasted me with a Fireball? That's the least powerful Mordred we're ever going to see. With the weapons he's got, he's going to level up faster than anyone you've ever seen. He's only been here a day, and he's already got a wagonload of followers."

"The other people in the wagon didn't attack us," said Stacy. "He could have been hitchhiking."

Julian let out an exasperated sigh. "The driver didn't even slow down. If you picked up a hitchhiker, and he pulled out a gun and started shooting at other cars, wouldn't you have at least some kind of reaction? Those were mercenaries."

"Are you even sure it was Mordred?" asked Tony the Elf.

"What kind of question is that?" cried Julian.

"Did you see his face? Did he look like Mordred?"

"Of course not! We all look different. That's part of the game. Look at my giant fucking ears. Look at your own!"

Tony the Elf folded his arms. "So what makes you think it was Mordred?"

Julian gawked at Tony the Elf like he wanted to pull him out of that tree and shake him until all of his stupid questions fell out. "He abducted my familiar and tried to kill me. Who else would do that?"

"It could have been anyone," said Tony the Elf. "A wizard who wanted a talking bird to keep his own talking bird familiar company? Maybe some opportunistic thief who knows how to move talking birds on the black market? In either of those two cases, they likely would have fired at you if they thought you were going to try and take away their prize. I know how strongly you feel about Ravenus, but we've got to do what's best for —"

"I'm telling you, man! It was Mordred!"

"Did he betray his identity some other way? Did he shout 'Burn in hell, Julian' or something when he fired at you?"

"No," Julian admitted. "He didn't say anything. He just smiled." He looked Tony the Elf in the eye. "But it was a knowing smile. He knew me, and he wanted me to know that he was going to enjoy killing me."

"I got that same vibe," said Stacy. "I'm pretty sure it was Mordred."

Julian glared at Tony the Elf. "You see? She has higher Intelligence and Wisdom scores than any of us. Are you satisfied now?"

"I believe you," said Tony the Elf. "But I still think we should be smart about this. One of us should still go back and let the others know where we've gone."

Julian shook his head and laughed. "If all you wanted was to bail on us, you can be my guest. We don't need you."

"Yes, you do," said Tony the Elf. "I'm the only tracker you've got, and I've got more Hit Points than any of you."

"Who then?" Julian's voice was calm but cautious, as if he was contented by the conversation finally moving forward and willing to consider whatever Tony the Elf had to say, but fearful that he might be the one chosen to stay behind.

Tony the Elf thought for a moment. "When we find Mordred, we may need to act quickly, and Dave is extremely slow."

Dave straightened in indignation. "I'm the —"

"I know. Your healing spells are invaluable."

Julian glanced nervously at Stacy. "So..."

"Stacy is a total badass," said Tony the Elf. "And under the right circumstances, her stealth may prove useful in avoiding a direct confrontation."

Julian swallowed hard. "I *have* to go. It's Ravenus."

Tony the Elf scoffed. "Of course *you* have to go. You don't get to run away while the rest of us go to save your bird."

"But if —"

"You said it yourself," Tony the Elf continued. "Mordred is dangerous, and he's only going to get more so the longer we wait. We need to go after him with everything we've got. You're not the most powerful sorcerer in the world, but you're all we've got for offensive magic. And you tend to think outside the box."

"But who else —"

"If anyone's going to stay behind, it'll need to be someone who is almost completely useless for anything but delivering a simple message."

"Who are you talking about?" Julian was close to shouting.

A yawn sounded from behind Tony the Elf, who stepped to one side.

"Hey guys," said Chaz. "What's up? What are you all talking about?"

Julian leaned toward Stacy and whispered, "I always forget he's here."

Stacy nodded.

Tony the Elf put his hands on Chaz's shoulders and looked him in the eye. "Chaz, I have a very important mission for you."

Chapter 19

"What if he ain't really sleeping?" asked Denise, staring at the red-robed halfling on the ground. "What if this is all some sort of *mind game* he's playing at?"

Randy squatted next to her. "How do you figure?"

"Maybe he's just waiting for us to let down our guard so he can make a break for it."

"So what if he is," said Randy. "It ain't that long a walk back to the city, and I'll be carrying him the whole way. He won't have any opportunities to run."

"And it didn't occur to you that maybe *that's* just what he wants?"

Randy was confused. "A lift into town?"

"Goddammit, Randy!" Denise poked Randy in the head with her pudgy finger. "You need to tell them two brain cells in your head that they need to get to fuckin'. You got an underpopulation problem going on in there."

Randy swiped away Denise's arm and stood up. "Did you have a point you was trying to make?"

"Supposin' we walk him in through the gate, and he starts a-hootin' an' hollerin' about how we done kidnapped him? What are you gonna tell them guards?"

"I'll tell them the truth."

"What? That we's from another universe, and we need this little hobbit to send us back home? Randy, you wouldn't believe some of the shit I've heard folks say just to get out of a speeding ticket, but none of it even compares to that steaming pile of horseshit."

"That *steaming pile of horseshit* just happens to be the truth."

"The truth don't matter if nobody believes it. It'll be his word against ours, and our word means jack shit. Trust me, Randy. You don't want to go to prison here. I guarantee you those cells are full of scarier things than even the biggest, baddest nigger you ever –"

Even a paladin has his limits. Randy felt no remorse for punching Denise in the face.

"What the fuck was that for?"

Randy gave Denise a stern look. "That was a warning."

"A warning? You 'bout broke my goddamn nose!"

"I don't like that word."

"I don't give a good goddamn what you like, you big fucking –"

This time, all it took was a look that carried with it the promise of a second punch to the face. Randy felt something he'd never felt in his whole life. Power. It felt amazing to see Dennis shut his mouth so abruptly. He suddenly understood how this feeling might corrupt someone. *Use it sparingly. Maintain humility.*

"Denise," Randy said gently. "Did you have a suggestion about how to proceed with Wister?"

Denise nodded.

"I'm listening."

Denise inhaled deeply before speaking. "The way I see it, we got two choices. We can either beat the truth out of him here in the forest, or –"

"I already told you we ain't –"

"*OR*," said Denise, raising her hands up. "We make sure he's genuinely unconscious."

"And how do you propose we do that?"

"Simple. We try to wake him up." Denise sucked sloppily on one of her thick, grimy fingers, then pulled it out of her mouth. It was dripping with saliva. "Ain't nobody can fake sleep their way through a wet willy."

It was a disgusting proposition, to be sure, but ultimately not a harmful one. Randy nodded his consent.

Denise plunged her finger into the halfling's ear and gave it a few good twists, provoking not even the slightest twitch of a reaction. Denise twisted more forcefully, like she was trying to bore into

Wister's brain.

"That's enough," said Randy.

Denise pulled her finger out. It was covered in a thick layer of orange gunk up to the first knuckle. She grimaced and hurriedly wiped it off on a tree trunk. "He's out cold, all right. No doubt about it."

Randy shook his head. "I could have told you that."

"But don't you feel better, knowing for sure?"

"I'll feel better when we get him past the city gate and into the Whore's Head. How do you reckon we're gonna do that?"

"We could tie each of his legs to one of our own, like we's doing a three-legged race. We make like he's drunk and needs us to walk him home."

"I'm twice the size of either one of you," said Randy. "Do you know how ridiculous that would look? I won't barely be able to take a proper step without tearing him apart at the crotch."

"I'm just thinking out loud."

Randy snapped his fingers. "I got it! He can sit on your shoulders, and we'll let his robes hang down over your face, so it looks like you're both just one normal-sized guy."

Denise shrugged. "It's worth a shot, I reckon."

Over the course of the next hour, Randy and Denise made several attempts to make Wister and Denise look like one person, but Wister, being unconscious, wasn't very cooperative, and his robes were barely long enough to cover Denise's face. His feet and Denise's arms were all clearly visible.

Eventually, Randy conceded to disrobing Wister entirely, which did little but satisfy Denise's morbid desire to check out his junk. After sitting the naked Wister atop Denise's shoulders, Randy attempted to wrap the robes around high enough to cover Denise's head and Wister's bottom, and low enough to cover Denise's arms and Wister's legs. Since Wister was more slender than Denise, Randy had to tie knots in the robe to keep it shut. Having done the best he was going to do, he stepped back to observe his handiwork.

"How do we look?" asked Denise, her voice muffled by the robes.

"Stop talking," said Randy. "I can see your lips moving under the fabric. It's breaking the illusion. Just give me a minute to take it in."

If he squinted and stretched his imagination to the point of tearing, he could almost convince himself that he was looking at a giant red squash which, for some reason, had short thick legs and the torso of a sleeping child. But to an observer who wasn't forcefully trying to delude himself, there would be no mistaking this for exactly what it was.

"Come on, man," said Denise. "It's hot in here. Is this disguise gonna work or not?"

"It ain't gonna work at all. Go on, get on outta there."

Denise's struggle to free herself made it look like the giant squash/child hybrid was about to give birth to a xenomorph. Randy couldn't help but laugh.

"Man, fuck you, Randy. This ain't funny. I can't hardly – Oh shit."

Wister slumped forward just beyond Denise's ability to stay balanced. They fell like a tall tree. Slowly at first, but picking up enough momentum on the way down to plant both of their faces hard into the ground. That should have been even funnier, but it really looked painful.

"Denise!" cried Randy. "Are you okay?"

"No, I'm not fuckin' *okay*!" Denise's shout was muffled this time by both the fabric and the ground, and it was funny again.

Randy kept his laughter to himself as he walked toward them. "You want some help?"

"Yes, goddammit! Get me the fuck out of – Oh no."

"What is it?"

"Oh please, no." Denise's voice sounded desperate. "Please, no. Stop!"

"Denise!" cried Randy, trying frantically to unwind the cloth from around Denise and Wister. "What's wrong?"

"Randy! Where the fuck are you?" Denise was flopping wildly and helplessly, like a fish on a dock. "Get me out of here! He's pissing in my goddamn hair!"

"Stop squirming around and let me help you." Her squirming and flailing was making it difficult to undo the knots in the cloth.

"It's everywhere." Denise's voice cracked, like she was about to cry. "It's all I can taste or breathe."

"Hang on. I just about... There you go."

The robes loosened up and Denise wiggled out of them as fast as she could. Once out, she greedily sucked in lungfuls of relatively urine-free air. Her hair was all wet and disheveled. She looked like she had just stepped out of the shower, even if she didn't smell like it.

"You all right?" asked Randy.

Denise sniffed. "That was humiliating."

"Hmph," said Randy. "You wanna talk about humiliating, try having your car keyed with the words *FAG MOBILE* on the hood in the school parking lot."

Denise grinned. "I remember that."

"Well I'm *so* happy that I could finally bring a smile to your face."

"Come on, man. I ain't had nothing to do with keying your car. It was Johnny Ross done that."

Randy nodded. "I had my suspicions. Still, you don't have to be so happy about it. You don't know what that was like. I couldn't afford to get it painted. I had to go and scratch up the whole hood with a screwdriver to make the words incomprehensible."

"I ain't smiling about that," said Denise, still clearly smiling.

"What then?"

"You remember when Johnny came back to school the following Monday, all banged up and missing a tooth?"

"Yeah," said Randy. "He looked like shit. They said he got hit by a car."

"Oh he got hit all right, but it weren't no car that hit him."

Randy looked quizzically at Denise. "Are you saying... You did that?"

"Let me ask you something, Randy. Did Johnny Ross ever so much as give you a dirty look after that?"

Randy shook his head.

"That may have had something to do with him wanting to hang on to the rest of his teeth."

Randy stared deep into Denise's eyes. "You did that... for *me*?"

"Pssh," Denise scoffed. "Fuck no. I just wanted to beat the shit out of somebody, and I figured I might as well do a public service as well."

"Is that why you became a cop?"

Denise shrugged. "Pretty much."

"You know something, Dennis? You got something like a heart in you."

Denise grinned again, still caught up in her memory of beating the shit out of Johnny Ross. "You should have seen him, blubbering like a little bitch."

Randy felt he should be sharing Denise's glee, but he just wasn't feeling it. "Come on. We need to get him back to the others."

Denise wiped some wet hair out of her face. "What we really need to get him is a fucking diaper."

An idea struck Randy.

"If we was to swaddle him up in his robes, do you reckon we could pass him off as a baby?"

"He ain't *that* small."

Randy squinted down at Wister. "What if you don't count his legs below the knees?"

Denise clutched the handle of her axe, her eyes open wide like an excited puppy. "You want I should chop his legs off?"

"What? No! I meant we could bend his legs, disguising his size in the swaddling."

Denise shrugged. "It ain't as foolproof as *actually* changing his size, but it might work."

It was completely light out by the time Randy was as satisfied as he was going to be with the sleeping baby disguise. They probably would have been better off half-assing it and using the dark to their advantage. Wister's height was easy enough to disguise by letting his legs hang freely behind a curtain of robes, though it made carrying him awkward. And that still didn't fix the problem of the seemingly enormous baby head, which was only fixable by obscuring most of it.

"What do you think?" Randy asked Denise.

"If we was just gonna wrap him up completely, why'd we spend so long at it?"

Randy was too tired for stupid questions. "Can he pass for a baby or not?"

"Sure," said Denise. "Or a fish, or a log, or any number of things you might wrap up in cloth and carry around."

As they trudged back toward the city, the halfling seemed to grow heavier in Randy's fatigued arms. Finally, they left the forest and had the city walls in sight. There were a few people, carts, and wagons coming and going through the North Gate, and the guards didn't seem to be asking too many questions or looking anyone over very carefully. But what if they were spotted coming out of the woods? What business did anyone have walking out of the woods with a baby so early in the morning? This was wrong. It was all wrong.

Randy stood up straight, shifting Wister's weight more comfortably in his arms.

"What are you doing, Randy?" asked Denise. "His feet is sticking out of the side."

"I can't go through with it," said Randy. "I just can't bring myself to deceive those men or break the law."

"Have you lost your goddamn mind? You bought enough weed from me to stuff a king-size mattress. And that's all while you was already on parole. Now ain't the time to get all uptight about the law."

"I'm sorry, Denise. I don't expect you to understand. This is just something I have to do." Randy uncovered Wister's face and walked briskly toward the North Gate.

Denise struggled to keep up with Randy. "What about all them folks back at the Whore's Head who's wanting to go back home to their families?"

"The law is the law. It must be upheld." Randy quickened his pace even further to escape Denise's perfectly reasonable arguments. A part of him knew that Denise was right, and that he was acting like a pompous windbag. For the life of him, he couldn't figure out why he felt so compelled to risk what might be everyone's only chance to go back to their normal lives for ideals that he'd never given a shit about up to now.

"Come on, Randy," Denise called out after him. Think this through. Don't be —"

"Hello? Sir? Excuse me!" Randy spoke loudly, both to drown out Denise's voice, and to deny himself the means to reconsider. Panting, he stopped in front of the guard. The muscles in his upper arms burned.

"Good morning, sir," said the guard on the left side of the gate. "What troubles you?"

The gate was wide open. Randy could just charge right through and lose this guy in the city's labyrinth of side streets. He shook the thought out of his mind and spoke before any further temptation had the chance to enter.

"I found this halfling in the woods!"

The guard glanced at his partner on the right side of the gate, then looked back at Randy. "Congratulations?"

"I suspect he ain't who he claims to be."

The guard squinted at him, his apparent confusion deepening. "Who does he claim to be?"

"Well he says his name is Wister, but –"

"Don't listen to him!" Denise had caught up faster than Randy had expected. "He's crazier than a rabid badger."

"I ain't crazy, Denise. And that's not nice."

Denise ignored him, instead addressing the guard who looked like he wished he was anywhere else. "Is he telling you wild stories about our friend Wister here?"

Randy had been doing a poor job explaining himself. The guard seemed relieved to hear something that made sense. "You are acquainted with the halfling?"

"No," said Randy. "Like I said, we found –"

"You bet your sweet ass we are," said Denise. "My buddy Randy here gets confused sometimes, on account of his mama dropping him on his head all the time when he was a baby."

"That's just not true! I am –"

"Has he told you how Wister's not really a halfling, but a human trapped in a halfling's body?"

"No," said the guard, looking quizzically at Randy.

Randy lowered his head. "It ain't like what it sounds."

"But that ain't all," said Denise. "He thinks *I'm* a human, too. And not only that, but a *man*!"

"It's the truth!" cried Randy. "You know it as well as I do. You're just trying to make me sound like a crazy person."

Denise shoved her breasts together and heaved them toward the guard. "Do these look like man-titties to you, boy?"

"No, ma'am," said the guard, holding his spear upright between himself and Denise. His partner on the other side of the gate stifled a laugh.

"You like these big titties, boy? I bet you'd like to put that spear of yours between them."

"I, uh..." The guard suddenly looked back to Randy. "I don't understand what you want me to do. I can't arrest this sleeping halfling for lying to you about his name."

"I don't want you to arrest him," said Randy.

"Then what *do* you want?"

"I just want to pass through the gate."

The guard's fist trembled with frustration. "Then why are we having this conversation? Do you need directions?" He tilted his spear toward the open gate. "Walk six feet in that direction. You can't miss it."

Randy was all too aware of how ridiculous he was being, but couldn't account for a reason behind it. He mustered up what little dignity he had left, bowed his head slightly, and said, "Thank you."

He hefted Wister over his left shoulder to give his arms a rest, then he and Denise passed through the gate.

"What was that all about?" the left guard asked the right guard, nearly shouting to be heard from the other side of the gate.

"Beats me," the right guard shouted back. After a moment, he added, "Say, Ridley. Would you ever fuck a dwarf?"

Denise stopped walking. She had that ass-kickin' look in her eyes.

"Ha!" said Ridley. "Certainly not that one. She smelled like piss."

"You don't have to tell me. I could smell her from here."

Denise started to turn around, but Randy was ready. He stopped her with a hand on the shoulder.

"You gotta ignore them, Denise."

"I ain't gotta do shit."

"Come on, man. They is officers of the *law*. You of all people got to see what they're doing. Don't even tell me you never baited nobody into throwing the first punch just so you could legally beat the shit out of them."

Denise's face was like a volcano of rage and frustration, threatening to erupt at any moment, but for a tiny plug of reason and self-preservation instinct. She needed another little nudge in the right direction.

"You tell me honest, Denise. Did it ever work out well for the other guy? *Ever?*"

Denise shrugged Randy's hand off her shoulder and stomped further into the city. "Cock-suckin' rent-a-cop motherfuckers."

"They ought to try the South Gate next time," said the right guard. "You know who would fuck a piss-soaked dwarf? Jennings."

"Oh, you didn't hear?" said Ridley.

"Hear what?"

"Jennings and Mosley got caught harassing some half-elf woman last night. They got caught by the commander himself."

The other guard whistled long and low. "I think I'd rather piss off Timmon Bloodsoul."

Chapter 20

Julian focused his concentration on a mental image of Ravenus, as if he might somehow pick up their empathic link like a radio signal if he tried hard enough. He knew that wasn't how it worked, and that he wasn't going to feel his familiar's presence until they were within a mile of each other, but they'd been walking for a while, and conversation had started to run dry.

"There's a crossroads up ahead," said Stacy.

"That's all we need," said Dave. "More uncertainty. Can you guys slow down? My legs are sore from trying to keep up with you."

As weary as Julian was of the sound of Dave's whining, he had to agree with his assessment of the crossroads situation. "How will we know which road to take?"

Tony the Elf picked up his pace. "I'll go ahead and see if I can't find any fresh wagon tracks turning left or right." He whistled. "Come on, Dave!"

Dave looked up, panting and sweating. "What?"

Tony the Elf's sheepdog, also called *Dave*, barked and discontinued urinating on a tree to run after his master.

It only took a few minutes to catch up to them, but apparently that was enough time for Tony the Elf to fail his Tracking skill. He shook his head as the rest of the party approached.

"I'm sorry, guys," he said. "I got nothing. The north/south road is more traveled, but there's a bit of traffic on the roads heading east and west. I can't tell how fresh any of the tracks are though."

Julian looked at the road heading west. It was large enough to accommodate a wagon, but only just. The trees loomed closer to the sides of the smaller roads than they did on the more heavily traveled main road.

"If Mordred was worried about being followed," Julian hypothesized aloud, "he might have ducked down one of these smaller roads."

"Hmph," said Dave. "Mordred's not worried about being followed. I think he only grabbed Ravenus to bait you into following him in the first place."

Julian nodded. He suspected Dave's reasoning had more to do with cowardice than it had to do with reason, but what he said wasn't untrue.

Tony the Elf had already come up empty, but he was still the only tracker in the group. Julian asked him, "What do you think?"

Tony the Elf shrugged. "I think it's a good thing I talked you into saving your Mount spells. We might have spent their entire duration deliberating about which way to go."

"We have no idea where any of these roads lead, right?" asked Stacy.

"Yeah," said Julian.

"And we have no idea where Mordred is headed?"

Tony the Elf nodded. "That is our current predicament, yes."

Stacy grinned. "Not a predicament. That's the solution."

"Go on," said Julian, hopeful that Stacy had put her high Intelligence score to work connecting seemingly random pieces of data together to form some larger picture that the rest of them were incapable of seeing.

"With nothing else to go on, the bigger, more traveled road makes the most sense. There's bound to be more stuff that way. Whatever Mordred wants, it will more likely be in that direction."

"More stuff," said Julian, not bothering to hide his disappointment.

"Hey, it's the best I can do with nothing to work with."

"What if he's trying to level up?" asked Dave, massaging his right leg just above the knee. "He'd be more likely to encounter more monsters on a less-traveled road."

Julian narrowed his eyes at Dave. He could see what was going on here. "You're just gainsaying our conclusions so that you have more time to rest your fat little legs."

"What?" said Dave, overplaying his offended outrage. "How could you even... I would never... Where do you get off accusing me of –"

Tony the Elf dropped to one knee and placed his palm flat on the road. "You two idiots shut up for a second." He squinted and cupped his right hand next to his ear, focusing it along the road leading eastward. "Somebody's coming."

Julian looked in that direction, but the road veered to the right and was soon obscured by the trees. They wouldn't get a good look at whoever was approaching until they were nearly right on top of them. Now that everyone was quiet, Julian could also hear the distant rumble of hooves and wheels on the road.

"We should hide," said Dave. "It might be Mordred."

Tony the Elf looked up at Stacy. "How many horses were pulling Mordred's wagon?"

"Just one."

"It's not Mordred," said Tony the Elf. "This wagon is being pulled by two horses."

Stacy nodded. "Impressive."

"I could have told you it wasn't Mordred," said Julian. "I still can't feel Ravenus."

Tony the Elf stood up. "Whoever it is, they're bound to know these roads far better than we do. We'll ask where each road leads to, and use that information to make our best guess as to which way Mordred might have gone."

Everyone halfheartedly nodded their consent. The plan didn't seem likely to yield much in the way of useful information, but hopefully it would be better than nothing.

They stood shoulder to shoulder, (or, as in Dave and Julian's case, shoulder to ass) so as to keep from being ignored. But they were ready to jump out of the way should the travelers speed up and threaten to run them over.

The rumbling grew louder as the wagon drew closer. A cloud of dust rose from the bend in the road, and from it emerged two white horses. Behind them, seated at the front of a large sturdy wagon, were two uniformed Cardinian soldiers.

The soldier on the left raised his right hand, and the soldier on the right pulled on the horse's reins. The wagon slowed to a halt twenty feet in front of them.

"What sad band of brigands are you who would impede the journey of the king's own soldiers?" demanded the soldier on the left.

"We're very sorry," said Julian. "We don't want to take up too much of your time. We just need —"

"Stand aside this instant before we throw you in with this lot!" The soldier cocked his head back. Julian took the gesture to mean that their wagon was full of prisoners.

"Come on, man," said Julian. "We just want to know where these roads lead."

The soldier leaned forward and spoke directly to Julian. "This is your final warning, *elf*."

"Let them go, Julian," said Tony the Elf. "We'll catch the next one."

Julian noticed then that he was the only one still standing in the wagon's way. Tony the Elf and Stacy stood on the right side of the road, and Dave stood on the left. Reluctantly, Julian stepped back to join Dave and let the wagon pass. Who knew how long they'd have to hang around before another wagon came along?

"Yah!" said the soldier with the reins, and the horses started moving.

"Hey," said Julian, determined to get something out of these pricks. "Can one of you at least tell me where you're coming from?"

"Ye mum's house," said a voice from inside the wagon. A black-skinned half-elf grinned down at Julian from above the paneling on the side of the wagon, which covered all but the very top and bottom of the iron bars. His hair was grey, but Julian suspected it might be white after a wash. "The line was pretty long, but she was servicing four at a time, so it moved quickly. Run along home and give her a kiss for me, hey?"

That was completely uncalled for. Julian had half a mind to jab that stupid grin off his face with his quarterstaff, but didn't imagine that would get him any closer to getting the information he needed, and might even get him thrown back there with him. "There's really no need for —"

"Gah!" cried Dave, jogging alongside the wagon as it turned onto the northbound main road. "He's got my beard!" He was banging on the side panel as his beard was being pulled under it.

"Stop the wagon!" cried Julian. "They've got my friend's beard!"

The soldier on the right turned around and laughed at Dave. "Such is the price of your friend's stupidity." Facing forward again, he addressed the driver. "Onward, Gareth."

"Oh my god!" cried Dave, picking up the pace as the wagon straightened out. "I think he's eating it!"

Those asshole soldiers weren't going to stop, and Dave wasn't going to be able to move much faster than he was now. It would only be a matter of seconds before he had his face ripped off while being crushed under a wagon wheel. Julian ran to offer whatever aid he could. He didn't carry a blade on him to cut Dave's beard, so he jabbed at the prisoners with his quarterstaff through the bars.

Someone grabbed the quarterstaff, and Julian immediately released his grip, not wanting to sacrifice his fingers to save a stick. Fortunately, the occupants of the wagon seemed to regard it a fair trade for what was left of Dave's beard. Dave stood panting on the side of the road with a large jagged chunk of the right side of his beard missing.

"Are you two okay?" asked Tony the Elf, running up to meet them.

Dave wiped the spittle off the chewed-away section of his beard. "Define *okay.*"

"What a couple of fucking assholes!" said Julian. He was madder than he could ever remember being.

"What do you expect?" said Tony the Elf. "They're criminals."

"I was talking about the soldiers."

Tony the Elf shrugged. "That's just the way it is. They've got the uniforms. They can be as dickish as they want to be."

"You know what?" said Julian. "Screw that. I'll be right back."

"What? Where are you going?"

Julian turned around to face the wagon as it picked up speed. "Horse!"

A sandy brown mare materialized next to him. He grabbed the saddle horn, slipped a foot into a stirrup, and hoisted himself up.

"Just let it go, Julian," said Tony the Elf. "They aren't worth it."

Julian didn't look back. "Ravenus is. Go, horse!"

The wagon had picked up speed, but Julian's horse quickly closed the gap between them, and was soon trotting off to the right of the soldier who had done most of the talking.

Julian knew his Diplomacy skill would serve him better than magic in his current situation, but he couldn't bring himself to sweet-talk these jerks. He'd go the other way with it. Reverse Diplomacy. He cleared his throat.

The soldier looked at Julian, then down at his horse. "Well well. So the elf knows a little magic trick. Very impressive. Fuck off."

Julian smiled to himself. They wouldn't last two minutes. He started to sing. "*Jimmy crack corn, and I don't care. Jimmy crack corn, and I don't care.*"

The soldier gave him a scornful look. "What?"

"*Jimmy crack corn, and I don't care. Jimmy crack corn, and I don't care.*" Julian didn't know anymore lyrics to the song, or even if it had more lyrics. But annoyance was what he was going for, and repeating the same line over and over again would yield greater results anyway. "*Jimmy crack corn, and I don't care. Jimmy crack corn, and I don't care.*"

"I don't care either. Now fuck off!"

It was working already. "*Jimmy crack corn, and I don't care. Jimmy crack corn, and I don't care.*"

The prisoner who had claimed to have been serviced by Julian's mother gaped at him as he continued to sing, then turned to his fellow prisoners. "The elf's gone and lost his fool mind, he has."

Julian sang louder. "*Jimmy crack corn, and I don't care! Jimmy crack corn, and I don't care!*"

The soldier's fists were shaking with rage. "Stop saying that!"

The dark-skinned half-elf nodded slowly, appreciating the frustration of his captor. He sang along with Julian. "*Jimmy crack corn, and I don't care! Jimmy crack corn, and I don't care!*"

If this song could drive Pee-Wee Herman to jump from a moving train, it could make this bastard crack. "*Jimmy crack corn, and I don't care! JIMMY CRACK CORN, AND III! DOOOOON'T! CAAAAAAAAAAAAAAAAAA–*"

"ENOUGH!" said the soldier. "Gareth, stop the gods damned horses." Once the wagon slowed to a stop, he looked at Julian, red-faced and breathing heavily. "What is it you want from me, elf?"

"I just want to know where you're coming from."

"Lighthouse Rock. We're transporting a group of pirates and thieves from the Barrier Islands to Cardinia where they will be hanged. Are you satisfied now, or would you like to know what I had for breakfast this morning?"

"And where does the westbound road lead?"

"It leads west."

Julian cleared his throat. "*Jimmy crack corn, and I–*"

"All right, all right! Enough! I've always known elves to be snobbish, but never flagrantly obnoxious."

"The westbound road?"

"A string of unpronounceable elven villages. How is it you don't know where your own people live?"

Julian ignored the question. "And what's to the south?"

The soldier shrugged. "Port Town, of course."

Julian bit his lower lip. "That's a pragmatic name. I take it that's a sea port?"

"Careful with this one, Sarge," said the conspicuously jovial prisoner. "He's a clever one, he is."

The soldier looked back at the wagon. "Keep running that mouth, Tanner. You've got less than a day before it stops running for good." He turned to Julian. "Yes, it's a sea port. Now are we done with the geography lesson?"

"Yes," said Julian. "Thank you."

As the wagon pulled away, Julian sat atop his horse and thought about his options. The elven villages didn't seem very promising. He couldn't see Mordred recruiting an army of elves, if building an army was even what he had in mind. Elves, to Julian's limited knowledge, were mostly peaceful people who typically liked to keep to themselves.

Lighthouse Rock and the Barrier Islands sounded like a better place to recruit a bunch of lowlifes for Mordred's hypothetical terror army, but even that sounded too small-time.

Port Town made the most sense. If Mordred did mean to take a boat to a different continent, the haystack he was hiding in would grow exponentially larger. And unless he was planning to steal a boat, they probably ran on some kind of schedule. There was a chance, then, that they might be able to catch up with him. He quickly conjured up three more horses. It was time to ride to Port Town.

Behind him, from the back of the prison wagon headed to Cardinia, Julian heard the black elf continue singing.

"Jimmy crack corn, and I don't care. Jimmy crack corn, and I don't care."

Chapter 21

It was mid-morning when Randy and Denise finally arrived back at the Whore's Head Inn, and Randy was exhausted. He wanted nothing more than to hand over this halfling, who seemed to have increased in weight to that of a hippo in his fatigued arms, instruct the others not to harm him, and fall into a nice deep coma.

To avoid needlessly waking anyone up, Randy decided to enter through the gap in the back wall rather than knock on the door. The precaution proved unnecessary. As soon as he entered, he had three sets of red, sleep-starved eyes glaring at him.

"Mornin'," said Randy.

"Don't you *mornin'* us," said Frank. "Where the hell have you two been all night?"

"We was in the woods. Y'all ain't had to wait up for us."

"What is this place?" said Denise. "A fucking boarding school? It's nice that y'all care so much about us, but we can take care of ourselves."

"No," said Frank. "We don't, and you can't." His passed to the halfling in Randy's arms. "Who's the little girl?"

Randy laid the body down on an empty table and shook some blood into his arms. "He's a boy. Well, a man really. He's one of them little fellers. Not like you, but the other kind. You know, like Tim."

Frank nodded. "A halfling. But *who* is he?"

"Well he says his name is Wis—"

"I'll tell you who the fuck he is," said Denise. She pointed a fat little finger at the halfling on the table. "That right there is fucking Mordred. Signed. Sealed. Delivered. You're welcome."

Everyone at Frank's table suddenly seemed a bit more awake. Everyone except for Frank, anyway, who just looked a little more tired and annoyed.

"Forgive me for being cranky and skeptical. I didn't get much sleep last night. Do you have any evidence at all to support this theory of yours?"

"Go on," said Denise. "Tell him about the Red Robes of Nu... Neutrinos? Nutrition?"

"Neutrality," said the bald man to Frank's right. Randy hadn't introduced himself to him the night before, on account of him seeming moody and standoffish. But now he looked to be wide awake and open to engagement. "Did he claim to be wearing the Red Robes of Neutrality?"

"You bet your shiny bald ass he did," said Denise.

Frank stifled a yawn. "I'm running on two hours of sleep here, Stuart. You wanna clue me in? What the hell are the Red Robes of Neutrality?"

"It's from the *Dragonlance* novels I read when I was a kid," said the bald man, Stuart. "In the world of those books, wizards wore different colored clothes to match their alignment. Good wizards wore white, evil wizards wore black, and neutral wizards wore the Red Robes of Neutrality."

"Why?" asked Denise.

"Why what?"

"Why did they wear colors to match their alignment?"

"I don't know," said Stuart. "Think of it like a uniform, I guess."

Denise's face betrayed no sudden clarity. "What if they was an evil wizard, but they didn't want nobody to know they was evil, on account of they wanted to earn somebody's trust in order to betray them later? Could they wear a white robe then?"

"What? Maybe. I don't know. Who gives a shit? The point is that he blew his cover by making a reference to books that don't exist here."

"He hasn't blown shit," said Frank.

"What are you talking about?" said Stuart. "*The Red Robes of*

Neutrality are clearly a reference to *Dragonlance*. What are the odds that some random halfling wizard would come up with that exact turn of phrase to describe his clothes?"

Frank yawned. "Not too long if the person who created him was a fantasy nerd." He looked around the room at all the sleeping bodies littering the floor. "Ask any of the halflings here, for instance, where their characters are from, and chances are they'll say *The Shire*. Mordred cut some corners when he made this world. Did you know there's a tavern in the Shallow Grave district called *Mos Eisley*?"

Stuart lowered his head. "I've heard rumors."

Randy frowned. "So this ain't Mordred?"

"The fuck he ain't!" shouted Denise.

"Shh!" said the heavyset woman on Frank's left. "Keep your voice down. People are trying to sleep in here."

"Don't you shush me, Mama Cass. I got a nice big chicken bone you can choke on."

While the big girl was clearly enraged at being likened to Mama Cass (though now that Denise mentioned it, the resemblance was uncanny), the others at the table appeared more confused, as if wondering what big chicken bone Denise had been referring to. Randy would have enjoyed watching her try to squirm her way through an explanation, but she was already near her breaking point, and he still had one last bit of evidence to present.

"There was also the matter of *Little Red Riding Hood*," said Randy.

Frank turned his attention from Denise to Randy. "What's that?"

"Well," said Randy. "It's a story about this little girl who's takin' this basket of goodies to her grandma's house, when she gets approached by this smooth-talkin' wolf, and –"

Frank stopped him with raised hands. "We are familiar with the story. What does it have to do with the unconscious halfling on the table?"

"When we first happened upon him, he was way up in a tree. Dressed as he was, Little Red Riding Hood was the first thing to pop into my head."

"That's completely meaningless," said Frank. "You've already established that his clothing is an allusion to a completely different fictional character."

"You ain't let me finish yet," said Randy. "The whole reason he was up in the tree to begin with was on account of there was this wolf barkin' up at him."

Frank sighed. "The Big Bad Wolf. I get it."

"Man, you don't even know!" said Denise. "This was the biggest, baddest goddamn wolf you ever seen. I'm tellin' you, that thing was bigger than a horse!"

Stuart shrugged. "Sounds like a dire wolf. Some animals in this world are bigger versions of their mundane, real-world counterparts. You get used to it."

"This weren't just no big wolf," Denise insisted. "It was blacker than Satan's asshole, and had glowing red eyes."

The big girl raised her eyebrows. "A *fiendish* dire wolf. That *is* pretty unusual. So how did you two heroes manage to escape a fiendish dire wolf?"

Randy and Denise looked at each other, then Randy looked back up at the big girl. "I just poked him with my sword and he ran off."

"Bullshit."

Denise pointed at the big girl. "Are you callin' my friend a liar, Large Marge?"

"My name is Rhonda, Pissbeard the Pirate."

"I believe him," said Stuart. "A paladin wouldn't lie."

"Randy may be queerer than a barrel of faggots," said Denise, "but he ain't no liar."

"Denise!" said Randy.

Denise shrunk back under the weight of all awake eyes in the room focused on her. "Forget I said that last part."

Randy's heart burned as everyone shifted their attention to him. It was like all of their eyes were magnifying glasses concentrating the sun's light on him at the same time.

"Is this really true?" asked Frank.

Randy lowered his head, then lifted it again to look Frank straight in the eye. "I don't rightly know what a *barrel of faggots* even means. But yes, I *am* a homosexual."

Frank rolled his eyes and even cracked a little smile. "I can assure you that no one here gives even the tiniest hint of a fuck about that. I was talking about the wolf story. You just poked it with your sword?"

"I was scared," said Randy. "And I ain't never stabbed nothing before."

"Nothin' but buttholes," Denise muttered.

Once again, every eye in the room focused on Denise, not one of them betraying any sign of amusement.

Denise looked at the floor. "Sorry."

"The *Little Red Riding Hood* connection is tenuous at best," said Frank. "Though a timid fiendish dire wolf raises some suspicion. That, along with the Red Robes thing is certainly enough to warrant further investigation. You did right by bringing him in." He looked over at the halfling. "Knocking him out might have been a little excessive though. Did you at least try to coerce him peacefully first?"

"We ain't laid a hand on him," said Denise. "At least, not until he went and passed out on his own."

Frank, Rhonda, and Stuart exchanged some uncomfortable glances.

Frank finally broke the confused silence. "You say he passed out without any provocation?"

Randy nodded.

"We ain't provocated shit," said Denise.

Stuart frowned. "I can't think of any game-related reason why that should happen."

Frank sighed and glanced at the sleeping halfling. "This story is getting stranger and stranger. I don't like it." He looked up at Randy. "Is there anything else?"

Randy patted the lump under his rough wool shirt. "There's one more thing."

Frank rubbed his temples. "Of course there is."

Randy pulled out the polished wooden stick and placed it in front of Frank. "This fell out of the tree he was hiding in."

Frank turned to Rhonda. "What can you make of it?"

"Goddamn, woman!" said Denise as Rhonda's eyes glowed with bright white light.

Rhonda stared at the stick for a full minute before her eyes returned to normal. "I picked up a powerful aura of conjuration magic."

"Powerful enough to summon a fiendish dire wolf?" asked Stuart.

"Possibly. I could cast an Identify spell to know for sure, but it will take time, and the components are expensive."

Stuart looked at the sleeping halfling. "Don't bother. I think I know what happened. We need to tie him up."

"What's your theory?" asked Frank.

"Mordred follows these two hillbillies into the woods —"

"Hey!" objected Randy and Denise.

Stuart ignored them. "While they're screwing around doing whatever, he climbs into a tree, summons the wolf, and commands it to attack him until it is struck with a weapon, at which point it is to run away."

"Why?" asked Frank. "What would be the point?"

Stuart shrugged. "Maybe he wanted to be brought back here to infiltrate the Whore's Head Inn."

Frank shook his head. "If Mordred wanted to infiltrate the Whore's Head, he wouldn't bother screwing around with wolves and wands. He'd just knock on the door and say 'Hi. I'm Bernie from Milwaukee. I got sent here a few days ago.'."

"Well then maybe he's testing the new recruits, running auditions to replace his Horsemen. I don't know what he's up to, but I can't think of any other reason that these two aren't currently little piles of fiendish dire wolf shit in the woods."

"And how do you explain him passing out for no reason?"

"I don't know," said Stuart. "I'm not claiming to have all the answers. All I'm saying is that we have some pretty compelling evidence that – Wait, where'd he go?"

Randy looked at the table he'd set the halfling on. It was bare. Before panic could start to set in, he heard a thud and a grunt behind him.

Denise stood over Wister, who was groaning on the floor and cradling his nuts.

Wister flipped over, pushed himself to his knees, and was about to make a break for it when Denise kicked him hard in the ass, sending him face-first into the floor.

"Where the fuck do you think you're going, Frito?" She jumped on the halfling's back and put him in a choke hold.

"What did you call him?" asked Rhonda.

"Let... go!" Wister forced the words through his constricted throat.

"Frito," said Denise. "You know, like the midget with the ring in them movies?"

"That's *Frodo*."

"Please... stop!"

"Maybe I got him mixed up with that guy from *The Godfather*."

Rhonda shook her head. "That's *Fredo*."

"Can't... breathe!"

"That Mexican painter lady with the unibrow?"

"Frida Kahlo."

Denise let Wister's once again unconscious body drop to the floor. "Well then who the fuck is Frito?"

"That's a corn chip."

Denise looked thoughtfully at the floor, then raised her head again. "Oh yeah. That's right."

"Did you have to choke him to the point of passing out again?" asked Stuart. "We could have questioned him just now."

"Sorry," said Denise. "Force of habit."

Stuart turned to Frank. "At least now we know he's a flight risk. All the more reason to tie him up and keep him under guard in the cellar until we can get a definitive answer, don't you think?"

Frank frowned. "We don't know it's Mordred. What if we're wrong? What if we keep him tied up in the cellar for a week, and then find out that he's not Mordred? What do we do with him then? Turn him loose so he can run to the authorities?"

"It's the only lead we've got," said Stuart. "And I think it's a strong one. Rhonda, what do you think?"

"I don't think I want to be around when everybody wakes up and finds out that we probably caught Mordred and then decided to let him go."

"I didn't say we should let him go," said Frank.

"Then how do you propose we contain him?" asked Stuart. "The walls in this place aren't even finished. And let's not forget that he's a spellcaster. Who knows what kind of magic he could use to slip away unnoticed? We need to keep his arms restrained so that he can't use magic. And we need someone on him around the clock to make sure he doesn't try anything."

Frank put his elbows on the table and cradled his head in his hands. "I just don't know."

"Don't stress yourself out about it," said Rhonda. "This decision isn't yours to make."

Frank nodded his head in resignation.

Randy cleared his throat. "If it's all the same to you folks, I'd like to be the one to keep watch over him. I know you's all good people, but I just want to make sure no harm don't befall him."

"I'm afraid that's out of the question, my friend," said Frank.

"And why's that?"

"Because you have somewhere else to be. Some gentlemen came by looking for you a little while ago. They banged on the door until we woke up."

Randy didn't like the sound of that at all. "Who was it? Don't nobody know me here."

"They were kingsguard," said Frank. "The king has requested a meeting with you, as you are the only known worshiper of the New God." He smiled. "You are to report to the royal palace immediately."

Randy swallowed hard. "Oh shit."

Chapter 22

Chaz trudged back up the road, tired, sweaty, and thirsty. He hadn't slept well, due to his lute making a lousy pillow, and his mouth still felt funky from not having brushed his teeth. He wanted a shower and a toothbrush, or at least a shot of hard liquor to swish around in his mouth.

What he didn't want was to be walking alone on Certain Death Boulevard with nothing to protect himself with but a lute and a sword that was about as intimidating as a dry stick of spaghetti.

He strummed his lute, trying not to think about what kind of terrible creatures lurked in the woods to either side of him, just waiting to jump out and eviscerate him. He knew there was at least one owlbear, whatever the fuck that was, roaming the wilderness, no doubt pissed off by its sudden inability to scratch its nuts. Judging by the size of those arms, it probably wouldn't need them to kick his ass.

The woods were quiet. The first sound Chaz heard, aside from the strings of his lute, came not from his right or left, but from behind him.

Chaz turned around. A wagon was approaching, pulled by two white horses. With a little charm and a little luck, he might be able to get himself a ride into town. Or he might get raped, or murdered, or both. After pausing to think about the owlbear with no arms and itchy balls, he decided to take his chances.

"Good day, gentlemen!" Chaz shouted as soon as he judged the two drivers to be within shouting distance. They wore uniform armor. Kingsguard. *That's good. Kingsguard were responsible for keeping order, and upholding the king's good reputation. They probably didn't rape and murder innocent civilians.* He looked up and down the otherwise empty road. *At least, not while anyone was there to witness it.*

"Get out of the way!" the soldier on the right shouted back at him.

In a way, that was comforting. Chaz felt that he could now exclude rape as a probable outcome of this encounter. Still, getting a ride seemed like an equally unlikely prospect. Fortunately, he had a backup plan. He stepped aside, allowing the wagon to go on its way if that's what the drivers decided. He strummed on his lute and began singing the theme song to *The Golden Girls*, which was the only song about friendship which came to mind on such short notice.

"Stop the wagon!" demanded the soldier on the left.

The horses stopped, and the two soldiers smiled as Chaz continued to play through to the end of the song.

"That was a lovely song. Wasn't it, Gareth?"

"Indeed it was, sir," responded the soldier holding the horses' reins. "Melted my heart, it did."

The superior officer leaned down and smiled at Chaz. "Did you really mean it? Would the biggest gift, indeed, be from you?"

"Absolutely!" Chaz couldn't believe how hard these two guys fell under his spell. Maybe bard wasn't such a shit class after all. In the wrong hands, this kind of influence could topple kingdoms.

"And what may we do for you, dear friend?"

"I could really use a lift into town."

"What do you think, Gareth? Do we have enough room in the back?"

"Always room for one more, sir."

Chaz was a little confused. "One more?"

"I'll need you to surrender your weapon."

"Of course," said Chaz, hurrying to unbuckle his sword. He handed it up to the officer in charge while the other soldier, Gareth, climbed down. "Do you need my lute as well?"

"The gods forbid!" cried the officer. "What better way to break the tedium of travel than with a string of delightful songs?"

Chaz took that to mean they'd expect him to play non-stop all the way to Cardinia. Still, it was better than walking.

Grinding chains crunched from on top of the wagon's roof as Gareth used both hands to turn a large crank on the side. As he did so, the back of the wagon opened up from the top outward, like the bow ramp of a Higgins boat, suspended on a chain at each of the top corners.

"What are you guys carrying in here?" Chaz shouted over the loud crunch of chain against chain. "Turnips? Potatoes? Melons?" He really hoped it wasn't manure.

The soldier grinned in a way that made the hair on the back of Chaz's neck stand up. "Rhymes with *melons.*"

Chaz couldn't think of any words offhand that rhymed with melons. *Ellens? Helens? Magellans?*

As the door descended further, shedding light into the shadowy interior of the wagon, Chaz saw chains feeding up into the ceiling. At the end of the chains were manacles. In the manacles were wrists.

The door slowly kept lowering, and wrists gave way to arms, then to curious, filthy faces all staring at Chaz. There was an orc with a chest full of scars and a steel prosthetic right leg, a goblin holding a thick tuft of coarse brown hair in one of his raised hands, and a curious-looking half-elf with charcoal grey skin and a wild mop of hair that might have been white if it were clean. All were standing with their arms raised as high as they would go.

"Felons," said Chaz when the top of the door touched the road and the chains stopped crunching. And there was rape, back on the table.

"That was a good one, Cappy," said the half-elf. "I was going to guess *bellends.*" This provoked suppressed giggles from his fellow convicts. "It's a near rhyme."

The soldier did not look amused. "You bunch of bellends won't be laughing tomorrow when your bodies are fed to the pigs."

"I expect not, sir. But do warn your wife not to choke on my bellend again. It's bigger than what she's used to." The giggles that followed this time were not suppressed in the least.

The soldier's face smoldered as he grabbed the hilt of his sword. After a few deep breaths, he relaxed, no doubt imagining the lunatic with a premature death wish swinging at the end of a rope the next morning. He looked at Chaz and smiled pleasantly.

"Come on then. In you go."

Chaz wasn't fooled for a second by the invitational tone in his voice. Still, he had to make at least a perfunctory effort to get out of this.

"You know what? I don't want to trouble you. I think I'll just walk after all." He took a step back, and into the breastplate of the other guard, Gareth, who had come around to flank him. *Fuck.*

"I believe Captain Reynolds just told you to get in the wagon."

"Good news, gentlemen!" said Captain Reynolds. "You'll make the last leg of your last journey with music." He turned to Chaz. "Don't be shy. They won't bite. Well the little gobber might. He's in here for eating his mother."

Chaz looked at the goblin.

The goblin grinned back at him, baring teeth which were filed to points. "She had ripe melons."

Making a mental note never again to attempt using his crappy first level spells on the king's soldiers for the purpose of laziness, Chaz slumped up the ramp and took the empty spot on the bench next to the orc, hoping that he was in for something like tax evasion.

The inside of the wagon stank something fierce. Who knows how many condemned men had soiled themselves on the way to the gallows in here. But it was nothing compared to trying to extract the last remnants of oxygen out of the fart cloud Cooper had left in the Bag of Holding while waiting for someone to remember that Chaz was still in there.

"Play loud," said Captain Reynolds, "So we can hear you up front." He stood with his hand casually resting on the hilt of his sword while Gareth went back around to crank the door closed again. He seemed to know that Chaz was waiting for an opportunity to jump up and bolt out of there, and seemed to be hoping he'd try.

As the chains lifted the top of the door, the chains inside the wagon, connected to the prisoners' manacles, slowly allowed them to lower their arms. As loud as those chains had sounded outside, they were even louder inside the wagon. By the time the door finally closed, cutting off Chaz's only hope of escape, everyone around him was sitting down on their benches. The crunching sound was still ringing in his ears when the wagon jerked forward.

When the wagon had achieved its cruising speed, someone banged on the wall from the outside. "I don't hear any music!"

"Play something," said the dark half-elf. "Keep it instrumental if you can. I need to think."

Chaz nodded. With certain death waiting for him in Cardinia, the only thing this guy had to think about was escape, and that suited Chaz just fine. He started plucking and strumming.

"What is that style of music?" asked the half-elf. "I've never heard anything like it."

"Surf rock," said Chaz.

The half-elf looked like he was about to inquire further, but shook his head and steepled his fingers, his eyes focused on a point of empty space between himself and Chaz.

Chaz continued playing, hoping to see some hint of inspiration on the half-elf's face.

The half-elf nodded slowly, like a plan was brewing in his mind. His gaze flickered almost imperceptibly quickly to the orc and back, then slowly down to the goblin on his left who was snacking on the hair in his hand like it was cotton candy.

Finally, he leaned in close to Chaz. "Whatever happens. Whatever you see. Do *not* stop playing. Do you understand?"

Chaz nodded. It sounded like some serious shit was about to go down, but he was in the unusually fortunate position of standing between two violently opposing parties who wanted exactly the same thing from him. He'd pluck that lute until his fingers wore down to bloody nubs if he had to.

"What's going on?" demanded the orc. Perhaps the half-elf's glance hadn't been as imperceptible as Chaz had thought.

"Easy, big guy," said the half-elf. He reached his foot back under his bench as far as it would go and rolled out a quarterstaff similar to the one Julian always carried around. He grinned up at the orc. "We're busting out of here."

The orc smiled broadly, exposing a mouth full of cavity-riddled teeth and tusks. "What can I do?"

"I need you to look outside," said the half-elf. "Alert me when we pass a tree with a bright blue stripe painted down the trunk."

The orc nodded. "I'm on it." He lowered himself awkwardly from the bench to the floor with his good leg and peered through the bars below the paneling.

The half-elf cleared his throat. "I'll need what's left of the dwarf's beard as well." He reached cautiously for the hair clutched tightly in the goblin's hand.

To absolutely no one's surprise, least of all the half-elf's, the crazy hair-munching goblin snarled and hissed as he jerked his hand away.

"Come on now," said the half-elf. "Think of all the people you can eat on the outside. Think about *Captain Reynolds.*"

The goblin gave it some thought, then reluctantly opened his hand.

The half-elf took the tuft of hair and started working at it with his hands, bunching it together and aligning the ends on one side.

He leaned toward the goblin. "And if you wouldn't mind snipping off a small lock of my own hair. Just a few strands will do. Don't eat them."

The goblin obliged, his wide open mouth next to the half-elf's head, like he was about to bite into his skull. He took a few strands of grey-white hair as close to the scalp as he could, held them taut, and yanked one of his sharpened teeth through them.

The half-elf winced. "Thank you." He sat up and rubbed his head where the goblin had bitten his hair off. He wound his own long and thin strands of hair around the top of the bundle of much coarser dwarf hair. The end result looked like an old-timey fingerprint duster. "Perfect."

Chaz was beginning to lose the flicker of hope he'd had in this plan.

The half-elf got down on the floor, looking through the bars of his own side of the wagon. After examining both ends of the quarterstaff he'd had hidden under his bench, he seemed to favor the bottom end, which he passed slowly and carefully through the bars.

Chaz's fingertips were getting sore from continuous and intense lute-playing, but he continued plucking those strings, forcing himself to ignore the pain by trying to figure out what the hell the half-elf was up to.

Occasionally, the half-elf would pull the bottom of the staff back into the wagon and examine the end, but Chaz couldn't think of what he might be looking for. It wasn't until the fourth such occurrence that Chaz noticed a difference.

The bottom of the quarterstaff was getting progressively thinner. The half-elf was grinding it to a point on the edge of the wagon wheel. It was a clever display of ingenuity, but Chaz still didn't see how it was going to help them escape. Even if they managed to catch the soldiers by surprise when the door opened, the chains would raise everyone's arms, leaving them all incapable of wielding a makeshift spear.

Chaz gulped. All of them, that is, except for *him*.

That was this crazy half-elf's plan? For Chaz to single-handedly dispatch two armored kingsguard with a sharpened stick?

Chaz's feelings must have been written all over his face. The next time the half-elf examined his spear tip, he glanced up at Chaz.

"What troubles you, bard?"

Chaz thought it best to get his thoughts out in the open, so that maybe the half-elf could put his cleverness to work on a better plan. "This plan isn't going to work."

"How can you say that?" asked the half-elf, only peripherally paying any attention to Chaz, most of his concentration still focused on further sharpening his spear. "You don't even know what it is."

"I figured it out."

"Did you now?" The half-elf smiled to himself as he slowly rotated the quarterstaff between his fingers.

"I can't do what you need me to do."

The half-elf pulled in his staff. The bottom wasn't a conical point as Chaz was expecting. It was narrow and pointed, like a hypodermic needle at the end of the plunger, or like one of those sticks people use to pick up trash on the side of the road. He looked at his work with a satisfactory nod, then up at Chaz.

"You're already doing what I need you to do. Just keep doing it." He looked down at the orc, still peering through the bars. "Have you seen anything yet?"

The orc grunted. He looked terribly uncomfortable. "Lots of fucking trees out there," he grumbled. "But none with a blue stripe."

"Of course not," said the half-elf. "I made that up."

The orc turned around. "You wha—"

The half-elf plunged the pointy end of his staff into the orc's right eye. The orc struggled for a few seconds, but the half-elf had the advantages of surprise, elevation, and two legs. He twisted the staff and pushed it in even further until the orc finally stopped moving.

"What's the matter, bard?" said the half-elf. "You look rather surprised for someone so intimately knowledgeable of my plan."

Chaz just continued to gawk, his fingers strumming on autopilot now.

"Push him this way," said the goblin. "I want his hair."

The half-elf shook his head. "You can have all the hair you want once we're free. I need him to stay on this side of the wagon." As if the orc wasn't quite dead enough for him, he gripped the staff with both hands and shoved it in just a little harder, then pushed it forward until the pointy part snapped off.

Chaz missed a note, making it sound like the lute was reacting to the grisly scene.

The half-elf wasn't yet finished molesting this orc's eye socket, it seemed. He took a knee and plunged two fingers in.

That was more than Chaz could handle. He stopped playing.

"Bard!" snapped the half-elf. "What are you doing?"

"What am *I* doing?" asked Chaz. "What the hell are *you* doing?"

Clunk, Clunk, Clunk. Someone was banging on the front wall again. "I don't hear any music!"

The half-elf pulled the broken spear tip out of the orc's eye socket and looked up at Chaz. "I'm getting us out of here. Now play your song!"

Chaz nodded and picked up his instrumental surf rock just where he'd left off.

The half-elf wiped off some of the blood and eye-goo from the spear tip on his pants, then picked up the bundled dwarf hair. He carefully inserted the pointy end of the spear tip into the wide end of the hair bundle. His fingerprint duster now had a handle.

Satisfied with the miniature broom he'd created, but apparently unsatisfied with the amount of mutilation he'd performed on the orc he'd brutally murdered, he knelt down and removed the orc's prosthetic leg. After separating it into its component parts. He discarded the foot and the part that fit over the stump, but kept the shaft, a foot-long steel pipe.

"Is this part of your plan?" asked Chaz, or do you just *really* not like him?"

The half-elf peered through the bars for a moment, then stood up. "Now's the time. We only get one shot at this. Are you ready?" He inserted the tiny broom into the metal pipe.

Finally, something made a little sense to Chaz. "A blowgun."

"You catch on quick, bard," said the half-elf. "Are you ready for your next assignment?"

"You want to request a song?"

The half-elf closed his eyes and shook his head. "No, I don't want to request a song." He bent down and slid what remained of the quarterstaff across the wagon floor to Chaz. "When I tell you to, you're going to shove this stick through the bars and into the wheel spokes."

"Okay." Chaz tried to rethink the half-elf's plan. They stop the wagon and get the soldiers to open the back door. The chains would still force the half-elf's hands up, so he'd have to keep the loaded blowgun in his mouth. It still seemed so far-fetched. He might get lucky and kill one of them, although Chaz deemed even that to be highly unlikely. What about the other one? Was he hoping they'd line up and he could blow the dart straight through the first guy's head? Again, he felt compelled to raise an objection.

"I don't get how you mean to take down two armed soldiers with a homemade dart," said Chaz. "Maybe you should think about this a little more."

"Maybe you should shut up and do what you're told."

Chaz looked down at the dead orc. "Okay."

The half-elf lay down on his stomach and looked forward through the bars. "It's time. Bard, put down your lute and get on the floor. Remember to wait for my word."

Chaz did as he was told, nervously setting his lute on the bench. He lay down parallel to the half-elf and held the quarterstaff with shaky hands. On his left, he could see the wheel spokes turning clockwise at a leisurely rate. Ahead of him, he could only see a horse's ass, and a bit of forest beyond. The road must be getting ready to veer right.

Clunk, Clunk, Clunk. Captain Reynolds was banging on the wall again. "I didn't tell you to stop playing, bard. If I have to stop this wagon, you'll be –"

The wagon jerked forward as a horse screamed in pain. The wagon was moving faster.

"Julian?" said Chaz.

The half-elf sprung to his feet, jumped onto the bars at the top of the wagon, and bunched his body up as close to the ceiling as he could. "Be ready bard!"

"Stop, you crazy animals!" cried Captain Reynolds. "Gareth, grab the reins!"

The wagon rumbled along the road, leaning left as the horses veered right. Chaz held the staff and got ready to shove it as hard as he could into the wheel spokes. They weren't trying to stop the wagon. They were trying to flip it.

"Now, bard!" said the half-elf. "Now!"

Chaz shoved with all of his might. His world jerked, spun around, and finally crashed. When it was finished, he decided that it probably hadn't been as dramatic as it felt like while it was happening. They hadn't flipped the wagon, so much as just tipped it over. The cage hadn't broken open, if that's what the half-elf had been going for, but there did seem to be a lot more chain spilled all over the place. The crank mechanism that controlled the back door and the prisoners' arms must have busted.

When he felt more orientated, he looked up to see the half-elf strangling the goblin to death with a length of chain and slamming his face down into the side paneling.

His second murder of the hour complete, the half-elf turned to Chaz, then sprung toward him like a pouncing cat.

"Shit!" screamed Chaz, curling into a ball and raising his arms over his face.

After a few seconds of not being murdered, Chaz peeked out from behind his arms. The half-elf hadn't been after him. He was holding Chaz's lute by the neck, waiting at the back door.

The half-elf kept his ear to the door for a moment, then pulled back and kicked it open. The chains offered no resistance, but the door stopped suddenly after only having opened about two feet wide.

"Ow!" shouted Gareth. "My face!"

The half-elf continued listening at the door, nodding slowly. When the time was right, he smashed the business end of Chaz's lute over the head of Captain Reynolds, who never saw it coming.

He pulled the lute into the wagon, where Captain Reynolds dropped in a heap at Chaz's feet. He repeated the move when Gareth stumbled into view. He armed himself with the captain's sword and rooted around under the captain's cloak until he produced a ring of keys.

After unlocking the manacles on his own wrists, the half-elf tossed the keys to Chaz. "Chain them up."

"You aren't going to kill them?" asked Chaz, trying not to sound like he was encouraging the idea.

"Of course not," said the half-elf. "Why would I?"

"You didn't seem to have any qualms about killing the orc and the goblin."

"They were in for rape and murder. It would have been irresponsible to set them loose."

"And what are you in for?"

The half-elf smiled, handing over Chaz's destroyed lute. "Remember what I said about Captain Reynold's wife?"

Chaz looked up from his lute. "You were serious about that? You fucked his wife?"

"He caught us in the act." The half-elf sighed. "But it was worth it."

"You called her a pig."

"She is a pig... sometimes."

"I don't understand what you mean."

The half-elf smiled again, like he was being deliberately obtuse, and was finally tired of the joke. "She's a wereboar. I have what you might call an *unconventional* sexual appetite." His eyes glazed over like he was lost in a pleasant memory. "She was in hybrid form at the time. You've never heard a woman squeal like that."

"That's so disturbing."

"We need to go before they wake up. We can't let them know which way we've gone."

"Does that mean you're not headed into town?" asked Chaz. He'd hoped to be able to make the rest of his trip in the company of such a capable fighter.

"We're absolutely headed into town," said the half-elf. "Cardinia is where the women are. It's too risky to travel by road. But there are other ways to breech the city walls."

"Such as...?"

"Such as shutting up and doing what you're told. Now let's go."

Chaz lowered his head. "Okay."

Chapter 23

The stout oaks and elms of the forest grew closer to the road the farther south they traveled, eventually giving way to spindly cypresses as the lush grass turned to muddy water. Where the hard-packed earthen road stopped and the wide cypress-planked boardwalk began, an old, weather-beaten wooden sign greeted the party.

WELCOME TO PORT TOWN

"We should dismount," said Dave. The boardwalk appeared sturdy, supported by living cypress trees on both sides and wide enough for a large wagon to travel on, but he didn't want to take any chances. The last thing he needed was to fall through and be trapped underwater under a panicky horse.

Julian nodded. "Their spell duration is about to run out anyway." He pointed at the sign on the side of the road. "We should take that, too."

"The sign?" asked Stacy. "What do we need that for?"

"We need to start taking souvenirs wherever we go," Julian explained. "If Chaz fails to tell everyone where we are, or if we've gone somewhere else by the time help arrives, they can find us by looking at the inventory on our character sheets."

"Not a terrible idea," said Tony the Elf. "But what will you tell people who question you for carrying around obviously stolen city property?"

"Two of us could carry it together, facing down," said Dave. He

181

didn't really like the idea of backing one of Julian's crazy schemes, but Tony the Elf needed to be taken down a notch. "Nobody would even know."

Tony the Elf shook his head. "You two fools do whatever you want. As long as we're just wasting time, I'm going to give my feet a rest." He sat down on a wide-capped cypress knee and began to remove his boots.

Julian looked at Dave. "Thanks."

Dave nodded. "Sure."

"Couldn't we just go to, like, a souvenir shop or something?" asked Stacy.

Julian laughed, which surprised Dave, as it was the exact sort of suggestion he'd expect to come out of Julian's mouth. Maybe he was finally learning the ropes.

"Where do you think we are?" asked Tony the Elf. "Disneyworld?"

"I was just trying to be helpful."

"Maybe we can find some cool keyring, or one of those caps with the Mickey Mouse ears."

"Keep talking, Tony the Elf," said Stacy. "Maybe you'll find my foot in your ass."

Julian raised his hand like he was trying to get the teacher's attention. "Hey guys, come on. Keep it civil. If we find something smaller and more portable when we get into the city, we'll ditch the sign." He grabbed the top left corner of the sign. "Grab the other side, Dave. On three, we'll both give it a good hard yank."

Dave grabbed the bottom right corner and prepared to yank.

"One... two..."

"What do you two think you're doing with that sign?" said an older man's voice from behind Dave.

Julian looked past Dave. "Jesus!" He quickly let go of the sign. "Um... Nothing, sir. It looked crooked, so we were straightening it out."

Dave turned around and saw a naked old man standing on the road. He looked like a fat David Attenborough who life hadn't been kind to.

"It doesn't look crooked to me."

Julian forced a cheerful grin. "You're welcome!"

"That sign has stood there since before I was born," said the naked old man, the tip of his withered old dick peeking out from a snow white tangle of pubes. "Before Cardinia opened the harlot legs of her own seaport. Back when this place meant something. Port Town may have fallen under hard times, but I'll not stand here and watch her be vandalized by outsiders."

He walked toward the sign as Julian and Dave backed away, stretched his arms up in the air, and, sprayed a jet of steamy, foul-smelling piss on one of the posts that held it up.

As he continued to saturate the post, he looked at Julian and pointed at his own piss stream. "Do you know what this means, boy?"

Julian shrugged, trying not to gag at the pungent odor. "I don't know, sir. Urinary tract infection?"

The old man redirected his stream to the other signpost. "It means that this is *my* town. You got that?"

"Yes, sir."

"I won't tolerate any other cats."

"Cats?"

The old man ceased pissing and walked nakedly toward Julian, whose face was locked in a fight-or-flight struggle. "Now come here and let me smell you."

"What? No!"

But it was too late. The old man gripped Julian by both arms and sniffed at his face and under each arm.

"Nyegh," said the man, releasing Julian and turning toward Stacy. "Is it you?"

Stacy took a step back. "I'm warning you, sir. Do *not* touch me."

The old man snarled. "Aye. Stand still then, so I can smell you."

"I, um... I suppose that's a fair compromise."

He sniffed at her face, but nothing in his face or his dong showed any sign of arousal. "Lift your arms."

Stacy reluctantly acquiesced, allowing the crazy old bastard to sniff each pit to his satisfaction. "This is starting to make me uncomfortable."

"Which one of you is it?" He started walking toward Tony the Elf, who was quickly re-lacing his boots. Dave the dog snarled and barked as he approached.

"Take it easy, Dave," said Tony the Elf. "We seek no trouble." He raised his arms. "Just smell me and be on your way."

"Aye," said the old man. "I'll be on my way once I find the pussy I smelled."

Stacy gasped. "I beg your pardon!" Dave couldn't tell if she was more offended by the naked man's crude language or because she'd already been ruled out.

The old man ignored her, concentrating on thoroughly sniffing Tony the Elf.

"Bah!" he said, evidently unsatisfied with the amount of 'pussy' coming from Tony the Elf's armpits. He snarled as he surveyed the scene until he locked eyes with Dave. "You! Halfbeard!"

Dave had grown accustomed to being ignored or forgotten, and had considered it a blessing in this case, but now he'd been re-discovered.

The man moved quickly and excitedly toward Dave, like maybe he was interested in more than a friendly sniff.

"Please!" cried Dave. "No!" He shielded his face with his forearms as the crazy naked man bounded toward him.

"Aha!" said the old man, grabbing Dave roughly by his left forearm. "I know a pussy when I smell one! Explain yourself, dwarf!"

Dave was dumbstruck with confusion, but felt compelled to at least try and beg for his life. "I'm sorry for being such a pussy! It's just that my legs are short and I'm always the last one to the fight. Please don't kill me!"

"Have you lost your fool mind, boy?"

Dave considered pointing out the irony in the question, but pussied out. "What?"

"I'm not interested in your legs," said the old man, shaking Dave's arm vigorously in front of his face. "What's this on your arm? Are you a wereleopard?"

Dave had had enough. He yanked his arm away. "Of course I'm not a wereleopard! What kind of question is that? Who the hell are you?"

The old man puffed out his wrinkly, sagging, pale chest. "I'm Doogan Merriweather, mayor of Port Town."

"Is that an elected position?" asked Stacy.

Mr. Merriweather ignored her, his mad eyes still focused on the band of leopard fur on Dave's arm. "Now explain that arm, son. You don't want to anger me."

This guy had some nerve. Sure, he was kind of terrifying at first. The shock of a naked old man showing up out of nowhere and demanding to sniff everyone is bound to throw anyone off their game. But that shock had passed now. He was elderly, unarmed, naked, and outnumbered. He wasn't in a position to demand anything.

Dave put his fists on his hips. "I don't have to explain shit to you, you crazy old bastard. Go piss on a post."

"Dave!" shouted Stacy and Julian simultaneously. Tony the Elf just shook his head.

Doogan Merriweather glared at Dave, the whites of his eyes turning yellow. Orange, white, and black fur sprouted out all over his face and body as he grew and changed shape. His fingernails and toenails grew into claws. His face became more feline, his mouth spreading wide in what looked like a maniacal grin as his teeth grew sharp and pointed.

Dave's bladder emptied into his armor.

"I'm so sorry, Mr. Merriweather!" Dave blubbered. "I'll tell you anything you want! My arm got hurt when a leopard attacked me. I didn't have any healing spells on me, so my friend patched up the wound with some leopard skin. When I healed my arm the next morning, I accidentally grafted the leopard skin onto my arm."

The giant tiger-man hybrid in front of Dave nodded once, then morphed back into his naked old man form.

"Fascinating," said Mr. Merriweather. "That wasn't so hard now, was it?"

Julian and Stacy were gawking. Dave the dog cowered behind Tony the Elf, who was glaring at Dave.

"That was amazing!" said Stacy. "Are you a... I don't even know the right word."

"I am a weretiger."

"That's so cool!"

"I apologize if I gave you a bit of a fright," said Mr. Merriweather. "I have a tendency to be overly territorial." He gave Dave a stern look. "And I *don't* tolerate sass talk from youngsters."

Dave's heart skipped a beat. "I'm sorry, sir!"

"So that explains why you don't wear clothes," said Stacy.

"That is correct, Miss..."

"You can call me Stacy."

"That is correct, Miss Stacy. I usually do my patrols in tiger form, but I approached you all in human form, so as not to alarm you."

"Of course," said Tony the Elf. "I can't think of anything less alarming than being sniffed by a naked old man."

"You mind that sass talk, boy," said Mr. Merriweather, pointing at Tony the Elf. He turned back to Stacy and spoke in a more jovial tone. "It's also the only form I'm able to speak in. Are you folks hungry?"

Dave was hungry as hell, but he held his tongue. Likewise, Tony the Elf's and Stacy's eyes were both screaming "YES! YES! YES!", but they deferred the question to Julian, who had the most to lose by lollygagging.

Julian nodded. "It would be my honor to buy you lunch, Mayor Merriweather. I'd love to know more about your town."

Mr. Merriweather smiled broadly, swallowing Julian's Diplomacy bait. "That sounds delightful! I know just the place. Follow me."

And just like that, he morphed into an actual tiger. His striped tail swaying like a charmed snake, he started walking down the cypress boardwalk.

Port Town was not a city for dwarves, or for people in heavy armor, or especially for dwarves in heavy armor. The entire town was on the water. The town's 'buildings' were just miniature barges tied to the expansive boardwalk, which formed the streets. From the looks of it, Dave imagined the whole city could disband at a moment's notice, leaving behind only a network of piers to bewilder any future travelers who happened to wander upon it.

Atop the flat roof of each of these buildings was a garden, boasting a rainbow of colorful vegetables. Citizens stopped what they were doing to wave at the tiger walking before Dave's group.

"Good afternoon, Mayor Merriweather!"

"How do you do, sir?"

"Merry weather we're having today, wouldn't you say, Mayor?"

To each, the mayor responded with a nod or a low, rumbling growl.

Human and half-elven children hopped down from their parents' rooftop gardens to run their fingers through the mayor's fur, provoking a purr that should have had them shitting themselves. Dave didn't care much for kids, but he had to force himself more than once to refrain from saying "What are you crazy little bastards thinking? Don't you know that's a man-eating wild animal?"

At the end of the main avenue floated a barge much larger than the other ones, about twenty yards wide and two stories tall. The sign over the main entrance read MERRIWEATHER INN. Clearly the family had their furry paws in more than just politics.

Two of the windows on the second story of the Merriweather Inn had blackened frames, as if they had recently been burned. Workers wearing scarves over their noses and mouths were prying off burnt pieces of wood.

"Trouble at the inn?" asked Stacy.

Mayor Merriweather let out a sharper, more terrifying growl, bordering on a roar, which nearly caused Dave to soil his armor again, but merely sent all the kids scampering happily away.

When the kids were gone, the mayor turned down a side pier and morphed into his human form. "Aye, there was trouble at the inn. Band of ruffians come in yesterday evening, all full of sass talk." His visible annoyance of the memory quickly faded. "But never you mind that. Prepare yourselves for the finest grilled fish to ever grace your gullet. Now I'll be in tiger form, as it's not proper for me to dine like this. But don't you worry. One-Eyed Pete will take care of you." Without waiting for a response, he took his tiger form and continued his way along the pier.

The barge they entered was longer than most, and boasted one of the more impressive vegetable gardens on top. A steady tendril of smoke flowed out of a chimney at the far end.

"Fisherman's Hole," said Stacy, reading the sign above the door. "Something in there smells good."

She wasn't wrong. The mingling scents of grilled fish, hot peppers, and sea salt incited a rumble in Dave's stomach to rival the mayor's growl.

"Mayor Merriweather!" said a kindly old woman's voice. "What a pleasant surprise! Come on in."

Dave followed Mayor Merriweather into the floating tavern, and the rest of the group followed behind him.

The heavyset elven woman behind the small bar had streaks of grey running through her brown hair, but her plump face remained youthful.

"I see you brought some guests," she said, watching as the rest of the group shuffled in. She turned to the far end of the tavern. "Pete! Throw some more fish on the grill! And bring out the mayor's bucket!"

"Righty-Ho, Maisy!" came an old man's voice from the kitchen.

"You good people make yourselves at home," said the elf woman, Maisy. "Pete'll bring you some food in just a minute. Can I get you something to drink?"

Dave was about to respond, but the Mayor cut him off with a sharp growl.

"Right away, Mr. Mayor."

Dave, Stacy, Julian, and Tony the Elf sat in chairs around a round wooden table. Dave the dog lay down behind Tony the Elf's chair, and Mayor Merriweather sprawled out on the floor next to the table.

They all sat quietly for a moment, until Julian couldn't wait any longer.

"This band of ruffians you mentioned earlier. How many did you say there were?"

The mayor looked up at him, snarling softly as if to say "You know I can't talk when I'm a tiger.", but then reconsidered. He held up a front paw and extended four long white claws.

"Four?" asked Julian.

Mayor Merriweather nodded and retracted his claws.

Stacy leaned in to whisper to the others at the table. "That's one less than we saw in the wagon, including the driver."

Tony the Elf tapped his fingers on the table. "You may have interrupted his recruitment. That's good. If we can keep him on the run, we might keep him from gaining as much in the way of followers and Experience Points as he would, left to his own devices."

"Hope you folks are hungry," said a man bursting in through the kitchen door carrying a platter of sizzling grilled fish in one hand and a massive bucket of raw fish in the other. His smile was as friendly as a man wearing an eye patch and an apron covered in blood could hope to offer. He placed the fish platter on the table and the bucket on the floor next to the mayor, who wasted no time gulping back an entire two-foot long tuna.

Dave hoped his assumptions were correct, that this man was One-Eyed Pete, and that the blood on his apron had once belonged to fish.

"And thirsty," said Maisy. She had a tray of tall cups made from the stalks of very thick bamboo, and a large wooden bowl. She placed it on the table next to the fish platter. The cups and bowl were full of beer. She placed one cup in front of Dave and each of his companions, and placed the bowl on the floor next to the mayor's fish bucket. Dave noticed words engraved at the bottom of each cup. He took a closer look at his own.

The small, but carefully etched letters spelled 'FISHERMAN'S HOLE'.

He sipped his beer. Light and fruity. Not a bad flavor at all, but nothing he'd be able to get drunk on.

The mayor took a break from devouring fish to lap up some beer from his bowl.

Maisy pulled a bunch of wooden chopsticks out of the front pocket of her apron, much cleaner than her husband's, and passed them around. Then she reached into another pocket and pulled out a handful of dried sardines.

She crouched down below the table. "Don't think I forgot about you." She tossed the sardines to Dave the dog, who happily accepted them.

"Thank you, ma'am," said Tony the Elf. "You are most generous."

"What brings you folks to Port Town?" Whether she was genuinely interested or merely suspicious, the question sounded more sincere than the typical pointless small-talk Dave was used to hearing from tip-hungry waitresses.

"We're looking for someone," said Julian. He looked down at the mayor, who was tearing a tuna in two with his claws and mouth. "Mr. Mayor. Did you notice anything peculiar about these ruffians?"

Mayor Merriweather's responding growl didn't sound friendly, and he remained focused on the task of tearing his fish apart.

"Best not bother the mayor while he's eating, son," said One-Eyed Pete. "There'll be plenty of time for talk once you've had your supper. Go on and eat your fish before it gets cold."

"Of course," said Julian. "I beg your pardon, Mayor Merriweather."

Dave had to admit the mayor was right. This was some fantastic grilled fish. Peppery and flaky, with a hint of lemon. He thought he could eat this every day of his life and never want for another food. Of course, he'd been hungry enough to eat his own boots before he started, so that may have enhanced the flavor as well.

Before long, they were all sitting around a pile of fish bones, completely picked clean of meat, while the mayor stretched out on his back next to an empty bowl and bucket.

Julian raised his eyebrows at the rest of the table. Stacy and Tony the Elf nodded their approval.

Julian cleared his throat. "Mayor Merri–"

"Mayor Merriweather!" cried a young half-elf who had just stormed in through the door carrying a bundle of blue fabric. "Thank the gods I've found you." He rushed over to the mayor and unfolded the cloth, revealing it to be a robe.

Mayor Merriweather morphed into his human form and wrapped himself in the robe. "What is it, Piper?"

"It's Dylan Swann, sir. He's climbed up to the crow's nest of the Second Wind again. Says he's going to jump if Mary Stillwater won't take him back."

"Drunken fool," grumbled the mayor. "These sorts of shenanigans are exactly the reason she left him in the first place. A pretty girl like that can do much better for herself than a degenerate, sass-talking drunk like him. And why does he always choose my boat to host his theatrics?"

"I can only speculate, sir. Yours is the tallest in the harbor, which amplifies the dramatics."

"It's not that tall. He's like to do more damage to my boat than he does to himself."

"Also, he probably counts on you to come get him down, so he won't have to make good on his threat."

The mayor nodded. "He'd better not. If he survives the jump, I'll make him wish he hadn't." He turned to Dave's table. "I'm sorry to cut this short, new friends. It seems a mayor's work is never done."

"But," said Julian. He was too late. Mayor Merriweather and his assistant were already out the door. "Well... shit."

"Mind your tongue, son," said One-Eyed Pete. "There are ladies present."

"I'm so sorry," said Julian, balancing his Diplomacy against his frustration. "I was out of line."

Maisy smiled at him. "What's this urgent business you have with the mayor anyway. Who are you looking for?"

Julian sighed. "The mayor mentioned some ruffians who rode into town yesterday evening. It may be one of them."

"They were a strange lot," said Maisy.

Julian perked up. "Did you see them?"

"Not personally, but nothing stays a secret in Port Town for long." She pulled a chair over from another table and sat down to share her gossip. "I heard these fellas rode into town like they owned the place, the leader up and demanding passage by ship, right then and there. But there weren't any boats scheduled to leave until this morning."

"They say he used words that I won't repeat," said One-Eyed Pete, "And some I just plain didn't understand."

Maisy put her hands on her hips. "But he changed his tone once Mayor Merriweather took his hybrid form."

Dave gulped. "I can believe that."

"So they left this morning," said Stacy. "On a boat."

"On four boats," said Maisy. "They left their room at the inn one at a time, each boarding a boat bound for different destinations."

Tony the Elf bit his lower lip. "Decoys. He sent his lackeys off in different directions so that we'd have to choose between splitting our own party or gambling on a twenty-five percent chance of following the right lead."

"Did you hear anything about one of these guys carrying a bird?" asked Julian.

One-Eyed Pete and Maisy looked at one another, then shook their heads.

"Don't recall hearing anything about a bird," said One-Eyed Pete. "But all of them were said to be carrying so many bags that they could scarcely walk down the pier."

Maisy shook her head. "That's no way to live your life. Shackling yourself to material possessions will only slow you down."

"So what happened at the inn?" asked Stacy.

Maisy grimaced. "Well it seems the last of them didn't take kindly to being told what's what by Mayor Merriweather the day before, so he decided to leave something for the town to remember them by."

One-Eyed Pete pounded the table with his fist. "He set a fire elemental loose in his room just before he left and boarded his boat, the coward!"

"Calm yourself, dear." Maisy put her hand on her husband's shoulder, and addressed the rest of the table. "It wasn't as bad as it could have been. Thank the gods Mayor Merriweather was here in town, rather than out on one of his fool border patrol missions. Everything his great, great, great grandfather worked so hard for might have been burnt to ashes."

Dave tried to imagine the scene. "A weretiger fighting a fire elemental. I wish I could have been able to see it."

One-Eyed Pete shrugged. "Wasn't much of a spectacle. He just turned into a tiger and tackled the thing through the window. The seawater snuffed it right out."

Tony the Elf tapped his fingers impatiently on the table. "We need to figure out which one of those guys is the real Mordred."

"If they left one at a time," Stacy reasoned, "then Mordred was probably in the biggest hurry to get away."

"Or he could have been the last guy," said Tony the Elf. "He might have felt betrayed, being intimidated by something he thought of as his own creation. Burning down the inn and running away sounds just like the sort of thing that Mordred might consider worth hanging around for."

Julian looked at One-Eyed Pete. "Do you know where each of these boats were headed?"

One-Eyed Pete rubbed his chin. "If I recall correctly, the first of them was headed west for Portland."

Tony the Elf smirked and shook his head, no doubt thinking about Mordred's lack of imagination when naming the seaports of his fantasy world.

"And the second one, I believe, was sailing south to Port City." Stacy and Julian also smiled quietly to themselves.

"The third boat was bound for Portsville."

Everyone at the table, except for the co-owners of the establishment, laughed like bursting dams.

"Where was the fourth boat going?" asked Stacy. "Portugal?"

"Were they on an im-*port*-ant mission?" asked Tony the Elf.

Julian wasn't laughing anymore, clearly anxious to get back to the task of tracking down Mordred... and of course Ravenus, but Dave had just thought of a port pun that he didn't want to go to waste.

"Was it captained by Mr. *Port*-tato Head?"

Nothing but stares and silence. If laughter was people, Dave would be a war criminal.

"The fourth boat," said a visibly bewildered One-Eyed Pete, "was headed to Meb' Garshur."

"Ooooh," said, Stacy. "Meb' Garshur. Sounds exotic."

"That's no place for a pretty young girl like you, dear." Maisy's voice was grave with warning. "If all they did to you was murder and eat you, you could count yourself among the lucky ones."

"Is it really that bad?"

"Stay away from that place, child. It's a cursed land. You'll find nothing in Meb' Garshur but orcish barbarians."

"Or even worse," whispered One-Eyed Pete, leaning in. "You might even find *Timmon's Tomb.*" His eye was wide as he let the last word linger a bit.

"I'm giving the girl a serious warning," snapped Maisy. "Now's not the time to go filling their heads with silly fisherman's tales."

"How can you say it's silly?" asked One-Eyed Pete. "That legend is older than either one of us."

"Exactly! I'm three hundred years older than you, and no one took it seriously when I was young."

"Excuse me," said Stacy. "If the place is so evil, why do you have boats going there?"

"King Winston the Wise opened up trade in an effort to strengthen peace along the border."

"Winston the Weak! Pish to the fool king and his peace," said Maisy. "How can you call that trade? We give them grain and corn to keep their armies well-fed, and lumber to construct their siege weapons."

"What siege wea—"

"And what do they give us in return? Poisonous herbs to weaken us for when they finally decide to invade."

One-Eyed Pete smiled. "She disapproves of my smoking."

"Invade?" said Tony the Elf.

One-Eyed Pete rolled his eyes. "There's not going to be any invasion. There are at least a hundred different barbarian tribes down there, all too busy fighting one another."

"Pish!" said Maisy. "Open your eyes, you old fool. The invasion's already begun. Just look at Shallow Grave. That used to be a thriving district of Cardinia until it was overrun by the dark races."

Stacy cleared her throat. "Can we maybe use a different term than *dark races*? And what's Shallow Grave?"

One-Eyed Pete glanced at his wife. Satisfied that she was going to allow him to field the question, he turned to Stacy. "Another part of the king's peace plan was to invite anyone who swore allegiance to the realm to live in Cardinia. It has not been one of his more popular actions among the common folk. Most who took him up on his offer have been orcs, and most of them settled in the part of the city known as Shallow Grave. But as much as people worry, I've not heard tell of any more crime or violence in Shallow Grave than in the rest of the city."

"You mark my words," said Maisy. "They're biding their time. When the invasion comes, King Winston the Weasel will see his once great city gutted from the inside."

A moment of silence passed. There was only so long anyone could stand to argue with a possibly racist four-hundred-year-old woman.

Tony the Elf cleared his throat. "I'd like to know more about Timmon's Tomb."

"Pish!" said Maisy, standing up. "With all the real problems in the world, you youngsters only want to concern yourselves with spooky fisherman's tales. Well some of us have work to do." She retreated behind the bar and started aggressively washing some dishes.

One-Eyed Pete grinned. "Don't mind her none. She grew up in the aftermath of the War of the Fractured Kingdom. She still remembers the raids and the ransoms." He looked at Tony the Elf. "Now lad, how is it an adult elf has lived so long without hearing of Timmon the Terrible or the legendary elf Simon Swiftheart? Did your father never tell you these tales?"

"My parents died when I was very young," said Tony the Elf. "They were eaten by bears."

Players would make up any kind of bullshit to avoid having to write a complicated back-story for their character. Dave didn't realize he was laughing out loud until he once again felt everyone's eyes on him.

"I'm sorry. I was thinking of something else." Another giggle bubbled up, which Dave failed to pass off as a hiccup. He stood up. "I'm just going to go to the bathroom for a while."

He hurried out of the floating tavern and took a walk along the pier. Thanks to Mayor Merriweather, Dave's bathroom needs had already been taken care of. He just needed some air.

In no hurry to make a further fool of himself, he wandered along the maze of piers, and was soon enjoying this oddly quaint town. The sea air felt good in his lungs. It was as close to Gulfport, familiarity-wise, he'd ever felt in this world. He looked out at the vast, calm sea and imagined that on the other side of it he might find Cancun, rather than some orc-infested shithole wasteland.

Dave passed a little shop called Leeches & Lures, which struck him as kind of horrifying until it occurred to him that it was probably a bait shop. Fishing sounded nice. He'd have to tell Julian about this place. Even if they didn't have the sorts of souvenirs he was looking for, having some fishing gear suddenly appear in their inventory might hint that they were on the coast.

He decided that he had better head back to join the others again, so they wouldn't think he'd fallen in the water and drowned.

The others were exiting the Fisherman's Hole as Dave approached.

"You guys get anything?" asked Dave.

Julian held up two of the bamboo cups. "I bought these. The name of the place is engraved on the bottom." He shrugged. "Better than nothing, I guess."

"I was talking about information," said Dave. "Did Timmon's Tomb turn up anything?"

"It's just your standard fantasy bullshit," said Tony the Elf. "Evil king obsessed with immortality. Betrayals. Vows of vengeance. Phantom ship. Yadda yadda yadda. About as original as you'd expect for someone who came up with Port Town, Portsville, and Port City."

"And Meb' Garshur," said Stacy. She froze. "Oh my god! That's it. Mordred's going to Meb' Garshur!"

Tony the Elf rolled his eyes. "Take it down a notch, rookie. You heard the elf lady. Even One-Eyed Pete didn't really seem to believe the story. This is how people entertained themselves before television."

"Au contraire, mon frere!" Stacy was *not* taking it down a notch. She was giddy with excitement. "Television is exactly what I'm talking about. Have you ever seen a movie or TV show in which people were talking about some creepy old legend, joking about how only a fool would believe in it, and they turned out to be right?"

Julian shook his head. "I can't think of any. The guy joking about it is always the first to get killed off."

Tony the Elf's eyes were no longer rolling. "Mordred would know exactly where to find the hiding place of Timmon's Eternally Beating Heart, because he's the one who hid it."

Stacy folded her arms. "Mm hmm."

"And he'd know the location of the tomb, and the altar, and all the details of the Forgotten Rites of Resurrection."

"Mm hmm."

"An undead lich king hellbent on destroying Cardinia could unite the orcish barbarian tribes."

Stacy looked admiringly at her fingernails. "Not bad for a rookie."

"Why would he do that?"

"How the heck should I know?" asked Stacy. "Because he's an asshole."

"He wants to kill us," said Dave. "We're the only ones here who know his true self. With us out of the way, nobody will know he's a big phony."

"He'd kill all of those innocent people for *that?*"

"None of these are people to him. They're sets of statistics on a sheet of paper. He made them. He can unmake them."

"We have to stop him," said Tony the Elf.

Julian frowned. "There won't be any boats leaving until tomorrow."

Tony the Elf tugged on his ears. "What can we do?"

Dave cleared his throat and pointed his thumb over his shoulder. "I saw a bait shop back that way."

Chapter 24

Tim woke to the smell of sweat and urine that was not his own. He had a splitting headache, and the sun was shining right in his face. Why was he outside? Why was he upside down? Why was he moving?

All of those questions were answered with a long, wet fart.

"Goddammit, Cooper! Let go of me!" Tim kicked his legs, freeing himself from Cooper's grip and, consequently, allowing gravity to slam his head into the road.

"Dude," said Cooper. "Are you okay?"

"No, I'm not fucking okay!" Tim rubbed the stinging pain in his head to a dull, but still excruciating, ache. He looked at his fingers. There wasn't any blood on them.

"I would have let you down gently if you'd asked before you started kicking."

"I'm sorry," said Tim. "I was too busy choking on fart."

"Hey. I didn't ask to carry your sorry drunk ass."

Tim looked up and down the road. Nothing but road and trees in either direction. "Where the hell are we?"

Cooper shrugged. "Somewhere south of Cardinia."

"Did we pass the Horsemen's house yet?"

"No," said Cooper. "I was too exhausted to keep going, so we spent a few hours sleeping in a tree. We haven't traveled very far at all."

Tim stood up. "Let's keep moving. It still smells like fart around here." He started walking. The pavement was warm on his feet. It must have been close to noon. "Do you have anything to drink?"

"I've got the Decanter of Endless Water." Cooper paused mid-step to squeeze out a little more fart.

Tim shook his head. "That's not the only Endless Decanter you've got."

"You've been turning into quite the little asshole these days. You think it's fun to go through every day with zero bowel control? Do you know what it's like to have rash from your taint all the way down to your knees?"

Tim cringed, forcing himself not to look at Cooper's legs. "All right, enough already. I'm sorry I said anything. Okay?"

"You know what?" said Cooper. "Fuck your sorry. It's not okay. You act like your problems are the only ones that matter. You're not even fun to drink with anymore. I spent an hour last night listening to you bitch and moan because the girl you like doesn't spend every waking moment of her life fantasizing about your tiny dick. I don't –"

"Shut up," said Tim. "What the hell happened here?"

Just around the bend in the road, two white horses stood in front of an overturned wagon.

"Shit," said Cooper. "What could have pushed a wagon over like that?" He squinted at the forest. "You think an owlbear could've done that?"

"No way. Those things are vicious. The fact that those horses are still alive is evidence enough to rule out owlbears."

Cooper laughed. "And Julian."

"Stay here. I'm going to go check it out." Tim unsheathed his dagger, slid the blade down his left shirtsleeve, and concealed the hilt in his palm. He walked in slow, even steps, so as not to spook the horses.

From inside the wagon came grunting and the rattling of chains. That didn't sound good. They might be better off just leaving this one alone. He was so focused on the sounds coming from the wagon, he neglected to watch where he was stepping and accidentally kicked something metallic and jingly.

As he looked down to find a ring of keys, all sounds from within the wagon stopped.

Fuck.

The wagon's rear door swung open sideways. The wagon lay on its side, meaning that the door was actually meant to lower down to form a ramp like on a Jawa sandcrawler. A man poked his head out, looked at Tim, then down at the keys, which he seemed much more interested in.

"You there! Fetch me those keys at once!"

His presence given away, Tim waved for Cooper to come over.

"I wonder if you've seen any of my friends walking along this road," said Tim. "Two elves, a dwarf, and a very attractive human woman?"

"Are you deaf, *runt?* Or just dimwitted? I just gave you an order."

"And *I* asked *you* a question."

The man raised his eyebrows. "Surely you jest! It will be a pleasant day in the frozen wastelands of Trabajar when Captain Cornelius Reynolds bargains for the obedience of a halfling!"

"Trabajar?" asked Tim. "Isn't that the Spanish word for *to work?*"

"I don't remember," said Cooper, who had just caught up to him. "All I remember from Spanish class is *sacapuntas.*"

Tim pretended not to notice the chained man's growing frustration. "Oooh, that's a good one. What is that, like, a bag of whores?"

Cooper snorted. "Nah. It only sounds dirty. It means *pencil sharpener.*"

"Will one of you two cretins stop blathering and fetch me those keys?"

"Who the fuck is this guy?" asked Cooper.

Tim shrugged. "I don't know. I think his name is Cornholius or something. He wants me to unchain him, but he's kind of an asshole."

"Careful," said Cooper. "Whoever put him in chains did it for a reason. He could be dangerous."

"You unchain us this instant," said Captain Reynolds. "Or you'll find out just how dangerous we can be."

"Us?" Tim kept his distance, circling the back of the wagon to get a better look inside. "There's more than one of you in there?"

One other soldier sat in the wagon, his chin resting in his palms and his elbows resting on his knees. From the bored and listless expression on his face, Tim guessed that Captain Reynolds was this man's superior officer, and it was the captain's ranting and raving that had gotten them both into their current predicament, and was now keeping them from getting out of it. But he dared not suggest a more diplomatic approach.

Tim gave him a little wave. "'Sup?"

"This is your last warning," said Captain Reynolds. "You will fetch me those keys right now, or else once I'm free I'll hunt you down like the dogs you –"

With a rustling of chains, both soldiers' arms suddenly jerked to the left. Both men were pulled to the hole in the roof of the wagon as Cooper came around the other side with a fistful of chains and broken gears.

Tim pushed the wagon's door out wider, then cleared his throat. "I'm going to ask you one more time." He started unlacing his pants. "Your answer will determine how soaked with halfling piss you get."

Cooper pulled up the front of his loincloth. "And half-orc piss."

"You wouldn't dare!" The expression on Captain Reynolds's face suggested he knew otherwise.

Tim was impressed at the captain's dedication to continuing to be a stubborn piece of shit. He didn't want to have to urinate on a fellow human being, but he needed information. A simple *yes* or *no* shouldn't be too high a price to pay to not be drenched in urine.

Tim enunciated every word carefully and clearly. "Have. You. Seen. My. Friends?"

Captain Reynolds's face trembled with rage and fear. "Do you know who you're talking to? I am one of the king's own soldiers. Urinating on me is the same as urinating on the king himsegblbghfrgb..."

Tim winced. "Dude, not in the mouth!"

Cooper's stream was strong enough to strip the bark off a tree, but Tim didn't appreciate the sheer volume produced until he saw it flowing back out of a man's open mouth.

By now, Tim really had to pee. Since Cooper had gotten things rolling, he supposed there was no point in not making good on his threat. He aimed high and was soon hosing down the captain's shiny breastplate.

"The gods have mercy!" cried Captain Reynolds, moving his head around to avoid Cooper's stream, which was following his mouth. "I'll have your heads for this!"

"I've never done this before," said Cooper. "I always thought my first time would be more... I don't know... erotic?"

Tim was all tapped out before long. He had traded longevity for power and accuracy. But Cooper was still going strong. It was going to come down to Cooper's Fortitude check against the captain's Willpower check.

Unfortunately, the captain's stubbornness prevailed as Cooper's stream wilted lower and lower, until he shook off the last few drops and lowered his loincloth.

Captain Reynolds may have won the battle, but it was a Pyrrhic victory for sure. A man can only be but so proud of himself while crying and kneeling in a puddle of half-orc piss.

Tim had one more idea that just might crack the fucker.

"Cooper," he said, rubbing his fingertips together. "I seem to have dripped a bit of pee on my fingers. Might you have anything on you with which I could wash my hands?"

"Sure," said Cooper. "Look in my bag." He dropped his fur and filth covered bag on the ground with his free hand.

Tim pushed aside all of the scroll cases containing their character sheets, which he had forgotten were in there, and pulled out the Decanter of Endless Water. He pulled out the stopper and let the cool clean water run over the tips of his fingers.

"Aaaaah," said Tim. "That feels really good. I do so hate the feel of pee on my skin."

"How about some for me?" Cooper put his hand out.

"Sure, pal!" Tim rinsed Cooper's fingers, avoiding eye contact with Captain Reynolds. He then poured the water over his own head. "Nothing like a cool shower to beat the summer heat."

"We'd better get on our way," said Cooper. "We've got a lot of ground to cover."

Tim stoppered the decanter. "That's true. And I certainly don't want to be around here once all of this piss has been festering in the sun for a while. You gentlemen take care."

Cooper picked up his bag and let go of the chains, not taking his eyes off the two men in the wagon. But the fight had been pissed out of them. Captain Reynolds continued sobbing while his subordinate, who had been spared most of the urine assault, merely shook his head in frustration.

They hadn't made it twenty feet down the road when Tim heard what he was waiting for.

"Wait!"

Tim stopped walking and smiled to himself, but he didn't turn around.

"We saw your friends."

That was worth turning around for. "Where? Which way were they going?"

"We met them at the crossroads south of here," said Captain Reynolds. "They seemed unsure of their destination. They asked where the different roads led."

"And what did you tell them?"

"I'll tell you after you've washed the piss off of us."

Tim found it interesting that the captain's demands had been lowered from releasing them to just giving them a wash. He'd done the math and come to realize that was the best deal he was going to get. There's no way Tim and Cooper would unchain two armored soldiers they'd just drenched in piss. He was on the ropes.

Tim turned back around and started walking again.

"Gods have mercy!" shouted Captain Reynolds. "Fine! Port Town is to the south. Elven villages to the west, and Lighthouse Rock to the east. Please show some decency!"

Tim nodded to Cooper, who pulled out the Decanter of Endless Water.

Captain Reynolds put out his hands eagerly in a way that made Tim suspicious. His intentions became clear as Cooper started strolling right up to him.

"Cooper! Stop!"

"Huh?" Cooper turned around about ten feet away from the rear of the wagon.

Captain Reynolds looked panicky. "We had a deal, halfling!"

"Shut up," said Tim. He looked at Cooper. "You big idiot. He was about to jump you and hold you hostage for the keys."

"I was not!" insisted Captain Reynolds.

Cooper frowned thoughtfully. "So... We're not going to rinse them off?"

"Use the geyser setting, fucktard."

Cooper glared down at Tim, then aimed the mouth of the decanter at Captain Reynolds. "Geyser."

Captain Reynolds, who had been standing with his knees bent, still ready to pounce, was knocked off his feet by the torrent of water that smashed into his breastplate. Cooper spent a full three minutes showering the two men and the entire interior of the wagon, until all of the piss had been either washed away or diluted.

It may not have been their preferred outcome, but the captain and his subordinate eagerly took what they could get, positioning themselves to allow the water to flow into their armor and through their hair.

As soon as Cooper deactivated the decanter, Captain Reynolds started running his mouth again.

"You sniveling cowards! I'll have your heads, and the heads of all your friends. I won't stop until –"

"Geyser," said Cooper. Captain Reynolds got blasted in the face with a quick burst of water, and fell back down on his ass.

"Are we done here?" asked Tim. "Good."

Tim and Cooper continued their journey southward in silence for a while. It was an uncomfortable silence because Tim was unsure of Cooper's mood. Time to test the waters.

"So is that the sort of story we brag about later, or the sort we vow never to speak of again and pretend never happened?"

"It's the sort you can shove up your ass," Cooper said without even looking down at him.

Fuck.

"Is something the matter?"

"I'm tired of you calling me a fucktard."

"Oh come on, man. Don't be such a crybaby. I was just busting your balls. We've been calling each other a fucktard since the third grade. That's what we do."

"It didn't feel like you were just busting my balls."

"You were about to get us both killed!"

"So there it is. You *weren't* just busting my balls."

Tim let out an extra-exasperated sigh. "I can't believe I'm hearing this, from you of all people. The king of insults is angered because I called him a mean name. As if I don't have enough shit to deal with right now."

Cooper snorted. "And once again it all comes back to *your* problems."

"What the fuck, man?" cried Tim. "Did we get fucking married last night? When did you turn into a nagging wife?"

Cooper stopped walking. "Hey, I just thought of something."

Tim looked up at him. "What is it?"

"Shut the fuck up."

Tim kept his mouth shut for a few minutes, even more uncomfortable in the silence. Cooper was pissed. Maybe he just needed some time or space or some bullshit. Tim could give him that, after they had taken care of a more practical matter.

"We should look at the others' character sheets. There might be some kind of clue as to where they've gone."

Cooper snarled, stopped walking, and dumped the contents of his bag onto the ground. They each picked up a scroll tube and opened it.

"I've got Katherine," said Tim. "Her stats look okay. She's still got the Bag of Holding. And a bunch of dead rats and a dead owlbear. I guess she's eating well."

"I've got Julian," said Cooper. "Full Hit Points. He's out of first level spells, but he's got some souvenir cups."

"Souvenir cups? From where?"

Cooper shrugged. "Doesn't say. It just says 'Souvenir cups' with a number two after it." He handed the paper to Tim and opened another tube.

Tim looked at Julian's inventory. There they were. Two souvenir cups. "That doesn't sound very urgent. If he's shopping for souvenirs, he must have gotten Ravenus back."

"Dave bought a set of fishing lures."

"Seriously?" said Tim. "How are his Hit Points?"

"He's full."

Tim and Cooper looked through the rest of the tubes, finding everyone to be at fourth level, as they'd suspected, and in full health.

Closing the scroll on his own tube, Tim smiled. "Looks like everybody is in ship shape."

Cooper grunted.

"Jesus Christ, dude. When are you going to let this go. I'm sorry, okay? We're best friends. Let's do a bro hug and put all this PMS shit behind us."

"I don't feel like best friends."

That stung more than it should have. "How can you say that? We just peed on a man together? What stronger bond can two men have?"

Cooper looked at Tim. "So what do you suggest we do?"

"Let's go back to town. Maybe pop into a pub for a celebratory drink."

Cooper threw all of the scroll tubes angrily into his bag and stood up. "I *knew* you were going to say that."

"Seriously, dude. What happened to you while I was out? Did you find Jesus and give up drinking?"

"Our friends could be in danger."

Tim laughed. "Danger? Our friends are sitting on some beach, fishing and drinking piña coladas in their goddamn souvenir cups. "

Cooper didn't share Tim's mirth. "You don't know that. They went after Mordred. He could have them locked in a dungeon somewhere, and all you can think of is crawling back into a fucking bottle."

"I can't believe you're giving me this lecture. *You* are the most degenerate, irresponsible drunk I've ever met."

Cooper folded his arms. "I don't abandon my friends."

Tim had had enough of this guilt trip bullshit. It was time to draw a line in the sand. "Fuck all this. You go and aimlessly wander the coastline all you want. I'm going back into town. By the time you finally pull your thick head out of your fat ass, *your friends* and I will be waiting for you back at the Whore's Head."

"Fine!" said Cooper. "And fuck you!" He turned around and started stomping away.

That wasn't the reaction Tim was hoping for. Served him right for trying to use reason with someone of such low Intelligence. The big idiot was on a wild goose chase. When the others finished their little impromptu vacation, they'd come back, and he'd still be searching for them under rocks or something. But fuck him. He could learn this lesson the hard way.

Still, Tim felt like he should say something.

"Fuck you too!" he called out to Cooper's back, then started the hopefully-not-too-long walk back to Cardinia.

"Hey asshole!" Cooper shouted a few seconds later. "Don't forget your character sheet!"

That was actually a good point. Tim turned around and got hit in the forehead by a hard steel scroll tube.

Cooper chuckled while Tim rubbed the floating lights out of his vision.

"Motherfucker!" Tim shouted. "That hurt, you know!"

Cooper just gave him the finger as he continued to walk away.

When the pain subsided, Tim packed away his scroll tube and started walking back to the city. When he came to the bend in the road where the overturned wagon had been, he cut through the woods. He was in no mood to hear anymore of Captain Reynolds's shit.

To make sure he didn't accidentally get lost, he stayed close enough to the edge of the forest so that he could see the road, but deep enough in so that he was confident he wouldn't be seen.

Among the trees, Tim felt much more aware of the potential danger he was in. He pulled out his dagger, but that did little to put him at ease.

He stopped briefly to check out the overturned wagon. It was still there, the horses still tethered to the front. If any monsters chased him right now, he could make a run for it and hope his pursuer chose to eat the horses instead. He scanned the trees behind him. No monsters. Ah well, it was still a good plan.

Now that he'd passed the wagon, Tim walked closer to the road, and finally left the woods entirely. Strangely, he didn't feel any less scared. There wasn't anything containing the monsters and bandits to the forest. Something could jump out of the trees any moment, and he'd be fucked.

He walked for half an hour, jumping at the sight of every bird flying out of a tree in his periphery and the sound of every cricket chirp. When he saw an approaching horse-drawn cart, he allowed himself to relax a little. He could at least pretend he was relatively safe for the next couple of minutes.

The driver was a heavyset human with a shaggy beard a dwarf might admire. In the seat next to him sat a heavy crossbow, no doubt to discourage those who might seek to relieve him of his wares. Wooden crates were stacked and secured with ropes in the back of the cart. When it got close enough, Tim could read the words BUCKLEY'S SUMMER ALE printed on the sides of the crates. A summer ale sounded like the perfect way to ease the rest of his journey. He didn't have any money to offer, but it never hurt to ask.

Tim smiled up at the driver as he drew closer. "Spare a summer ale for a weary traveler?"

The driver spat in Tim's direction. "Spare this, runt." He threw a fast-food soda cup, which Tim was able to swat out of the air before it hit him in the face.

Tim kicked some dirt at the wagon as it passed. "Screw you, man! Why does everyone in this stupid world have to be such an —"

Where the fuck did he get a fast-food soda cup?

Tim got on his hands and knees and inspected the cup closely. This was no fantasy world cup. It even had a plastic lid and straw. He ran his finger along the side. It was waxy. Rolling the cup over with that same finger, he nearly had a heart attack when he saw what was printed on the other side.

Arby's

Tim picked up the cup and pulled the lid off. There was still a bit of watery brown liquid at the bottom. He poured it onto the tip of his tongue, then spat.

"Blegh. Fucking Pepsi."

Why was there an Arby's cup here? Would Mordred have put an Arby's in his fantasy world? No. He might be a fat stupid asshole, but he took the game far too seriously to throw a modern fast-food restaurant into his beloved creation. But what else could it be? Who else could have...

Tim looked up toward the city. "Goosewaddle."

Chapter 25

Katherine floated in total darkness, surrounded by dead rats, globs of coagulated blood, and some horrible, armless, brainless bird-bear hybrid monster. She was starving. The dead creatures' blood had gone stale, providing her no nourishment. So much for that plan.

What the hell was she doing? She'd vowed to herself to never get in this bag again. And yet here she was. She was probably going to die in here. Who sees a nasty old blood-smeared bag on the side of the road and says "Hey, I think I'll pick that up." Nobody.

She had no idea if it was day or night outside. How long would it take for her to starve to death? Days? Weeks? What a shitty way to go. She should have just let the sun fry her.

And then an even worse thought occurred to her. What if she didn't die? What if she lived forever, eternally starving in this void. Panicking, she rummaged through her bag, looking for something she might be able to kill herself with. There was nothing.

The hunger was bad, but the loneliness and boredom were worse.

A rat floated by close enough to grab, so Katherine grabbed it. She threw it as hard as she could. It collided with another rat and stopped, the second rat zooming off like a struck pool ball.

If she had pool balls, she could set up a cool game of zero gravity 3D pool. That would be kind of awesome. She'd have to build, like, a bunch of green felt blocks, some with pockets and some without, in different locations and... Holy shit, she was losing her mind. If she had a pool cue, she could stake herself in the heart with it.

"Come on, Katherine," she said to herself. "There's a way out of here. You've just got to think. You're a smart girl. When you put your mind to it, there's no obstacle you can't – What the fucking fuck!"

Someone grabbed her wrist. The next thing she knew, she was in some kind of dark dungeon, standing face to face with a black-skinned, white-haired elf, who was still clutching her wrist.

After a brief wide-eyed, confused exchange of gawking at each other, the elf glanced down at the wooden table next to him. On top of the table lay a dagger with a long, slender black blade.

A second passed. With his free hand, the elf grabbed for the dagger, and Katherine bit his throat out. Elf blood, as it turned out, was exquisite. It was thinner and sweeter than rat or rabbit. She sucked down gulp after gulp after gulp until she started to feel bloated.

Once Katherine had a good belch and wiped her mouth off on the elf's clothes, she started thinking about her next move. She was in a small room. The only exit was a wooden door. It looked old, but sturdy.

This guy had probably discovered the bag on the side of the road, detected that it had magical powers, brought it home, and was hiding out in here so he could keep all the loot inside for himself.

The elf stared at her, its mouth and dead eyes both open wide, as if it was shocked at the assumptions she was making.

"What?" said Katherine. "It's not because you're black. This was no hate crime. You were clearly reaching for a weapon with which to stab me. I was acting in self-defense."

The elf continued to stare at her.

"I have black friends." She thought for a moment. "Well, *a* black friend... on Facebook. To be honest with you, I don't even know who she is. She posts all the fucking time though. Always about Jesus. I want to unfriend her, but I don't. Because I'm not a fucking racist."

Katherine sighed. It was damage control time. At least she didn't have to do it with her bare hands this time. She grabbed a fistful of his hair with one hand, and the dagger in the other.

"For the record, I'd do this if you were white too." She drove the dagger into the elf's skull, then worked it back and forth, up and down, and in a circular motion to give the brain a good scramble.

After she'd wiped the blood and brains off on his sleeve, she brought the Bag of Holding down over his head. Then she chucked the dagger in as well.

With her ear to the door, Katherine listened closely for any outside activity, but didn't hear anything. Judging by the dankness of the air, the lack of windows and the generous splotches of black mildew all over the dull, rusty orange brick walls, she guessed that she was underground. Opening the door probably wouldn't fry her with sunlight. Still, she stood to the side as she pushed the door ajar.

No light outside either. Not even torches. That was fine for Katherine. As a vampire, she could see in the dark. But this elf guy must have really been going out of his way to secretly check out his newfound Bag of Holding.

This stupid bag may be more trouble than it's worth. She needed a place to hide it. If she turned into a bat or a wolf, she could just absorb it. But she needed to talk to someone to figure out what time of day it was outside.

"What if..."

She set the bag on the ground and took a couple of steps back from it. The room she was in was pretty small, so she opted for her normal-sized wolf form rather than the huge version. She picked up the bag with her mouth, careful not to tear or puncture it, then changed back into a half-elf.

The bag was gone. It was part of her. That was weird. Did that mean that all of those dead bodies were floating around inside her? *Ew.* But just think of the practical implications. If she ever got back home, she could make a killing as a heroin mule. Or maybe something less horrible. She'd think more about that later. Right now, she had to find out where she was, and if it was safe to leave.

Katherine opened the door wider and stepped out to find a hallway of rough grey brick, which did a much better job of hiding the mildew. The room she had come out of was at the end of the hallway, so she walked in the only direction there was to go.

She soon came upon a T intersection with a door on the right. She could go straight, turn left, or see what was behind the door. Listening at the door, she could tell there were definitely people in there. That was good enough for her. She pulled the door open.

"Excuse me. I was wondering if –"

"AAAAAHHHHHHH!" screamed a black female elf, completely

naked and bent over a modest wooden bed. Her small, jet black breasts bouncing in rhythm as her man took her from behind.

"What? Who?" The male elf took a little longer to come to grips with what was happening.

"Oh my god! I'm so sorry!" Katherine slammed the door shut.

"You there!" shouted the male. "Stay where you are!" He sounded pissed.

"It's cool," said Katherine. "Take your time." As long as she'd been stuck in this world, Katherine had never seen a black elf. She'd seen elves with different skin tones, but none were jet black like these, and here there were three of them. She wondered if she was in one of *those* neighborhoods.

The door swung open. The male elf stepped out, his white hair sweaty and sticking to his skin.

"Who are you? How did you get here?" He had thrown on a blue silk robe, but he was still pitching a pretty good sized tent.

"I'm really sorry," said Katherine. "I should have knocked. If you two want to, like, finish up or whatever, I can wait down the hall."

"Quiet, mongrel!"

"Whoa! Not cool, man. Look, if you could just tell me what time of day it is, and how to get out of here, I'll be out of your hair."

The female elf stepped out in an identical robe to her man's, which Katherine found kind of tacky, but a little bit adorable.

"Who is she? What does she want?"

The male elf sneered at Katherine. "She claims to have trespassed into our lair simply to ask the time."

"Actually, that's not what —"

"Quiet, mongrel!" said the female.

"Come on, guys. Cool it with the *mongrel*, huh? That's kind of frowned upon where I come from."

The female elf looked Katherine up and down. "You are not drow."

"No, I'm Katherine. Were you guys *expecting* a third party? 'Cause, you know, that's cool."

"How is it that you can see with no source of light?"

The male elf laughed. "Six of her fathers were probably dwarves."

Katherine got up in his face. "What the fuck is your problem, man? I haven't said anything about you being black, have I?" She gasped. "Oh shit, I just did. I'm sorry. Can we start over?"

"Put her in the cell," said the female elf. "We'll see how coy she acts after she talks to The Extractor."

The male elf grabbed Katherine's wrist and started walking. She walked with him, thinking about how easily she'd taken out the last black elf who'd grabbed her wrist.

Katherine had no doubt she could take these two elves down just as easily, but she didn't want to kill anyone she didn't have to. She could run away, but she didn't know where the exit was, and if it was still daytime outside, she could be stuck down here for hours with legions of these people trying to hunt her down. It was less trouble to just comply. A little guided tour on the way to the cell might even give her a better layout of the lair.

No such luck. The walk to the cell was a short one. It was just another little room along the hallway opposite the door to the room where these two had just been fucking. The cell door was just like the others, with the exceptions of having a small, barred window and iron braces mounted for a crossbeam.

The female elf opened the door, and the male shoved Katherine into the cell. He then struggled to pick up the thick oaken crossbeam, which was leaning against the interior wall.

The cell was sparsely furnished, the only amenities being a hole in the floor to shit in, and the saddest excuse for a bed Katherine had ever seen. It wasn't at all like the bed the two elves had been fucking on. This one was more like just a frame of scrap lumber containing a hole-ridden cloth sack full of straw, with a ratty grey blanket thrown on top. The walls were the same rusty orange as the first room she'd come from, only with a thicker, blacker coating of mildew.

The door slammed shut behind her. She turned around, put her hands on her hips and watched the two elves through the window as they hefted the crossbeam into place.

"I don't suppose either of you would be willing to tell me the time."

The female elf was breathing hard. That crossbeam was a sturdy chunk of wood. She shook her head and smiled mock-sympathetically.

"Your time is up, mongrel. Whatever appointment you're in such a hurry to get to, you aren't going to make it."

Chapter 26

The royal palace was easy enough to find. The central tower was tall enough to be seen silhouetted against the sky even as far away as the Whore's Head Inn. Up close, the white stone of the tower sparkled with flecks of some blue mineral which dazzlingly reflected the sunlight.

The walls surrounding the royal palace, which Randy now stood outside of, were decidedly less dazzling. They were half again as tall as the outer city walls. The top five feet of them looked to have been added on later. The brickwork was different, darker, with rusted swords and barbed spearheads poking out at downward angles through the mortar. Anyone trying to scale this wall had better be packing a pair of Kevlar gloves.

Randy made his way counter-clockwise around the perimeter of the wall until he came to a gate. The two guards at either side of the gate stood at attention, their spears and shields held as straight as their spines. They appeared to take their jobs a lot more seriously than the guards along the outer city wall did. A human on the left and a half-orc on the right, they eyed Randy stoically as he approached.

Randy attempted to hide his nervousness with a cheery smile. "Good morning."

"State your name and business," said the human guard.

"My name's Randy Perkins," said Randy. "I'm um... I'm currently unemployed."

The guard closed his eyes and breathed deeply, like he was having one of those mornings. When he spoke again, it was slow and deliberate, like he was talking to a child. "Please tell me the purpose of your visit to the palace."

"I'm here to see the king."

"Oh, is that all? Then by all means, go on through."

Randy smiled. "Well thank you very much." As soon as he took a step forward, the two guards' spears formed a large X blocking his way.

"I was joking," said the guard.

Randy didn't know what to say. He put his palms up. "You sure got me good."

"What business do you have with His Majesty?"

"He requested I come here, on account of I'm a pal..." Randy's mind was drawing a blank. What was that word? "Palindrome? Platypus? Pallywog?"

The two guards looked at one another. The half-orc mouthed the word *pallywog.*

"You are a paladin of the New God?" said the human guard, cutting off Randy's train of thought.

"That's right!" said Randy excitedly. "How did you know?"

"Lucky guess."

Randy noticed that the spears had not been taken back. "So... Can I go in and see the king now?"

"Describe him," said the guard.

"The king?"

"The New God."

"All right," said Randy. He thought for a moment. "He's nice. And gentle. And, um..."

"What does he *look* like?" The guard's voice was showing signs of impatience.

"Look like?"

"Surely, if you've devoted your life to this New God, you must have seen him."

"I ain't seen him face to face, but I seen plenty of paintings and statues and such."

"Statues?" the half-orc guard finally spoke. "The New God has only existed for a day. What sculptor dare attempt to chisel out the likeness of a god in such little time?"

"Please, tell us then," said the human guard. "What does the New God look like, based on these paintings and statues?"

Randy thought hard to pick out what all the different pictures of Jesus he'd seen in his life had in common. "Well, he's a skinny feller, with light brown hair, a little long in the back, and a nice full beard." The guards looked at each other. Randy was losing them. "Let's see, what else? He's got shiny blue eyes and he wears this blue toga thing, and —"

Both guards broke out in laughter.

"Please," said the human guard when he caught his breath. "Stop, just stop. I can't take anymore."

Now Randy was the one getting impatient. "What is y'all two laughing about?"

"I honestly don't know," said the half-orc. "This is one of the saddest displays I've ever seen. Blue toga!" He started laughing even harder.

The human guard was laughing so hard he had to use his spear to remain standing up. "This is..." He caught his breath. "This is even worse than the description that crazy old lizardman gave us."

Randy put his hands on his hips. "Is y'all gonna let me in or not?"

"Of course," said the human guard. "Far be it from us to deny His Majesty counsel on matters of such consequence." He called into the gateway. "Open the gate, Henry!"

"Well that's more like it," said Randy. "Thank you very much."

"Borgarth, relieve the heretic of his weapon and throw him in with the others."

"Heretic?" cried Randy. "Others?" Before he knew what was happening, the half-orc guard was upon him, starting to unbuckle his scabbard. Randy tried to struggle free, but the guard's hands were strong. "You get your hands off me this instant!"

The half-orc, Borgarth, place a firm hand on Randy's shoulder, instantly suppressing the struggle, and looked him in the eye. "Are you going to be a good little prisoner and come quietly, or are you going to make me really enjoy my job?"

Randy had had the shit beaten out of him enough times to be able to catch his meaning. He lowered his head. "I'll be good."

The open gate revealed a beautiful, meticulously maintained garden leading toward the palace proper. Randy considered making a run for it, but had a feeling that Borgarth was hoping he would do just that.

"Should I alert Sergeant Moore to identify the prisoner?" asked Borgarth.

"Is that the big colored feller?" asked Randy. "Run and fetch him. He'll tell you I ain't no heretic."

The human guard laughed. "I wouldn't bother with this one. Not after the toga thing."

"You don't understand," Randy pleaded. "I need to see the king."

"You'll see him soon enough," said the human guard. "Before your trial, you will be given the opportunity to confess your heresy and beg for a swift execution."

Randy swallowed hard. "Well that's... generous."

"Come on," said Borgarth, jerking Randy forward by the back of the neck.

Randy allowed himself to be guided around the back of the palace, down a stone stairway, and through a sturdy iron door.

The interior was more brightly lit than what Randy had expected for a dungeon. Being on palace grounds, prisoners here were not simply locked away and abandoned. Two guards, a dwarf and a human, stood at attention as Randy and Borgarth approached a barred cell door.

"Brought us another cleric of the New God, have you, Borgarth?" said the human.

Borgarth snorted. "Show some respect, Mayfield. This one's a *paladin*."

The dwarf shook his head. "Aye, it's times like these when the crazies really start to come out of the stonework."

"Hammerford," said Mayfield. "Open the door, and allow our new guest to join his brothers of the faith."

The dwarf, Hammerford, took a ring of steel keys off a peg mounted on the wall. "Come on, sir paladin. In you go." He turned the key and started to open the barred door.

"NOW!" cried one of the inmates from within the cell.

A crowd of prisoners flooded out of the cell at once, knocking Hammerford backwards. Borgarth and Mayfield looked at one another and shook their heads.

Borgarth shoved Randy aside, set his spear against the wall, grinned, and cracked his knuckles as the prisoners tried to rush him.

The first was a fat human man, not too far removed from Randy's true-form physique. Borgarth got down on one knee to give him a good solid punch in the gut. The wave of fat rippled out from the epicenter of the punch, causing waves to ripple across his fat face. The prisoner dropped to his knees and fell flat on his face.

Next in line was a halfling who almost managed to sneak past Borgarth under the cover of shadow. But the big half-orc caught the tiny halfling by the arm, picked him up, and hurled him like a sack of oranges at another human prisoner, fitter than the first, but not so fit as to be able to shake off the force of a thrown halfling. They both collapsed to the floor and did not try to stand again.

Finally, a wild-eyed, wrinkled lizardman ran at Borgarth, snapping his teeth and thrashing at the air with his clawed fingers.

Randy backed up against the wall. The human guard from outside had mentioned a crazy old lizardman, but to see him up close, in the scaly flesh, was something he hadn't adequately prepared himself for.

Planting his right fist in his left palm, Borgarth braced himself, then elbowed the lizardman in the side of the head as soon as he got close enough. The poor old reptile spat out teeth as his forked tongue flapped from his mouth until his head slammed against the wall. He was out cold.

Borgarth grinned at Randy. "Prison breaks truly are my favorite part of the job."

Randy surveyed the carnage. At least an equal number of prisoners had tried to escape the other way, and were dealt with in similar fashion by Mayfield and Hammorford.

Those prisoners who were conscious and able to walk grudgingly filed back into the cell. The three guards dragged the rest in by their arms, legs, or in the case of the lizardman, his tail.

"Are you waiting for an invitation?" Mayfield asked Randy. "Or do you also require assistance?"

Randy shook his head and hurriedly followed the fresh blood smear trails into the cell. The door slammed shut behind him.

Mayfield and Hammerford bade farewell to Borgarth, then sat down to continue a card game which had apparently been interrupted by Randy's arrival.

Inside the cell, Randy couldn't hear himself think over the moans and wails of the injured prisoners.

"Send for a healer!" cried a half-elf who had been stopped by Mayfield and Hammerford. "You brutes broke my leg!" He winced as he touched his broken shin.

"And my nose!" honked the fat human, tears running down the sides of his blubbery face.

"You're a bunch of clerics and paladins, aren't you?" said Mayfield. "Heal yourselves." He reached for a box on a shelf above their card table.

The fit human and the halfling who had been thrown at him grabbed the bars of the cell door and started shaking it. "No!" cried the human. "Not the stone!"

Randy's heartbeat quickened as the Mayfield ignored their protests, pulling a small, round stone out of the box. He braced himself for whatever was about to happen next.

Mayfield placed the stone on the table, and he and Hammerford continued their card game in silence. Randy found that very underwhelming.

The human continued to shake the cell door, but the halfling gave it up, a disgusted look on his face when he turned around.

"What's with the rock?" asked Randy.

"It's a Silence Stone," said the halfling. "We can wail in agony all we like, and those two bastards won't be bothered in the least. They can't hear us."

"Can you, you sons of whores!" shouted the man shaking the door.

"Barton!" shouted the halfling. "That's enough already! It's noisy enough in here as it is."

Finally, Barton succumbed to the futility of his action and gave up shaking the door.

The halfling covered his ears, trying to drown out the wailing and crying of his fellow inmates. "This will be the only sounds we hear until the sweet release of the king's justice."

Randy sat down on a hard, splintery unfinished wooden bench. "Why did y'all lie about being clerics for Jesus?"

"You're going to preach us a sermon, *paladin*? You're as guilty as the rest of us."

"No I ain't."

Barton grinned. "You can cut the act, Pally. You've got nothing to gain by earning the trust of we fellow charlatans."

"I'm telling you, I *ain't* no fellow charlatan!"

"I believe you," wheezed the fat man through his broken nose.

"You've believed every one of us, Waddles," said Barton. He turned to Randy. "He's not even in here for heresy. He's here by choice. He demanded to be brought in, so that the representative of the New God should not suffer alone."

The fat man, who may or may not have actually been named 'Waddles', knelt before Randy. "If it please the New God, I beg for you to lay your hands on me."

"Right here in front of all these people?" Randy had sympathy for this poor bastard. Lord knows he'd traveled down that lonely road enough times himself. "There's actually some debate where I'm from whether that pleases the *New God* or not."

Barton laughed. "You are, without a doubt, the most profoundly sad excuse for a phony disciple I've ever seen."

Randy glared at him in frustration.

"He wants you to heal him," explained Barton. "Fix his flattened nose."

"Oh," said Randy. He smiled at Waddles. "In that case, I'd be happy to."

Barton rubbed his hands together. "Fantastic." He stood up and addressed the other inmates. "Behold, fellow clerics of the New God! Bear witness to his great healing power, flowing through the righteous hands of our new paladin brother... I'm sorry. What was your name?"

"Randy," said Randy.

"*Randy!*"

All eyes in the cell were on him. Some were curious. Others embarrassed. A few just because there was little else of interest going on in the cell.

"It's okay, Waddles," said Randy. "You ain't got to be afraid."

Waddles scooted forward, heavy breaths whistling through his broken nose.

Randy placed both hands atop Waddles's hot, sweaty head and closed his eyes. "In Jesus Christ's name, I heal you."

Again, Randy felt the same warmth flow from his heart, down his arms, and through his hands. Waddles's nasal whistle grew louder and shriller, like a boiling kettle, until it stopped suddenly. Worried that he'd accidentally killed Waddles, Randy opened his eyes.

Waddles was very much alive. His breathing had silenced because his nose was whole again and the air was flowing freely. Tears in his eyes, he took several more deep, silent breaths, just to demonstrate that he could.

"Waddles!" said Barton.

Waddles stood up and glared at him. "My name is *Wettle*."

The rest of the inmates murmured among themselves.

"Did you see that?"

"I can't believe it!"

"Could it be true?"

"Heal me!" cried the half-elf with the broken leg, which had turned a nasty shade of purple by this point. He tried to stand on his good leg, but fell over onto the bad one. "Yeeowwww!"

Randy stood up. "Hang on, man. I'll come over there to you." He looked at his hands doubtfully. "I'm only first level, and I don't know how much of this healin' juice I got in me. But I'll do my best."

He walked over to where the half-elf was writhing and wincing on the floor, knelt down next to him, and laid a hand on his cheek. "In Jesus Christ's name, I heal you."

The half-elf winced even harder as his bones shifted beneath his skin, but then a wave of calm washed over his face as the purple faded from his shin. He hopped to his feet and started dancing, then stopped to grab Randy's hand and kiss it.

"It's a miracle," said Barton. "I've seen real, faithful clerics study for months and not be able to elicit this much healing power from their gods. The New God has only existed for one day."

Randy went on to heal everyone else in the cell, even those with only minor scratches or abrasions, each time being certain that he must be getting close to depleting his daily allotment of healing.

When it was done, Randy had been hugged, kissed, squeezed, and shaken more than he'd been in his whole life prior to this.

Barton knelt before him. "I humbly beg you accept my apology, Sir Randy. You have given us so much this day. How may we serve you?"

Exhaustion had caught up with Randy. "I just want to go to sleep for a little while."

Barton ripped off his shirt, displaying a nice, smooth chest and a satisfactory set of abs.

"I appreciate the gesture," said Randy. "But I weren't kidding. I'm seriously tired right now. I ain't slept all night."

Barton bundled his shirt into a ball. "Lay your head on this, Sir Randy." He placed the balled-up shirt on the wooden bench. "I would be honored to bring you whatever meager comfort I can. I shall stand watch and make sure no harm befalls you while you rest."

"As will I," said the half-elf.

"And me," said the halfling.

"You can count on me," said Wettle.

One by one, all of the other inmates stood in a semicircle, shielding Randy from whatever unlikely evil might befall him here in this locked cell. It was a nice gesture at any rate.

Randy lay on the bench, his mind racing with wonder. *Had it really been a miracle? How was he healing so much? Was the real Jesus acting through him?* It was too much, and he briefly worried that he wouldn't be able to sleep. That worry sorted itself out in a matter of minutes when sleep descended on him like a summer storm.

Chapter 27

"Stupid Tim and his stupid alcoholism." Cooper plodded further southward, grumbling about how stupid everyone was for splitting the party.

"Stupid Julian and his stupid bird."

"Stupid Dave and his stupid… uh… general suckiness."

"Stupid bard guy and his stupid name that I can never remember."

"Stupid Katherine and her awesome vampire tits."

Cooper was supposed to be the stupid one. So why wasn't he the one wandering around aimlessly in the wilderness while everyone else searched for him? Why was he the only one who seemed to be thinking beyond the next –

He'd made it to the crossroads. On one side of him, a smaller road broke off to the east. On the other side, a small footpath led into the forest which he probably wouldn't have noticed if he hadn't stopped to look around. And, of course, the main road continued heading south.

Cooper tried to think back on the directions Captain Pisspot had given them.

"Poortown to the south, and Schoolhouse Rock to the east," he said to himself. "Wait, no. That's not right. Lighthouse Rock. That's it."

He thought for a moment, trying to reason out which road would more likely lead him to his friends.

"Lighthouses are near water, which might explain the fishing lures. Poortown sounds like it sucks. Probably some third-world shithole. Fuck that. East it is."

The forest grew closer to the eastbound road than it did to the main road. Anything could jump out from the trees at any moment. A lone traveler would be wise to have his weapon out, clearly visible and ready to use.

Cooper's axe remained firmly strapped to his back. He *wanted* something to jump out at him, just so he could beat the shit out of it. He'd resort to his axe if it was necessary, but he was in more of a punching mood. A bear would be good. Or a crocodile. He could rage out and swing it around his head by the tail. That would be fun.

Or better yet, a whole horde of kobolds. He could punch those little fuckers left and right until they were piled up on either side of the road.

But there was nothing. No bears, no crocodiles, no kobolds. Nothing. Cooper was alone with his thoughts, and those made for some pretty shitty company.

He thought about how much traveling his C&C characters had done over the years. He would state that he wanted to travel to Bumblefuck, Wherever, and the Cavern Master would roll some dice behind the screen and say something like "You arrive just before nightfall." He'd never considered how fucking boring it must have been for them.

Jerking off was always a time-honored means of killing time. He'd even excused himself once in the middle of combat to go rub one out in the bathroom because Dave was playing a wizard and couldn't keep track of what all his spells did. Sure enough, when Cooper returned to the table, it was still Dave's fucking turn.

That wasn't really an option here though, as stopping to wank would defeat the whole purpose of wanking by making the journey exactly that much longer.

Could he walk and jerk off at the same time? He doubted it. Honestly, was any man that talented? To put himself in the proper frame of mind, he would have to think up a scenario in which he was having sex while walking.

He was at an airport, and it was on fire. Flames raged at either end of the moving walkway, trapping him and that smoking hot Indian girl who works at the Taco Bell on Highway 90, forcing them to keep walking in the opposite direction until the firefighters rescued them. And she wanted his cock in the baddest way.

Cooper reached under his loincloth. Not even a semi. This was too fucking stupid.

He was on a treadmill, and the smoking hot Indian girl who works at the Taco Bell on Highway 90 was his personal trainer. As an incentive for him to keep moving, she...

No. That was even worse.

He and the smoking hot Indian girl who works at the Taco Bell on Highway 90 were running away from a particularly swift-moving glacier, but they couldn't run away from their passion.

"What the fuck is wrong with me? Oh, thank fuck. There's the lighthouse."

Lighthouse Rock, the top of which now visible above the treeline on the side of the southward-curving road, was pretty much as advertised. It was a lighthouse built atop a big-ass rock that Cooper hoped he wouldn't have to climb. After another mile of walking, the trees thinned out and the road straightened, revealing a tiny village at the base of the rock. So tiny, in fact, that Cooper could only make out one small cottage. If his friends were here, they should be easy enough to find.

Smoke from a wood fire mingled with salty sea air to form a smell that Cooper found quite pleasant. Approaching the cottage, he also smelled grilled fish and suddenly realized how hungry he was.

"Hello?" he called out before getting too close. Given his appearance, it wasn't a stretch to think that someone might mistake him for a marauder and shoot him on sight.

"Come around back!" an old man's voice responded.

Cooper circled wide around the left side of the cottage, taking in the waterfront view. The sea was vast, with only a single island visible to the south. He could just make out a lighthouse at the top of that one as well.

While the cottage was modest, the pier stretching out toward the island was anything but. The wood used to build that could have been used to build a house ten times the size of this old shack. It looked even more impressive when compared to the tiny rowboat tied to the end, bobbing up and down on the waves.

"Don't get many travelers 'round this way," said the old man. "You hungry, big feller?"

Cooper turned around. An old gnome wearing a set of grey overalls and a fisherman's cap was standing behind a grill, flipping a fish with a set of wooden tongs.

"I'm fucking starving," said Cooper.

"Well come on over and have a seat. The fish won't take long."

A weathered wooden table sat on short legs, only six inches off the ground. Cooper sat next to it in the grass.

"Do you live here?"

"Aye," said the gnome. "My name's Waldo. I'm the lighthouse keeper."

Cooper looked around. There was no sign of anyone else. "All alone? Isn't that kind of dangerous?"

Waldo brought over a smoking, sizzling fat fish and set it on the table. "I've outlived a wife and two sons. When the gods see fit to take me, I'll be ready."

Cooper leaned over and blew on the fish, showering it with as much spit as cool air. He looked up at Waldo, who was raising his fluffy white eyebrows at him. "I'm sorry. This is your lunch. You go first."

"You go on and help yourself. I'll grill up some more."

Having been as polite as he was capable of, Cooper shrugged, picked up the fish by the tail, and tore the front half off with his teeth.

"You weren't joking about being hungry, were you? I'd better throw on a few more."

Waldo walked over to what appeared to be a wishing well built of cobblestones and mortar. At two feet high, it came up to his chest. He placed a foot on a protruding stone near the bottom, then hoisted himself over the rim and jumped in.

"What the fuck?" said Cooper.

Waldo splashed, but didn't sink. It wasn't a well after all. Just a shallow pool. He bent over, waited, and then struck down suddenly with both hands. When he stood again, he had a fish in his hands at least as big as the one Cooper was eating. He threw it out of the pool to flop around on the ground. Twice more, he did the same thing. Satisfied, he climbed out of the pool and tossed all three fish onto the grill, where they spent the remainder of their short lives flopping wildly until they succumbed to smoke and flame.

"Thank you for the fish," said Cooper, hoping he wasn't putting this old guy out too much.

Waldo adjusted some of the wood under the grill with his tongs. "Think nothing of it. It pleases me to have company other than soldiers and prisoners."

"Prisoners?"

"The royal navy uses the cell carved into the bottom of the rock to hold captive pirates, brigands, and whatever riff-raff they pick up at sea, until they can be picked up by soldiers from the city. I keep them fed. Every now and again I get some folks to share their tales, but most of them are too preoccupied with their impending execution to be interested in talking. Just had three in here this morning. The half-drow was a nice enough feller, as far as their kind goes."

Cooper felt he'd reached another dead end. "So I don't guess you've seen any other travelers come this way? A couple of elves, a dwarf, a human bard? Maybe they might have had some fishing gear?"

Waldo shook his head. "No. No one like that. Just soldiers and prisoners."

"Shit." Cooper nibbled at what remained of his fish. All he could do now was check out Poortown.

The island in the distance caught his eye. As long as he was here, he supposed it was worth asking about.

"What's that island over there?"

Waldo turned around and shielded his eyes from the glare of the sun. "That's the first of the Barrier Islands. They separate the Great Sea from the Bay of Meb' Garshur. There's eight of them in all, between here and Port City."

Cooper's head jerked up. "Port City?" That sounded like a place where people might do some fishing. He looked at the island again. He'd have to go that distance eight times. "Fuck, that's going to be a hell of a swim."

"Speak not such nonsense!" said Waldo. "Use my boat."

Cooper had already imposed enough on this lonely old man. Taking his boat was too much. "I couldn't."

"You seem a strong young lad, both in body and spirit. But that's far too great a distance to swim. By the gods, it's farther than I'd ever want to row even. Since the royal navy built that pier, I do most of my fishing from there. I have little use for that old boat these days."

Cooper dug through his bag, scraping together the last of his money. He laid five gold coins down on the table. "At least let me pay you for it."

Waldo smiled, then pushed four of the coins back toward Cooper. "You overestimate the value of such a modest vessel. I'll keep one coin to ease your conscience, and return it when you bring my boat back to me."

"You're a hell of a guy, Waldo."

"There's just one more thing," said Waldo. "Now don't you go anywhere just yet." He hurried into the back door of his cottage.

Shit. He was probably getting some lube. *No such thing as a free lunch.* Cooper had maxed out his Swim skill, being one of the few that was based on Strength. He looked back at the island. It didn't seem quite as far away now that he thought about having to jerk off a geriatric gnome for a boat.

Waldo returned with a large roll of paper. The nice kind that Julian sometimes wrote magic spells on. He unrolled it on the table. It was blank, not that Cooper would have been able to read it anyway.

"What the fuck is this?"

"All that rowing is bound to build up an appetite," said Waldo, heading back to the grill. With his wooden tongs, he grabbed each of the three fish, and placed them one by one onto the paper, which he then rolled up.

"You've been generous enough," said Cooper. "This is too much."

"There are plenty of fish in the sea, friend. Too few decent folk."

"In the sea?"

Waldo furrowed his brow. "In the world."

Cooper decided it would be best if he stopped talking now. He shoved the wrapped-up fish into his sack and walked down to the pier alongside Waldo. "I'm sorry to eat and run like this, but I have to find my friends."

"Think not of it," said Waldo. "Safe travels, and may the gods watch over you on your quest."

Cooper climbed down the ladder and into the little boat. It was probably big enough for Waldo and a good-sized catch, but Cooper felt like he was sitting in a toy. The oars felt like oversized spoons in his hands. But to its credit, the boat held his weight.

Once Cooper was settled, Waldo untied the rope and tossed it down into the boat at Cooper's feet.

After a final thank you, Cooper took a deep breath, then started rowing toward the first of the Barrier Islands.

Chapter 28

"We've been walking forever," said Chaz. "I don't even think we're heading toward the city anymore."

Tanner continued forward, almost silently, at his brisk pace. "Stop your whining. We're almost there."

"Almost where? We're in the middle of the fucking woods, and it's getting dark."

"Don't worry. I'm half-drow. I can see perfectly in all but total darkness."

Chaz stopped walking. "Well I'm human, and I can't see shit. Hold up. I'm going to light a torch." He was digging through his bag for his flint and steel when Tanner's charcoal grey face got right up in his own.

"Are you out of your mind? An open flame in a dark forest? Are you so desperate to be eaten by monsters? Why not strip down and slather yourself in honey while you're at it?"

Chaz was tired, his legs ached, and he was starting to get a little scared. He didn't care how whiny he sounded. "If we'd just gone in through the gate, we could have —"

Tanner swiped the torch out of his hand and bonked him over the head with the soft top of it. "Are you finished?"

Chaz pushed out his lower lip and nodded his head.

"Very good." Tanner handed the torch back to Chaz. "Now follow me, and for the grace of the gods keep your mouth shut."

Chaz did his best to keep up, though he could barely see or hear which way Tanner was going. He tripped over roots and got slapped in the face by branches and spider webs until he almost tackled Tanner, who had stopped for no discernible reason.

Tanner smiled at Chaz. At this point, he was pretty much all eyes and teeth. "We're here."

Surely he didn't mean their final destination. This place didn't look any different than the rest of the forest, save for a large flat rock on the ground which Chaz found to be a very inviting place to sit down.

"So what are we doing?" asked Chaz. "Taking a break?"

"I'd like to get us out of the dangerous forest," said Tanner. "As soon as you kindly remove your ass from the hatch."

"Huh?" Chaz stood up. "Hatch?"

Tanner got on his knees and tried to push the stone sideways. "It leads down to the abandoned part of the drow lair. It's prone to flooding during the rainy season, and nobody really uses it anymore because they've burrowed more modern, more luxurious tunnels since then. I might be the only person who's been in this part of the lair in the past two decades." The rock wasn't budging.

"Why do you go down there?" asked Chaz.

"Different reasons. Sometimes to escape a jealous husband, or a night patrolman. Sometimes just for a quiet place to read. Do you want to give me a hand?"

"Oh, sorry." Chaz got down next to Tanner, placed both palms on the rock, and pushed.

"It's been over a year since I've used this entrance," Tanner grunted. Finally, the rock started to shift sideways. It whined and groaned on its rusty pivot, revealing a hole, and the top rung of a ladder leading down.

"What if they heard that?" asked Chaz.

"Who?"

"The drow."

"I'm telling you, friend. The place is sealed off. No drow has been here in over a decade." Tanner started down the ladder. "Pull the hatch shut after you."

Against his better judgement, Chaz climbed into the hole, even darker than the forest. The hatch proved easier to close than it had been to open, but no less noisy.

Making his way down the ladder with only his sense of touch to guide him, it seemed to take forever. He had no idea how far down he was climbing. Finally, he felt solid ground.

"Feel better now?" asked Tanner.

"I guess."

"Maybe it's time you lit that torch."

Chaz knelt on the earthen floor to rummage through his bag. Ironically, lighting a torch proved to be a complicated task while not being able to see, especially since it was something he hadn't ever done before. He found a brick and a steel bar, which he clanked against each other a few times, but produced no sparks.

"What's taking so long?" asked Tanner. "What are you doing?"

"I'm trying to start a fire."

"Here. Let me try."

Chaz held up the bar and brick until Tanner's groping hands found them.

"What in the seven hells is this?" said Tanner.

"What?"

"It's no wonder you can't make a spark. This is a whetstone."

"It felt dry enough to me."

"I can't even... Give me that bag."

Chaz waited while Tanner dug through his every worldly possession.

"What's in all these flasks?" asked Tanner.

"Oil."

"What do you need so much godsdamned oil for? Are you planning to deep fry a dire boar?"

"My friends told me it's, like, the most useful thing in the game."

"Game? What are you – Never mind. Just stop talking. Here's the flint. Hold up the torch."

Chaz pawed around on the ground until his hand found the torch. "Here."

Tanner felt the top. "Wrong end, stupid."

"I'm sorry! I can't fucking see!" Chaz turned the torch around. "There."

Shink. Shink. Shink.

On the third attempt, the sparks ignited, and the top of the torch burst into flames. Tanner gave Chaz an annoyed glare, and they both stood up.

"Shit," said Tanner.

A dozen black elves, dressed in identical black, studded leather armor, armed with identical black-bladed short swords, surrounded them on all sides. At the entrance of the chamber stood a male and female elf, both with the same jet black skin, both wearing identical blue silk robes, like they were an insecure teenage couple at the mall.

"I told you there would be others," said the female.

"Your prediction was sound, Vivia. But how did you know they would enter here."

"It was the only logical explanation. Too many of us have forgotten this place even exists. It's a weakness in the security of our lair." She started barking rapid-fire orders at the soldiers.

"You, tell the Extractor to gather his tools. I want to know exactly what the trespassers know, and what it is they want."

"Right away, princess," said the soldier who'd been given the task. He hurried past her through the exit.

"You, have the engineers seal off this hatch at once."

"As you command."

"The rest of you, escort the prisoners to —" Vivia collapsed into her boyfriend's arms. She was breathing hard, and her eyes were wide with terror. "Mittens! No!"

Chaz looked to Tanner, who only shrugged. The other soldiers also appeared to have no idea what was going on.

The soldier nearest her cleared his throat. "Awaiting orders, princess."

Vivia looked at him like she only half-remembered where she was. "Put these two bumbling fools in the cell with the other one. Then report to my father." She grabbed her lover's hand. "Come, Alessandro." Together they hurried out the door.

One of the soldiers grabbed the torch out of Chaz's hand and snuffed it out on the floor.

Chaz held his hands up in surrender as they took away the rest of his belongings and patted him and Tanner down for hidden weapons.

A soldier on either side of him grabbed each of his arms firmly, but not too roughly, and started marching him through the darkness. They walked for what must have been at least thirty minutes, turning left and right, always at perfect right angles. Even if he was able to see, Chaz knew he'd be hopelessly lost in this place.

The soldiers escorting Chaz let go of his arms and halted, as did the rest of the surrounding footsteps, leaving him completely devoid of sensory input. He might as well have been all alone in that stupid Bag of Holding again. Taking in a big lungful of air, he decided that he was happy he wasn't.

CLUNK. The sound of heavy wood on stone.

SCREEEEECH. A solid door opening on long-neglected hinges.

Chaz was gripped by the shoulders and shoved forward. A second later, Tanner was shoved into him. The door closed behind them. Two soldiers grunted as they heaved a wooden crossbeam into mounts on the door. Then footsteps fading away.

Neither Chaz nor Tanner moved. According to Princess Vivia, there was supposed to be a third prisoner here in the cell with them. Not knowing who, or what, or especially where, that prisoner was scared the shit out of Chaz.

"Didn't the princess say something about there being another intruder?" whispered Tanner.

"That's what I was just thinking."

"Hello?" Tanner whispered just a little bit louder.

There was no response.

Chaz's hands were trembling. "I'm really starting to freak out, man."

"Calm yourself," said Tanner. "I've gotten myself out of worse binds than this."

"Bullshit."

"Have the drow all gone?"

"I don't know," said Chaz. "I think so."

"That'll have to do."

Chaz heard the clink of iron on stone, and the room was suddenly as bright as day.

Tanner was grinning at him. In his hand was a foot-long iron stick, the top of which glowed like a 100-watt bulb.

"What the hell is that?" asked Chaz.

"A sunrod. I keep one in my boot in case of emergencies."

"Then why'd you make me go through all that shit with the torch?"

"Because these are expensive," said Tanner. "Besides, how was I supposed to know you don't know how to light a torch?"

"That was so embarrassing. Everyone was watching me that whole time."

"Don't feel bad. I was picking my nose in the beginning."

Chaz laughed nervously. "That sounds like my friend, Coo—"

Tanner grabbed Chaz's shoulder. He was looking at something else.

Chaz followed Tanner's gaze to a rickety wooden bed. There was the third prisoner, covered from head to toe in a shabby burlap blanket. Whoever he was, he was a big motherfucker.

"Do you think he's sleeping?" asked Chaz. "Or dead?" He didn't know which he would have preferred.

"We should find out," said Tanner. "Pull away the blanket."

"Fuck that. *You* pull away the blanket."

"I'm holding the light."

They needed to stop wasting time that could better be spent thinking of a way out of here. Chaz was not at all interested in seeing the Extractor's tools, or finding out exactly what they were meant to extract. "Fine. I'll do it."

They weren't in a big cell, but Chaz took such tiny, careful steps toward the sleeping prisoner that it seemed to take forever.

"Come on!" Tanner whispered at him.

Having reached the end Chaz guessed the feet would be, he pinched a bit of the blanket and tugged gently at it.

The other side of the blanket fell away, revealing the most hideous sight Chaz had ever seen. It was some kind of horrific beast which had been butchered to death in the worst ways possible. It's hide was a mixture of fur and feathers. A wormy tongue hung out of its open beak. One of its eyes looked to have been gouged out with a hand spade, leaving a gaping hole in its hollowed out head. The eye which remained was no less frightening, staring at Chaz in mad terror.

He was about to scream when Tanner clapped a hand over his mouth.

Was that the hand he'd been picking his nose with?

"Calm down," said Tanner. "Are you calm?"

Chaz nodded. Tanner removed his hand.

"What the fuck is that?" Chaz whispered.

"It's just an owlbear," said Tanner. "And it doesn't look like it's in any shape to harm us."

"What happened to its face?"

"And where are its arms?"

Chaz had been too terrified by the creature's mangled face that he hadn't noticed that both of its arms were missing... *Its arms!* "They're in the woods, just south of Cardinia."

Tanner looked at him quizzically. "Is that a joke?"

Chaz shook his head. "I saw them there yesterday."

"Hmm… That *is* peculiar."

"Princess Vivia!" said Chaz. "She thinks we're partnered up with this thing?"

Tanner frowned. "That doesn't make a whole lot of sense."

"Oh my god. Do you think the Extractor did this?" He grabbed Tanner by the shoulders. "We've got to get out of here!"

Tanner slapped Chaz hard. "Get a hold of your wits! You said yourself that the owlbears arms were removed no later than yesterday. It's a good bet that its eye and arms were removed at the same time. Ergo, the Extractor is not likely responsible for this."

Chaz nodded. "Okay. That makes sense."

"Having said that, we are in agreement that escape is currently our most prudent objective." He looked through the small barred window. "Now, let's see what we have to work with. It would be very helpful if you had a fishhook, a roll of twine, and a small candle."

"I have none of those things."

"Why am I not surprised?" Tanner rubbed his chin and thought some more. "I wonder if the owlbear's beak is strong enough to pry those hinges off."

Chaz clapped his hands over his face. "We're going to die in here."

"Hey Chaz," said a familiar female voice. "What are you doing in here?"

Chaz looked up. Katherine was standing in the corner of the cell, where he was pretty fucking certain she hadn't been standing a moment ago, holding a dead black cat with white paws, which was dripping blood on the floor.

"Katherine?"

"I seem to be the only one of us not yet acquainted," said Tanner. He smiled and offered his hand to Katherine. "Hello, Katherine. I'm Tanner Goodwyn." After shaking Katherine's hand, he shook one of the dead cat's limp front paws. "And you must be Mittens."

"Mittens?" said Katherine.

Chaz gasped. "Oh no!"

Katherine looked back and forth between Tanner and Chaz. "What the fuck is wrong with you two?"

"The drow princess became very distraught a short time ago," said Tanner, "about a certain *Mittens*, who I assume you were killing at the time. A sorceress can sense the death of her familiar."

"Oh my god," said Katherine. "I feel like such an asshole. I thought it was just a stray."

Chaz shook his head. "We are *sooooo* fucking dead."

"Do either of you guys know what time it is?" asked Katherine.

"Who gives a shit?" said Chaz.

"Why can no one give me a straight answer about this?"

"It was getting dark just before we arrived," said Tanner.

"Perfect. We should leave then."

Chaz balled up his fists in frustration. "Ya think?"

"I just need to do one thing first." Katherine held Mittens up against the wall and punched its face into a mushy pulp. With her fingernail, she painted the word *SORRY* low on the wall, along with a sad face, and placed the mutilated cat corpse underneath it.

Tanner grimaced. "That was... unexpected."

"Can we maybe stop thinking of more ways to piss off the drow," said Chaz, "and start thinking of ways to get out of here?"

Katherine evaporated into a pink mist which flowed through the barred window of the cell door, where she coalesced back into her normal, half-elven form. She easily lifted the crossbeam from its mounts and set it down against the wall.

"Come on," she said. "There are some stairs leading up not too far from here."

Chapter 29

The bar of the Merriweather Inn was classier than the Whore's Head Inn. Every surface of the floor, walls, and bar, every stick of furniture, including the grand piano in the corner, was crafted out of the same reddish-brown polished cypress.

Rupert, the bartender, rapped his knuckles on the bar three times. "Resistant to water, fire, termites, you name it. Tough as nails, this wood. Just like our mayor."

"Is that right?" said Stacy. Her eyelids were getting heavy, and Rupert's impromptu course on the virtues of cypress wood wasn't making them any lighter. She put her quarter-full beer glass down on the bar and stifled a yawn. Rupert immediately moved it to a coaster and wiped up a tiny drop left behind.

Tony the Elf had retired to his room to work on his epic fantasy novel which Stacy learned, against her will, was absolutely not based on his experiences here, because no one would take that seriously. More out of politeness than interest, she'd asked him how far into it he's gotten. He was still in the world-building stage, he'd told her, developing a magic system, drawing maps, determining the alliances between all the noble houses. Stacy took that as nerd-speak for "I haven't actually written anything yet."

That left her alone at the bar with Dave, who was, at the best of times, about as exciting as downing half a bottle of Benadryl.

Stacy swigged back the remainder of her beer and placed a silver coin on the bar next to Dave. "I'm going to go see what Julian's up to."

Dave nodded and grunted an acknowledgement.

The night air was warm and muggy, with very little breeze coming in off the sea. If Stacy was going to spend any significant amount of time here, she'd need to invest in some lighter casualwear. This patent leather Catwoman outfit, with its excessive amount of buckles, straps, snaps, and hidden pockets, was great for hiding an extra blade and a set of lockpicks, and it was the perfect frame with which to showcase her new smokin' hot bod. Hell, according to her character sheet, which she'd looked over more carefully at the bar to distract herself from Dave's aura of dullness, it even counted as armor, so it might even deflect a sword strike or two, as unlikely as that seemed. But it didn't breathe very well, and it made going to the bathroom at least a twenty-minute commitment.

She found Julian sitting at the end of a long pier, swinging his feet above the water and staring out at the bloated yellow moon, no doubt hoping to catch the silhouette of black wings against it.

"Copper piece for your thoughts?" she said. It was a dad-worthy joke.

"Hey, Stacy," said Julian. "What are you doing out here? Couldn't sleep?"

"I was hanging out with Dave. I came out here to avoid falling asleep."

Julian smiled, but there was sadness in his eyes.

"How about you?"

"Hmph," said Julian. "I couldn't sleep even if I *could* sleep. Does that make sense?"

Stacy nodded. "Yeah, the elf thing. I got it. Still worried about your bird?"

"Ravenus." Julian's voice had the slightest trace of annoyance in it.

"I'm sorry. I didn't mean to sound —"

"It's okay. I'm sorry. I know it sounds crazy for me to care so much about a *bird*, but —"

"I don't think you're crazy. Ravenus isn't just a bird, and I shouldn't refer to him like that. I know you two have some kind of special bond."

"He's my friend."

Stacy sat down behind Julian and slipped her hands under his arms and wrapped her arms around his chest. "I'd like to be your friend, too. We could have a special bond." She kissed the back of his neck.

Julian's body went rigid, and neither of his hands was on her thighs. His heart was beating so fast she thought it might explode.

She eased off and leaned back a bit. "Can I ask you a personal question?"

"Sure," said Julian, his voice an octave higher than normal.

"Are you gay?"

Julian shook his head. "No."

"Do you have a girlfriend back home?"

"No."

"Are you saving yourself for Jesus or whatever?"

Julian laughed. "No."

Stacy was not in a laughing mood. She stood up. "Then what the fuck is going on here?"

"What? What do you mean?"

"Are you not attracted to me?"

"No!" said Julian. "I mean yes. I'm super attracted to you. I mean, look at you." The conspicuous bundle of serape over his crotch provided evidence of his sincerity.

Stacy folded her arms. "Then what's the problem?"

"I told you. I'm worried about Ravenus."

"Don't give me that shit. I had a guy try to feel me up once at his own mother's funeral."

"That's pretty messed up."

"So what's *really* the problem?"

Julian looked down at the water. "It's Tim."

"I thought so," said Stacy. "So it's bros before hoes? One of you stakes a claim, and I have to choose between a drunken man-child and eternal celibacy?"

"We're not exactly bros. I only met him a few hours before we got sent here. It's just that he really seems to be on edge these days, and I don't want to push him over."

"He's got it no worse than any of us. We're all in the same boat here."

Julian looked up at her. "That's another thing. I was kind of into you before you got sent here."

"You were?" Stacy sat down next to Julian.

"I thought you were pretty, and smart, and funny, and I thought it was cute how you freaked out when we wrecked your boss's office with a giant scorpion."

Stacy smiled. "That's really sweet. But I don't see how it constitutes a problem."

"I liked the real you, as you were," said Julian. "I mean, I still like you as you are now, but here's the thing. You don't even know the real me. What if you just like me because I rolled a high Charisma score?"

Stacy scooted a little closer to him. "You're thinking too hard on this. I'm not asking to exchange vows. We don't know what we're going to be up against tomorrow. I'm scared, and kind of lonely here."

"I feel lonely too sometimes," said Julian. "Cooper's the only one I really knew before coming here."

"I just want to lose myself for a few minutes, forget about this place."

Julian nodded.

Stacy leaned in closer, her lips brushing against Julian's ear, and whispered. "Tim's not around. We've got the whole pier to ourselves. We've got a big, full moon, and the sound of the waves lapping against the shore."

Julian laughed nervously. "I guess this is what the other side of Diplomacy feels like."

Stacy stretched around to kiss him. It was an awkward angle, but she could manage it until she got him on his back. His lower lip trembled as she touched it with her tongue and ran a hand up his thigh, burrowing under the bunched up pile of serape.

Julian's lips parted, letting her tongue inside. Then he jerked away.

"What the hell is that?" Stacy heard him shout just before she hit the water.

Not expecting a late-night swim, Stacy gulped down some seawater as she flailed about trying to reorient herself. She broke the surface, hacking to get the water out of her lungs, and swam for the nearest ladder.

Julian was waiting for her at the top, his hand reaching down to offer assistance. "I'm so sorry!"

Stacy wanted to punch him in his blue balls, but resisted the urge. "Something catch your eye?" She accepted his hand and climbed back onto the pier.

"Look," said Julian, pointing at the moon, which was now obscured at the bottom by something square, with a little stick poking out of the top. It was like the silhouette of a cheese cube on a toothpick.

"That *is* odd," said Stacy. "I don't know about throw-a-girl-off-a-pier odd, but certainly out of the ordinary."

Julian smiled at her. "I did no such thing. I was startled, and you lost your balance." He looked back at the strange silhouette on the moon. "Do you think we should tell someone?"

"I don't know if it's worth waking anyone up over."

"You just came from the hotel bar, right? The bartender should still be awake." Julian started walking. "I'll feel a lot better about it when someone tells me 'Oh, that's nothing. Happens all the time.'."

Stacy followed him, seawater sloshing around in her boots.

When they got back to the Merriweather Inn, Dave was the only patron left at the bar. The bartender's eyelids were heavy, suggesting he wasn't accustomed to working so late. He looked pained to see two more customers walk through the door.

"Excuse me, sir," said Julian.

Rupert sighed. "What'll you have?"

"I'd like you to come outside and take a look at something."

The bartender narrowed his eyes at Julian, his right arm reaching down for something under the bar. "I hope you folks aren't bringing trouble into Port Town."

Considering Julian's vague request from the Rupert's point of view, Stacy could see how he might think he was being lured outside to be mugged. "Just look out the window," she said. "Something's going on with the moon."

Keeping his eyes on them, the bartender made his way to the window on the rear wall of the Inn's lobby. He peeked out the window, stared for a moment, and then his jaw dropped.

"Merciful gods!" he said. "The legend is true."

"What is it?" asked Dave, waddling over to have a look.

Rupert turned around, running his fingers through his oily hair. "The Phantom Pinas!"

"The phantom *what?*" said Stacy.

Julian stepped back out of the doorway to have another look at the moon. "All I see is a square with a stick poking out of the top."

"Those be her junk sails," said Rupert, hurrying toward the front entrance. "I have to sound the alarm." He walked past Stacy and Julian and out of the inn.

Stacy looked at Julian, then at Dave, who was still looking out the window. "Did anyone understand a single thing that guy just said?"

"Not a thing," said Julian. "But he's freaking the hell out about it, and that's making me start to freak out."

Dave stroked what was left of his beard. "Didn't that old guy at the pub before mention something about a —"

A bell clanged loudly from outside. Rupert must have reached the town alarm.

After a seemingly impossibly short response time, a big tiger came bounding down the polished cypress stairs. Stacy forced herself not to scream.

When it reached the bottom of the staircase, the tiger morphed into the naked old mayor.

"What's the problem? Is there a fire?" He looked at the bar. "Where's Rupert?"

"He's outside," said Stacy. "He's the one ringing the bell." And he was still ringing it.

Mayor Merriweather looked at Stacy disapprovingly. "You're dripping water on my floor, missy."

Stacy remembered how fast Rupert had wiped up that drop of condensation from the bar, then considered that against the puddle at her feet. "Sorry."

The mayor stomped toward the inn's front door. "What's all this hullabaloo?"

Julian stepped forward. "We saw something on the moon and came in to ask the bartender about it. After he looked out the window, he started ranting and raving about some phantom and his legendary junk."

"His penis in particular," added Stacy.

"What?" said the mayor. He narrowed his eyes at Dave. "Has he been drinking?"

Dave shook his head.

Mayor Merriweather frowned and nodded. "He better not be. He's been dry for going on ten years now. Some folks just can't hold their liquor, and I won't stand for none of his nonsense again."

"There actually is something going on with the moon," said Julian. "As long as you're up, maybe you should come out and have a look."

Piper, the mayor's assistant, ran out into the lobby, holding one of the mayor's robes in front of him. "Mayor Merriweather! Don't forget your WOOOO!" He slipped in the puddle Stacy had left behind and hit the floor hard.

The mayor snatched his robe out of Piper's raised hand and glared at Stacy. "There now, you see?"

Stacy held her palms up apologetically. "I said I was sorry."

Mayor Merriweather, grizzled old man-tiger that he was, had no fear of walking into a trap or being jumped by muggers like his barkeep had. He tied the front of his robe as he strutted past Stacy to join Julian outside. Stacy followed.

The mayor looked out at the moon. He squinted, then his eyes widened in shock. "Sons of Rapha," he whispered. "It can't be."

"What are those little orange lights around it?" asked Julian.

That was a new development. The moon, and the mysterious square shape obscuring a little more of it now, was surrounded by what looked like random, tiny bursts of flame.

"Those be the breath of dragons."

Dave and Tony the Elf emerged from the inn, and townsfolk were beginning to gather on the piers outside their respective barges.

"Tell me that ain't what I think it is, Doogan," said One-Eyed Pete, arriving on the scene with his chubby elven wife. Stacy got the feeling things must be pretty serious for him to be addressing the mayor by his first name.

"I'm afraid it is," said Mayor Merriweather. "Evacuate the city."

Chapter 30

"Sir Randy," said Wettle. "Wake up. The guards bring another false cleric even as I speak."

Randy had already been awake for a few minutes, but was trying to get whatever rest he could while his incarceration kept him from doing anything productive.

"Now don't y'all try to make a break for it this time. Just stand straight and tall, and I'll see if I can sort this out."

"Good morning, Sergeant Moore," said Hammerford. They must have put their magic rock back in its container.

"What's good about it?" boomed a familiar deep voice. "A full day has passed, and still I have nothing for the king. His Majesty likely thinks me a fool for having claimed to bear witness to a disciple of the New God. Throw this one in with the other heretics." He stopped in front of the door. "Are the prisoners riotous?"

"You don't have to worry about them." Randy knew that voice right away. It was Borgarth, the half-orc guard who'd escorted him to his cell the day before. "They tried to break out yesterday. We beat them to within an inch of their lives."

When the door opened, the prisoners stood straight and tall, just as Randy had instructed them. The half-orc guard was accompanied by a wild-eyed, shabbily-dressed half-elf and Sergeant Moore, the big colored feller who had first witnessed Randy heal Denise.

Before Randy could say anything, Sergeant Moore laughed. "This is what you call beaten to within an inch of their lives? You've gone soft, Borgarth."

"Impossible," said Borgarth, walking into the cell. "Half of these cretins couldn't walk yesterday."

Wettle pointed to Randy. "He healed us! He is truly –"

Borgarth punched him in the gut. "The prisoner speaks not until he is spoken to!"

"Stop!" said Sergeant Moore, finally meeting Randy's gaze. "It's you!"

Borgarth looked first at Randy, then at Sergeant Moore. "You know this one, sir?"

Sergeant Moore glared at Borgarth. "This is the one I seek, you ignorant swine! This is the paladin of the New God. Why was I not informed of his arrest?"

"He wasn't... He didn't..." Borgarth huffed and blubbered a little more before he was able to form a coherent sentence. "We sought not to bother you. His description of the New God was almost the exact opposite of what you gave us. He described the New God as skinny and hairy."

Sergeant Moore furrowed his brow as he turned to Randy. "Is this true, paladin?"

"Like I was telling Mr. Borgarth and the other gentleman, I ain't never seen Jesus with my own eyes before. I was only going by artists' depictions of him and such."

"These depictions sound nothing like the description given to us by the prophet Goosewaddle?"

"You mean the professor? That little gnome guy?"

Sergeant Moore raised his eyebrows. "You are acquainted?"

"We are," said Randy. "Now he's a nice enough feller, and I don't want to get nobody in trouble, but I don't reckon he's actually seen Jesus any more than I have."

"His description was confirmed by the High Priestess Dailana, guardian of the *Sacred Tome of the Gods*. The image appeared on a previously blank page just as the prophet described it. She declared it a miracle."

Randy felt his heartbeat quicken. He was almost afraid to ask.

"What does he look like?"

"He is hairless and cherub-like."

"Cherub?" said Randy. "Is that like them fat babies with wings?"

Sergeant Moore frowned. "The description I was given of the New God made no mention of wings."

Randy thought for a moment. "So Professor Goosewaddle described the New God as being pudgy and bald? That sounds more like Buddha than Jesus. I don't want you to take offense, but is he *white*?"

"He is."

"Well that's one mystery solved. Folks back home will be pleased, I suppose."

"We have no more time to waste," said Sergeant Moore. "You must meet His Majesty at once."

"Can I just ask a small favor first?"

"What is it?"

Randy looked around the cell at his fellow inmates. "I think these folks has all learned a valuable lesson. How 'bout you let them go?"

"These men stand accused of blasphemy against the New God, the god you yourself follow. They will stand before the High Court and face judgement for their sins."

"Jesus would forgive them."

"The decision is not mine to make," said Sergeant Moore. "You may petition His Majesty for a royal pardon if that's how you feel your time is most wisely spent."

"All right, I'll do that."

"Thank you, Sir Randy," said Wettle. "Good luck to you."

Borgarth glared at Wettle, but made no move to strike him.

Sergeant Moore produced a black velvet bag from under his cloak and pulled it down over Randy's head, placed his hand on Randy's shoulder, and led him out of the cell.

"Why I gotta wear this bag on my head?" asked Randy. The answer was pretty obvious, but he was nervous and wanted someone to talk to him.

"You are not yet authorized to know your way around the palace." Sergeant Moore's grip on Randy's shoulder was gentle. He only applied slight pressure to indicate a turn. There were a lot of turns. They went up and down staircases of varying heights, around corners, sometimes even stopping suddenly, then turning around and going the opposite direction. Occasionally, the scent of food overpowered the old-sweat smell inside the bag.

From what he remembered looking at the palace from outside, Randy guessed that they had already walked much farther than what should be necessary to get from any one point of the palace to any other. Either Sergeant Moore was hopelessly lost, which Randy found doubtful, or this was an added measure of security protocol intended to keep potential spies or assassins from knowing the most direct route to the king. It occurred to Randy that such a measure might be counterproductive if used on a particularly clever spy with an acute sense of direction and a photographic memory. It would be just like handing him a map of the whole palace.

He would have liked to share that observation with the sergeant, but couldn't think of a way to say it without it sounding like some sort of veiled threat.

Finally, they stopped. Randy was grateful that he'd gotten a good night's sleep.

A door opened in front of him and the air which flowed out was cool. Randy couldn't wait to get the bag off his head and properly breathe some of it in.

Sergeant Moore guided Randy through the doorway, and Randy heard the doors close behind him.

"You again," said a man's voice. Any man who would talk so casually to someone as imposing as Sergeant Moore must be a king. "This is the paladin you spoke of?"

"It is, Your Majesty."

"Then for the love of the New God, take that filthy bag off his head."

Randy hadn't realized just how hot and stuffy that bag was until he breathed in the sweet, cool air of the king's audience chamber. Sweat ran down both sides of his face.

The circular room was covered in white marble from floor to ceiling. Two thirds of the perimeter was exposed to the outside, allowing cool air to circulate the scent of hyacinth flowers. Randy knew he was at the top of the high tower. He'd seen the vines hanging down the wall from the outside. From up here, he could see clear past the city walls.

A bald servant quickly approached and wiped his face with a cool, moist towel.

"Thank you," Randy said to the servant. He looked up at the man in the chair. He was dark skinned, and younger than Randy was expecting, maybe in his early forties. He had a receding hairline, but a pharaoh's beard. Randy had no doubt in his mind that he was looking at the king of the realm. "And thank you, Mr. King." There were some snickers from some important-looking people seated around a large polished-granite table.

The king smiled. "Mr. King. I like that."

"You will address His Majesty as *His Majesty*." Sergeant Moore was not smiling.

"I beg your pardon." Randy was sweating again. "Thank you, His, I mean *Your*, Your Majesty."

The king looked at Sergeant Moore. "Has he provided a description of the New God to you which matches that of the prophet's?"

"There were... *discrepancies*, Your Majesty. But I have witnessed his power with my own eyes, as have all those he was imprisoned with."

"Well," said the king. "If you can't trust a room full of criminals, who can you trust?"

"Your Majesty, please. If you hear what —"

"Show me."

Sergeant Moore bowed low. "Very well." He removed his cloak, folded it, and placed it on the marble floor. He unbuckled his breastplate and set it gently to the side. Finally, he pulled his thick, padded shirt over his head, revealing a massive brown chest.

Randy forcibly pushed away impure thoughts, but wondered how far the sergeant was going to keep stripping down.

To Randy's disappointment and relief, the strip show was over. To his horror and bewilderment, the self-inflicted violence show had begun.

Sergeant Moore pulled a dagger from the sheath attached to his waist, and carved a nice, big line from his right shoulder, diagonally down to his abdomen, painting the lower half of his body in blood, which spilled down and pooled on the floor at his feet. And ain't a one of them folks at the table said peep about it.

The king turned to Randy and cocked an eyebrow. "Let's see what you've got, paladin."

Randy walked jerkily toward the sergeant like he wasn't fully in control over his own legs. In truth, he was just trying to keep from throwing up. Why couldn't he have just pricked himself like he did with Denise? If it was meant to display how much faith he had in Randy, it was far more than Randy had in himself.

Stopping at the edge of where the blood puddle was slowly expanding, Randy leaned over and was just able to reach Sergeant Moore's shoulder. It felt cooler than it should, and his face was paler. He'd better hurry this up.

"In Jesus Christ's name, I heal you." He forced the words out unceremoniously, but felt the magic flow out of his hand. The river of blood slowed to a trickle, then merely a drip. Warmth returned to the sergeant's shoulder as full color returned to his face.

The king stared at Randy and Sergeant Moore for a long time, but his face betrayed nothing of what he might be thinking. He finally said, "Clean him."

Randy was at a loss for what to do. He didn't have a towel or a sponge or anything. He'd just have to do his best. He spit in his palms, rubbed them together and started wiping down from the sergeant's chest to his abdomen, willing himself not to get aroused. But the man did have some fine, hard muscles. For all of his effort, he was just making more of a mess, smearing blood everywhere.

Sergeant Moore, who hadn't so much as moved a muscle through this entire ordeal, now glared at Randy.

"Don't look at me like that," said Randy. "I'm doing my best."

Sergeant Moore jerked his head to the side, which Randy took as an indication that he should back off.

Randy stepped back and found that two more bald servants had been patiently and uncomfortably waiting behind him, one with a stack of folded towels, and the other with a basin of clean water. He stood with his red, sticky hands held out in front of him while the servants wiped away enough blood from Sergeant Moore's torso to show that he'd been completely healed.

"Impressive," said the king. "Turn and face the High Priestess."

Sergeant Moore turned to his right precisely ninety degrees.

An elven woman wearing a gown of aquamarine scales nodded her head. "What we've witnessed cannot be denied. Truly this man acts as a servant of the New God, Jesus Christ."

The king looked at Randy, who responded with a nervous grin. "I suppose a new god must take what he can get." He snapped his fingers and another bald servant emerged from behind a column near the throne. These little guys were everywhere, like the king's own Oompa Loompas. "See that the sergeant is thoroughly bathed and well fed. Sergeant Moore. You are dismissed."

Sergeant Moore genuflected in the pool of his own blood. "It has been an honor to serve Your Majesty."

Randy certainly wouldn't have minded being thoroughly bathed and well fed, but he had a feeling the king's business with him had only just begun.

As the single bald servant escorted the sergeant out of the audience chamber, a swarm of them came out of nowhere armed with towels and buckets. Most of them converged on the massive pool of blood, but a few of them crawled behind the sergeant, mopping up his bloody footprints.

"What is your name, paladin of the New God?" asked the king.

Randy thought it best to give his proper formal name when addressing a king. "Randal Perkins, Your Honor."

The king cocked an eyebrow.

"I'm sorry," said Randy. "Force of habit. Randal Perkins, Your *Majesty*."

The king shrugged. "'Your Honor' has a nice ring to it. I'm sure I've been called worse." He looked past Randy but pointed down at him.

Before Randy knew it, two little bald guys had wet towels wrapped around his hands and forearms. Instinctively jerking his hands away, he was shocked to see that they were as clean as they'd ever been. Even stranger, so were the towels.

"That was amazing," said Randy. The servants bowed and retreated behind him.

The king nodded. "Keepers of the Cloth have served the palace for ten generations. They are trained from birth in the matters of loyalty, subtlety, and cleanliness, in that order of importance."

Randy turned to look behind him. There was no trace of the two servants who had cleaned his hands. It made some kind of sense. They was even more subtle than they was clean.

The king cleared his throat. "If I may have your attention?"

"I'm sorry, Your Majesty. Go on."

"My sources inform me that you frequent an establishment known as the Whore's Head Inn. Is that correct?"

"That is correct, sir. I actually kinda live there."

"Forgive my curiosity, but how is it a man of such piety and profound moral character would choose to spend his time in a place of such ill repute?"

"That's where my friends are," said Randy. "I couldn't very well count myself a man of profound moral character if I was to abandon my friends."

"Loyalty is indeed important, but –"

The chamber door swung open, and a golden eagle flew into the audience chamber, screeching at the king. Randy let out a little yelp.

The king smirked at Randy, then addressed the giant, luminous bird. "Desmond, you're scaring my guest."

The eagle took human a human form so much like the king's, except for the pharaoh beard, that they might be related. "He is right to be scared, Winston."

A look of concern broke the cool, casual demeanor the king had been putting forward. "What has you so shaken up, little brother?"

"Timmon Bloodsoul lives again. He heads this way, even as we speak, to make good on the promise he made to our forefathers."

The king maintained his serious face for a time, then laughed out loud. "Are you back on the poppy?"

"Heed my warning, Winston. You must flee the city at once."

"I will do no such thing. This is preposterous!"

"I saw him with my own eyes."

The king laughed again. "And how did you recognize a man you've never seen, who most sane people don't believe ever truly existed? Was he holding a sign? Did he introduce himself? *Hello. I'm Timmon Bloodsoul. I've come to end your lineage.*"

Things had been sounding pretty serious. Randy didn't know who Timmon Bloodsoul was, but he sounded like bad news. The king's humorous derision of his brother's news helped him breathe a little easier. He cracked a little smile, enough to show the king he appreciated the joke, but not so much as to insult his brother.

Desmond's face was dead serious. "He rides the Phantom Pinas."

Randy laughed out loud. Desmond's deadpan act had caught him completely off guard. "He rides the phantom penis. Oh man, why is that so funny? What is that, like, a dance move?" He thrust his pelvis back and forth. "Look at me. I'm ridin' the phantom penis!"

Both the king and his younger brother stared down at Randy. Neither were smiling now. The king even looked like he might have aged five years in the past ten seconds. Randy held his breath to keep from laughing.

The king turned to his brother. "How can you be sure?"

"I saw his junk in the moonlight."

All of Randy's held breath and laughter exploded out through his nose. "I'm sorry!" Tears rolled down his cheeks. "I'm so sorry. Don't mind me."

"Who *is* this tittering buffoon?" demanded Desmond.

The king frowned down at Randy. "This is the only known paladin of the New God."

"Oh, big brother. Surely you tell a taller tale than I."

"It's true. He invoked the name of –"

The chamber door flew open again. "Your Majesty!" A burgundy-suited man ran in clutching a rolled up piece of paper.

The king rolled his eyes. "What is it now, Quelby?"

"This message arrived by falcon from Port City." Quelby held out the paper to the king, who snatched it out of his hand and unrolled it.

The king's eyes darted left and right at an increasingly frantic pace as they made their way down the page. He let out a long exhalation and crumpled the letter in his fist.

"What is it, brother?" asked Desmond. "What news from Port City?"

"There is no Port City."

Desmond laughed nervously, as if hoping for a punchline to follow. "What do you mean?"

"Ten thousand orcs descended on the town in the night. They burned the place to the ground and commandeered every seagoing vessel they could get their filthy claws on. They're headed north along the Barrier Islands." He tapped his fingers on the arm of his throne for a moment, then looked out across the granite table. "Balharr. Lock down Shallow Grave at once."

A tall, unusually handsome half-orc stood erect at the far end of the table. "Permission to speak freely, Your Majesty."

"You may."

"This will not win you any favor with the orcs of Shallow Grave."

"That's why I need *you* to convince them it's for their own protection."

"The men I would require for such a task would be better used fighting the enemy. The residents of Shallow Grave long to prove their gratitude and loyalty. Giving them this opportunity to fight alongside us as brothers would go far in integrating them into our society."

"I'm more concerned with their *actual* brothers."

"I have blood ties to Meb' Garshur," said Balharr. "Do you doubt my loyalty?"

The king put his hands on the arms of his throne and leaned forward. "That all depends on how resistant you are to following your king's direct order."

Balharr's fists were balled up at his sides, but he bowed low. "As Your Majesty commands." He marched out of the room.

When he was gone, the king let out a long exhalation, as if he hadn't been sure how that whole thing was going to play out.

He looked down at Randy. "I shall expect to see you on the wall above the South Gate. There will be much need for your gifts. For now you are dismissed."

Randy raised his hand. "Your Majesty?"

The king sighed. "What?"

"I was wonderin'. Them folks you got locked up in the dungeon? Do you think you might pardon them?"

The king furrowed his brow. "You mean the men who blasphemed against the god you serve?"

Randy nodded. "Them's the ones. I seen a change in their hearts, and Jesus is a god of forgiveness."

"I don't have time for this." The king waved his hand like he was shooing away flies. "Fine. Whatever. Release the prisoners into the paladin's custody." He looked out at the table. "Sorbin."

As Randy was escorted out, a man with a long white beard and a powder blue robe rose from his place at the table. "Your Majesty."

"Summon the prophet. Tell him to bring some more of those… What were they called? *Roasted Beef Sand Witches*? And more of the seasoned potato curls. We have a siege to prepare for."

Chapter 31

The sign above the entrance to what had formerly been known as "Professor Goosewaddle's Potion and Scrolls Emporium" had been replace by a sign which simply read "Arby's". Severed wires dangling from the bottom suggested this was a genuine sign which Goosewaddle had stolen, and that the light emanating from it was produced through magical means.

Business was booming. Tim had been standing in line for hours, more out of curiosity than any desire to eat Arby's food again so soon. The street was littered on both sides with creatures picnicking on the sidewalks, enjoying their roast beef sandwiches, while angry magic shop owners threatened to blast them with Lightning Bolts if they didn't stop blocking their storefronts.

The line moved slowly, and Tim was stuck between a centaur and a bugbear, one of whom had a serious gas problem. It was like the universe had conspired to make sure Tim was farted on at all times.

When he finally made it through the doorway, Tim discovered that the sign wasn't all Goosewaddle had swiped from some no-doubt-currently-very-confused-and-angry franchise owner. Four booths, the likes of which would not be found elsewhere in this world, occupied the space where once stood hefty oaken racks full of potions, ointments, and minor magical knick-knacks. On each table there were two plastic squeezy bottles, one red and the other white; Arby's sauce and Horsey sauce respectively, a napkin dispenser, a set of salt and pepper shakers, and for some reason a bottle of Tabasco sauce.

He also discovered why it was taking so goddamn long. There was only one guy working the counter. Beads of sweat shone high on his forehead along his receding hairline. The pit stains on his uniform green polo shirt ran down to where it was tucked into his lame-ass triple pleated khakis.

Anyone who can steal and magically teleport signs, food, condiments, furniture, and presumably kitchen equipment, could also swipe himself a couple of uniforms. But a few details gave this guy away as the genuine goods. He was wearing a pair of modern eyeglasses, which Tim had never seen in this world. His name tag read "Paul Gonzales (Manager)", which screamed "I'm from Earth." But the biggest clue was how ineptly this poor schlub was dealing with the angry minotaur who was currently shouting across the counter at him.

"Two gold pieces for so little food!" the minotaur boomed. "How can you call that a *value* meal?"

Paul Gonzales (Manager) did his best to answer without crying. "I'm sorry, sir. I don't set the prices. Please don't kill me."

"Is there a problem here?" said Professor Goosewaddle as he flew in from the staircase and hovered above the counter, his hands crackling with electricity. He wore the same green polo shirt as Paul, but his fit more like a wizard's robe, the bottom hanging past his toes. "If you find my prices unreasonable, there are a multitude of other dining establishments in the city."

The minotaur hung his big head and placed two gold coins on the counter. "I'll pay." His voice was low and mopey.

The situation diffused, Professor Goosewaddle grabbed a cup, filled it with Mountain Dew from the fountain, and floated above the crowd to the one empty booth, no doubt reserved for him.

The better part of an hour passed while Tim impatiently waited for his turn. Occasionally, a young girl named Jennifer would bring food out from the room Tim had once teleported to Earth from. She might have been pretty if her face wasn't covered in sweat and terror.

"Welcome to Arby's," said Paul Gonzales (Manager). "How can I help you?" His voice was much calmer than it had been with his previous customers. Tim's lack of fangs, claws, antennae, or horns probably had something to do with that.

"Two Arby's Roast Beefs and a large curly fry."

The manager swallowed hard, gawking down at Tim. He looked like he wanted to say something not roast-beef-sandwich-related, but after a quick glance in Goosewaddle's direction, he thought better of it.

"Anything to drink?"

"Nah," said Tim. "Brought my own."

"That'll be three gold pieces."

Tim patted his pockets, suddenly remembering something very important. "Fuck. I don't have any money."

The manager shook his head. He was breathing hard. "I'm very sorry, sir." He looked past Tim. "Next."

Tim stood on his tip-toes and leaned closer. "Come on, Paul. Hook a brother up." He hoped his use of modern American colloquialism would sway the manager, or at least fuck with him.

Paul glanced in Goosewaddle's direction again, then leaned down to get right in Tim's face. His breath smelled like Scope and Marlboro. "Are you... Do you know where I'm from?"

"Gulfport? Biloxi? D'Iberville?"

Paul stopped breathing Tim was pretty sure his heart stopped beating for a second. "You have to get me out of here!"

Tim made a mental note that he said 'me' rather than 'us'. He guessed Jennifer could go fuck herself as far as Paul was concerned. Typical fast food manager.

"I can't help anyone on an empty stomach."

"Listen, kid. I'd love to *hook a brother up*." Paul's attempt at hip urban slang was less convincing than if the minotaur had said it. "But if my till comes up short, the boss... I don't know what he'll do to me."

"Dude, chillax." Tim would never use the word *chillax*, but he was intentionally going as heavy as he could on the slang. "Your boss and I are tight." He turned around to face Goosewaddle's booth and shouted, "Yo! Goosewaddle!"

The restaurant went completely silent, save for the echoing slurp of the professor's Mountain Dew.

Goosewaddle turned around slowly to see who dared address him so informally in his own restaurant. When he saw Tim, his eyes lit up.

"Tim! Welcome! What do you think?"

Tim nodded. "I like it. A little taste of home."

"Come over and join me when you've gotten your food."

"Will do." Tim turned back to Paul. "Throw in an order of mozzarella sticks, and I'll see what I can do."

When Tim's food was ready, he carried his tray to Goosewaddle's booth, where he ran into an invisible force field, upturning his tray and spilling all his food on the floor.

"Fuck."

"Oh dear," said Professor Goosewaddle. "My apologies." He snapped his fingers.

Tim reached out for the force field, but it had been deactivated. "Don't sweat it. I've eaten off the floor of the Chicken Hut." He piled his curly fries and mozzarella sticks back onto the tray. At least the sandwiches were wrapped.

"Tell me, Tim," said Goosewaddle. "How did you hear about this place?" It sounded like he was more interested in marketing data than small talk.

"Someone threw a cup at my head."

Goosewaddle rubbed his little hands together. "Outstanding!" Tim could practically see dollar signs in the old gnome's eyes.

Tim unwrapped his sandwiches and removed the top buns. "I notice you kidnapped yourself a staff." He gave each sandwich a generous squirt of Arby's sauce, careful not to let any of it near his curly fries. Whatever cockroach shit or dire rat hairs they might have touched on the floor, he'd be damned if they'd be sullied by sauce.

"*Kidnap* is a strong word," said the professor. "I merely borrowed them against their will."

Tim spoke through a mouthful of roast beef sandwich. "That's kind of the textbook definition."

"I'm going to compensate them for their time and service," said Goosewaddle defensively. "I just need them to train a goblin staff." He leaned over the table and grinned. "Goblins will work for next to nothing."

"Sounds like you've learned the ins and outs of the fast food industry pretty well."

"I have learned much. Your world is a strange and fascinating place. I have seen – Oh dear. Just a moment." He reached down, then produced a sleek, black shiny rectangle.

Tim nearly choked on a curly fry. "Is that a fucking smart phone?"

Professor Goosewaddle pursed his lips as he looked at the screen. "A message from the king."

"Wait," said Tim. "Did you just get a fucking text?"

Goosewaddle climbed onto the table and stood up. "If I can have everyone's attention."

The din inside the restaurant calmed down. "The restaurant is closed for the rest of the day."

The din returned, only now it was louder and decidedly more grumbly.

Goosewaddle raised both hands over his head, each engulfed in a raging blue ball of fire. That shut everyone up. "It is the king's decree that you must all return to your homes immediately. A city-wide state of emergency has been declared."

That didn't sound good. Tim washed down a mouthful of curly fries with stonepiss. He didn't know if the citizens were reacting to the king's authority or Goosewaddle's, but everyone cleared out of the restaurant like cockroaches when the light goes on.

"Paul! Jennifer!" shouted Goosewaddle.

The clang of a pan against the floor rang out from Goosewaddle's workshop, quickly followed by Jennifer. She and Paul stood at panicked attention.

"Yes, Professor," they said in unison.

"I need twenty roast beef sandwiches and as many curly fries as you can fry in the meantime. These are for the king, so make them presentable."

Without a word, Paul and Jennifer retreated into the workshop.

Goosewaddle slumped down into the booth, idly picked up one of Tim's mozzarella sticks, pulled a hair off of it, and put it in his mouth.

"What's going on?" asked Tim. "And since when are you so close to the king?"

"I told you," said Goosewaddle. "I have learned much in your world. I was able to share valuable information with His Majesty about the New God."

Tim laughed. "You mean Jesus?"

"The same."

"What *valuable information* could you possibly have given the king about Jesus?"

"On one of my journeys, I was invited to attend a ritual at the house of the New God."

"Is that right?" said Tim. He was giggling on the inside. "What did you think?"

"Honestly? As far as divine worship rituals go, I found it a bit dull."

"You're telling me. Imagine trying to sit through that shit when you're six."

Goosewaddle stroked his beard. "There was a lot of sitting, yes. And standing. The kneeling was the worst. It was hard on my old knees, and I couldn't see anything."

"This is fantastic. Keep going."

"Some passages were read from some sacred text, then the High Cleric spoke candidly to the congregation about his interpretation of those passages. It was a little difficult to follow. He attempted to liven things up with humor, but he was no bard."

"Were you dressed like that?"

Goosewaddle ignored the question, his mind focused on his recollection. "I started to nod off, and was about to make for an exit, but temple enforcers were patrolling the aisles, passing baskets from one aisle to the next, in which the worshippers would put coins or folded pieces of paper. All I had to offer was two cockatrice feathers, so I put those in."

"I'm sure they were appreciated."

"Indeed. Cockatrice feathers are rare and valuable."

"I'll bet," said Tim. "So what happened next?"

"Something very peculiar," said Professor Goosewaddle. "The entire congregation stood up at once and began grappling each other by the hand, but wishing peace upon them."

Tim was really enjoying this. "It would have been worth sitting through this just to watch your reaction."

Goosewaddle rubbed his little hands together. "I haven't gotten to the best part. While I was still contemplating the ritualistic grappling, people started forming lines to ingest the *flesh and blood* of the New God."

"They did *not!*"

"They did!"

Tim looked at the restaurant door, then at the doorway leading to Goosewaddle's workshop, where Paul and Jennifer were busily making the king's sandwiches and curly fries and having an argument in hushed tones, then finally across the table at Professor Goosewaddle himself. "Did *you* ingest the flesh and blood of the New God?"

"I didn't want to at first, but the people I was sitting next to urged me forward. As I stood in line, I watched other people eat the tiny discs of god-flesh. Everyone seemed very calm about it, so I figured 'How often do you get the chance to eat a god?'. Truth be told, it wasn't as horrifying as it sounds."

"You don't say," said Tim. "Tell me. What does a god taste like?"

Professor Goosewaddle's eyes lit up. "Ah! This is the sort of valuable information I was able to pass along to the king, and what led me to recognize the New God later when I saw him on the magic screen box."

"Hold on," said Tim. "You're starting to lose me. What is it, exactly, that you *learned?*"

Goosewaddle looked left and right, then leaned across the table and whispered, "The New God's flesh is made of bread."

That should have been hilarious, but Tim was starting to feel the latent pangs of Catholic guilt.

"And his blood," said the professor. "His blood was infused with enough spirit to kill a dwarf."

Tim felt an uncomfortable sense of embarrassment, like when that one kid still believes in Santa Claus years after everyone else in the class found their toys hidden in the garage, and it's so sad, even the bullies won't make fun of him. He didn't know whether he felt more embarrassed for Professor Goosewaddle, the king, or the Catholic Church. But he knew this was going to end badly if he let it continue.

"Listen, Professor," said Tim. "There are some things you need to understand about my world."

"Indeed. There is still much to learn."

"Religion, for example, is different there than it is here. A long time ago, people made up stories to explain things they didn't understand, and over time, –"

"Twenty Arby's Roast Beefs!" said Paul.

"And ten large curly fries," said Jennifer. Each of them held two large, paper Arby's bags. "Would His Majesty like anything to drink with that?"

"Better safe than sorry," said Professor Goosewaddle. "He likes the Dew of the Mountain."

Tim stood in front of the exit. "Professor. We need to talk about this before you go."

"I mustn't keep His Majesty waiting any longer," said Professor

Goosewaddle, taking the filled cup from Jennifer. "You should run back to your tavern."

"But I need –"

"Paul, Jennifer. Get some rest. You'll find pillows and bedrolls in the room upstairs. You both did a fine job today."

"But Professor," said Tim. "You need to hear –"

"City-wide state of emergency," said the professor. "Such a declaration is unprecedented in my lifetime. I understand you're eager to share to share your culture and history with me, as am I eager to learn it. But now is not the time. The king demands nourishment. We shall speak of this again soon."

"But –"

Professor Goosewaddle bowed his head curtly. "Good bye for now." He vanished with a little pop and puff of blue smoke, which Tim suspected he may have added to his Teleportation spell for a little extra flair.

"Well, fuck."

As soon as the professor was gone, Paul sat in a booth and started sobbing. Jennifer sat in a different booth and laid her head on her arms. She looked more exhausted than anything.

Tim went back to his own booth and finished his curly fries.

Chapter 32

Katherine wasn't sure what had happened to Chaz's lute, but from the way he'd been griping since their escape, she suspected it might be lodged up his ass.

"How much farther is it to Port Town?" Chaz groaned. "I'm tired, and I can't see."

"I don't rightly know," said Tanner. "I'm not exactly sure where that drow secret exit let out. It was clever of them to put the door higher up in the tree, rather than at the base."

"Yeah, real clever. Didn't you say you had some business to take care of back in Cardinia?"

Tanner shrugged. "Something came up."

"Uh-huh," said Chaz. "Something like your skinny black dick?"

"Chaz!" said Katherine. She slapped him on the back of the head.

"Jesus!" cried Chaz. "That hurts. Is that, like, a vampire thing?"

"You're being rude and vulgar."

"The only reason he's hanging around is because he wants to get in your pants. You have to know that."

"Tanner has been a perfect gentleman."

"So was Millard."

"And was he trying to get in my pants?"

Chaz laughed. "No. He only murdered you."

"It sounds to me like somebody's jealous." Katherine would be lying if she said she didn't enjoy the attention, but it was getting a little pathetic.

"Oh please," said Chaz. "Don't flatter yourself. I'm just telling you like it is. Any guy can act like a gentleman when they're trying to get in your pants. I mean, even *I* was a gentleman when..."

Katherine glared at him. "I'm sorry, Chaz. Were you saying something?"

"Ha ha!" said Tanner. "No right way to finish that thought, mate."

Chaz trudged along sulky and silent.

Katherine didn't want to be that hard on him. "Why not pass the time with a song? Where's your lute?"

"The *gentleman* smashed it over a soldier's head."

"Oh."

"Traveler up ahead," said Tanner. "One of you should ask him how far it is to Port Town."

"Why one of us?" asked Chaz. "Your mouth seems to be in fine working order."

"Aye, it is that," Tanner said with a wink at Katherine. "But many folks don't take kindly to drow, even half-drow, such as myself."

"Chaz?" said Katherine. "Would you like to go talk to the traveler, seeing as how you have the highest Charisma score?" She didn't want to use geek-speak, but Chaz could do with feeling useful for once.

"I'm pretty sure your Charisma score is higher since you turned into a vampire."

Tanner smiled. "What a peculiar conversation we're having."

There was only so much pampering Katherine was prepared to offer Chaz. If he wanted to feel sorry for himself all night, that was fine with her. The pity train just left the station.

"I'll go," she said. "You two hang back."

The traveler was human. He was carrying a backpack almost as big as himself, and a sturdy hiking stick. He might have had his every worldly possession in there. Katherine didn't want to spook him, so she waited until she was close enough for him to see her before addressing him.

"Hello."

"Aye?" The traveler eyed her warily and did not stop walking. He was at least ten or fifteen years older than her, but his legs were strong.

Katherine changed direction and walked alongside him. "Are you coming from Port Town?"

"Aye."

"How long a walk is it from here to there?"

"At a brisk pace, you can make it in two hours. Get a good look, lass. It may no longer be there come sunup." He couldn't possibly expect her not to follow up on that, but he was still walking.

"And *why* would Port Town no longer be there come sunup?"

Though he failed to slow his pace, he at least did Katherine the courtesy of looking at her. "Timmon Bloodsoul approaches."

"Um... Who?"

"Never mind this guy," said Tanner, approaching from the other way.

"You stay back!" The traveler stopped dead in his tracks, brandishing his hiking stick at Tanner. "I don't seek trouble from no drow."

"You see?" Tanner said to Katherine. "What did I tell you?"

Katherine put her hands on her hips and raised her eyebrows at the old man. "You are out of line, sir. Drow are not all like that."

Tanner gave her a funny look. "Say that again."

"I said 'Drow are not —'"

"Drow," Tanner corrected her.

"Drow?"

"No, you're saying it wrong. *Drow*, rhymes with *cow*."

"I thought it was *drow*, rhymes with... uh... *grow*."

Chaz looked as cheerful as he had all night. "You were about to say *bro*, weren't you?"

"Chaz! Shut up!" Katherine turned to Tanner. "I totally was not." She was grateful that her blood no longer flowed, because she'd be beet red right now. Careful to get the pronunciation right, she faced the bewildered old man and repeated herself. "*Drow* are not all like that."

"Actually," said Tanner. "They kinda are. But I'm only *half*-drow."

"Tanner!"

"A soul cannot be half-corrupted," said the old traveler. "You walk in darkness."

"Well it's fucking nighttime, isn't it?" said Katherine.

Chaz and Tanner both smiled at her. The old man did not.

"Let's get out of here," said Tanner. "Leave this crazy old man alone with his fisherman tales."

"Aye, crazy am I?" The old man pointed a bony finger at one of his wide, blue eyes. "I know what my own eyes have seen, and they seen his pinas, sure as they see you standing there now."

"Hold up," said Chaz. "You saw his *what*? Like, he just whipped it out?"

Tanner folded his arms and cocked his head to the side. "You honestly expect me to believe that you saw the Phantom Pinas?"

Chaz scratched his head. "So is that, like, it got cut off, but he can still feel it? Wait… Then how did you see it?"

The old man raised his arms and his voice. "I saw his junk, *flapping in the wind!*"

Chaz shook his head. "I'm so confused."

"Pish!" the old man said, clearly disgusted with the three of them. "Travel south if you must. You'll know the truth of my words soon enough." And with that, he continued his journey north.

Katherine, Chaz, and Tanner continued southward.

"Have you really never heard of Timmon Bloodsoul?" asked Tanner.

Katherine shook her head.

"When I was a child, my father would tell me that, if I misbehave, Timmon Bloodsoul would get me. I guess your parents were more the positive reinforcement type."

"I don't have any recollection of my parents," said Katherine. "Chaz said they were rapists. I guess that kept them pretty busy. So you really think that old man was crazy? We don't have to worry about Timmon Bloodsoul and his spirit penis?"

"Phantom Pinas."

"Whatever."

"Trust me," said Tanner. "If the Phantom Pinas actually turned up, you'd see a lot more than one crazy old man fleeing northward."

There was an easy enough way to check that. Katherine took her bat form, flapped her way above the trees, and saw exactly what she was hoping she wouldn't. About a twenty minute walk away from them, there was a multitude of people heading their way. Men, women, and children, burdened with as much of their belongings as they could carry. It was an exodus.

Katherine flew down to the others and changed back into a half-elf. "It's real."

"What's real?" asked Tanner.

"All of it. Timmon Bloodsoul. The ghost dick. All of it. There is a crowd of frightened people coming this way right now."

"We should turn around," said Chaz.

"What if my brother's down there?"

"Then he's probably in that crowd heading north, just like we should do."

"I have to find out." Katherine took her bat form again and flapped high over the trees. She flew as fast as she could over the crowd, keeping an eye out for Cooper. He'd be the easiest to spot. There were maybe three hundred people in all before the crowd started thinning out in the back, and she didn't see anyone who looked like Cooper or Tim.

Whatever virtues Tim and his friends possessed, suicidal bravery wasn't one of them. They were probably all back at that shitty tavern, drinking their shitty beer. Katherine turned around, and rescanned the crowd more casually on her return flight. And there they were.

How could she have missed such a mismatched group of travelers on her first pass? She flew off to the side, into the forest, so as not to spook anyone with her transformation. Once back in half-elf form, she pushed her way through the crowd until she saw her brother and his friends again. Cooper had finally thrown on a shirt, which was nice. He and Tim were holding hands, which was a little weird, but kind of cute. Tim was probably drunk and needed the guidance.

She walked up behind Cooper and punched him jovially in the shoulder. "Hey, shithead. You miss me?"

When Cooper turned around, he – or rather *she* – was the biggest, most brutish human woman Katherine had ever seen outside of a Walmart.

The little half-elven girl, who was most certainly not Tim, looked up at the woman. "Who's that, mommy?"

"I'm so sorry!" said Katherine. "I thought you were a man."

The woman gasped.

"I mean a half-orc!"

SMACK! The big bitch had a hell of an arm on her.

"See here, now!" said the elf, sporting a wispy Fu Manchu style mustache. "That's my wife you're talking to!"

"I... I..." Katherine stammered at the family of four. Wait a minute... That wasn't right. Elven father. Human mother. Half-elven kid. What was this dwarf doing here? She might not have been so quick in her assumption if this short, hairy meatball hadn't been tagging along. She looked down at him. "Who the fuck are you?"

"I'm Griswald," said the dwarf. "I don't actually know these people. I just didn't want to travel alone."

The group turned their backs on Katherine and resumed their journey.

Chaz and Tanner weaved their way through the crowd toward Katherine like salmon swimming upstream.

"What was that all about?" asked Tanner.

"Just a misunderstanding."

Chaz hugged himself and shivered. "I think we should follow the crowd. Safety in numbers and all that."

"I need to find Tim."

Tanner pursed his lips in thought for a moment. "Is your brother the suicidally brave sort? Is it in his character to face certain death on principle alone?"

Katherine shook her head. "No."

"Then would it not be reasonable to assume that he and his companions would have fled at the first hint of danger?"

"That's exactly what I would have assumed," said Katherine. She glanced at the people walking past her. "But if that's the case, then where are they? Like Chaz said, the safest place is with the crowd. Unless..."

"Unless?" said Tanner.

"Chaz, do they still have that flying carpet?"

Chaz looked at the ground. "Yeah."

"Well that's it then. They probably just took to the sky and high-tailed it out of there."

Tanner's eyes were wide. "Your brother has a flying carpet?"

"Yeah. So?"

"That's worth more money than I've ever seen."

Katherine smiled. "When we find him, I'll take you for a ride." She, Chaz, and Tanner started walking with the current, headed back north to Cardinia.

"You know something?" said Chaz. "I'm starting to get sick of this fucking road."

Chapter 33

Cooper's arms felt like wet noodles which were, somehow, also on fire. He'd been rowing all day and all night. The rising sun revealed nothing but yet another of the goddamn Barrier Islands. It seemed wrong that the most relaxing parts of the journey involved walking along the beach with a boat on his head, but he was grateful to see that opportunity approaching.

This was the sixth or seventh island Cooper had washed up on. He couldn't believe he'd originally planned to swim. With the next island so close, he redoubled his efforts, rowing as hard as he could until he felt the crunch of the boat's hull against sand. He allowed himself a small break to drink from the Decanter of Endless Water, then stepped out of the boat and into the shallows.

Placing the boat over his head the way he'd come to find most comfortable, he began walking southward along the shoreline of the island, dragging an oar in each of his exhausted hands. He couldn't see where he was going, but was able to navigate by making sure he never veered from where the water met the sand.

Cooper trudged along the beach, dreading the moment he would have to put the boat back in the water and start rowing again, when he heard a voice from up ahead.

"You there! In the name of the United Forces of Meb' Garshur, I demand you surrender your vessel!"

Cooper lifted the boat off his head and let it fall on the sand next to him. "In the name of what?"

"The United Forces of Meb' Garshur," repeated the orc twenty yards up the beach. He was flanked by an orc on either side of him.

"Gesundheit."

"Drop the oars and step away from the boat," said the leader.

All three of the orcs wore an identical roughspun woolen tunic with some kind of symbol painted poorly on the front. It might have been a fist dripping blood, or it might have been a rhinoceros taking a dump. These guys were no Picassos. Their clothes were dripping wet, and though they made an effort to look threatening, Cooper could tell they were just as exhausted as he was. These poor fuckers had been swimming. The good news Cooper took from this was that he must be getting close to the southern mainland. The bad news was that a fight was inevitable.

"I have a counter proposal," said Cooper. "How about you go fuck yourself?"

"So be it."

"Seriously? I didn't think —"

"Scab! Grunt! Draw your weapons!"

"Oh, right," said Cooper. As Scab and Grunt drew their shortswords, Cooper decided to even the odds. "I'm really angry!"

His vision tainted pink, Cooper could already see the look of fear in the two henchmen's eyes.

"If you cannot stand against a single half-orc," said the leader, "how will you breach the walls of Cardinia?" His underlings still hesitant, he employed a different strategy. "It's this or keep swimming."

Scab and Grunt charged at Cooper, shortswords held high above their heads. Cooper swung an oar at the one he'd arbitrarily decided was Grunt, snapping it in half against the side of his head and dropping him to the sand.

With a battle cry that was something between a lion and a goat, Scab swung his sword down with both hands at Cooper, who barely had the presence of mind to try to block the blow with his remaining oar. The sword sliced through the oar and into Cooper's shoulder, but he hardly felt it.

"FUCK YOU!" said Cooper, and punched Scab in the throat.

Scab dropped his sword and grasped at his neck with both hands. Cooper tackled him and punched him in the face until his head was little more than a pulpy red stain in the sand.

"For Meb' Garshur!" shouted Grunt, who had recovered from his oar wound.

Cooper felt the burn of jagged steel dig into his back muscles. It pissed him off. He swung his arm around wildly and caught Grunt in the knee, dropping him to the sand again. As Grunt screamed, Cooper drove the broken oar handle into his mouth, effectively staking his head to the beach and shutting him the fuck up.

Cooper breathed hard as his vision returned to normal. He couldn't go on any more. He'd have to take a nap.

"Tut tut," said the remaining orc, reminding Cooper that there had, in fact, been three.

Fuck. Cooper stood up on wobbly legs and staggered backwards a few steps.

The orc leader was holding the business end of the oar which Cooper had cracked over Grunt's head. Making a show of just how unconcerned he was about Cooper, he unceremoniously jerked the other end of the oar out of Grunt's gaping maw. "Everyone knows that the best way to deal with a barbarian is to wait for him to wear himself out. But I was hoping to not have to do my own rowing." Placing the pieces together, he whispered something that Cooper couldn't make out, and the oar was suddenly whole again. He looked up at Cooper. "I'll give you one final chance to continue your miserable existence. Row for me, and I'll let you live."

"Sorry," said Cooper between labored breaths. "I was continuing my miserable existence in the opposite direction." He dropped his remaining oar handle and reached for the greataxe strapped to his back.

The orcish fighter/wizard/asshole was similarly equipped. The greataxe he produced appeared to be in a much better state of repair than the chipped and rusted blades of Scab and Grunt's shortswords. It even made Cooper's axe look like a piece of shit in comparison. The double blades were shiny silver and designed to look like angel's wings. A silver skull adorned the top, with a spike jutting through it. The edges of the angel wing blades were engraved with words that Cooper couldn't read.

Cooper had never seen such an impressive-looking weapon. "Sweet axe."

"This is Soulreaper," said the orc. "I would hate to sully her blades with the filthy blood of such an unworthy opponent, so I will repeat my offer one last time."

Cooper's guts churned. Coming out of a Barbarian Rage always did a number on his insides. Relief came in the form of a loud, extended fart, which he and the orc leader awkwardly endured.

"It would appear that my ass has made plain my thoughts about your offer."

The orc leader huffed and held up his weapon. "Very well. Send my regrets to Scab and Grunt when you see them in –

YAAAAARRRRGGGGHHHH!"

His face was obscured by a flapping mess of black feathers.

Cooper was almost as surprised as the orc leader, but jumped on the opportunity he was presented with. With all of the power he could muster in both arms, he brought his greataxe down hard between the orc's shoulder and neck, cutting down to what must have been near the lung on his opposite side.

The avian assailant, whose identity Cooper would confirm when he got the chance, disengaged from the orc's face, but not without a souvenir. A gloppy string of blood and nerve followed the bird from where the orc's eye used to be.

Somehow, that motherfucker was still standing. Still screaming in agony, he took a wild swipe at the bird, but it appeared his depth perception was off.

Cooper buried his axe in the big bastard's head, finally bringing him down. He left the axe in the orc's head and picked up Soulreaper. It felt incredible in his hands. Perfectly balanced, with a grip that felt like it had been designed specifically for his big, clumsy hands. Not a bad day's work.

"Scrawww!" said the bird, hopping excitedly on the beach.

"Are you Ravenus?"

"Scrawww!" the bird repeated.

This wasn't going to do. Cooper was all but certain he'd found Ravenus. The bird was big like Ravenus. It sounded like Ravenus. It had the predilection for eating the eyeballs of its enemies like Ravenus. And it seemed unlikely that some other random bird would swoop out of the sky to help him in a fight. Still, he wanted to be sure. With no way to communicate, he'd have to think outside the box.

Cooper sat down on the beach, opened his bag, and took out all of

the scroll tubes containing his and his friends' character sheets.
"Come here."

The bird squawked at him some more, clearly not understanding
him. Cooper repeated his command with a gesture.

After some more squawking and flapping, the bird finally hopped
forward. Cooper grabbed it, shoved it into his bag, and held the
opening shut.

While his bag pulsed like an erratically beating heart, Cooper
opened the scroll tubes until he found his own character sheet. Down
at the bottom was a short list of his possessions. At the bottom of
the list, he read the word *Ravenus*.

"Sweet." Cooper opened his bag, and Ravenus wobbled out,
gagging and choking.

When he finally caught his breath, Ravenus continued squawking,
hopping, and flapping.

"I'm sorry," said Cooper. "I had to know."

Ravenus just squawked louder.

"Dude. I don't fucking understand you."

Squawk squawk squawk. Flap flap flap.

Cooper was about to shove him back in the bag when he noticed
that only one of Ravenus's wings was flapping. "Are you hurt? Is
there something wrong with your wing?"

Ravenus turned his head in the direction of his flapping wing.
"SQUAAAWWWK!"

Cooper followed Ravenus's gaze. "I don't know what you want
from me. I told you, I can't fucking under— Hooooooly shit."

About half a mile up the beach, an army of orcs was marching
toward him. There were hundreds of them. On the water, luckier
orcs traveled in boats ranging from humble rowboats like his own to
larger sailing vessels.

Cooper stood up to get a better view. A few of the groups at the
head of the march stopped in their tracks, pointing at him.

"Oops."

It was time to get out of there. Cooper grabbed the mended oar
and lifted the boat over his head. Across half a mile of sea and sand,
he heard one word shouted simultaneously by at least a dozen voices.

"BOAT!"

"Oops."

Cooper lifted the boat and looked back. Sure enough, the whole goddamn orcish army was running at him.

Fuck.

Mustering what little strength he had left, he ran into the water until he was deep enough so that his weight wouldn't drag the boat on the sea floor. By the time he hopped inside, orcs were already jumping into the water after him.

With his one oar, Cooper rowed like a motherfucker. He had no direction in mind but *away from all these fucking orcs.*

Ravenus hopped up and down on Cooper's bag, squawking and flapping again.

"Yeah, no shit," said Cooper. "I fucking see them."

The bird was insistent, and it was driving Cooper nuts. He was trying to communicate something again, but Cooper was damned if he could figure out what it was.

Ravenus stopped flapping and squawking, and ducked into Cooper's bag. A moment later, Cooper could hear a faint clinking sound as a bulge in his bag bobbed repeatedly up and down. Ravenus was tapping the Decanter of Endless Water with his beak.

"What? Are you fucking thirsty?" asked Cooper. "I'm kind of in the middle of something here. Do you think you could give me a minute?"

Clink clink clink. Clink clink clink.

Cooper looked back. The orcs were swimming faster than he was rowing, and his arms were just about to give in to exhaustion.

Clink clink clink. Clink clink clink.

"You know what? Fine." Cooper set his oar down in the boat. If they wanted his boat that bad, they could fight him for it. Even with the advantages of higher elevation, not having to fight while swimming, and his badass new axe, he knew it would only be a matter of time before they overwhelmed him. But maybe he could take down enough of them to make the others reconsider.

He reached into his bag and pulled out the Decanter of Endless Water. Holding it over the side of the boat, he started pouring water into the sea. "Here. Drink up."

Ravenus stepped out of the bag, looked at the decanter, then up at Cooper.

"Squaaawwwk!"

"Dude, hurry it up. We're about to start fighting soon."

Ravenus flapped and squawked more furiously than ever.

"WHAT. THE. FUCK. DO. YOU. WANT. FROM. ME. ASSHOLE?"

Finally, Ravenus gave up his tantrum. He flew up to Cooper's head and raked a talon across his forehead, drawing blood.

"Mother*fucker*!" shouted Cooper. But Ravenus had already flown away.

Cooper turned around and found the bird flying in a tight circle behind the boat. "You want some water, shithead? I've got your water right here." He aimed the decanter at Ravenus and shouted the command word, "Geyser!"

Instead of blasting Ravenus out of the sky, the jet of water propelled the boat forward like an outboard motor. He was cruising, hopping waves as the little rowboat rocketed further out to sea.

"Hell yeah!" Cooper shouted as the approaching orcs got farther and farther away.

Ravenus flew down and landed on Cooper's shoulder.

"You know something, bird. You're all right."

Chapter 34

At the mayor's behest, most of the citizens had evacuated Port Town. Those with property untethered their barges and headed westward to Portsville. Those without started walking north, seeking whatever security they could get behind Cardinia's city walls. Only the Merriweather Inn remained. It was built on a barge just like the other buildings, but it was far too big to move out of the way in time.

Mayor Merriweather had tried to convince Julian and his friends to leave as well, but Julian refused. Tony the Elf watched over Stacy and Dave while they slept, and Julian sat with the mayor on the roof of the inn.

Potted plants, some vegetable and others decorative, lined the short wall on three of the four sides of the roof, but the southern wall, with its view of the sea, was kept clear. From the wear on the wicker chairs they sat on, Julian guessed that the mayor spent a lot of time up here.

"You really believe that skinny elf who set fire to my inn is responsible for waking Timmon Bloodsoul?" asked Mayor Merriweather.

"I'd bet my life on it," said Julian. He sighed. "I guess I'm betting all our lives on it."

"And what good will it do you to die here? I'm an old man. This inn is all I've got. You young folks have futures, or you could anyway. The world we know is about to be cast in a dark shadow. It'll need good young people to fight for a brighter future."

"This is the world you know," said Julian. "If my friends and I ever want to see the world *we* know again, we have to take that elf alive." He intentionally left out his primary motivation of finding Ravenus.

The mayor shook his head. "None of what you said makes a lick of sense to me, but I suppose having some company beats dying alone."

Julian was trying to remain optimistic. Mayor Merriweather wasn't helping. "I'm going to zone out for a couple of hours. Give me a jostle if anything happens."

"Suit yourself."

The moon had moved since Julian had first spotted the flying boat. The only indication he had of its current location was the occasional flash of fire from one of the dragons flying around it. He stared into the dark night sky and fell into a trance.

*

When he came to, dawn was just breaking and he had a much better view of the thing. It was a boat. One of those older, Asian-style boats with the sails supported by a series of long poles sticking out horizontally from the masts.

It was enormous, even bigger than the Merriweather Inn, flying slowly on a cloud of green mist. Huge, slow, terrifying. It reminded Julian of the Star Destroyer in the opening scene of *Star Wars*.

The good news was that the boat, and its entourage of four red dragons, each half as big as the boat itself, did not appear to be interested in Port Town. The bad news was that it was easily less than a mile away, but Julian felt no sign of Ravenus.

"Looks like we may get through this alive after all," said Julian, joining Mayor Merriweather at the west-facing edge of the inn's roof.

"Aye, if you keep your voice down." He rubbed his bristly chin. "He's headed straight for Cardinia, as the raven flies."

Julian grabbed the mayor by the lapels of his robe. "Did you see a raven?"

"Get a hold of yourself, boy!" said the mayor. "It's an expression."

Julian let go. "I'm sorry. I just —"

"Who ever heard of such nonsense? Getting yourself all worked up over a bird while there's four red dragons close enough to —"

The brisk, pre-morning air reverberated with a thunderous reptilian scream. One of the dragons had broken formation and was beating its great leathery wings in their direction.

"Well, shit," said Julian.

"Mind your tongue, boy," said the mayor. "And you might want to take cover." With that, he morphed into his man-tiger hybrid form.

Julian ducked behind the wall and peeked over the top. Squinting, he could just make out a figure riding on the dragon's massive head.

"Doogan Merriweather!" bellowed the figure atop the dragon's head. "I created you, and now I will end you! Prepare to suffer the wrath of Mordred!"

Well that settled that.

As the dragon got closer, Julian recognized the figure on its head, Mordred, as the same elf who had blasted him with a fireball, but with one significant difference. He was now wearing an eye patch.

"Ravenus!" Julian's sense of optimism was renewed. Ravenus must have escaped, and he left his captor something to remember him by. Good for him.

"Fly, Falkor!" shouted the dragon-riding elf. "Burn the inn to the ground!"

"Well, shit," Julian said again.

The mayor growled at him.

"Sorry." While Julian waited to be roasted, he considered Mordred's choice of name for his pet dragon. Falkor. The luck dragon from *The Neverending Story*. There was something sad about that. Mordred honestly saw himself as a bullied little boy striking back at his oppressors.

Falkor's head was about the size of a van, all scales, horns, and teeth. When he opened his mouth, Julian could see a flame at the back of his throat.

Julian crouched close to the wall and shut his eyes. The heat from the fire was intense, but not so much as it had been when he was actually engulfed in a fireball. When he opened his eyes, he saw that the entire eastern half of the roof was on fire. The chairs he and the mayor had been sitting in were completely incinerated. *Hang on.... Where the hell was the mayor?*

Julian looked up. Falkor was flying in an upward spiral. Mayor Merriweather was hanging on to the dragon's back, near the base of the tail, and climbing toward its head.

"That crazy son of a…" A thought occurred to him, and he

shouted up at the Mayor. "Don't kill the elf!"

Unable to offer much in the way of assistance in a dragon fight, Julian did what he thought was the next best thing. He picked up a potted plant and hurled it down on top of some flames. The moist soil snuffed out that one little section of fire. The roof was well-stocked with potted plants. Julian tried to choose the ones he assumed were decorative before the ones which were edible, but wasn't particularly picky about it. As he fought back the fire, he kept an eye on the mayor.

"Julian!" said Dave, hurrying up the stairs. "Are you okay?"

Julian smashed a potted orchid on some fire. "Yeah. Give me a hand, would you?"

Dave nodded and grabbed the nearest pot, a tomato plant. "Why are we doing this?" He smashed the pot down at his feet.

"What the hell, Dave? I'm trying to put out the fire!"

"Oh. Sorry. I just woke up." Dave waddled closer to the flames and raised his hands. "Water!" Streams of water flowed down from points in the air, as if poured from invisible pitchers. It was much more effective at containing the fire than Julian's pots had been.

Julian turned his attention back to Mordred, Falkor, and Mayor Merriweather.

The mayor had reached the dragon's head, and was getting very close to Mordred. Julian couldn't see exactly what happened next, but it must have caused Falkor some discomfort, because he jerked his head to the side, sending both passengers plummeting toward the sea.

"Shit," said Dave. "That's a hell of a fall. Do you think they'll survive that?"

"I hope so," said Julian. "I guess it depends on how many Hit Points they've got."

Julian's attention was so focused on the two falling figures that he didn't notice Falkor again until he swooped down to snatch Mayor Merriweather out of the sky.

Mordred hit the water with a loud, smacking splash, causing Julian to wince. He felt a little bad that he winced for Mordred, but not for Mayor Merriweather. It was a matter of being able to relate. He'd felt the sting of a belly-flop on the water before, but he'd never been devoured by a flying reptile.

A second splash came from directly below them. Julian looked down. Stacy had jumped out the window and was swimming out to Mordred's point of impact.

"Help!" cried Mordred, flailing his arms wildly in the sea, trying to keep his head above the rolling waves. "Help me!"

Julian looked at the sky, fearing Stacy might have to compete with a dragon to rescue Mordred, but Falkor seemed to have lost interest in all of them. He was flying back toward the big flying boat and his fellow dragons.

"It's dawn," said Tony the Elf, joining Julian and Dave on the roof. "Dave, start praying." He slapped Julian on the back. "Hell of a way to start the morning, eh?"

This seemed like an odd time for Tony the Elf to suddenly become friendly. Maybe he didn't have a clear understanding of what just happened.

Julian kept his eyes on Stacy. "Mayor Merriweather just got eaten by a dragon."

"Yeah, I saw that."

"You don't sound too upset."

"Are you kidding?" said Tony the Elf. "I'm ecstatic!"

"What the hell did Mayor Merriweather ever do to you?"

"I don't give a shit about Mayor Merriweather, or this town, or dragons, or any of this shit." He grabbed Julian by the arm and shook him enthusiastically. "We've got the magic dice, and we've got Mordred. He identified himself!"

"We don't have Mordred yet," said Julian. "Should we help her?"

"How good a swimmer are you?"

"I spent a summer as a lifeguard when I was in high school."

Tony the Elf let out one of those sighs that made him seem like the Tony the Elf that Julian was more familiar with. "I mean your character. How many ranks in the Swim skill do you have?"

"None that I know of."

"Swim is a Strength-based skill. What's your Strength score?"

"Not great."

"Then you'll just be one more drowning asshole that she has to haul back to shore."

Julian wanted very much to test his Strength score by throwing Tony the Elf off the side of the building.

Stacy, meanwhile, had reached Mordred, and was beginning the slow process of swimming him back to the nearest pier. It took a long time, but Julian and Tony the Elf were waiting to relieve Stacy of her burden when she arrived.

"Sit on him," said Tony the Elf. "Pin his arms down."

Julian sat on Mordred and held his wrists firmly.

After some initial coughing and gasping, Mordred looked up at Julian. He'd lost his eye patch at sea, and the vacant space in his ocular cavity was very disconcerting to look at. "Thank you for –"

"And don't let him talk!" said Tony the Elf.

Julian didn't know how to keep Mordred from talking, as he was all out of limbs.

"Thank you for –"

Julian spat in his face. It was all he could think of.

"Ew! Stop that. What are you hrmfrmfhng!" Whatever he'd meant to say was muffled by Tony the Elf's socks in his mouth.

"Okay, get off him."

Julian stood up.

Tony the Elf pulled Mordred up and quickly tied his hands behind his back with some rope he'd found on the pier. "As long as he can neither speak nor move his hands, he shouldn't be able to cast any spells."

"You stupid piece of shit," said Stacy. Julian was relieved to see that she was, in fact, speaking to Mordred. "I want you to take a good, hard look at this."

She grabbed Julian by the back of the neck and smooshed his face against hers. Her tongue wagged around in his mouth like an octopus looking for its keys in the dark. It was one of the least passionate kisses Julian had ever experienced. To further her point, she grabbed Julian's wrist and clapped his hand over her tit, which he found about as erotic as slapping a colostomy bag.

When Stacy was done using Julian like a RealDoll, she shoved him aside and got up in Mordred's face. "Let's get this one thing straight. You and me? Never. Gonna. Happen." She turned her back on him, thought for a moment, turned back around, and belted Mordred squarely in the nose. His body went limp. He only remained standing because Tony the Elf was holding him up.

"So," said Julian. "That just happened."

"Mordred and I had a little talk on the way back," Stacy explained. "We're all good now. Where's Dave?"

Stacy slung Mordred's unconscious body over her shoulder as they walked back to the Merriweather Inn, where Dave had just finished praying in the lobby.

"We should get back to the Whore's Head," said Tony the Elf. "At the speed that big boat is flying, we should be able to beat it to Cardinia if we travel by horse. We can get Mordred to send us back home before all hell breaks loose in the —"

"Help me!" said an old man's raspy voice at the entrance of the inn.

"Jesus Christ!" cried Dave.

"Mayor Merriweather?" said Julian. He wouldn't have recognized the old man if not for the tattered remains of his robe. His body was covered in blood, gore, and what appeared to be chemical burns.

Stacy dropped Mordred on the floor and shoved a chair across the floor toward the mayor. "Sit down. Dave, get over here!"

Dave placed a finger on the least sticky part of the mayor's naked body. "I heal thee!"

Mayor Merriweather groaned. The blood and gore remained, but the burns faded.

"I heal thee!" Dave said a second time, and the burns faded even more. He repeated the incantation until the burns disappeared completely. "You've sure got a lot of Hit Points."

Mayor Merriweather looked down at his erection. "It's been a while, old friend."

"What happened?" asked Stacy. "How are you still alive?"

The mayor smiled up at her. "I'll give you a little bit of the wisdom my mother passed down to me. Always chew your food before you swallow. That goes double if you're eating a weretiger."

Tears rolled down Stacy's face as she laughed.

Tony the Elf tapped his foot impatiently. "Guys. We really need to be on our way."

"You folks saved my inn," said Mayor Merriweather. "I can't let you leave here empty handed."

"Thank you," said Tony the Elf. "But that really isn't —"

"Wait right here," said the mayor. He walked down the hall and into a room, and closed the door behind him.

"Let's get out of here," Tony the Elf whispered.

Stacy glared at him. "Don't be rude. He wants to thank us. And who knows? He might give us something cool."

"Old people don't give cool things," said Ton the Elf. "He's going to give us a box of raisins or expired coupons for a casino buffet."

"You're kind of an asshole."

"The only thing I'm interested in walking out of here with is tied up and sleeping on the – "

"Over the years," said Mayor Merriweather, returning with a fresh robe and carrying a small wooden chest. "I've acquired a collection of special objects that I seldom have occasion to use."

"*Special* objects?" said Tony the Elf, suddenly seeming less in a hurry to leave.

Mayor Merriweather placed the chest atop the bar and opened the lid. He pulled out a folded grey cloth and placed it on the bar in front of Stacy.

"You move with the grace of a cat, your footsteps as quiet as falling snow. This is for you."

Stacy unfolded the cloth and held it up. It was a plain, grey cloak. "Wow. Thank you. It's beautiful."

Tony the Elf smirked as Stacy tried to mask her disappointment. He'd been right. This senile old man was giving them shit he found lying around his bedroom.

"Pussy scented dwarf!" said the mayor.

"Dave's fine," said Dave.

"You are sturdy and immobile."

"Um… Thanks?"

The mayor pulled a flat iron bar out of the box and placed it before Dave. "Take this rod and use it wisely."

"Awesome."

"Elven Ranger," said the mayor, looking at Tony the Elf. "It's a dangerous world out there. Face it in good health." He pulled out a medallion on a thick gold chain. The image of a lion's head was engraved on the front.

"Super," said Tony the Elf. "I shall take this, and forever pity fools."

Stacy glared at him.

"And last, but certainly not least," said the mayor, "the mighty sorcerer."

Julian could only assume he was talking about him. "That's kind of a stretch."

As you grow more powerful in your art, you will often find yourself the preferred target of your enemies, who rightfully fear you."

"Oh?"

"Choose the time to make your presence known." Mayor Merriweather placed an unadorned silver ring on the bar in front of Julian.

"That's nice," said Julian, slipping the ring on his finger. He smiled politely. "Simple. Elegant. Thank you very much."

"The command word is 'fade'."

"Fade?"

"Whoa!" said Dave.

"Julian?" said Stacy. She was looking right at him, but she looked confused, and her eyes didn't seem to be focused on him.

Julian looked down at his new ring, only to find it missing, along with his finger, hand, and arm. "What the hell is going on? Where am I?"

"Calm down, boy!" said Mayor Merriweather. "It's just a simple Ring of Invisibility."

"For real? Sweet!" Julian brushed Stacy's arm with the tips of his fingers. She yelped and shivered like she was covered in spiders. "This is the coolest thing ever!"

"Perhaps you're not as powerful a sorcerer as I was led to believe," said the mayor. "Don't worry. You'll get there."

"Hold on," said Tony the Elf. "Is all this stuff magical?"

"Of course," the mayor said with a gleam in his eye. "Did you think I just collected some random junk from my bedchamber?"

Tony the Elf put on his new gold chain, making him look like a first level rapper. "What does mine do? I don't feel any different."

"That is an Amulet of Health," said the mayor.

"So what? It gives me a Constitution bonus?"

Mayor Merriweather furrowed his brow. "I suppose that's one way of saying it."

Stacy slapped Julian's invisible hand when he touched her arm again, then put on her cloak. "How do I look?"

"Amazing," said Julian.

Stacy smiled. "Thank you!"

"No, I mean I can barely see you at all, except for your face and feet."

Stacy's cloak had taken on the colors of the bar, like a chameleon, making her difficult to focus on. She wasn't straight up invisible like Julian, but as long as she stood still, she was pretty close.

"That is a *Cloak of Elvenkind*," said Mayor Merriweather. "Elves are a race known for their grace and subtlety."

"WoooOOOoooOOO!" said Julian, lifting Dave's helmet from his head with invisible hands and making it seem to hover in the air. "Ghost helmet! WoooOOOoooOOO!"

"Of course," the mayor continued, "That's a generalization."

Dave snatched his helmet from Julian's hands and put it back on his head. "What's this thing?" he asked, picking up his flat iron bar.

Mayor Merriweather smiled. "That's an Immovable Rod."

"Not really," said Dave, waving the bar around.

"There's small button on the side. Give it a push."

Dave pushed the button, and the hand holding the bar seemed to become stuck where it was. When he let go of the bar, it hung in midair. Julian had seen a lot of strange stuff during his time in this world, but for some reason, he found this the most unnatural.

Dave pushed on the rod until his feet started slipping backwards, but the rod didn't budge.

Julian slipped off his ring and became visible again. "That's incredible." He gripped the rod with both hands and tried to yank it out of the air. It was as solid as a brick wall. "What is it for?"

"It's applications are limited only by your imagination," said the mayor. "Use it as a step to reach an apple just out of reach. Use it to anchor your horse while you take a nap. As a last resort, you could even use it to block a door while you make an escape. I've been using it to hang my winter coat."

Julian pushed the button on the side of the rod, and it succumbed once again to the force of gravity. He handed it to Dave.

"This is all very generous," said Stacy. "But really, it's too much."

"Nonsense!" said the mayor. "You saved my inn. I can't thank you enough."

"We really need to head out," said Tony the Elf.

Julian nodded. If Ravenus had escaped, he'd most likely made a beeline for the Whore's Head Inn.

Stacy picked up Mordred, and they all thanked Mayor Merriweather one last time.

"Fare thee well, strangers," said the mayor, standing at the entrance of the Merriweather Inn as they walked up the main pier. "Should you ever come back to Port Town, you'll never want for a place to rest."

When they reached actual land, Julian summoned five horses. After assisting Dave onto his horse, Julian, Stacy, and Tony the Elf worked together to secure Mordred's still-unconscious body onto one of the other horses. They needed him alive, but not necessarily comfortable. And they needed to work fast, so they could get as far ahead of the Phantom Pinas as possible before the horses timed out. When they were finished, Mordred lay face-down across the saddle in a tangle of ropes binding his hands and feet, and looped several times under the horse's belly, around Mordred's underarms and shoulders, and tied off on the saddlehorn.

Satisfied that Mordred was secure, they mounted and rode full-throttle toward Cardinia. Dave the dog followed enthusiastically.

After just a few minutes of riding, their path was blocked by the enormous dead body of Falkor, the red dragon. Julian would have loved to hang out for a while and take a closer look at an actual dragon, but Tony the Elf, who was leading the way, didn't even slow down. He jumped his horse over the dragon's neck and continued galloping northward.

The next obstacle they came to was not so easily ignored. Tony the Elf reined his horse to a halt once they were in sight of the crossroads. Pouring out from the eastbound road onto the main road were hundreds and hundreds of orcs.

Chapter 35

Randy led his band of the king's ex-prisoners to the Whore's Head Inn. The twelve men had taken to calling themselves his disciples, which Randy was not at all comfortable with, but he believed their motivations were pure.

Loud, cheerful music greeted them as they bypassed the front door and walked around the inn to the gap in the wall. Two bards, one with a fiddle and the other with a set of pipes, played their instruments fervently near the door leading down to the cellar.

The mood of the patrons didn't seem to match the jolly tune in the air. There was no singing or dancing. Most everyone was sitting at tables, listlessly nursing their beers.

"Tough crowd!" Randy shouted over the music.

Frank looked up from his seat on the bar. "Randy!" His gaze darted to the musicians, then back at Randy.

He hopped down and walked briskly toward Randy. They met at a table in the center of the dining area.

"Who are these men?" asked Frank. Even at the same table, Frank had to raise his voice to be heard over the music.

"They're just some... friends." Randy scanned the room. Everyone was staring at him and the twelve strangers he'd just brought into the place. Did they think... *Oh no!* Best get that clear straight away. "This ain't, like, an orgy or nothin', if that's what you're thinking."

Frank grimaced. "That had not even begun to cross my mind."

Something was odd though. Randy couldn't shake the feeling that something wasn't quite right. Then it hit him. "Where's Denise?"

"Randy, listen." Frank's tone suggested that Randy wasn't going to like what he had to say.

"Stop the music."

"Just hear me out."

Randy turned to the musicians. "Stop the music!"

The two bards glanced nervously at each other, but continued to play.

"Randy," said Frank. "Just give me a minute to explain."

Randy stared coldly at Frank. "Rutger. Tobin. Please stop the music."

"Right away, teacher."

Two scrawny bards wouldn't put up too much resistance against Randy's two largest 'disciples'.

The music stopped suddenly and was replaced by Denise's muffled shouting.

"I said *wake up*, motherfucker! I'll break every goddamn finger you got!"

"No!" said Randy, running to the cellar door. He kicked it as hard as he could, but it didn't budge. Trying the handle, he found it to be unlocked. "Denise!"

"Aw shit," said Denise. "You stay outta here, Randy!"

Randy took the stairs three at a time. What he found at the bottom was a grisly sight.

Denise's knuckles were swollen and bloodied, but not half so much as the little halfling's face.

Wister was still tied to the chair, still unconscious. Fresh blood dribbled out over crusted dry blood from his nose and mouth. His right eye was purple and swollen shut, and his left eye wasn't much better.

"I'm sorry, Randy," said Denise, backing up against the wall. "We put this to a vote. You need to respect the democratic pro—"

Randy punched her as hard as he could in the face, relishing the crunch of her nose. He resisted the urge to heal Wister right then and there. These people had to see what they had allowed to happen.

He picked up Wister, still tied to the chair, and walked him up the stairs. He was met with gasps and averted eyes when he pushed open the cellar door.

"I know this looks bad," said Frank.

"It *is* bad," said Randy.

"We want to go home. You're not thinking straight because you're a paladin. The game has given you a rigid set of morals."

"I don't need to be no paladin to see this is wrong," said Randy. He pointed at Wister. "Last I checked, that's still a human being, and this is still America!"

"Actually, neither of those things you just said is true."

Randy spoke louder, addressing the whole inn. "Y'all know you done wrong. And I *know* you know you done wrong, on account of you had them two bards playing outside the door so you didn't have to hear this little guy getting the shit beat out of him."

He placed his hand on Wister's feverish, sweaty forehead. "In Jesus Christ's name, I heal you." Wister's head cooled as the swelling subsided from his eyes. Within seconds, he was perfectly healthy, but still unconscious.

"I can't let you cut him loose," said Frank.

"I don't intend to cut him loose," said Randy. "I'll give him a proper interrogation when we return."

"We who? And return from where?"

"There's still the matter of your atonement. The Lord has provided an opportunity for all of you to clear your souls."

The mood of the inn lightened as a murmur of light laughter spread through the crowd.

Frank smirked. "What, do we have to say ten Hail Marys?"

"No," said Randy. "You need to fight. The city is about to get besieged by orcs, and the king's army ain't big enough to fend them off. I've volunteered us to help defend the city."

The murmur of the crowd rose, but no longer had any trace of laughter.

"You did *what?*" said Frank.

"It's time to stop pretending. We get to be heroes for *real!*"

"Are you out of your goddamn mind?" asked Frank. "There's no way we're going to risk our lives to defend some imaginary city."

Randy nodded. "I reckoned you might say that. You should know that failure to show up will be regarded as an act of treason, and I will be compelled to report you."

From the look in Frank's eyes, Randy could tell that he both believed him and understood the gravity of being arrested for treason.

"Randy," Frank pleaded. He gestured at the silent crowd. "A lot of these folks have families they need to get home to."

"And what about the people of this city?" demanded Randy. "You think they don't have spouses and kids, or eggs, or larva, or whatever?"

"This is a game, Randy. None of this is real. What happens here doesn't matter."

"It's gonna matter when this city is overrun with orcs, and Timmon Bloodsoul shows up with his magic penis."

Wettle cleared his throat. "It's the Phantom Pinas."

"We're so close," said Frank. "We've got the dice. We've got Mordred. Don't ask us to die in this game."

"We don't know that's Mordred," said Randy. "And now that you done beat him into a coma, it may be a while before we is able to find out for sure. In the meantime we still need a place to live. And from what I gather, this Timmon Bloodsoul ain't coming to establish no change in government. He's coming to kill us all."

"Then we can flee north."

Stuart, the bald man who was familiar with the *Dragonlance* books, stepped forward. "I don't think that's Mordred," he said, looking at Wister.

"What are you talking about?" said Frank. "*You* were the one who was so adamant about him being Mordred before. *You* convinced us!"

"And now I'm not so sure."

"What about the *Red Robes of Neutrality*?"

"I'm not saying it's definitely not him."

"Then what *are* you saying?"

"I know the legend of Timmon Bloodsoul and the Phantom Pinas," said Stuart. "I don't know how I know it. Must be a Local Knowledge check or something. But Randy's right about this guy being bad news."

"So what's that got to do with the halfling tied to the chair?"

"Do you really think it's a coincidence that one of the biggest bads in the world is headed our way, out of the blue, right after Mordred showed up? The king thinks he's coming for him, but if Mordred's pulling the strings, I've got a hunch he's actually coming for us."

Frank folded his arms. "So what do you propose we do?"

"If we're going to have to square off with Timmon Bloodsoul, I'd rather do it with the king's army backing us up."

Frank frowned. "It's just as well, I suppose. Randy here hasn't left us much choice in the matter."

"What do we do with him?" asked Stuart, nodding down at Wister.

Frank glanced up at Randy, then looked away, like he was having thoughts he'd prefer Randy wasn't privy to. "You really don't think this is Mordred?"

Stuart shrugged. "I honestly don't know."

"Then we should hold on to him for the time being, if that's okay with the paladin." Frank looked up at Randy.

Randy nodded. "For the time being." He picked up Wister by the chair and started down the steps.

"Some of you guys come and help me lug all the weapons crates out of the cellar," said Frank. He and a few others followed Randy down the stairs.

Having placed Wister as comfortably as possible in the corner, Randy nudged Denise with his foot. "Come on, you. Wake up. It's time to go."

Denise groaned as her eyes opened.

"What the hell happened to her?" asked Frank. "She looks like her face got hit by a truck. Did you do that to her?"

"I did." It only now occurred to Randy how bad the scene looked.

"What kind of paladin punches a woman in the face?"

"I deserved it!" said Denise. "I... I talked back to him."

"Denise!" Randy knew that Denise only blurted out the first thing that popped into her head to cut off Randy from exposing her secret, but why did the first thing to pop into her head have to make him look like some kind of habitual domestic abuser?

Frank shook his head. "I don't even know what to say."

"This ain't how it looks," said Randy. He wanted so badly to tell everyone the truth, that Dennis was not only a man, but a dirty cop, an attempted child rapist, and to point out that he'd just admitted to thinking talking back to a man was justification for hitting a woman. But he'd made a promise to keep Denise's secret, and he was compelled to honor that promise. He'd have to diffuse this situation by some other means. He reached down to lay his hand on Denise's head.

"Don't you touch her!" said the big girl, Rhonda.

Randy jerked his hand away and backed off as Rhonda rushed forward to help Denise to her feet.

"I was just gonna heal her."

"She's had enough of your *healing*. You're never going to touch her again." Rhonda escorted Denise up the stairs. Denise, for her part, said nothing in Randy's defense.

Gus, the gay half-orc who Randy had been itching to have a long conversation with now that he was out of the closet, shook his head at him as he picked up a crate full of pieces of armor. As he and the others hauled crates up the stairs, Frank took Randy aside.

"There's something you're not telling me, isn't there?" said Frank.

"What makes you think that?" said Randy.

"You're not the brightest bulb on the Christmas tree."

"Thank you?"

Frank smiled. "But I don't think you're a bad person."

"You don't even know me."

"I don't have to. You punched Denise in the face before you healed the halfling."

"That is correct." Randy didn't know where Frank was going with this.

"Something doesn't add up," said Frank. "Paladins are held to a strict moral standard. If you willingly commit an evil act, such as punching a woman in the face for talking back to you, you should have been immediately stripped of your healing powers."

"That makes sense."

"I'll respect your privacy on the specifics, but just tell me this. There's more to you and Denise than meets the eye, isn't there?"

Randy nodded. "There is."

"You're not the most popular guy at the Whore's Head Inn right now."

"I recognize that."

"Maybe, for your own safety, it's best that we travel separately to South Gate."

That sounded a lot like a threat, but Randy gave Frank the benefit of the doubt and took it as genuine concern for his wellbeing. "I won't leave you alone with Wister."

"I understand that," said Frank. "I'll lead our people out first, then you come along in a little while with your new friends."

Randy nodded and sat down on the floor.

Frank patted him on the shoulder. "See you at South Gate." He hopped up the stairs and closed the door behind him.

Randy sat in silent contemplation. His *disciples* weren't friends. They were nice enough folks, but they revered him without even knowing him. The closest thing he'd had to actual friends were the folks at the Whore's Head Inn, and now they all thought of him as some sanctimonious piece of wife-beating white trash who was sending them off to face certain death.

He waited until the bustle of people donning their armor and readying their weapons died down, then trudged up the stairs to meet his disciples.

Chapter 36

In exchange for some intentionally vague promises, Tim had managed to score himself two big bags full of Arby's roast beef sandwiches and curly fries. He'd even pilfered a bottle of ketchup and a bottle of Arby's Sauce from off a tabletop.

He was out of booze and out of money, but otherwise feeling pretty good. His head beginning to clear, the thought about what Randy and Dave had told him in the car on the way to the Beauregard Casino, and what Cooper had told him in the bar two nights ago.

There was no point denying it anymore. Tim was a fuckup, and the only person who could change that was him. He'd start with a peace offering of roast beef sandwiches and curly fries to the people of the Whore's Head Inn. They were a forgiving bunch, and nobody could resist Arby's.

The streets were damn near deserted as Tim hugged his two Arby's bags and walked briskly toward the Collapsed Sewer District.

Approaching from the rear, Tim first noticed that the trunk of the piss tree was bone dry.

"Nobody thought to water you today? Hang in there, buddy. I'll be back before you know it."

The next thing he noticed was how quiet the Whore's Head Inn was. No low murmur of conversation. No clink of glasses. Nothing. It was eerily quiet, as if everyone was waiting for Tim to step inside before they shouted "SURPRISE!", or murdered him or something.

He briefly considered arming himself, but decided against it. This was a peace offering, after all.

"Hello?" he called inside. There was no answer. That was weird. This place was never empty. "Don't kill me. I've got Arby's." He stepped in through the gap in the wall. Not another living soul in sight. "Where the fuck is everybody?"

It was getting late in the evening, when everyone was usually coming back from their various assigned tasks and money-making jobs. This place should be hopping right now. Judging by some strewn articles of clothing, upturned supply crates, and the amount of unfinished beer glasses on the tables, Tim guessed there had been a sudden evacuation sometime in the early afternoon, but what could have prompted that, unless...

"Those motherfuckers. They did it."

Tim was both giddy and nervous at the same time. He calmed his nerves with the aid of an unattended glass of beer. He tried to think of other possible explanations for everyone to just up and leave the Whore's Head Inn all at once, but couldn't come up with any. There was only one possible explanation. They'd found Mordred, and forced him to send them home.

A wave of panic washed over Tim as he munched on a curly fry. Had he missed the bus? Had he gotten left behind? He shook the thought out of his head. They wouldn't do that to him. He'd been kind of an asshole lately, but not that big of an asshole. They were good people. They would have thought up some kind of contingency plan for those who weren't currently at the inn.

And that's another thing. He wasn't the only one who wasn't here when everyone left. He knew for a fact that Cooper wasn't in the city. And Dave, Julian, and Stacy were out on some fishing trip. Even if they'd leave Tim behind, they wouldn't leave Julian and Stacy. Everybody liked Julian and Stacy. All he had to do was to hang around and wait for the next bus.

Tim couldn't wait to meet Stacy again on the other side. The first things he'd do when he got back would be shave, take a shower, and put on some nice clothes. Not too nice. Keep it casual. He'd ask her to... The Olive Garden. Perfect. The one in D'Iberville. Casual, ironic, and it wouldn't put her on the spot about it being a *date* date. It would just be two friends sharing a meal and a common memory after coming through a – "What the fuck was that?"

Tim scooted his chair back. Wooden chair leg scraping against wooden floor. The same as the sound he'd just heard, but it was coming from the cellar. It appeared that he wasn't here alone after all.

Tim armed himself with a dagger in one hand and a roast beef sandwich in the other, giving him some options as to how he could face whoever was in the cellar.

As quietly as he could, he tiptoed to the cellar door and pulled it open slowly. He didn't know why he was bothering to be so quiet, as he knew all along what his next move was going to be.

"Hello?"

There was no answer except for more frantic scooting of chair legs on the floor. Were there more than one person down there? Maybe a poker game? Why weren't they answering him? "Who's down there?"

Still no answer. Just more scooting. That was weird. Tim abandoned his original intention to keep his dagger hidden until he knew he needed it, and held it out in front of him. He kept the roast beef sandwich ready, and held out hope that he'd be able to offer that instead.

"I'm coming down there," Tim called down the stairs. "And I'm prepared to defend myself."

He focused entirely on his Move Silently skill. Whoever was down there knew he was coming. Announcing that, in retrospect, had possibly been an error in judgement. But he could still get the jump on them if they didn't know exactly when he was going to show himself.

As Tim crept slowly down the stairs, he imagined he'd get a bonus modifier to his Move Silently check because the continued scooting of chairs on the floor would help to mask what little sound he was making.

Maybe it would be better to hold his dagger by the blade, ready to throw it. He might be able to get in a Sneak Attack from a distance. No, that was a stupid idea. If whatever was down there was hostile, and he didn't kill it with that first strike, he'd be armed with nothing but a roast beef sandwich.

Then again, the crate where they kept the daggers was pretty close to the bottom of the staircase. Jump. Throw. Roll. Grab another weapon. Tim grinned to himself. Some Rambo/James Bond shit was about to go down. He twirled the dagger in his fingers until he was holding it by the blade.

At the bottom of the stairs, Tim took deep breaths to steady his nerves.

Three… Two… "Surprise, motherfucker!" Tim jumped out into the open, spotted a target, and let his dagger fly.

A halfling, bound to a chair and gagged, stared back at him in wide-eyed terror as the dagger thudded into the wall right next to his head.

"Un-fucking-believable," said Tim. "I missed a stationary target? Hang on… Who the fuck are you?"

As far as good times to make shitty attack rolls, this was probably one of the best. He might have killed that poor little fucker, who looked like he was already having a pretty rough day. As Tim looked around, he noticed another gaping flaw in his plan. The crates full of weapons were all gone. The cellar was empty except for the captive halfling and the big wooden dildo-stake.

"I'm sorry, dude," said Tim. He pulled his dagger out of the wall. "Stop squirming so I can help you."

The halfling sat rigidly still as Tim cut the bandana tied around his head, then spat out a second wad of fabric that had been stuffed into his mouth. "Thank you!"

"What are you doing down here? Who did this to you?"

"I was taken prisoner by a female dwarf."

"Dennis," said Tim. "That fucking douche." He looked down at the dildo on the floor. "Did he… I mean *she… touch* you?"

"*Touch* me?" said the halfling. "She did a lot more than that!"

Tim held up his hands. "Oh Jesus, stop. I don't even want to know." The story began to play out in his mind. Everybody goes home, but Dennis chooses to stay. He can do whatever the fuck he wants in this world, more or less free of consequences. As soon as they're all gone, he wastes no time setting up his own little gimp-cellar. Motherfucker was probably out there right now trying to kidnap another halfling – or worse, an actual child – for his collection. That sick, sadistic fuck.

"Please let me out of here before she comes back."

"You bet." Tim started cutting away at the ropes. "You get as far away from here as you can. I'll take care of that dwarf bitch. You'll never have to worry about her again."

The grateful halfling stretched out his limbs and massaged his wrists. "Thanks, Tim."

"Don't mention it," said Tim. He held up his roast beef sandwich. "Do you want a sandwich?"

The halfling stared perplexedly at the sandwich.

Tim grinned. Of course this poor bastard didn't recognize it. He probably didn't even know what a sandwich was. The tinfoil wrapper surely didn't make it any clearer. He unwrapped the sandwich and offered it again. "It's food. You eat it. Delicious. Yum yum."

"I... Where did you..." The halfling's growling stomach stopped his train of half-asked questions. "Thank you." He took the sandwich and ripped away a quarter of it with one bite.

"Pretty good, huh?"

"Delicious," said the halfling. "Yum yum." He took another bite.

"I've got some curly fries upstairs if you want to try those as well."

The halfling looked down at the chair and dildo. "I really should be going. This has all been very traumatic."

"I understand. You take care of yourself. I'm really sorry this happened."

Tim escorted the halfling up the stairs and out of the building through the gap in the wall.

He was kind of a hero. He'd just rescued another person from a life of captivity and abuse from a sick asshole. The only feeling more satisfying than that would be seeing the look on that nutless fucker's face when he came back and found his gimp had been set free.

The only question left then would be whether he should just kill her straight away, or get medieval on her ass. Tim didn't think long on that one. He didn't have the stomach for torture. He'd just straight-up kill her.

This was the first step in Tim turning his life around, and it felt good. He helped himself to another abandoned beer and a roast beef sandwich.

Chapter 37

Randy stared out the window of the top floor of the right hand tower of South Gate. He and Professor Goosewaddle were there by the King's request. Occasionally, one of the residents of the Whore's Head would glare up at him from the rampart.

"Lower the gate," said the king. His voice was low and grim, but resolute.

"Brother, you can't," said Desmond. "There are still refugees coming from Port Town. Women and children, Winston."

"That's exactly what the orcs are counting on. They mean to exploit my merciful reputation. My scouts reported that the orcs aren't advancing up the road. They're staying under the cover of the forest on either side. Any minute now, they'll start pouring out of the forest as near as they can to the wall, and we won't have time to lower the portcullis. If they take control of the gate towers, the city is as good as lost."

"That's no army, brother. It's a mob. We have wizards and sorcerers on the walls. A few well-placed fireballs will scatter those orcs like the cockroaches they are."

"Has your vision failed you? Or have you just not noticed the giant flying boat sailing this way? The one flanked by three red dragons?

There's a six hundred-year-old lich at the helm seeking to end our bloodline. We can't waste spells on orcs."

The king turned to the guards manning the gate crank, who appeared to be stalling until the argument was settled. "Your king gave you an order. Lower the gate!"

It took three soldiers to push the shafts sticking out of a central axle which fed the heavy iron chain connected to the top of the gate. They each gripped their shafts and started pushing counter-clockwise.

As the gate started lowering, Randy gripped the stone ledge and leaned forward. The nearest refugees sprinted to beat the closing gate, in many cases discarding belongings they had deemed important enough to travel for miles with. Sadly, the ones with children seemed to be lagging the farthest behind. They weren't going to make it. Randy had never felt so helpless. He wanted to plead with the king to keep the gate open a little longer, but if his own brother couldn't convince him, Randy surely wouldn't be able to either. Besides, Randy knew the king was only looking out for the people already within the city walls. The responsibility to make decisions like this was something Randy was grateful he'd never have.

Desmond, the king's brother, morphed into a golden eagle and flew out of the south window. Randy was mildly curious about where he might be flying off to, but his attention was drawn to Professor Goosewaddle, staring gravely southward, not at Desmond or the doomed refugees, but at the approaching boat.

Part of why Randy liked the professor was that he never seemed to take things too seriously, like he'd lived long enough to brush off as trifles what younger folks often viewed as tragedies, always maintaining a sunny and cheerful disposition.

That wasn't how he looked now. The professor looked old, tired, and even a little scared.

"Something on your mind, Professor?" asked Randy. He knew it was a stupid question, but he had to break the tension.

"Dragons," said Professor Goosewaddle, not taking his eyes away from the flying boat.

"They pretty badass?"

"They are extremely powerful, and vastly intelligent. But they are mortal. Put enough arrows in them, and they'll drop out of the sky."

That sounded good to Randy. He frowned. "I feel like there's a *but* coming."

"But they're also selfish and fiercely independent. It's rare to see two red dragons of that size working together. Seeing three seemingly subservient to one master makes me wonder if all the arrows and spells in the world would be enough to fell that ship."

Desmond was returning, gripping a screaming toddler by the arms in his gold talons. Randy and Professor Goosewaddle stepped to the side to let him in.

"Have you lost your mind?" said the king. "I can't fight a war with this noise!"

Desmond took his human form. "I thought, since you were about to make him an orphan, you'd be best suited to raise him." Without waiting for a response, he turned back into an eagle and flew out of the window again. Parents were raising their children above their heads, trying to get his attention.

"Desmond, come back!" the king shouted over the wails of the child. "Gods have mercy. Somebody take this child downstairs!"

"As you command, Your Majesty," said one of the three guards manning the gate crank. Randy suspected he was just happy for an excuse to get the hell out of there.

With the gate now completely lowered, a crowd of refugees was pooling at the base of the wall, all shouting to be let in.

"Fire!" shouted a soldier on the rampart to Randy's right.

As the king had predicted, orcs had begun to charge out of the forest where it was nearest the wall. They were met with a barrage of arrows, dropping a few of them instantly. But for the majority of them, a single arrow wasn't enough to take them down. Orcs poured out of the forest faster than the archers could kill them.

"Fire!" An identical situation broke loose to Randy's left.

Dead orc bodies were piling up along the base of the wall, but they were dropping closer and closer to the huddling refugees, and the torrent of orcs flowing out of the forest showed no signs of letting up. The night air was alive with the twangs of bowstrings, orcish battle cries, the screams of terrified refugees... and the pounding of heavy boots racing urgently up the stairs.

"Your Majesty!" said a high ranking soldier, judging by the quality of his armor.

The king winced. "What is it now?"

"North Gate has been breached."

"They're attacking from the north, too? How did they get in?"

"Not *in*, Your Majesty. The breach was from the inside. They got *out*."

The king balled up his fists. "That pigheaded bastard! He had one job! Do nothing. How hard is that?"

"Who?" said Desmond, who had returned with a little half-elven girl. "What happened?"

"Balharr, my most cunning general, has taken it upon himself to disobey a direct order. That's treason. I'll have his pig head on a pike!"

"Calm down, brother," said Desmond. "This is partially your fault for keeping him penned up when there's a war to be fought. You denied him his purpose. He only wants to serve you. That's not treason."

The news-bearing soldier cleared his throat. "There's more, Your Majesty. They wear tunics identical to the enemy's." He lowered his eyes. "Complete with the Bloodfist of Meb' Garshur."

Randy knew what the receiving end of betrayal looked like, and that's what he saw in the king's tired eyes. He'd been frustrated and madder than hell just a second ago, but now he was heartbroken.

"There must be some mistake," said Desmond. "Balharr is a good man, Winston. He wouldn't do this."

The king looked down at the scared half-elven girl hiding behind Desmond's leg. "This is a disaster. I've failed my people in every conceivable way. Go, Desmond. Save what children you can."

"Excuse me," said Randy. "I'm sorry to interrupt. But if Balharr was gonna betray you, why would he sneak out the back? Why wouldn't he just march his orcs up here, chuck all us out the window, and force the gate open?"

The king furrowed his brow and pursed his lips. "That is an excellent question."

"Steady on, men!" cried the soldier giving commands on the western side of the south rampart. "They're falling back!"

Randy poked his head out of the window. Sure enough, the torrent of orcs pouring out of the forest had slowed to a trickle, each one getting three or four arrows in the chest as soon as he cleared the trees.

As the screaming and shouting died down in the immediate vicinity, more distant screaming and shouting could be heard coming from the woods. After a moment, orcs began running out of the forest farther away from the wall in every direction. The archers on the wall all looked at each other, collectively shrugged, and started casually picking off orcs as they came within bow range.

"What in the Abyss has gotten into those fool orcs?" said Desmond, having returned with another child.

"Bedlam," said the king, gazing out at the sudden change in the tide of battle. "Complete and utter chaos. I'm afraid I owe Balharr an apology." The cry of a baby brought his attention downward. "Quickly, raise the gate!"

Randy ran to the crank and manned the third shaft himself. Together, he and the two soldiers turned the crank clockwise, and the gate began to rise.

"Your Majesty," said Professor Goosewaddle. "By my estimation, the Phantom Pinas should be within range of your more advanced spellcasters' Fireballs."

The king joined the professor at the window. "Can you hit it from this range?"

"I believe I can, Your Majesty."

"Then fire at will."

Professor Goosewaddle rubbed his hands together and licked his lips. He closed his eyes, cupped his hands in front of him, as if cradling an invisible globe, and mumbled some words in a language that Randy didn't even come close to recognizing. When he opened his eyes and hands, a marble-sized, but intensely bright orange sphere hovered in place for a second, then darted away so fast that Randy almost couldn't follow it.

Upon reaching the flying boat, the sphere exploded into a massive, fiery orb, which did little but expose the even more massive invisible orb surrounding the boat. Some sort of force field.

"Just as I feared," said Professor Goosewaddle. "The Pinas is protected."

Randy did not giggle.

But somebody else finally seemed to get the joke. A deep, hollow laugh echoed out from the boat. It was your quintessential "Muhuhahahaha!" evil villain laugh, and it grew louder with each bellowing repetition, drowning out all other sounds, until it abruptly stopped.

The night was dead silent. No one dared breathe. The huddled masses at the gate stopped pushing their way in. Those refugees still on the road stopped in their tracks.

A ray of green light, like the beam of a searchlight, shone out from the front of the boat onto the people frozen in fear, standing in the open gateway. The light scanned west along the base of the wall, shining on the multitude of arrow-riddled orc corpses, which began to twitch and moan.

"Lower the gate," whispered the king. His voice trembled.

Nobody moved.

The green beam locked on the gate again, then scanned along the eastern part of the wall, shining its evil magic on the piles of dead orcs.

"Lower the gods damned gate!"

The bad-news soldier assisted the two others in turning the crank counter-clockwise, but they were far too late.

The crowd at the gate screamed. Those already inside the walls fled deeper into the city. Those on the outside of the walls ran back out onto the road or into the forest. Undead orcs swiped their powerful arms at anyone who got too close, but didn't chase after them. They appeared to have their priorities in order, and those all amounted to securing the open gate.

Archers on either side of the gateway fired their arrows, but they were ineffectual against the undead. When the gate was low enough, two dozen orc zombie hands grabbed the bottom and shook it back and forth until they had pulled it free of the tracks it slid down on and crashed onto the ground. Hundreds of orc zombies flooded into the city.

"Your Majesty," said the bad-news soldier. "It's no longer safe for you here. We must get you to a secure location."

The two soldiers who had been manning the gate crank drew their swords and took defensive positions at the top of the stairs, ready to hack away a path of undead orc if need be.

"Go, Winston," said Desmond. "We'll find a way through this, and your people will need you more than ever."

The king shook his head. "I've done it again. I played right into his hand." He allowed himself to be escorted to the stairs.

Things had gone from bad to not-so-bad to really bad in a very short amount of time. Randy had been trusting the king's wisdom to get them out of this like a person might trust the pilot of an airplane that's clearly headed into a mountain and all the engines are on fire.

He couldn't let the king leave without giving them some kind of guidance. "Um..." he said. "Your Majesty? Is there anything specific you'd like us to do?"

The king looked up at him and smiled sadly, his eyes full of resignation and despair. He shrugged. "Pray?"

Chapter 38

By the time the orcs had finished filing through, Julian's Mount spells had long since expired. Julian, Dave, and Stacy lay low behind some trees and listened to Tony the Elf whine about not being able to get back to the Whore's Head Inn.

"We shouldn't have hung around to take Mayor Merriweather's junk."

"It's called being a decent human being," said Stacy.

Julian slipped his new ring onto his finger. "Fade." He disappeared. "This isn't junk. This stuff is cool."

Tony the Elf rolled his eyes. "You guys are missing the point. I want nothing more than to be a decent human being. That's why I'm trying to get this one-eyed prick back to the Whore's Head Inn, back to the magic dice. We can all go back to being decent human beings. And we're not going to be able to take any of this *cool stuff* with us."

"Julian," said Stacy. "Give me your ring. I want to go on a little scouting expedition. See if I can find out anything."

Julian slipped the ring off his finger and reappeared. He didn't like the sound of Stacy going off alone. This is exactly the way the party kept getting split. If someone was going to get lost, he'd much rather it be Dave or Tony the Elf. "Why you?"

"Because I'm awesome." She'd snatched the ring out of his fingers before he'd seen her hand move. She was a quick one. "Fade."

"Be careful," Julian said to the empty space just above the Stacy-shaped patch of flattened grass.

"Don't worry," said Stacy's disembodied voice as the grass stood up. "I'll be right back."

Dave shook his head. "There goes another one."

"She'll be okay," said Julian. It was more a statement of hope than belief. "She's smart. She's quick. She's quiet."

"She's overconfident," said Tony the Elf. "Maxed out stats aren't going to help her if she tries to take down a bazillion hostile orcs by herself at first level."

Julian looked for some sign of Stacy. Footprints in the grass, frightened grasshoppers jumping away, anything. He saw nothing but the endless procession of orcs. "She's not going to fight them. That's why she brought the Invisible Ring with her."

"Ring of Invisibility," Dave corrected him.

"Whatever."

"I'm just saying, that's what it's called. An invisible ring would be just that. A ring that you couldn't see."

As if Julian didn't have enough on his mind. He was in a quandary about his feelings for Stacy and his loyalty to Tim, Ravenus was still missing, and he was currently weaponless and unprotected near a horde of pissed-off orcs. He didn't need Dave's petty bullshit right now. "Names can carry more weight than just the literal meanings of their component words. You can't just call any cranky farmer a Grim Reaper, can you?"

"You can if you're making a terrible joke."

"You'd know. Okay, what about the Bag of Holding? That could literally describe any bag in existence. That's what a bag does. That's its only purpose. It holds shit."

"So what's your point?"

Julian thought for a moment. It seemed they had both lost track of what this argument was about. *Bag of Holding. Grim Reaper. Word meanings. Invisible ring.* He was back on track. "My point is, if the book had called it an Invisible Ring, you wouldn't be bothered about it."

"And *my* point," said Dave, "is that it's not called an Invisible Ring. It's called a Ring of Invisibility."

"That wasn't your point. Your point was that Invisible Ring would have been an intrinsically inappropriate name, due to the literal meaning of –"

"Jesus Christ!" said Tony the Elf. "Would you two please just shut the fuck up? Is there seriously so little of interest going on around you right now that you feel compelled to bicker about such trite bullshit?"

"That's just what I was trying to get across to Dave," said Julian.

"No, seriously," said Tony the Elf. "Shut the fuck up." He jerked his head to the side. "Listen."

Julian listened, and soon heard what Tony the Elf was hearing.

"Shit. Shit. Shit. Shit. Shit. Shit. Shit." It was Stacy, and she was rapidly getting closer.

Tony the Elf drew his twin machetes and hid behind his tree. He gestured for Julian and Dave to do the same.

Dave grabbed his mace with both hands and crouched down.

Julian, having no weapon, was only able to comply with the second part of the request. He reasoned that whatever Stacy was running from wasn't making enough noise to be the entire orc army. So that was good.

Not wanting to use up any more of his spells until he absolutely needed to, he decided to get creative. He scooped up a handful of dirt, thinking he might be able to temporarily blind an opponent.

"Shit. Shit. Shit. Shit. Shit. Shit. Shit." Stacy ran past, fully visible, and at least three somethings were crashing through the woods behind her. She stopped dead in her tracks and turned around to face them.

Three orcs ran into view, and Tony the Elf drove his twin machetes deep into the slowest one's bare back. It let out a silent scream as it dropped, suggesting that Tony the Elf had punctured both of its lungs.

The fastest orc continued after Stacy, but the one in the middle turned around, seeming to recognize they'd been ambushed.

Julian flung his payload of dirt, but didn't quite reach the confused orc's face. They both watched as dirt trickled down his muscular, scarred chest.

The orc didn't scream a battle cry as he raised his rusty sword, like Julian expected. He merely snarled, which was cut short when Dave bonked him on the head with his mace. He shook it off and followed through with his swing at Julian, but only managed to strip some bark off a tree as Julian ducked behind it.

Tony the Elf brought one machete down hard on the orc's sword arm and plunged his second one into its throat. Blood gurgled out of its neck and down Tony the Elf's arm as the light of life faded from its eyes.

"Stacy!" said Julian, just barely remembering to keep his voice down.

Julian and Tony the Elf ran in the direction the fastest orc had gone. Dave waddled behind them. They found the orc lying dead on the ground, its body hacked into a bloody mess, but there was no trace of Stacy.

Suddenly, she materialized out of thin air with her sword poking the dead orc in the ass. "How about that?" she said, looking at the silver ring on her finger.

"What the hell was that?" said Tony the Elf. "You said you were going on a scouting mission."

Stacy looked up from her ring. "I did. On my way back, I found these four orcs relieving themselves in the woods."

"Four?" asked Dave, noting the body count.

"I killed the first one while he was *watering a tree*, if you take my meaning. So anyway, I thought I'd do my part, you know? I figured they should be pretty easy to take out one by one if they couldn't see me." She held up the hand, displaying the Ring of Invisibility. "Did you know this thing stops working when you attack something?"

"Yes," said Dave and Tony the Elf.

"No," said Julian. "That *is* useful information, though."

Tony the Elf shook his head. "What did I tell you? Overconfidence. You're not going to last long if you keep pulling stunts like that. You're lucky they didn't call the whole goddamn army over here."

"They were too greedy," said Stacy. "As soon as the leader saw me, he shushed his buddies. They wanted the ring."

Julian looked over at the endless column of orcs, then back at Stacy. "Did your scouting mission yield any results?"

Stacy folded her arms and smiled smugly. "As a matter of fact, it did. Just a bit farther ahead, the orcs are branching off to either side of the road and continuing north through the forest. I'm guessing they're trying to get as close to the city as possible without being seen."

"And this is helpful to us *how?*" asked Tony the Elf. He was still using a scolding tone of voice, like he wanted to continue driving home the point that Stacy's little scouting mission had been irresponsible and reckless, yielding no useful results and putting them all in serious danger. He was kind of a dick that way.

"If they're going far enough off into the woods so as not to be seen from the road, then we should be relatively safe from being seen if we can get on the road."

"That's your plan?" said Dave, having finally caught up to the rest of them. "Stand out in the open, surrounded by thousands of orcs?" He and Tony the Elf would make the perfect couple.

"Why not?" said Stacy. "If we're spotted on the road, we can always just summon some horses and outrun them." She looked at Julian. "Do you have enough of those spells left?"

Julian nodded. "If we double up."

"Aside from being suicidally insane," said Tony the Elf, "your brilliant plan made no mention of exactly how you expect us to get to the road from here. Are we supposed to tunnel under the column of orcs?"

Julian wanted to tell Tony the Elf to take it down a notch, but he was more curious about Stacy's response.

"Screw that noise," said Stacy. "They're not walking as densely together in the forest. We'll just go through them." She tapped a finger on the Ring of Invisibility as if it was the most obvious thing in the world.

Julian anticipated Tony the Elf's next question, and fielded it in his place to keep him from being an asshole. "We've got one ring. There are four of us."

"And a prisoner," said Dave.

"And a dog," said Tony the Elf.

Stacy shrugged. "It's true, this is not an ideal situation, but you must know I wouldn't have brought up the idea if I hadn't already figured out a way around the most obvious problem. Give me some credit, guys!"

Tony the Elf smiled. "I can't wait to hear this. How are all of us going to get all of us past all of those orcs without being seen?"

Stacy grinned. "Simple. I'll piggyback you across one by one."

Tony the Elf laughed. "I think that's the best thing I've ever heard."

"If you've got a problem with my plan, spit it out."

"Okay," said Tony the Elf. "Here's a problem. Look at you, and look at Dave. He is a concentrated mass of meat and iron. You try to put him on your back, and he'll snap those little chicken legs of yours like dry spaghetti."

"Someone else underestimated me once." She looked down at the bloody remains of the orc at her feet. "Oh look. There he is now."

Tony the Elf smiled and nodded. "I'll admit to being curious." He looked at Dave. "Go and hop up on there, Big D. Let's see what Little Miss Badass can do."

"Little Miss Badass," Stacy said to herself. "I like that. I may adopt it." She squatted low on the ground. "Come on, Dave. Don't be shy." She shot him a quick glare. "But don't get too frisky either."

"What... I..." Dave stammered.

"I'm just messing with you. Climb aboard, big guy."

Dave climbed onto her back, and it was like watching a Saint Bernard mount a Chihuahua. That is, until she stood up.

No grunt. No strain. Stacy's legs unfolded as easily as if they weren't even supporting her own weight, much less Dave's. Together, Dave and Stacy looked like an old-timey television set turned upside down and walking on its rabbit-ear antennas.

She hopped up and down a few times, just to show off.

"I might be able to take you boys two at a time." After a moment of reflection, she said, "That came out wrong. Forget I said that."

After Tony the Elf agreed to Stacy's plan, on the condition that he was the last one to be ferried to the road, they followed the orcs northwest at a safe distance until the orcs turned north.

"Looks like this is as far from the road as they're going to get," said Stacy. "Who's first? Julian?"

Julian felt like he should at least raise some token objection to having to go first, but he knew he was the obvious choice. He was the lightest, and the one best equipped to escape danger if caught alone. He nodded his consent.

Willing himself not to get an erection, Julian climbed onto Stacy's back. He wrapped his left arm loosely around her neck, so as not to choke her, and gripped her right shoulder. In his right hand, we wielded the sword he'd taken from the orc Stacy had killed.

"Fade", said Stacy, and they both disappeared.

"Good luck," said Dave.

"Be careful," said Tony the Elf. "You're not as much of a badass as you think you are."

Stacy's hair brushed Julian's chin as she turned to face Tony the

Elf. "You guys don't go anywhere. I'll be back before you know it."

Being invisible and carried was like being inside one of those 4D theaters they have in amusement parks, like an incredibly detailed simulation of existence.

Stacy didn't bother trying to be too stealthy, because the orcs were making plenty enough noise to provide cover. They were being particularly loud a little ways north. Julian couldn't make out exactly what was going on, but a group of them appeared to be engaged in combat with something much larger than they were.

"Sweetums," said Stacy.

That was weird. This was hardly the time to be putting him on the spot like that. But in the interest of their safety, Julian played along. "Yes, *Pumpkin?*"

"What? Ew. No no no no no. They're fighting a Sweetums. A big furry monster, like Sweetums from the Muppets. I saw one earlier, while you were zoned out on the carpet." She changed course and started jogging toward the shouts and screams and roars.

After a few steps, Julian had a clearer view of the fight. Half a dozen piles of gore, which presumably used to be orcs, lay in the immediate vicinity of a wounded and enraged owlbear. Twice as many living orcs jabbed at the beast with swords and spears, and even more were gathering behind them.

"Just so you know," Julian whispered. "That's called an owlbear."

"That's a stupid name. I'm calling it Sweetums."

Julian would have argued that, while the concept of the creature itself was a stupid one, the name owlbear was very appropriate. He would have argued that, had he not had more pressing issues to discuss, such as...

"Hey. Why are we running toward the Sweetums?"

"There should be a nice big gap on the other side of the fight. Now keep quiet." Stacy picked up her pace until she was sprinting.

Helpless to do anything else, Julian watched the fight and held his sword ready, hoping he wouldn't have to use it.

One unlucky orc rushed at the owlbear with his spear, missing the creature entirely, and finding himself within grabbing range. The owlbear picked him up with both hands, clamped its beak over his head, and ran its claws down the sides of his body like a cat scratching post made out of meat.

When the owlbear's claws reached down to the orc's leg, it grabbed hold of his calf, tore the head free with its beak, and proceeded to beat back the other orcs with the headless body of their former comrade. The orc flail wasn't a particularly effective weapon, but it did give those orcs nearest the owlbear a healthy coating of blood and gore.

"All right!" Stacy whispered excitedly as her pace slowed back down to a jog. "We did it!"

"Huh?" Julian had been so transfixed by the sight of orc entrails flying around, he hadn't realized that they had successfully breached the orc line. "Oh. Nice job."

"We got lucky with that one." Stacy spoke normally now that they were far enough away from the orcs. "I've still got to do this a few more times, and I won't be able to count on Sweetums as a distraction."

"Now that we're alone," said Julian. "Can I ask you a question?"

"Sure."

"What did Mordred say to you while you were in the sea that got you so riled up?"

Stacy slowed down to a walk and let out a heavy sigh. "He said he created this world just for me, that everyone in it was just another failed attempt at perfection."

"Straight eighteens," said Julian. "The perfect character."

"He said he was saving that character for someone special. Someone who would be his queen. Like I'm supposed to be honored to have been chased into the women's restroom of an Olive Garden. It's just like Tim. Where do these guys get the idea that you can just claim a woman as your territory like a dog pissing on a fence post?"

"Did he say anything about Ravenus?"

Stacy looked like she was about to sigh again but checked it. "No. He didn't mention Ravenus."

"I had to ask."

"I know."

When they came to the edge of the forest, Stacy let go of Julian's legs. Julian became visible as his feet touched the ground.

"Thanks for the lift."

Stacy materialized in front of him, the Ring of Invisibility in her hand. "Don't mention it." She looked back into the forest. "Guess it's time for round two."

"Be careful out there," said Julian. "There's no rush. Take your time, and get back to me in one piece."

Stacy nodded, smiled at Julian, and vanished.

Just like that, Julian was alone, surrounded by orcs on all sides, and who knew whatever other kinds of horrible beasts, any one of which could jump out at any time to tear him apart.

He felt a quick peck on the lips. "I'll be right back."

Chapter 39

The air was warmer than usual, and something sharp was poking Cooper in the head. He opened his eyes to find Ravenus pecking at him.

"Fuck off, bird!" He missed Ravenus as he swatted at his own face.

Looking down at his crotch, he found the Decanter of Endless Water gushing out from between his legs, where he'd placed it when he felt himself getting drowsy.

"Hey Ravenus. Check it out. Looks like I'm getting rid of a Big Gulp."

The water arched out from his crotch into the sea, and onto a group of naked children who were playing and laughing.

"That's kinda fucked up."

"Good morning," said someone behind Cooper.

Cooper tilted his head back until he had an upside-down view of a group of humans and half-elves standing behind him. Their clothes were more brightly colored than what Cooper was used to seeing. They were all armed with long spears or bows, but didn't appear to be hostile. His autopilot system had worked. He was on a beach.

"Which way is Cardinia?" He deactivated the Decanter of Endless Water.

A large human man, wearing nothing but a turquoise linen skirt, his fat, sun-bronzed belly tattooed with symbols that might have been a language, stepped forward. "You're on the wrong side of the sea, mate. You're a mile west of Portsville."

"Portsville? Shit! Hold on... Where the fuck is Portsville?"

The group of beachgoers looked at one another before the skirted man spoke again.

"Your companion tells us you were drifting blindly in your sleep. This is not a good idea. A few degrees in another direction, you might have washed up on the beaches of Meb' Garshur. There you would have been killed for sure. Even here it is not safe to carelessly display possessions of such great value, especially while you sleep. You are fortunate that we did not kill you ourselves, take your belongings, and feed your body to our pigs."

What was Cooper supposed to say to that? "Um... Thank you?"

The fat man shrugged. "You survived by one vote. Maka did not want to kill you in front of the children."

"Thanks, Maka."

A slender half-elven woman with dark hair, wearing a near-translucent matching purple skirt and shawl, and an emerald navel ring, bowed her head gracefully.

Cooper made a mental note to send Ravenus on a little scouting mission once they got back on the water, so that he could rub one out to Maka.

"There are other ways to express one's gratitude," said the fat man.

Cooper was barely paying attention, mesmerized by Maka's ample bosom. "I was just thinking the same thing, dude."

The fat man cleared his throat. "AHEM!"

Cooper jerked his head away from Maka. "Oh, sorry." He stood up and turned his boat around in the sand, pointing it back out to sea. "So what's that you were saying about how to get to Cardinia?"

Some of the Portsvillians chuckled, which made Cooper feel uneasy.

The fat man grinned widely. "The way is simple. Head north by northeast until you reach the north shore, then follow the coast eastward until you reach Port Town. From there, you can take the road north to Cardinia."

Cooper was relieved. For a minute there, he thought they had been trying to extort some kind of offering from him, which he would have been happy to give if he didn't absolutely need every single thing he had on him. "Cheers." He pushed his boat into the water.

The group on the beach tittered among themselves.

"Excuse me, sir!" the fat man called out after him, sudden alarm in his voice.

Cooper turned around. "What? What'd I do?"

"Surely you don't mean to cross the Great Sea in *that*."

"Sure I do," said Cooper. "Why the fuck do you think I just asked you for directions?"

"You are indeed brave, friend, but this is not a voyage to be made in a one-oared rowboat. You will require passage on a larger, more sea-worthy vessel." The fat man smiled like a dirty cop about to solicit a bribe. "For a reasonable price, my friends and I can book you passage on the next ship to Port Town. That's a nice decanter you have there. We just might be able to get enough for it."

So it was extortion after all. Cooper couldn't fault them for taking advantage of his apparent predicament to the end of relieving him of a little coin, but they were asking for a permanently enchanted magic item in exchange for a boat ticket to Poor Town. They took him for a dumbshit.

The joke was on them. They had obviously not figured out his preferred method of boat propulsion, thinking instead that he was just some weird fucker who liked to sleep on the beach with a fountain of water gushing out from between his legs.

Cooper sat down in his rowboat, facing the beach, with the Decanter of Endless Water resting on his lap.

The group on the beach closed in a bit, some of them appearing to be riding the line between *holding* and *brandishing* their weapons.

"Sir," said the beach party's spokesperson. "Please be reasonable. You'll never survive this journey. It just isn't possible."

"Do you know what a bidet is?" asked Cooper.

The Portsvillians looked blankly at one another, then back down at Cooper.

"I'm afraid we're unfamiliar with that word," said the fat man. "Please enlighten us. What is a *bee-day*?"

"It's a device for washing assholes," said Cooper. "It works like this." He pointed the Decanter of Endless Water at the group and said the command word. "GEYSER!"

The force of the water pushed Cooper's little boat quickly out to sea while simultaneously drenching the Portsvillians.

A few arrows sailed over Cooper's head as the boat ramped over wave after wave. He guessed there were probably a lot more that would have hit him, but got deflected by the gush of water.

Once he was safely out of arrow range, he deactivated the decanter. "Ravenus."

Ravenus was perched on the front of the boat. He looked at Cooper.

Cooper pointed at his own eyes, pointed out to sea, and flapped his arms. "I need *you*... to *scout*... for *danger ahead.*"

After a moment, Ravenus nodded. He flew away, leaving Cooper alone at sea.

Cooper lay on the floor of the boat and pulled up the front of his loincloth. "Why yes, Maka, I *do* like it weird."

Chapter 40

"Being a vampire is tougher than you think," said Katherine. "You get these great powers, and you think *Now I'm a big badass*, but you're completely reliant on other people. Take travel, for instance. I'm in this stupid bag again after I vowed never to – Are you paying attention? Ew. Your ascot's slipping."

Katherine adjusted the ascot she'd made out of fabric torn from the black elf's cloak to cover the hole she'd ripped out of his neck.

"There you go. All fixed."

She wasn't crazy. She was passing the time talking to an elf who she understood all too well was not alive. He was just a focus for her to talk to herself.

Crazy people don't know that what they're doing is crazy. Katherine was fully aware that what she was doing was crazy, and so she could therefore not be.

"What was I saying? Oh, right. I mean, I'm trusting my life to *Chaz* of all people. I'd be better off taking my chances with a parasol. And do you know how embarrassing it is to have to step into a bag while all those strangers are watching me, while *he's* watching me?"

"..."

"No, not Chaz. I don't give a shit about Chaz. I'm talking about Tanner."

"..."

"Oh, I don't know. I mean, sure I like him. But do I *like* him like him? It's really too early to tell, isn't it? Take it from me, Bub. You don't want to rush these things. But yeah, he's cute, and smart, and we're both half-elves."

"..."

"I'm not saying that matters. I'm just saying it's something we have in common. We could swap clothes or whatever."

"..."

"Fuck you!"

"..."

"I'm sorry. You're right. It's just this bag. It gets to me, you know?"

"..."

"Nah, he's cool. He even gave me a little good-bye wave. It was sweet. But I'll tell you this much. I will fry in the fucking sun before I let that smug Stacy bitch see me step into a bag."

"..."

"I don't care. I've got my limits, and I won't –"

Katherine felt a hand grasp her ankle. "I'll talk to you later."

The road rushed up fast to hit her in the face. She rolled over onto her back and wiped her hair out of her eyes to find she was surrounded by old people clapping enthusiastically.

Chaz held the Bag of Holding out to his side and took a deep bow.

"Dude, what the fuck?" said Katherine. "Put the bag on the ground before you pull me out. Don't hold it up in the air and dump me out like a sack of potatoes."

"I'm sorry," said Chaz. "I –"

"And what's with grabbing me by the leg?"

"Well I didn't want to specify *Katherine's arm*. What if the bag takes that to mean I *only* want your arm?"

A shiver ran up Katherine's spine. "Ooh. That's a good point."

"Thank you."

"Why are we not in the city yet? Who the fuck are all these geriatrics?"

Chaz scowled. "*Tanner* said we should hang back and escort the elderly citizens."

Katherine clapped her hands together. "That is *so* sweet!"

"What?"

"Where is he?" Katherine stood up and shoved two old men out of her way to break free from the crowd. "Whoa!"

Stacy and Tanner were walking together. Stacy was telling him something which required growling and clawing at the air, and he was completely enthralled.

"Uh-uh, mamacita!" said Katherine. "You need to back that shit up right now."

Tanner stopped laughing.

Stacy stopped clawing and sighed. "Looks like someone let the Kat out of the bag."

Katherine got up in her face. "And what the *fuck* is that supposed to mean?"

"Your name is Kat, and you were just released from a bag."

Katherine stepped back. "Fine." She looked at Tanner. "Whatever she was saying about me, it's a goddamn lie."

"She hasn't mentioned you," said Tanner.

"Then what was with all of the clawing and growling?"

Tanner smiled. "Stacy was regaling me with tales of the mayor of Port Town. Quite the character, he seems."

Subject change! With her vision not rage-focused on Stacy and Tanner, Katherine noticed that Dave, Julian, and that other elf guy who insisted on being called *Tony the Elf* had joined them on the road. Tony the Elf had an unconscious, bound and gagged third elf slung over his shoulder. Tim and Cooper were still missing.

"Have you guys seen Tim?"

Dave shook his head. "He and Cooper weren't in Port Town. We thought they might be with you."

"They weren't with me. I've been in a fucking bag all day."

"They're probably back at the Whore's Head," said Julian. "You know those two."

These old folks walked even slower than Dave. Katherine suggested stuffing them all into the Bag of Holding and flying them into the city, but the idea was not well-received.

Distant in the northwestern sky, the big flying boat loomed, orbited by dragons, like a giant floating atom. It was a strange sight for a while, like when the Hale-Bopp comet was visible in the sky back in the late 90s. But just like the comet, Katherine eventually grew accustomed to it being there.

She tried to keep her mind focused on the tongue-lashing she was going to give her brother when she finally caught up with him, but Stacy's incessant yapping kept her distracted.

Blah blah blah... We put out a fire. Blah blah blah... We captured a guy who may or may not be Mordred. Blah blah blah… A tiger-man clawed his way out of a dragon's asshole. Blah blah blah… We got some new toys.

And the worst part was that Tanner was eating that shit up. Katherine couldn't interrupt without coming off like a total bitch, but she didn't know how much longer she could go on listening to –

"Cardinia!" one of the old people shouted.

Katherine looked up. There it was on the horizon. Vast city walls silhouetted against moonlit clouds. There seemed to be a lot of frenzied movement on top of the walls, like little ants scurrying about after someone poked the hill with a stick, but Katherine couldn't make out any more detail than that from this far away.

Before long she could hear the sounds of battle. Orcs were storming toward the gate and being mowed down by arrows. Humans, half-elves, and dwarves pounded on the gate, screaming for it to open.

This went on for a time before a tiny orange speck of light zoomed out from the top of the left gate tower to the flying boat, where it exploded into a massive ball of fire which seemed to have no effect but to make the old people *ooh* and *aah.*

An evil laugh erupted from the boat, and it returned fire with a sickly green spotlight, which it scanned along the base of the wall like it was searching for something. It didn't seem like much of a big deal to Katherine, but the screaming from within the city grew louder and more intense.

"What is that?" asked Stacy.

Tanner shrugged and shook his head. Then his eyes widened as he stared at the boat. "The dragons have been released!"

Katherine watched as the three dragons flew toward the city walls. One approached from the east, another from the west, and the third flew down toward the crowd huddled at the gate. All three dragons vomited massive plumes of fire indiscriminately onto soldier, civilian, and orc.

The masses atop the walls changed from ants into fireflies. Burning bodies fell – or jumped – off of the walls. More often than not, they stayed put where they landed. That is, until the green light from the ship shone on them.

"They're getting slaughtered," said Tanner. "We have to help."

"Help how?" said Tony the Elf. "If the king's whole army can't stop them, what can we do?"

"We can take out one of those dragons."

"How?"

Tanner smiled at Stacy. "The same way Mayor Merriweather did."

Katherine frowned, trying to remember the finer points of Stacy's story. "You're going to let it eat you, and then claw your way out of its asshole?"

"Of course not. I'd be dead in an instant."

Stacy looked from Tanner to Katherine. "But *you* could do it! You could get in there and turn into a big wolf and tear it apart from the inside."

"Fuck that shit!" said Katherine. She looked at Tanner. "Did you mean —"

"No no no," said Tanner. "Powerful as you are, that's far too risky. But we will need someone to use as bait." He looked at Tony the Elf. "What about your prisoner?"

"No can do," said Tony the Elf. "We need him alive."

Katherine wasn't going to be the one to suggest using one of the old people. She'd gotten bad enough looks for wanting to ferry them over the wall in a bag. *Bag… BAG!*

"I have a dead elf in my bag!" she blurted out before considering how such an announcement might be received.

"You have a what?" asked Stacy.

"Excellent," said Tanner. "Dave, I'll need your Immovable Rod, your breastplate, and your mace."

"Um…" said Dave. "Okay."

While Dave removed his armor, Katherine dumped the body of the dead elf onto the road. Everyone gawked silently down at it. It only then occurred to Katherine that this was one of Tanner's people.

"Did you make that ascot?" asked Tanner.

Katherine nodded.

"Nice work."

"I can make you one."

"Another time." He addressed the whole group. "I'll need any swords or spears anyone can spare."

Julian laid down an old rusty sword, and Tony the Elf tossed down a spear in similar condition.

One of the old men knelt before the pile of offerings and gently laid down an ancient-looking leather scabbard containing a sword with a tarnished hilt. "It belonged to my grandfather."

"Keep your grandfather's sword, sir," said Tanner. "Pass it down to your grandson. My own blade will be sufficient."

With that, he proceeded to pound the shit out of Dave's breastplate with Dave's mace.

"Hey man!" cried Dave. "What the fuck are you doing? I need that!" But he dared not get too close to the crazy black half-elf wielding his mace.

"It's for the greater good," said Tanner. Having bent the breastplate to the point of uselessness, he took the spear with both hands and started punching holes in it.

After about twenty minutes of hammering, bending and twisting metal, Tanner had something that resembled an iron football, only with blades poking out in every direction. At the center of the football was Dave's Immovable Rod, wrapped up so tightly that it didn't even rattle.

He flipped the dead elf over on the road so that he lay face down. "The more squeamish of you may want to look away."

No one looked away.

Tanner shrugged, then shoved a protruding spearhead into the base of the elf's skull, up into its brain.

"Well I suppose that's that," he said, standing up to admire his handiwork.

"That's that?" said Dave. "What the fuck is that?"

"A baited hook," said Tanner. "Now all we need to do is cast our line and reel us in a dragon."

The road was becoming a dangerous place. As two of the dragons continued to rain fire down on the city, the third was flying in a zig-zag pattern across the road, lighting up orcs and townsfolk, and it was getting closer to them with every pass.

Under Tanner's instruction, Katherine and Julian carried the mutilated elf corpse to the edge of the forest on the left side of the road, taking care not to mangle it any more than it was already mangled, while Stacy and Tony the Elf shepherded the old folks into the woods on the right.

"Here's how this works," said Tanner. "Katherine, I'm going to need you to fly Julian and our unfortunate friend here up a few feet above the treetops. Julian, I'll need you to put your finger into the hole at the bottom of the... *thing*, and push the button on the Immovable Rod. When he's suspended in the air, both of you come back down here."

Julian wrapped the edge of his serape around his hand before lifting the contraption by the shaft of the spear poking up through the bottom of the dead elf's head. "I hope this works, because it's pretty gross."

Katherine wasn't exactly sure what all this was adding up to, but she did her part. She took her giant bat form and lifted Julian by the arm he was holding the elf with.

"Ow. Ow. Ow. Ow. Ow," said Julian as Katherine flapped. "OW! Okay okay, bring me down!"

When they reached the ground, Katherine changed back into a half-elf. Julian's face was bleeding from a small cut on the side of his face.

"What happened?"

"Your unsteady flying happened," said Julian. "As soon as the thing went rigid, I got sliced in the face."

"I'm sorry."

"Don't be," said Tanner. "That means it's going to work."

Julian looked up at the suspended elf corpse. "I think I get what you're going for, but that's clearly a dead elf hanging from a ball of spikes. It's hardly tempting."

"That's what you're here for," said Tanner. "If all I needed was a button-pusher, I would have invited the whining bard. I need a sorcerer to bring that body to life."

Julian frowned. "I think you severely overestimate the power of my sorcery."

Tanner laughed. "I don't mean literally. He's got a spearhead in his brain, after all. But surely you know how to cast the spell Mage Hand."

"Yeah, I can do that. It's a Zero-Level spell."

"I don't know what that means."

Julian looked back up at the dead elf. "Wait a minute. You want me to *Weekend at Bernie's* this guy?"

"Again," said Tanner. "I have no idea what you're talking about."

"You want me to wave his arms around and stuff so that he looks alive?"

Tanner smiled. "Precisely!"

Julian shrugged. "I've participated in stupider plans. So what then? We shout insults about his mother and hope for the best?"

"I was thinking you might cast a Magic Missile at him."

"You really should have checked with me about whether or not I had all these spells you need before you went through all the prep work."

"*Every* sorcerer knows Magic Missile."

"Well what if I'd used them all up already?"

Tanner shrugged. "Then I guess we'd shout insults about his mother and hope for the best. Can you cast the spell or not?"

"Yeah, I've got it."

"Good," said Tanner. "Get your ass up that tree, then, and use it."

"Why do I have to climb up a tree?"

"You want the spell to come from as close to the decoy as possible," Tanner explained. "And you need to see your target, hopefully without him noticing you. You'll have more cover in the trees than you would from the road."

"What can I do?" asked Katherine.

"Catch your friend when he jumps out of the tree."

"I'm going to jump out of the tree?" asked Julian.

"We'll see how long you want to linger in that tree when there's a red dragon flying your way."

"Point taken." Julian pulled himself onto the lowermost branch of the tree beneath the decoy and started climbing.

Katherine watched Julian climb for a while, then looked at Tanner. "You really think this will work?"

"If the dragon takes the bait, the dwarf's armor should hold the blades in place while protecting the activation button from accidentally being pushed. With any luck, he'll slice himself all the way down the esophagus before he realizes what's happening to him, and the device will be lodged in his gut. The more he thrashes about in agony, the more he tears himself apart from the inside. Even if he manages to remain perfectly still, he'll be out of the fight. One less dragon to –"

"Motherffff—Ow," Julian's voice said from a suddenly flattened sapling.

"Julian?" said Katherine. "I didn't hear you cast the spell or call down or anything. And how am I supposed to catch you if you're invisible?"

Julian materialized on the ground. "I panicked! As soon as I hit him with the Magic Missile, he looked my way, and my brain told me to take every defensive measure I could at once. That included fleeing and activating the ring."

"Y-y-you really hit him?" Tanner's voice was trembling with excitement. "Hurry up. Start moving the elf's arms!"

Katherine and Tanner helped Julian up and over to a position directly below the decoy.

"Mage Hand," Julian groaned. His fingers pointing down, he pinched the air like he was holding two beer bottles by their caps and waved his arms up and down. When Katherine looked up, the dead elf's arms were waving just like Julian's, suspended in the air by their middle fingers.

Katherine wondered if that gesture translated. The dragon's angry roar in response, she felt, was inconclusive evidence.

Tanner took Katherine's hand and squeezed it tight. If her heart could beat, it would have been pounding.

Just like that, the visible sky through the gap in the forest canopy was replaced by flashes of scaly underbelly, which came to a halt like a rabid dog having reached the limit of its leash.

If the dragon's anger roar was loud, its pain roar was deafening.

"Let's get out of here!" Tanner shouted, keeping his grasp of Katherine's hand as he ran for the road.

They followed Julian, who was sprinting like his ass was on fire.

Clearing the forest, they met Dave, Chaz, Stacy, Tony the Elf, and a bunch of old people who had come out of hiding to watch the spectacle.

The dragon did as Tanner had predicted. It thrashed its tail, beat its wings, set fire to a semicircle of trees, but did not move more than a few feet in any direction.

Breathing fire soon gave way to vomiting blood as the creature's wings flapped weaker and weaker gusts. Its final roar was like that of a wounded walrus. Finally, it went limp, hanging in the air with only its head and the tip of its tail swaying inches off the ground.

The old people clapped enthusiastically.

Chapter 41

They were all dead. All of Randy's new friends from the Whore's Head Inn. All of his "disciples". Every one of them gone now, and it was all his fault.

Looking down at the ramparts, all Randy could see were charred, smoldering bodies lying all over each other, their efforts not having made a lick of difference. The air was thick with smoke and the scent of roasted meat. It turned Randy's stomach.

The dragons were setting every flammable building in the city alight, zombies were running rampant in the streets, and the big flying boat was practically on top of them now. Professor Goosewaddle had thrown every spell he could think of at it, but hadn't so much as scratched the hull.

"You done fucked up good this time, Randy."

Randy turned around to find Denise, completely unharmed, standing at the top of the stairs. "Denise! You're okay!"

"No thanks to you."

"How did you survive the fire?"

"By not being in it," said Denise. "I got down off the wall as soon as your back was turned."

"You're a coward," said Randy. "You know that?"

"So says the hero hiding up here in the tower."

"I was here at the request of the king. Ain't that right, Professor?"

Professor Goosewaddle nodded.

"You tell yourself whatever you got to say to get through every day, but it's this new self-righteous bullshit act you been running is what got all them folks out there killed tonight."

Randy's eyes and cheeks burned with shame and frustration. "I know."

Denise looked like she was going to say more but shook her head. "Don't matter none now. What's important is that we're still alive."

That wasn't what Randy needed to hear. He stared despondently out the window at the bodies on the rampart. The boat shone its green light along the bodies and up the gate tower. When it shone on Randy, he doubled over with a sudden wave of nausea.

"Listen, Randy," Denise continued. "This party's gone to shit. We need to get back to the inn, and you need to let me do what I got to do to get Mordred to send us back home."

Randy's insides were churning. He wanted to throw up, but nothing was coming out.

"Well, well," said a raspy voice at the door. "Look who it is."

"Friend of yours?" said Professor Goosewaddle.

Randy looked up. The man at the door was badly burnt. Randy might not have recognized him if not for the smoothness of his shaven head. "Stuart?"

"How's the view from up here?" said Stuart. "Can you see my dead wife?"

"Stuart," Randy choked up the words, delirious with pain. "I'm sorry."

"My wife is dead, Randy. I wanted to come up here and tell you that."

"Well," said Denise, gazing down at the wall. "You're half right."

"What?" Stuart limped to the window. "Rose!"

Randy shook off the pain as best he could and grabbed Stuart by the leg. "No, Stuart. That ain't Rose."

Stuart wrested his leg free, kicked Randy hard in the face, and climbed out the window. The pain in Randy's probably broken nose was nothing compared to the pain in his twisted guts.

Denise shook her head. "You know, you see that shit play out in every zombie show or movie, and you think real people would know better. Guess I was wrong."

Randy contemplated using divine power to heal his nose, but it felt selfish when so many others had suffered so much more. He put the thought out of his head.

"Goddamn, them zombies can pack a punch," said Denise. "Um... We can go ahead and cancel Stuart's ticket home."

The pain in Randy's guts began to subside, but there was no relief to his crushing despair. He'd had everything he ever wanted in life. Friendship, camaraderie, respect, acceptance. He'd been part of something. He'd mattered. And now it was all gone. "I... I didn't know it would be so... so hopeless."

"Despair not, my friend," said Professor Goosewaddle, producing a worn, Naugahyde-covered book from within his robes.

Randy's vision was blurry through tears, but it looked like... "Is that a *Bible*?"

"I've been reading up a bit." The professor opened the book and scanned down a page. "Ah, here it is. Psalms 34: 17 and 18."

"Aw shit!" said Denise. "That's the one from *Pulp Fiction*, ain't it? Goosewaddle's 'bout to fuck some shit up!"

Professor Goosewaddle ignored Denise and read his selected passage. "When the righteous cry out, the Lord listens; he delivers them from all their troubles. The Lord is close to the brokenhearted; he saves those whose spirits are crushed."

Denise frowned. "That ain't the one from *Pulp Fiction*."

"Of course!" said Randy. "It's just like the king said." He smiled at Denise. "I know how to make this right!"

"Randy, you already done shit in the chili. There ain't no making this right."

Randy bowed his head and folded his hands. "Our Father, who art in heaven, hollow be thy name."

"Hollow?" said Professor Goosewaddle.

"Thy kingdom come. Thy will be done on earth as it is in heaven."

"Jesus Christ, Randy," said Denise. "This ain't the time."

"Give us this day our daily bread,"

"Bread!" the professor spoke in a reverent whisper.

"...and forgive us our trespasses..."

"Come on, Randy. Shit in one hand and pray in the other, you know? We gotta bounce!"

"...as we forgive those who trespass against us..."

"They're coming up the stairs!" said the professor. "Guard Randy!"

Randy heard the lumbering footsteps climbing the stairs, but dared not open his eyes. "And lead us not into temptation..."

"You back the fuck up!" shouted Denise. This was followed by a grunt and a crash.

"...but deliver us from evil."

The groans of at least a dozen zombies rose from the direction of the staircase.

"Randy, I need your help!"

Randy's heart quickened.

"Forthineisthekingdomthepowerandthegloryforeverandeveramen!"

When he opened his eyes, he saw Denise standing at the top of the stairwell. She held her axe in front of her, but seemed to have reservations about using it. She kicked zombies back down the stairs as each one lunged at her.

"I can't hold them back much longer!"

"Hang on!" said Randy. "I'm coming!"

"This way!" shouted Professor Goosewaddle from outside the east window. He was on a knotted rope, climbing up to the roof.

Denise waddle-ran past Randy and looked out the window. "That rope ain't tied to nothin'!"

"It's magic!" the professor's voice called down. "Hurry!"

The idea of climbing a magically suspended rope must have been preferable to facing whatever was coming up the stairs, because Denise didn't hesitate long before grabbing the rope and pulling herself out of the window.

The front of the zombie crowd reached the top of the stairs, and Randy's worst fears were realized when he recognized familiar faces.

Frank, even in death, continued to lead his people. Half of his face, and his entire beard, had burnt away, but it was definitely him. His little zombie-gnome groans had a certain distinction. Randy could hear Frank's voice in them.

Behind Frank were two soldiers, their armor having been warped by dragon fire, and their forearms little more than blackened meat on bone. They had tried to shield themselves from the flames.

Gus, the queer half-orc who Randy had been eager to talk to again, stood head and shoulders above the rest of the zombies piling into the top floor of the gate tower. He shoved his way past the soldiers and stepped over Frank, his dead eyes staring, hungry for Randy's living flesh.

"I'm sorry, Gus," said Randy. He grabbed the rope and pulled himself up just in time to pull his foot away from Gus's grasp. Gus fell forward out of the window and plummeted to the wall, where he crushed two more zombies. The rest of the zombie crowd at the window reached up for Randy as he scooted up the rope.

Randy looked up. It was indeed disconcerting to see the top of the rope sticking up like a middle finger to gravity. But up was the only way to go, so Randy climbed.

Denise and Professor Goosewaddle were both hugging the top of the conical roof. The blue wooden shingles looked fine from ground level, but up close, they showed signs of severe decay.

The angle of the roof also presented a problem. It was a little too steep for Randy's liking. He slowly marine-crawled his way to the top and joined the others.

"Now what?" asked Denise.

"Just hold tight and wait for Jesus," said Randy.

"Wait for – Randy, have you lost your goddamn mind?"

"He'll come." Randy had no logical reason to believe his prayer would work. Praying had never solved any of his problems back on Earth. His mama had tried to pray the gay out of him, but that hadn't worked for shit. But for some reason, Randy had absolutely no doubt in his mind that this prayer had been heard and would soon be answered.

"Bullshit," said Denise. "It don't do you no good mumbling *Our Fathers* when what we really need is a *Hail Mary*."

Randy nodded. "I suppose it couldn't hurt. Hail Mary, full of grace—"

"Shut the fuck up, Randy," said Denise. "I meant like in football. A last-ditch act of desperation. A long pass into the end-zone, hoping that one of your receivers can – What the fuck are all those people doing?"

The roof of the South Gate tower provided an excellent view of the city, all the way to the royal palace. Randy, too, thought it odd that people had stopped running away from the chaos at the gate, and now seemed to be running toward it.

"Maybe they figured they ain't got nothing to lose, and decided to stand up for themselves?"

"Doubtful," said Professor Goosewaddle. "They're unarmed, unorganized, and still clearly terrified. They're running *from* something."

The tower shook as a giant white leg stepped out from behind the palace. Giant, that is, in relation to the palace. It was actually pretty short for the plump white body it was connected to.

"Holy fucking shit," said Denise. "It's the Stay Puft Marshmallow Man."

That had been Randy's first thought as well when the massive creature lumbered out onto the main avenue, but something about it was wrong.

"Uh-uh," said Randy. "Stay Puft wears a sailor's hat and a blue sailor's collar. That thing's wearing a white scarf and a chef's hat." He gulped. "It's the Pillsburg Doughchild."

"Have you two lost control of your senses?" asked Professor Goosewaddle, his old eyes welling up with tears. "Do you not know the face of the New God, Jesus Christ, when you see it?"

"The what?" Pieces started falling into place in Randy's mind. That cheap, Naugahyde-covered bible. Goosewaddle had swiped that from a church. His peculiar reverence for bread. He'd taken Holy Communion, gotten it fixed in his mind that Jesus's body was made out of bread, and jumped to a conclusion when he'd seen an ad for biscuits or crescent rolls somewhere. The game had created the image of its new god according to the description that Goosewaddle had provided the High Priestess. "Oh no. Professor, we've made a terrible mistake."

Denise's face was a mask of confusion and terror. "What did you do, Randy?"

The towering mass of sentient dough smiled and waved at the screaming Cardinians as it waddled toward the South Gate. With each step, the flaming skeletons of the city's more stalwart buildings collapsed in on themselves.

"Foolish mortals!" boomed a voice from the bow of the flying boat, which had stopped advancing. It hovered just above the western part of the southern city wall. A figure stood, dressed in black armor, its glowing red eyes peering out from the shadow of a great horned helmet, its skeletal hands raised in clenched fists.

"Is this the best resistance you can offer? This impressively large, yet oddly adorable *golem*? Your efforts insult your future king. The sun has set on the day of the living. Once my dragons reduce your pitiful champion to a smoldering pile of ash, I shall rule a city of the dead. Dragons, attack!"

Between the seismic damage caused by the giant dough monster and the fire damage of the dragons, the city was in pretty bad shape. Wooden buildings caught a moment of reprieve as the two dragons refocused their attention on their new target.

"Jesus! Watch out!" Randy cried as the dragons beat the smoky air with their red leathery wings, each of them gunning for the Doughchild from opposite directions.

The New God raised his massive dough head, looked at Randy with its vacant, black, circular eyes, and gave him a friendly wink. He seemed blissfully unaware of the dragons closing in on him.

The dragons inhaled deeply as they approached, filling their internal furnaces with air, then spewed out twin plumes of fire down on the unsuspecting Doughchild.

Randy nearly lost his hold on the tower roof when the New God fell to his doughy knees, shielding his face from the blasts with arms that were soon aflame.

"NOOOOOOOO!" Randy cried as the dragons retreated to recharge their lungs. He closed his eyes and pressed his face against the tiles. He couldn't stand to watch Jesus burn.

"Look!" said Professor Goosewaddle. "He is risen!"

Randy opened his eyes.

The New God had gotten to his feet again, his face no longer cheerful. His black eyes were now semicircular in shape, tilting down toward his nose. The curvature of his mouth had reversed downward. He had his angry face on.

He held his arms out to his sides, and his burnt skin flaked off like the outer layer of a croissant, revealing fresh doughy skin underneath. The smoky air now had a trace of buttery goodness.

When the dragons circled around for their second pass, the New God was ready for them. The significance of his crucifixion-like posture only became clear to Randy when he opened his hands to reveal holes in his doughy palms. Randy was confused, ashamed, scared, and hopeful at the same time.

"This is just all kinds of wrong," said Denise.

The dragons made their charge, sucking in great lungfuls of pastrified air, preparing to rain down another fiery assault. When they opened their mouths, their flames were blocked by jets of red fluid shooting out of the Doughchild's crucifixion wounds. They resisted at first, but the New God was unrelenting, shooting more blood out of his palms than should have been possible.

After a moment of turning their heads against the spray, the dragons seemed to have a change of heart. They each faced the palms directed at them with open mouths, greedily gulping down as much of the New God's blood as they could. The Doughchild was smiling again.

"Wretched lizards!" cried the figure on the flying boat. "You're supposed to *attack* the golem, not drink its blood!"

The New God stopped shooting blood out of his hands, and the dragon to his right lazily flew toward him and swiped at his face with one of its huge, clawed forearms. It missed by at least ten feet, and the dragon was promptly swatted out of the air by the same hand it had just been drinking from.

The dragon slammed into the bottom of the right gate tower, which collapsed down on it. Rising up from the rubble on unsteady legs, it stood eye-to-eye with Randy. The eye, which was nearly as big as Randy, suddenly grew even wider. The dragon's scaly cheek puffed out for a second, just before it threw up all over the shambling horde of zombies and fell over.

"Well I'll be goddamned," said Denise. "That motherfucker's trashed."

Randy thought for a moment. "You mean like *drunk*?"

"I mean fuckin' shitfaced. Come on, Randy. I'm a cop. You think I can't spot a drunk dragon when I see one?"

Randy glared at Professor Goosewaddle. "That ain't blood, is it?"

Goosewaddle looked back at him defensively. "You know as well as I, the New God bleeds wine."

"Of course he does."

The other dragon seemed to be faring a little better. The Doughchild had dealt with it in similar fashion to the first one; it was struggling to its feet near a dragon-sized pile of former wall, but at least it hadn't – *Ew.*

Randy was at a better angle to see the torrent of vomit which erupted from the second dragon's mouth. This one had apparently eaten more recently than the first. Randy was able to recognize partially digested halves of livestock in the red soupy mess raining down on the zombies below.

The screams coming from the base of the tower grew louder and more intense, which surprised Randy. He figured they'd have all turned into zombie groans by now. One particular cry stood out from the rest.

"Rose!" Stuart's voice cried out. "Rose!"

How could he still be alive? He was in bad shape before he climbed out the tower window and got mauled by zombies. His voice wasn't half as surprising, however, as the one that answered.

"Stuart! What happened? OH MY GOD! WHAT IS THAT?" Rose had no doubt just spotted the hundred-foot-tall dough monster.

Randy looked over at the vomit-covered zombies near the second dragon. They weren't shambling. They were all kind of just standing there looking confused and horrified. They were... *alive*.

"Randy!" said Professor Goosewaddle. "You've done it. The New God's blood is returning life to the dead!"

"Impossible!" bellowed the enraged captain of the flying boat. "What manner of magic is this?"

With a wave of his bony hands, the boat's sails pivoted on their masts. The boat changed course and started moving again. The jagged, pointy bowsprit was pointed right at the New God, who was, once again smiling and waving at the screaming, blood-covered masses.

His anger turned to laughter as his boat flew toward the New God. "Enjoy your last breaths of life, mortals! Your sorcerer's tricks are no match for the Phantom Pinas!"

"Oh no!" said Randy. "He's gonna ram Jesus!"

"Uh-uh," said Denise. "Don't no man poke his pinas in *my* Lord and Savior! Professor, move the rope!"

Randy followed the path the boat was taking. With the aid of Goosewaddle's rope, Denise might have a chance at boarding, but... "How you gonna get past that force field?"

"Look at all them arrows sticking out of the bottom. That shield blocks magical attacks, but it don't do shit against regular stuff."

Professor Goosewaddle repositioned his rope, and Denise jumped and grabbed hold of the nearest end.

"I'm really angry!" she shouted. Her muscles ballooned out until she looked like a very short linebacker. She swung along the magically suspended rope one hand after the other, like a gorilla at the zoo, just as the boat was coming in range.

"Oh fuck!" she shouted as the rope went limp and she plummeted toward the ground, where she smacked into a large puddle of Jesus blood. Randy hoped that would sort her out.

"Oh dear," said Professor Goosewaddle. "The anti-magic field canceled out the rope spell. I really should have thought of that."

The Pillsburg Doughchild took no evasive action as the bowsprit of the Phantom Pinas plunged deep into his belly. His little black eyes grew to twice their normal size as his mouth gaped open.

Randy watched in horror as the flying boat pierced through the flesh of this god he had accidentally called into being. "I'm sorry, Jesus."

But the boat had not pierced the flesh, as became evident when the New God's belly expanded outward again, hurtling the Phantom Pinas, bow over stern, back over the city wall.

"HEE HEE!" bellowed the New God, cheerfully rubbing his belly as the Phantom Pinas crashed into the ground outside.

The citizens had mostly gotten over the initial horror of having just been resurrected from the dead and covered in blood, or they were willfully postponing the shock to cheer for the New God, and wrestle their still-undead friends and family members into puddles of dragon vomit.

The New God helped out, shooting jets of fresh wine-blood into wandering groups of zombies. He shot one jet into the top floor window of the left gate tower, just below where Randy and Professor Goosewaddle were still clinging to the roof.

"Aaaaahhhh!" Frank screamed.

"Jesus Christ!" shouted Gus.

As more and more people were resurrected and had time to come to terms with what was going on, shouts of praise and thanks overtook the shouts of alarm and shock, until it seemed like everyone in the city was celebrating at the New God's doughy feet. Even the orcs who had arrived with hatred in their hearts now laid down their weapons and bowed low before the giant Doughchild.

One person, however, was feeling particularly cheery. Timmon Bloodsoul marched through the destroyed South Gate, his skeletal hands crackling with purple lightning. As soon as the New God was in his line of sight, he thrust his hands forward, unleashing a barrage of purple bolts.

"I have underestimated you people," said Timmon Bloodsoul as the New God dropped to his knees, his doughy flesh burning and bubbling in a shell of purple electricity. He advanced. "I was not expecting to face a lesser-god, but it matters not. I am Timmon

Bloodsoul! Even gods are at the mercy of my awesome power! Let this be a lesson to any who would –"

The lightning stopped. Timmon Bloodsoul looked at his hands as new flesh began to grow on them. He removed his helmet, exposing a youthful face and flowing blond hair. He looked down at his feet. He was standing in a puddle of dragon vomit. "I… I'm… *alive.*"

THWACK THWACK THWACK THWACK THWACK THWACK THWACK THWACK

The fletching of fifty or more arrows sprouted out of Timmon Bloodsoul's face, neck, and armor at once. For a moment, he stood still like a half-elven cactus, then fell face-first into the puddle of dragon puke, the restorative powers of which apparently only work once.

"You reckon it's safe to get down now?" Randy asked Professor Goosewaddle.

The professor's eyes still looked tired, but they had their cheerful gleam back. "Safe as it will ever be, I expect."

By the time the professor had retrieved his rope, and he and Randy climbed down the side of the tower, the New God's flesh had once again been completely restored, and the citizens of Cardinia were happily munching away at the bread he'd just molted.

"Randy!" the New God called down. He looked even more enormous from ground level.

The crowd grew silent. All eyes followed the Pillsburg Doughchild's gaze to Randy.

"Yes, um… Jesus?"

"I must go now and take my place in the heavens. Your faith has inspired others, and I have many prayers to answer."

Randy had never felt such a complex mix of emotions. He was at a profound loss for words. "Okay."

"Remember," said the New God. "Nothing says lovin' like helping your fellow man." With that, he pointed his arms at the ground and sprayed blood onto the cheering crowd. The blood shooting out of his hands and feet propelled him upward.

Randy watched him ascend until he was just another star in the night sky.

Chapter 42

Tim lay on the deck chair at the front of his boat in the middle of Bay St. Louis, near enough to civilization to restock his beer cooler, but far enough out to sea to be beyond all the bullshit. The boat rocked gently, like a cradle, as Golden Oldies played softly from the radio in the cabin. He had the sun on his bare chest, a cold summer lager in his hand, and a line in the still bay water. There was neither a worry in his head nor a cloud in the sky.

Well, that wasn't entirely true. There was one small worry in his head, and it concerned the one small, dark cloud in the sky. Some kind of meteorological anomaly. It didn't belong there. It was a smudge on his perfect day, like a drop of turpentine on a beautiful oil painting.

Whichever way he positioned his chair, his eyes were still drawn to that fucking cloud, and it was getting closer, creeping toward him across the otherwise pristine blue sky.

"Tim."

It wasn't enough that the cloud had to hover over him like an asshole. Now it was interrupting Neil Diamond. Tim closed his eyes, hoping that if he ignored the cloud, it might go look for someone else to talk to.

"Tim."

Nope. Sorry, talking cloud. Go take that shit somewhere else. I'm fishing.

"Shocking Grasp."

Huh?

Tim awoke to the sensation of blowing a cattle prod. The crowd of people standing around him vibrated back and forth in his field of vision as a gazillion volts of electricity racked his body.

"WHAT THE MOTHER FUCK!" Tim said when Rhonda finally let go of the back of his neck.

"Sorry 'bout that," said Rhonda.

"I fucking pissed my pants! Do you know how embarrassing that is?" Probably no more than the pool of vomit on the table. Tim noticed that the side of his face was wet and sticky. He should have stuck to beer.

"I authorized it," said Frank. "We couldn't wake you up, and we need to talk."

Tim twitched as the residual effects of Rhonda's spell worked their way out of his body. "Where the hell have you guys been?"

"We've had a hell of a night," said Frank. "It's a long story."

That sounded like a perfect opportunity to mend some fences. Tim forced a smile. His heavy head tilted toward the Arby's bag on the table. "I brought you guys a present."

When Tim lifted the handles, the sides of the bag tore free from the bottom, the paper having been externally digested. The individually wrapped roast beef sandwiches had not been properly stacked, and the pile collapsed outward into Tim's puddle of shame.

"There's still a few good ones on the top."

Frank frowned for a moment at the pile of sandwiches marinating in booze and bile, but seemed to have more pressing issues on his mind.

"There was a halfling tied up in the cellar," said Frank. "What happened to him?"

Tim nodded slowly as his mind sorted out what, in the recent past, had been real, and what had been a dream. *Talking cloud, dream. Halfling in the cellar, real.* "Halfling. Yeah, I saw him. I cut him loose."

Frank shook his little fists. "Why would you do that?" He sounded very distressed.

"I was trying to be a decent person," said Tim. He suddenly remembered something. "Hey! I brought you guys sandwiches!"

"Tim!" Frank slapped him lightly on the cleaner side of his face. "I need you to stay focused. This is important."

Tim waved Frank's hand away. "Hey, man. Cut that shit out. I just woke up. There's, like, a million people in here. Can't you fire a question at someone else?"

"Rhonda. Hit him with another Shocking Grasp."

Tim stood up on wobbly legs and backed away from Rhonda. "Whoa! Hey! Hold the fucking phone, man!" He looked at Frank. "What's gotten into you guys? What's with all of this Gestapo shit? Dude in the cellar said Denise was down there dildo-raping him."

"That's a goddamn lie!" said Denise.

"Well it seemed pretty fucking credible to me, *Dennis*."

Denise pointed a fat little finger at Tim. "Hey! You watch your –" She put her hand down, seeming to realize that she was only drawing more unwanted attention to herself. "Ain't I told y'all that little halfling was faking sleep? Tough little sonofabitch."

"Think, Tim," said Frank. "Did he say anything else? Like where he might be going? *Anything?*"

"I don't... No." Tim shrugged. "I just gave him a sandwich and sent him on his way."

Frank buried his face in his hands and did something between a laugh and a cry. "You gave him a sandwich. That's fantastic."

"What are you all even doing here?" asked Tim. "When I got here, the place was empty. I figured you guys found Mordred and fucked off back home."

"You stupid asshole."

"What?" Tim was taken aback. That wasn't a very Frank-like thing to say.

"The halfling *was* Mordred."

"We don't know that for sure," said Randy.

Frank took a few deep breaths. "Yes we do, Randy. Everything adds up to him being Mordred. The Red Robes of Neutrality. Little Red Riding Hood. Conveniently waking up when he sees the opportunity to trick some dumb little shitbag to cut him loose."

"Dude," said Tim. "Take it down a notch. It was an honest mistake. How the hell was I supposed to know it was Mordred?"

"You knew we were looking for him!" Frank shouted in Tim's face. "You knew he could look like anyone! Who the fuck else would we have tied up in a goddamn cellar?"

"I thought –"

"No!" said Frank. "You don't think. You drink. And you bitch, and you moan, and you whine, and you routinely fuck up the simplest tasks given to you. Let me ask you this. Why are you here alone? Where the hell is Cooper? Where are the rest of our people, who you claimed to be delivering character sheets to? Did you even do that?"

"They were fishing," said Tim. "I didn't think it was worth the trip, so Cooper went on alone." The words sounded so wrong as they fell out of his mouth.

"Fishing?" Frank shook his head. "In the middle of a goddamn war? And you entrusted their character sheets with the dumbest motherfucker to walk the earth?"

"You've got a beef with me, Frank. And maybe I fucked up. Don't drag Cooper into it."

"I'm sorry," said Frank. "The second dumbest. I don't care what your character sheet says. *You* are, without a doubt, the most skullfuckingly brainless sack of primordial shit to ever crawl out of the sea."

Tim took in all of the silent gazes. Even Randy and Denise were gawking at him. Not a single one of these assholes spoke a single word in his defense. They probably felt the same way Frank did. Maybe Frank was right. He could feel the drying vomit on his face crack as he looked down at his piss-soaked crotch. Frank was definitely right. He was a first-class, Grade-A fuckup. "I'm sorry."

Frank shook his head. "That's not good enough this time. You're a liability. Pack your shit. I want you out of here before –"

"Whassup, muthafuckas!" said Stacy, waltzing through the gap in the back wall of the inn with a body slung over her shoulder.

There were some other people behind her, but Tim ducked behind the bar before he could make out who they were. He couldn't let Stacy see him like this.

"Stacy!" cried Randy. "I'm so glad y'all are all right."

"Did you see the Stay-Puft Marshmallow man?" asked Stacy excitedly. "What the hell happened here?"

"Actually," said Denise. "That was the Pillsburg Doughchild."

"*Actually*," said Randy. "That was Jesus. Sort of."

What the fuck were they talking about?

"That was the most awesome shit I've ever seen!"

"Who's that?" demanded Frank. His voice was still angry.

Stacy cleared her throat. "Ladies and gentlemen of Earth. I present to you..." She let out a small grunt, like she was shifting the weight of the body she was carrying. "Mordred!"

There was a moment of intense silence.

"Mordred!" Stacy repeated. After another moment of silence, she said, "I kind of expected a different reaction. More of a *You go, girl!* or at least a *Yay!* Honestly, anything at all would have been nice. What's going on?"

"You've made a mistake," said Frank. "That's not Mordred."

"Sure it is."

"I don't think so. We had Mordred here a little while ago before some *fucking idiot* cut him loose."

"You had someone else here who claimed to be Mordred?" Stacy sounded skeptical, but Tim suppressed the tiny sliver of hope that tried to seep into his heart.

"He hadn't fessed up yet, but all the evidence pointed to him. Denise here was conducting an interrogation when we all got summoned to the South Gate."

"Well I don't know who you were interrogating," said Stacy. "But it wasn't Mordred. This is Mordred. He didn't even try to hide it. He told me all about how he created this world, and all the people in it, and how he finally rolled the perfect character, me, and how he wanted me to be his queen and rule this world together with him."

"She's right," said Tony the Elf. "He's the real deal."

Tim had heard all he needed to. He hopped up on top of the bar.

"Uh-oh!" He rang the bell above the bar and shouted back at an imaginary chef in an imaginary kitchen. "Fire up the ovens! We got to bake some *humble pies.* Ooh, baby, we got a hungry crowd in here tonight!"

"I'm sorry," Frank muttered.

"What's that, Frank? I didn't quite catch it." Tim lay down on the bar. "Let me crawl my primordial sack of shit out of the sea so I can hear you better." He let his tongue hang out of his mouth as he inchwormed his way across the bar, smearing a trail of piss behind him. "Blegh, blargh, blaugh, blegh." The crowd who had woken him lowered their heads and endured the spectacle. The newcomers, including Stacy, Katherine, Butterbean, Dave, Julian, Tony the Elf, and some black dude, watched in stunned silence. "I'm sorry, Frank. Could you say that again?"

"I'm sorry," Frank repeated, more loudly and clearly. "I'm a big enough man to admit when I'm wrong. I owe you an apology."

Tim frowned. "Just think of that poor little halfling you tortured for no reason at all." He shrugged. "But you know what? Water under the —" *Hold on a second... Butterbean?*

Katherine's wolf stood docilely next to her. Neither of them was trying to kill the other. Also, there was something off about Katherine. She looked a little dumpier somehow.

"Katherine?" said Tim. "Are you... *alive?*"

"Yeah!" said Katherine. "Isn't it cool?"

"What... How..."

Katherine shrugged. "Fuck if I know. I just walked into town as a vampire, trying my best to avoid stepping in these red puddles that were *everywhere*. You know, so I don't ruin my shoes. And then these two drunk orcs are dancing around, not watching where they're going, and they knock me on my ass right into a puddle. I'm getting ready to kick some ass, because I'm never going to get this shit out of my jeans. And then, just like that, my heart starts beating. I won't lie. It scared the shit out of me."

"That's terrific!"

"It is what it is. I'm going to miss flying. But it's nice to be able to drink again."

"Well how about that." Tim sat up on the bar and rubbed his hands together. "Bring forth the guest of honor. Let's see what ol' Mordred has to say for himself."

Stacy hefted the unconscious elf into a sitting position on the bar. "One Mordred. Order up!" She took a step back and stood next to Julian.

The elf had a scrap of cloth tied around his head, obscuring his left eye.

"What happened to his eye?"

Julian tugged on his ears. "The best theory we've got is that Ravenus took it when he escaped."

"Where's Ravenus?"

Julian frowned. "I don't know."

Tim pulled a pair of socks out of the elf's mouth and held them up. "Um... Who do these belong to?"

Tony the Elf raised his hand. "Those are mine."

Tim flung the socks in Tony the Elf's general direction, then looked down at the captive elf. "Should I kick him awake, or would you prefer the honor, Rhonda?"

"That won't be necessary," said the elf. He looked up at Tim with his single eye. "Hello, Tim."

The crowd gasped.

Tim's heart skipped a beat. "Mordred."

Mordred bowed his head. "I suppose I should congratulate you on thwarting my plan to take over the city. I must admit, I was not expecting poor Timmon Bloodsoul to have to go up against the Michelin Man."

"Stay-Puft Marshmallow Man," said Stacy.

"Pillsburg Doughchild," said Denise.

"Jesus," said Randy.

Tim frowned. "Is someone going to fill me in on this?"

"Ah, the New God everyone's been talking about," said Mordred. "A very clever ploy. Invent a new god that you have unique knowledge of, and he's yours to command. I would never have allowed it, of course. But the game, left to its own devices, tends to have its bugs. I expect that trick will only work once, though. Now that others have witnessed his power, you can bet that clerics and paladins will be lining up to join his flock. I'm afraid that you'll be a run-of-the-mill paladin again, Randy."

Randy shrugged. "I can live with that. I don't like all that attention anyway."

Mordred smiled at Frank. "So, noble leader. You've finally captured Big Bad Mordred. What do you propose to do with me?"

"You're going to send us all back home," said Frank, "so we can try to salvage what we can of our real lives."

"Sure thing," said Mordred. "Untie my hands and hand over the dice."

Frank slowly pulled the dice bag out of his vest's inner pocket. Mordred stared at it hungrily.

"Stop," said Tim. "Something's not right. He's got a funny look in his eyes."

Randy raised his hand. "Excuse me."

"Randy, this isn't fucking school," said Tim. "If you've got something to say, just spit it out."

"I was just thinking..."

"I'm sure you'll be home in time for COPS."

Randy glared at him. "I was just *thinking*," he repeated. "What's to stop Mordred from just saying his own name when you give him the dice?"

344

"Well thank you, Randy, for planting that idea in his head."

"Don't be too hard on him," said Mordred. "That's precisely what I was planning to do. You'd have to be a complete moron not to expect that."

Tim looked at his feet. "I've had a bit to drink tonight."

"Shit," said Frank. "I can't believe I was about to hand over the bag. If Mordred gets back to Earth..."

"He can take over the game again," said Julian.

Mordred smiled. "He *is* a clever one. It looks like you good people have a bit of a conundrum."

"No," said Dave. "This isn't a problem at all."

Mordred's grin flickered. "And how's that?"

"Command!" said Dave. "It's a first level clerical spell. We'll just Command him to say our names." Tim relished the look of panic that spread over Mordred's face while Dave continued. "We'll have to wait until morning to get started, and it might take a few days, but between me and however many other clerics we have here, we should be able to get everyone home within a week."

Frank must have noticed Mordred's change of mood as well. He was actually smiling. "I never thought I'd say this, but I can't wait to be five foot three again."

"I can't wait to have balls again," said Denise, drawing the attention of everyone in the room. Even Mordred snapped out of his funk to give her a puzzled glance.

Julian's eyes widened. He whispered something to Stacy.

Stacy's jaw dropped as she clapped her hands. "Come on!" she said, grabbing Julian's arm. Together, they squirmed their way through the crowd and out of the inn.

Tim frowned. "What the fuck is up with those two?"

"It's disgusting," said Mordred. "They're completely shameless."

"What are you talking about?"

"Nothing," said Katherine. "He's just trying to fuck with you."

For some reason, Tim suspected that Mordred was being more upfront with him than Katherine was.

"What is going on with Julian and Stacy?" Tim asked Mordred. "Are they..."

"Morning, noon, and night," said Mordred. He was grinning again. "She's insatiable. It's like she's got a bomb in her uterus that will explode if he doesn't keep resetting the timer."

Tim's heart started pounding. "Resetting the timer? You mean, like, with his dick?"

Mordred rolled his eye. "Yes, Tim. With his dick."

"You knew about this, Katherine? You all knew?" Tim had only meant to address the group that Julian and Stacy had been traveling with, but he noticed that nearly everyone in the room had taken a sudden interest in their own feet. "Jesus Christ! How long has this been going on?"

"Tim," said Frank. "She's a grown woman. She can make her own choices."

"You can do better than her anyway," said Katherine. "She's kind of a bitch."

Mordred grinned at Tim, a twinkle in his eye. "He's resetting that timer right now, Tim. It requires a long, slender tool. I don't think you could reset that clock with your tool even if she let you try."

Dave took a step toward Mordred. "You want me to shut him up for you? We won't need him until morning anyway."

Tim shook his head. "Nah. It's cool."

He walked along the bar to the shelves where the stonepiss bottles were stored and took one. He unstoppered it and took a swig. Vomiting and napping had put him back in a pretty good position for a second wind.

"You want that drink now, Kat?"

Katherine looked left, then right, at all the eyes staring back at her. "Um… sure."

He took another bottle off the shelf, walked back over to the end of the bar where Mordred was still tied up, and tossed the unopened bottle to Katherine. She caught it awkwardly with both hands. She was certainly not a vampire anymore.

Tim took another swig from his bottle, then addressed the crowd. "Let's raise our glasses to Julian and Stacy."

"Come on, Tim," said Frank. "Don't do this."

"What?" Tim said in his best innocent voice. "I'm serious."

"You're embarrassing yourself."

Tim laughed. His throat was raw. "Look at me, Frank! Take a good, hard look. I'm covered in my own vomit and urine. I'm past the point of self-embarrassment."

"Well then think about the rest of us. You're making everyone very uncomfortable."

"What's everyone got to feel uncomfortable about?" asked Tim. "Are you all *resetting her clock*? I thought it was just Julian."

"I can't let you talk that way about Stacy," said Randy. "I know you's upset, but she's our friend."

"You too, Randy? How do you prep your tool for that? You make her wear a flannel shirt and a trucker hat? Or do you just use the tool in the cellar?"

The crowd parted as Randy stepped to the front. "I'm gonna give you one last warning."

Tim held up his hands defensively. "You're right, Randy. That was out of line. I'm sorry." He jiggled his bottle. "Just the booze talking." He gulped some back. "I'm not trying to dis-*purge* anyone's character. I'm happy for them both. Hell, I'm punched as please."

Katherine had tears streaming down her cheeks. She mouthed the words *Please stop.*

Tim winked at her. *Backstabbing bitch.* He paused momentarily to swig back some stonepiss and remember where he had left off in his speech. Nothing came to mind. He started again.

"Julian and Stacy. Theirs is a fairytale romance, born here in a fairytale world. I don't know about you, but that brings a tear to my eye." This line was added on the spot to account for the actual tears welling up in his eyes. "And do you know how my favorite fairytales end?"

Dave's face turned pale. "Tim! Don't!" He knew how Tim's favorite fairytales ended, but his fat little dwarf legs couldn't do shit about it.

Tim crouched next to Mordred and smashed his bottle against the bar. "Happily. Ever. After." He grabbed Mordred's hair with his left hand and shoved the broken end of the bottle into Mordred's neck. He got in a good solid twist before someone's hands pulled him away.

It was Denise. She threw Tim against a wall and kicked him repeatedly in the gut and ribs.

"Stop it!" cried Katherine, trying to push Denise away. Without her vampire-enhanced Strength, it was a futile effort. She grabbed a handful of Denise's hair and yanked hard.

"Ow! Ow!" cried Denise. She stopped kicking Tim. "Okay! Let go of my hair!"

"Randy!" cried Frank from where Mordred was bleeding out on the bar. "Get over here and heal him!"

"In Jesus Christ's name, I heal you!" said Randy a moment later. "It ain't working. Mordred was right. I'm just a run-of-the-mill paladin now."

"Let me try," said Dave. "I heal thee! Shit, it's no good. He's lost too much blood."

"It was just one stab," said Frank. "Even with his Sneak Attack bonus, how much damage could he have done?"

Tim spat out a gob of bloody phlegm and grinned. "Coup d'état rules, bitches! Hit Points don't matter. It's a Fortitude Save or die."

"It's *coup de grâce*, you fucking idiot," said Frank. "Do you have any idea what you've done?"

"I don't know, Frank. I'm pretty drunk."

"You've damned us all here forever!"

"Oh, right. Yeah, I knew that."

Frank turned a livid visage to Katherine. "I can't guarantee your brother's safety." His words were barely above a whisper, but audible in the pin-drop silence of the room. "I can't even guarantee I won't kill him myself. You need to get him out of here right now, before –"

"Look who I found!" sang Stacy as she sashayed back into the inn accompanied by Julian, Cooper, and Ravenus. "Holy shit."

Cooper looked at Mordred, blood from his neck still trickling out in pulses over the side of the bar, then to Tim, sitting against the wall, his clothes stained with his own urine, vomit, and now blood.

Tim nodded at him. "Hey, Coop. 'Sup?"

"What the fuck happened in here?"

"We've only been gone, like, five minutes," said Julian. "Everything was cool when we left."

"Tim here had himself a little tantrum," said Frank. "Because Julian left the inn with *his girl*." He emphasized the last part with finger quotes.

Stacy stomped toward Tim. "You selfish little shit!"

Tim braced himself for another ass kicking, but Katherine stepped in Stacy's way.

"That's my brother. You need to take a step back."

Stacy got up in Katherine's face. "Don't forget. You don't have your superpowers anymore."

Butterbean growled.

Katherine smiled at Stacy. "But I *do* have a big fucking wolf. Now back off."

The silent air was as thick with tension as it was with the combined smells of Tim and Cooper.

"Is something amiss, sir?" Ravenus asked Julian.

"You could say that, Ravenus. Tim just killed Mordred."

"And who, exactly, is Mordred?"

"The dead elf on the bar."

Ravenus looked. "He's the one that kidnapped me! I ate his eye."

Julian smiled sadly. "I thought you might have."

"I'm not one to celebrate the death of a fellow living creature," said Ravenus. "But I can't honestly say I share the level of bereavement I see here."

"We needed him to get back home," said Julian. "The magic dice only work for him."

Ravenus nodded and looked over at Mordred's dead body. "That does make your goal more inconvenient."

"It makes our goal impossible."

"Not at all!" said Ravenus. "Chin up, sir! You can always seek out one of the other ones."

Julian looked curiously at his bird. "One of the other *whats?*"

"Mordreds, of course."

"There's only one Mordred, and he's over there bleeding onto the floor."

"There were at least three who captured me, sir."

"What are you talking about?"

"It was a curious thing to witness. Three bodies in the back of the wagon, but only one of them was able to function at a time. They were different races, but their mannerisms suggested, to me, that they shared the same spirit."

"I knew it!" shouted Denise. "Wister really *was* Mordred. That's how I wound up punching that tree. The little fucker knew the jig was up, and he went and switched bodies on account of he didn't want to feel a punch in the face. And that's also why we couldn't wake him up. He'd done given up on that body until Tim showed up."

Frank looked down at Tim. "That's just remarkable. We had two bites at the apple, and you let one go and killed the other."

Julian thought out loud. "The one you had here couldn't have been one of the three in the wagon. That makes at least four Mordreds."

"How many dice are in the bag?" asked Tim.

"Fuck you," said Frank. "That's how many."

"Then there are fuck you minus one Mordreds roaming around out there."

"What are you talking about?"

Tim laughed weakly. "That's why his spirit split. When he fell out of the penthouse window, he threw all of his dice in desperation, hoping at least one of them would activate before he splattered all over the pavement."

Frank took the bag out from inside his vest, and dumped the dice onto the bar. "There are six dice. That makes five Mordreds left."

Tim grinned. "You're welcome."

"You want some thanks?" said Frank. "I'll give you some thanks. I'm going to let you walk out of this bar alive. But my gratitude ends there. I don't want to see your stupid face or hear your whiny voice ever again. Are we clear?"

"Come on, Tim," said Katherine. "Let's go."

A few people looked like they wanted to say "Goodbye", or "Fuck you", or something, as Katherine walked Tim out the front door of the Whore's Head Inn, but no one actually said anything, except for the random black guy.

"Katherine, wait. I'm coming with you."

"You don't have to do that, Tanner," said Katherine. "Stay if you want."

Tanner, the black half-elf, turned to look at the crowd, then back at Katherine. "I don't actually know these people."

"Oh yeah. I guess that's true. Come on then."

Tim wasn't going to give the patrons of the Whore's Head Inn the satisfaction of seeing him blubber like a little bitch, but he couldn't hold out much more than a few yards after they were out the door. Tears and snot started to flow. "I fucked up, bigtime, didn't I, Kat?"

"Yeah you did, Tim."

Tim wiped his sleeve across his nose and sniffed. "I'm sorry, Kat."

"I know, Tim. You always are."

The End.

ABOUT THE AUTHOR

Robert Bevan has been living and teaching English in South Korea for the past fourteen years. He is the unashamedly self-published author of the bestselling Caverns and Creatures series of comedy/fantasy novels and short stories. He and his family live in Gimpo, up near The Wall, protecting the realms of men from Norks and wildlings.

www.caverns-and-creatures.com

www.facebook.com/robertbevanbooks

Made in the USA
San Bernardino, CA
22 April 2017